ONCE UPON TIME,
    THERE WAS A WIZARD...

THEN IT ALL WENT TO HELL.

CURSE WORDS VOLUME #3: THE HOLE DAMNED WORLD, FIRST PRINTING. JULY 2018. Copyright © 2018 SILENT E PRODUCTIONS, LLC. All rights reserved. Published by Image Comics, Inc. Office of publication: 2701 NW Vaughn St., Ste. 780, Portland, OR 97210. Contains material originally published in single magazine form as CURSE WORDS #11-15. "CURSE WORDS" its logos, and the likenesses of all characters herein are trademarks of SILENT E PRODUCTIONS, LLC, unless otherwise noted. "Image" and the Image Comics logos are registered trademarks of Image Comics, Inc. No part of this publication may be reproduced or transmitted, in any form or by any means (except for short excerpts for journalistic or review purposes), without the express written permission of SILENT E PRODUCTIONS, LLC or Image Comics, Inc. All names, characters, events, and locales in this publication are entirely fictional. Any resemblance to actual persons (living or dead), events, or places, without satiric intent, is coincidental. Printed in the USA. For information regarding the CPSIA on this printed material call: 203-595-3636 and provide reference #RICH–801974. For international rights, contact:foreignlicensing@imagecomics.com.
ISBN: 978-1-5343-0752-0

CURSE WORDS

VOLUME THREE: THE HOLE DAMNED WORLD

CREATED BY

CHARLES SOULE &
RYAN BROWNE

COLORS BY
ADDISON DUKE &
RYAN BROWNE

LETTERS BY
CHRIS CRANK

BOOK DESIGN BY
RYAN BROWNE

PRODUCTION BY
ERIKA SCHNATZ

LOGO BY
SEAN DOVE

ELEVEN

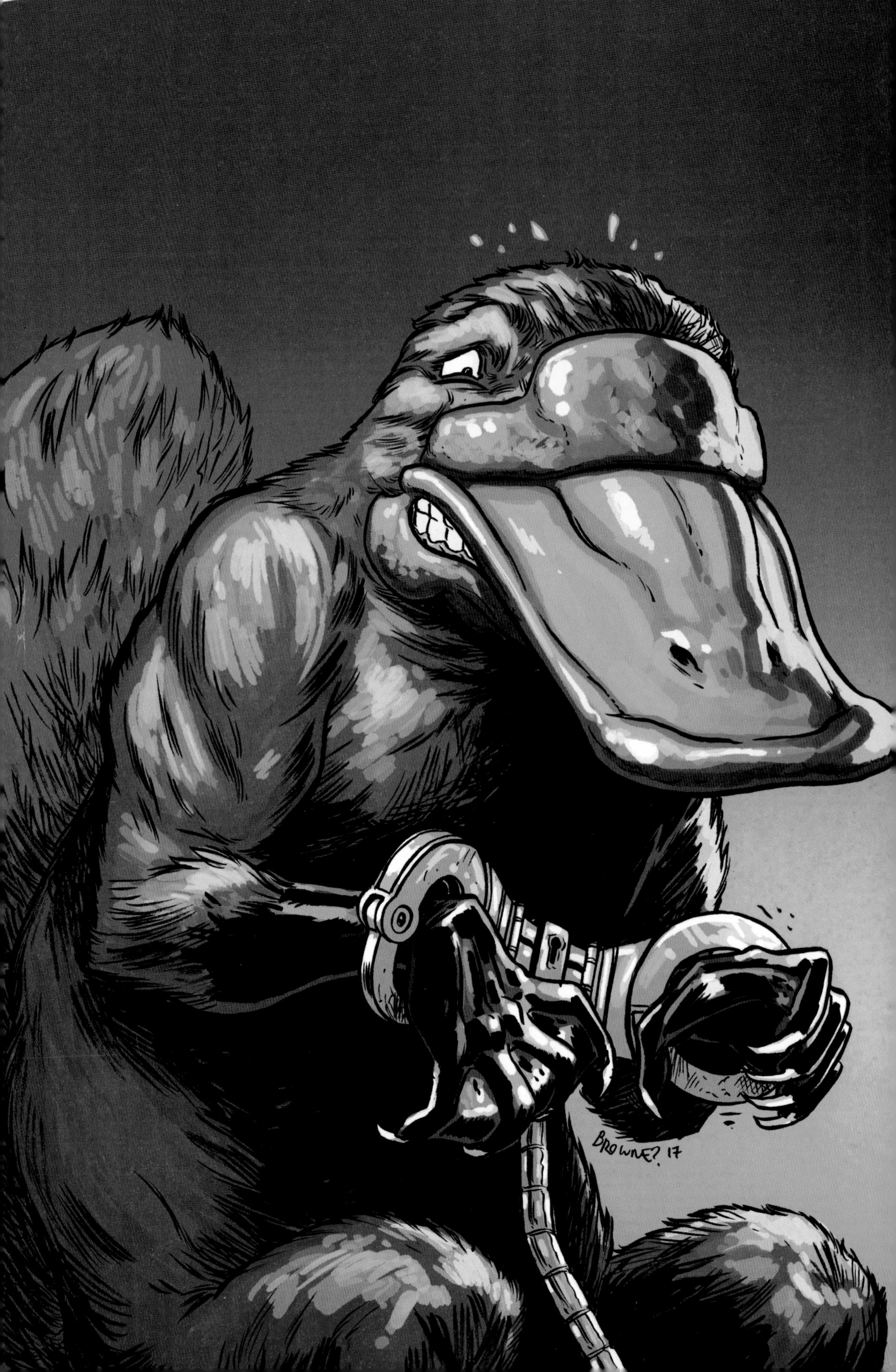

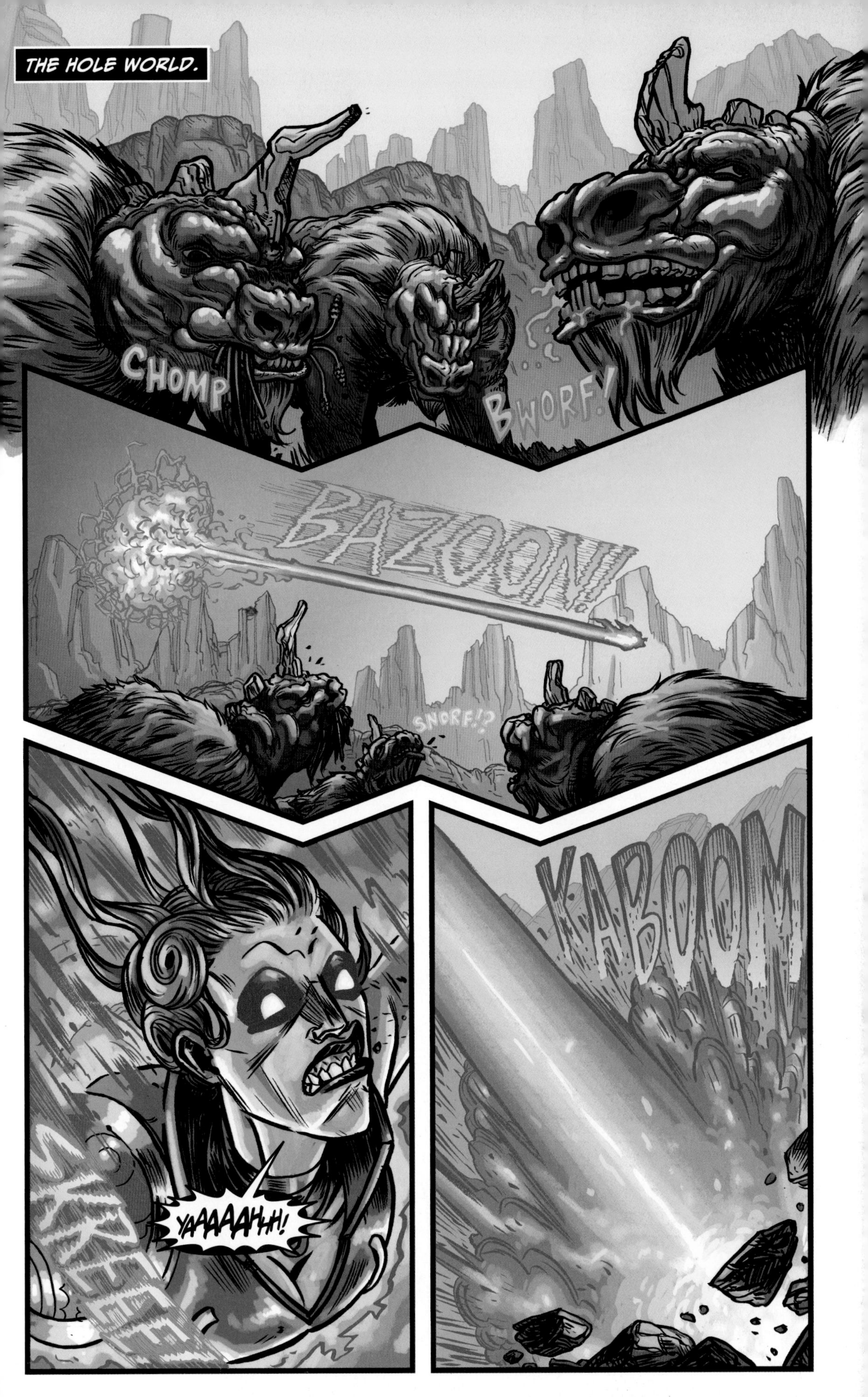
THE HOLE WORLD.
CHOMP
BWORF!
BAZOOON!
SNORF!?
YAAAAAHHH!
KABOOM

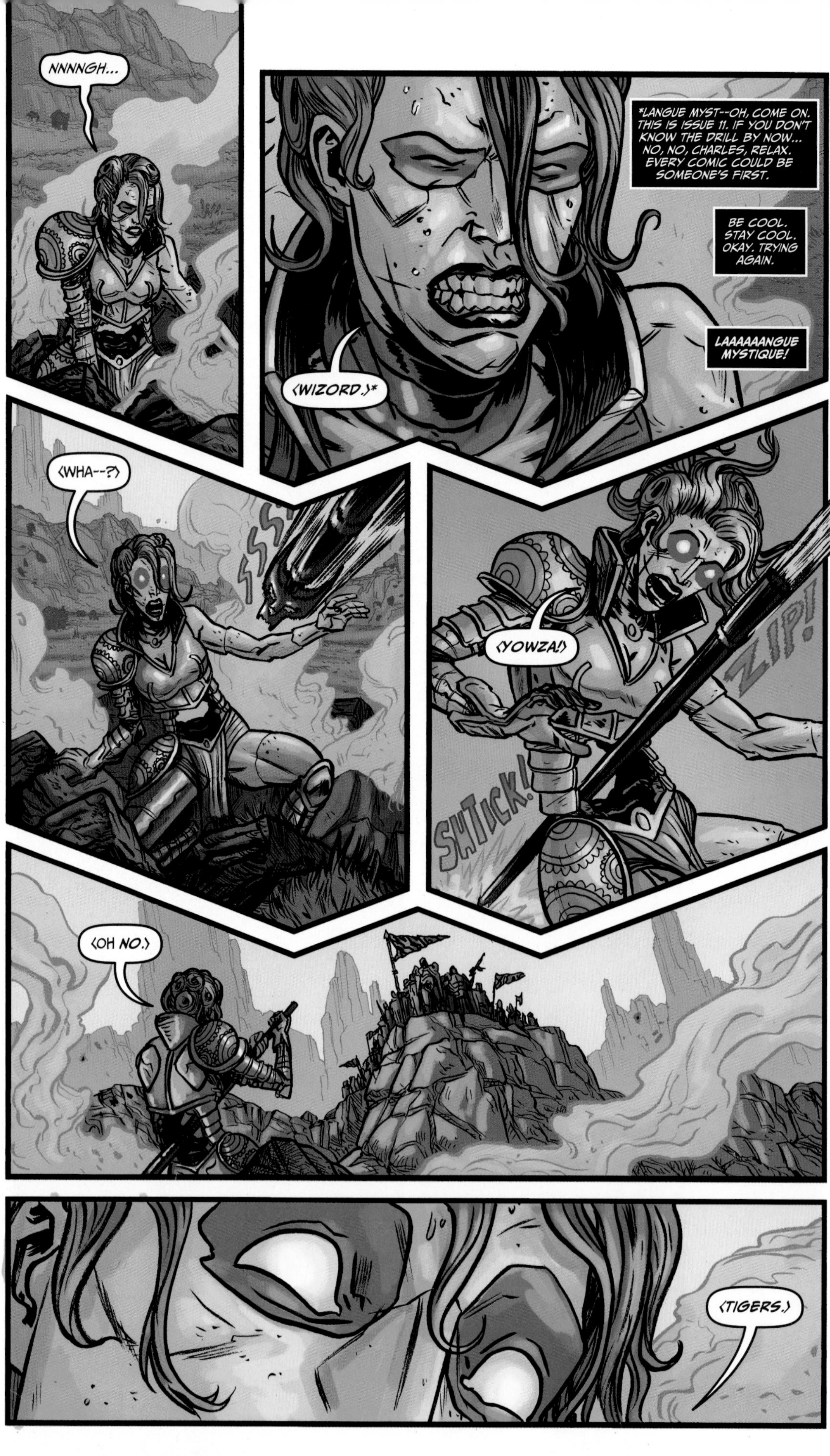
NNNNGH...
*LANGUE MYST--OH, COME ON. THIS IS ISSUE 11. IF YOU DON'T KNOW THE DRILL BY NOW... NO, NO, CHARLES, RELAX. EVERY COMIC COULD BE SOMEONE'S FIRST.
BE COOL. STAY COOL. OKAY. TRYING AGAIN.
LAAAAAANGUE MYSTIQUE!
‹WIZORD.›*
‹WHA--?›
‹YOWZA!›
ZIP!
SHTICK!
‹OH NO.›
‹TIGERS.›

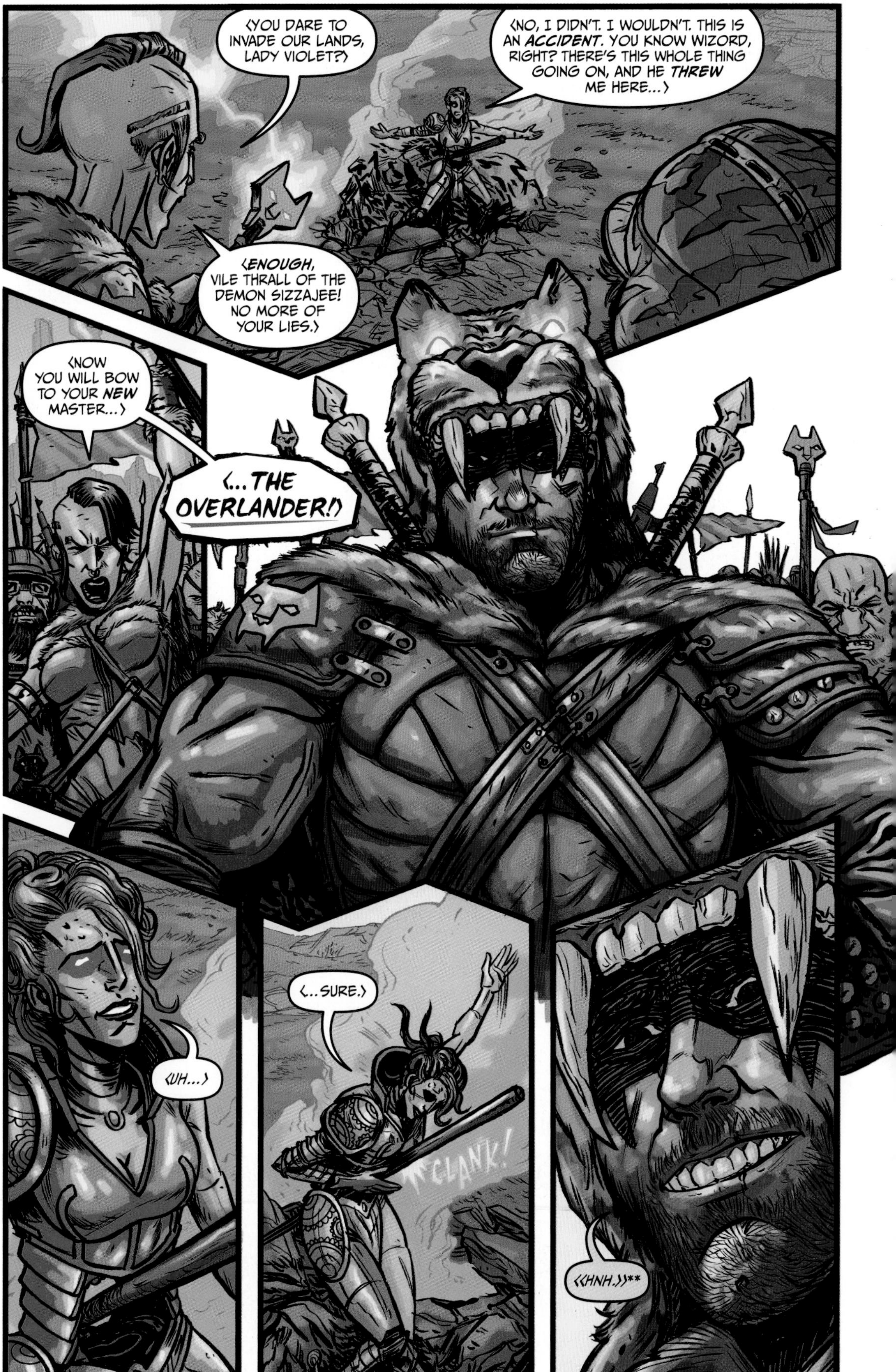
‹YOU DARE TO INVADE OUR LANDS, LADY VIOLET?›
‹NO, I DIDN'T. I WOULDN'T. THIS IS AN ACCIDENT. YOU KNOW WIZORD, RIGHT? THERE'S THIS WHOLE THING GOING ON, AND HE THREW ME HERE...›
‹ENOUGH, VILE THRALL OF THE DEMON SIZZAJEE! NO MORE OF YOUR LIES.›
‹NOW YOU WILL BOW TO YOUR NEW MASTER...›
‹...THE OVERLANDER!›
‹UH...›
‹...SURE.›
CLANK!
‹‹HNH.››**
**TIGER TALK.

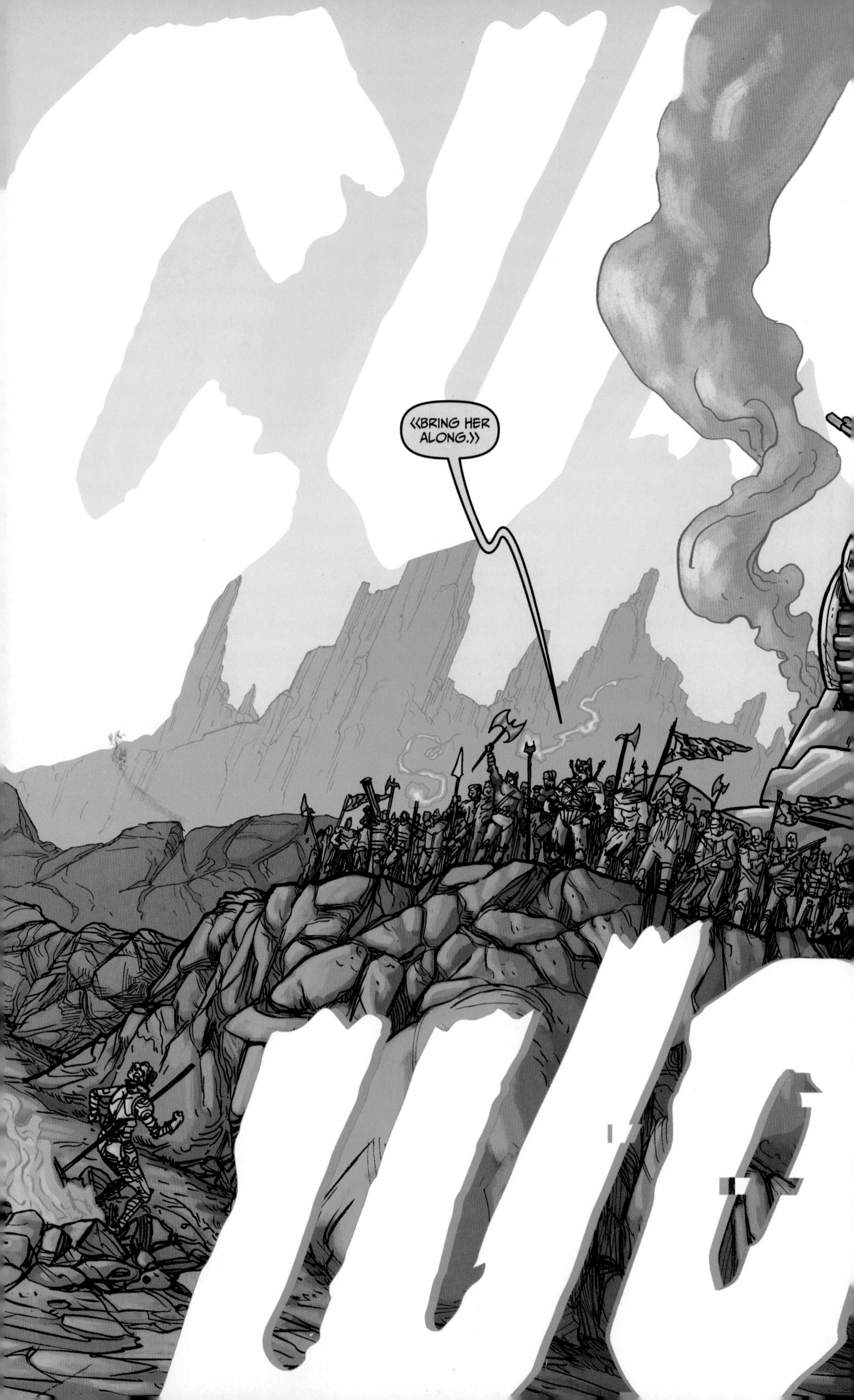

<<BRING HER ALONG.>>

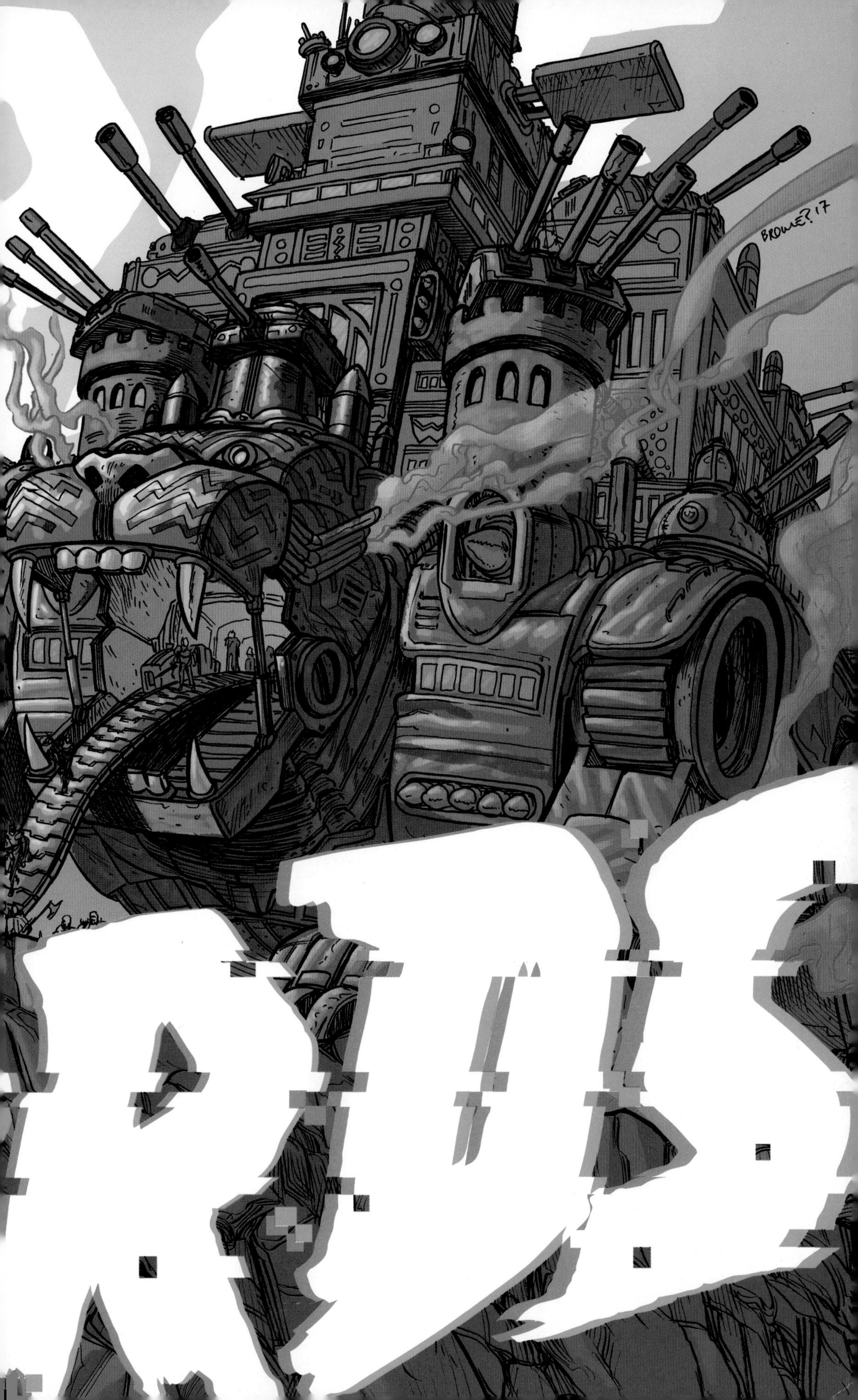

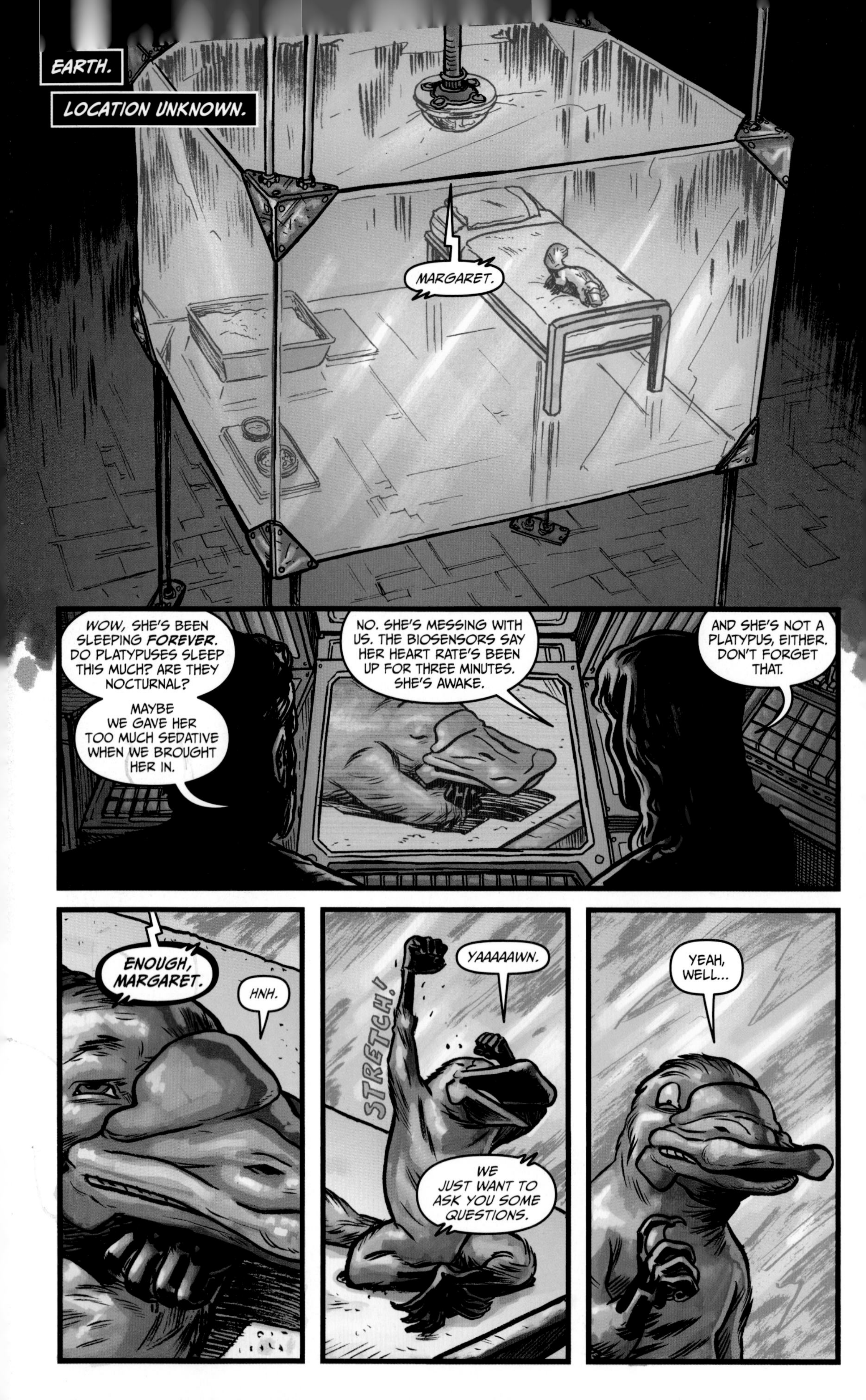
EARTH.
LOCATION UNKNOWN.
MARGARET.
WOW, SHE'S BEEN SLEEPING FOREVER. DO PLATYPUSES SLEEP THIS MUCH? ARE THEY NOCTURNAL?
MAYBE WE GAVE HER TOO MUCH SEDATIVE WHEN WE BROUGHT HER IN.
NO. SHE'S MESSING WITH US. THE BIOSENSORS SAY HER HEART RATE'S BEEN UP FOR THREE MINUTES. SHE'S AWAKE.
AND SHE'S NOT A PLATYPUS, EITHER. DON'T FORGET THAT.
ENOUGH, MARGARET.
HNH.
YAAAAAWN.
STRETCH!
WE JUST WANT TO ASK YOU SOME QUESTIONS.
YEAH, WELL...

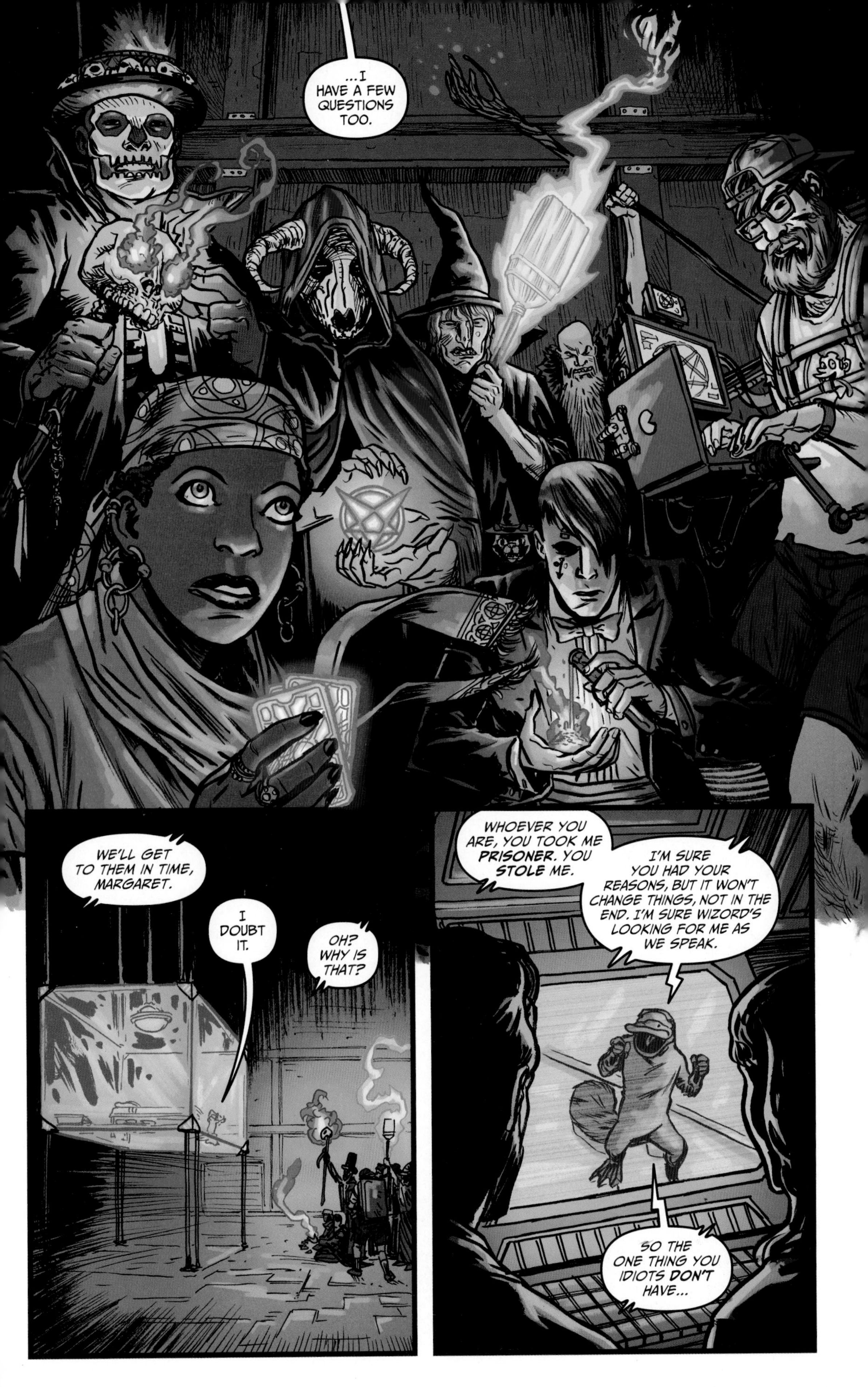
...I HAVE A FEW QUESTIONS TOO.
WE'LL GET TO THEM IN TIME, MARGARET.
I DOUBT IT.
OH? WHY IS THAT?
WHOEVER YOU ARE, YOU TOOK ME PRISONER. YOU STOLE ME.
I'M SURE YOU HAD YOUR REASONS, BUT IT WON'T CHANGE THINGS, NOT IN THE END. I'M SURE WIZORD'S LOOKING FOR ME AS WE SPEAK.
SO THE ONE THING YOU IDIOTS DON'T HAVE...

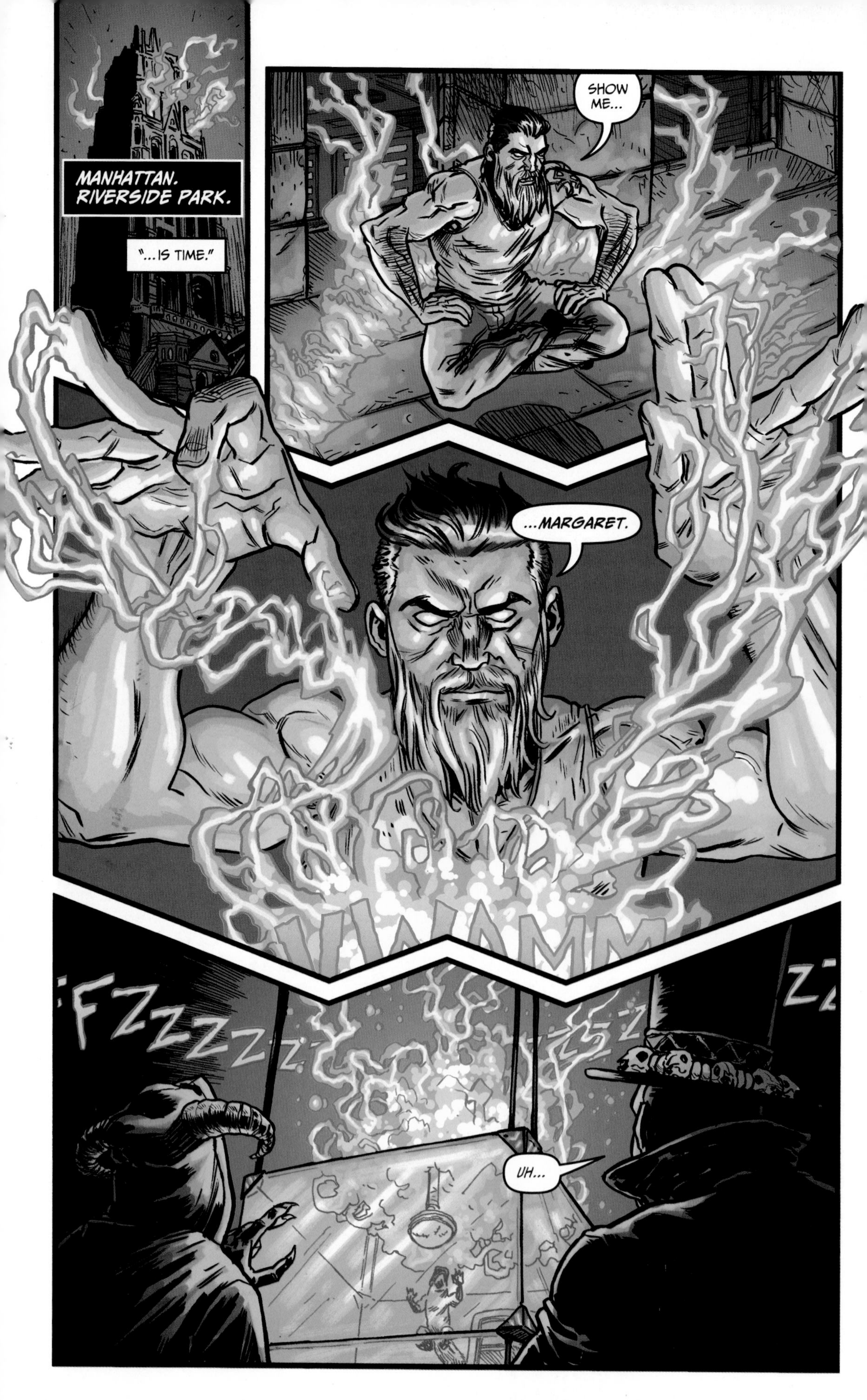
MANHATTAN.
RIVERSIDE PARK.
"...IS TIME."
SHOW ME...
...MARGARET.
VWAMM
FZZZZZ
ZZ
UH...

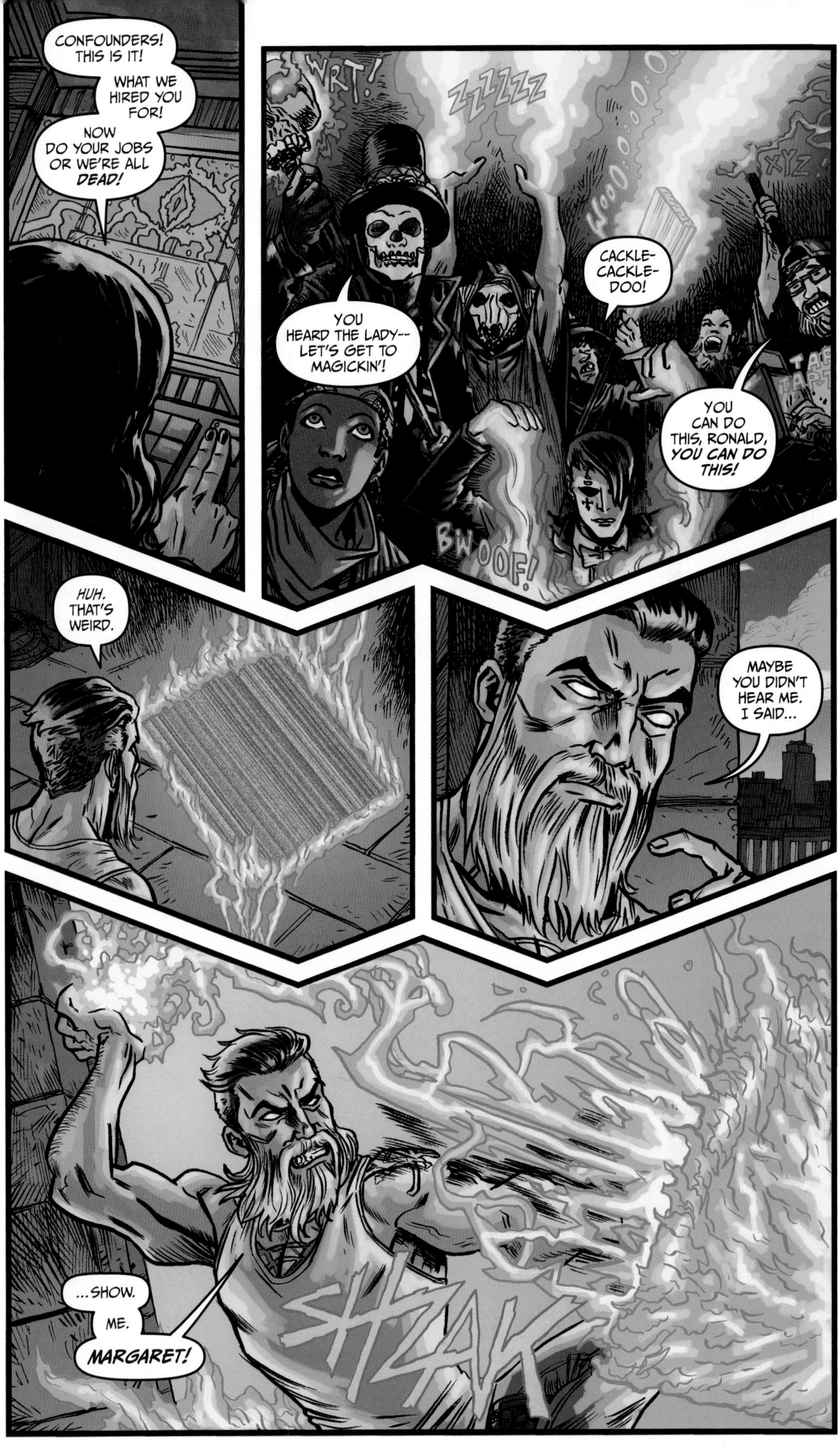
CONFOUNDERS! THIS IS IT!
WHAT WE HIRED YOU FOR!
NOW DO YOUR JOBS OR WE'RE ALL *DEAD!*
WRT!
ZZZZZZ
WOOOOOOO
XYZ!
YOU HEARD THE LADY-- LET'S GET TO MAGICKIN'!
CACKLE-CACKLE-DOO!
YOU CAN DO THIS, RONALD, *YOU CAN DO THIS!*
BWOOF!
HUH. THAT'S WEIRD.
MAYBE YOU DIDN'T HEAR ME. I SAID...
...SHOW.
ME.
MARGARET!
SHZAK

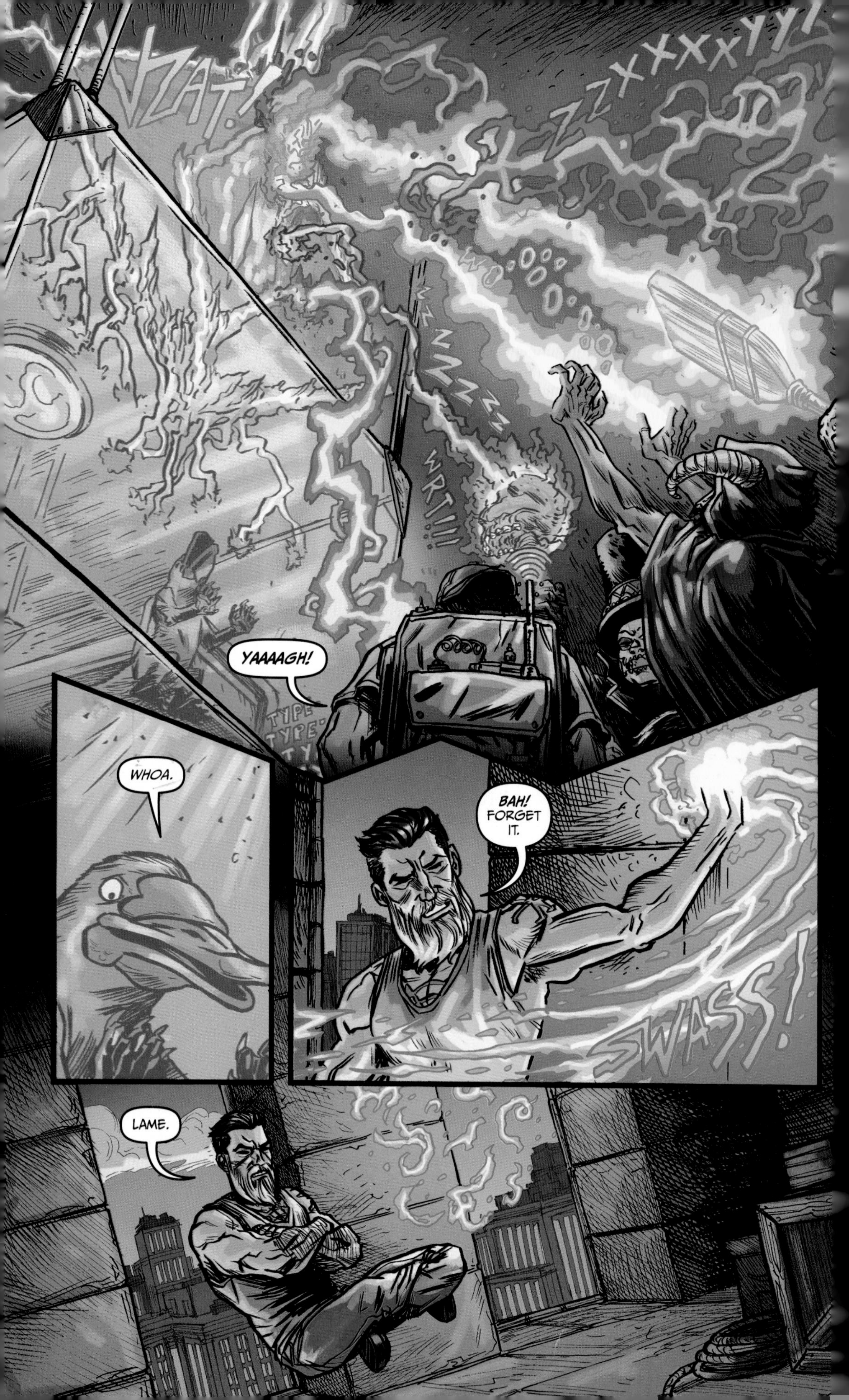
ZZZXXXXXYY!
WOOOOOO
ZZZZZZZZ
WRT!!!
YAAAAGH!
TYPE TYPE TY
WHOA.
BAH! FORGET IT.
SWASS!
LAME.

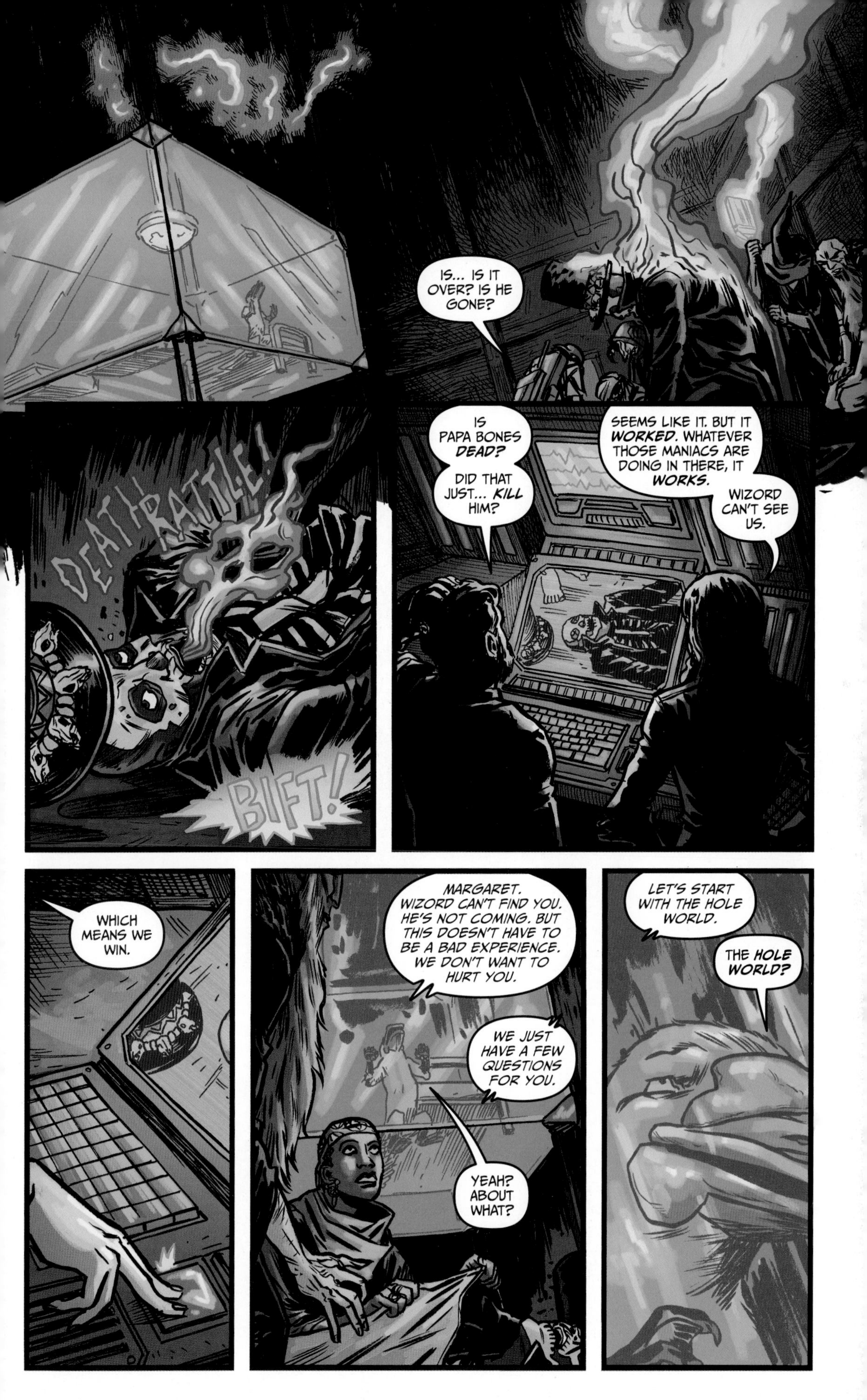
IS... IS IT OVER? IS HE GONE?
DEATH RATTLE!
BIFT!
IS PAPA BONES DEAD?
DID THAT JUST... KILL HIM?
SEEMS LIKE IT. BUT IT WORKED. WHATEVER THOSE MANIACS ARE DOING IN THERE, IT WORKS.
WIZORD CAN'T SEE US.
WHICH MEANS WE WIN.
MARGARET. WIZORD CAN'T FIND YOU. HE'S NOT COMING. BUT THIS DOESN'T HAVE TO BE A BAD EXPERIENCE. WE DON'T WANT TO HURT YOU.
WE JUST HAVE A FEW QUESTIONS FOR YOU.
YEAH? ABOUT WHAT?
LET'S START WITH THE HOLE WORLD.
THE HOLE WORLD?

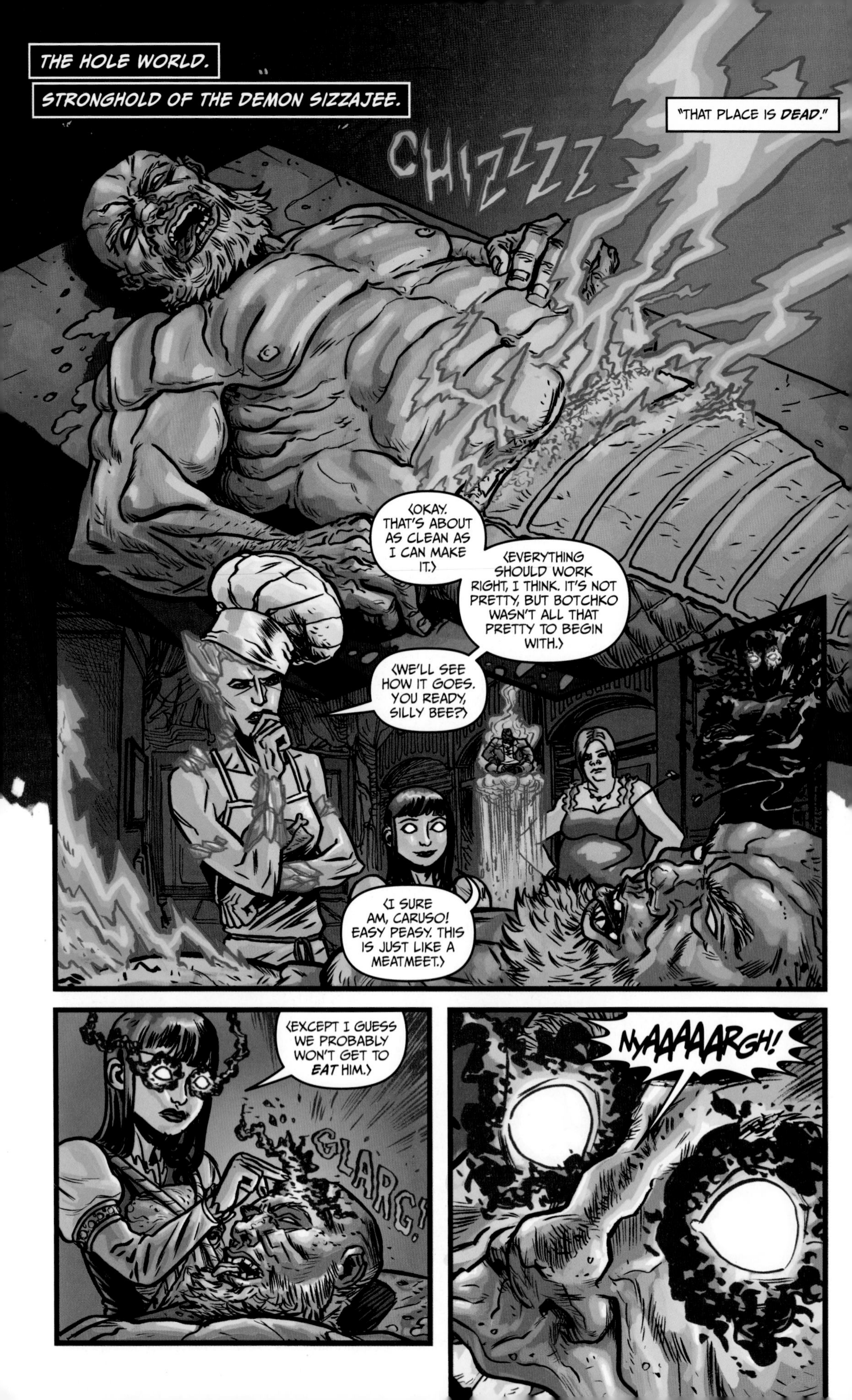
THE HOLE WORLD.
STRONGHOLD OF THE DEMON SIZZAJEE.
"THAT PLACE IS DEAD."
CHIZZZZ
‹OKAY. THAT'S ABOUT AS CLEAN AS I CAN MAKE IT.›
‹EVERYTHING SHOULD WORK RIGHT, I THINK. IT'S NOT PRETTY, BUT BOTCHKO WASN'T ALL THAT PRETTY TO BEGIN WITH.›
‹WE'LL SEE HOW IT GOES. YOU READY, SILLY BEE?›
‹I SURE AM, CARUSO! EASY PEASY. THIS IS JUST LIKE A MEATMEET.›
‹EXCEPT I GUESS WE PROBABLY WON'T GET TO EAT HIM.›
GLARG!
NYAAAAARGH!

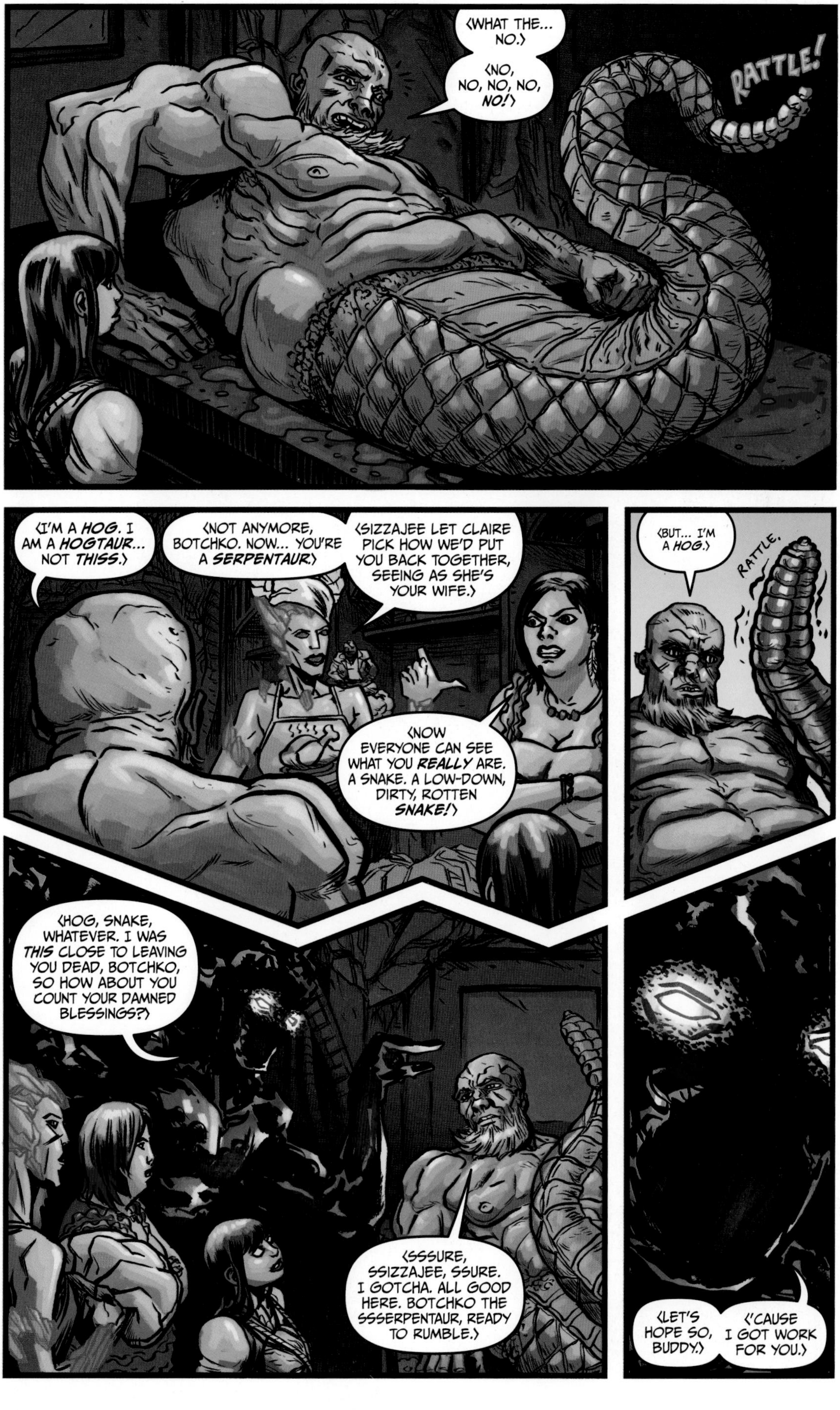
‹WHAT THE... NO.›
‹NO, NO, NO, NO, NO!›
RATTLE!
‹I'M A HOG. I AM A HOGTAUR... NOT THISS.›
‹NOT ANYMORE, BOTCHKO. NOW... YOU'RE A SERPENTAUR.›
‹SIZZAJEE LET CLAIRE PICK HOW WE'D PUT YOU BACK TOGETHER, SEEING AS SHE'S YOUR WIFE.›
‹NOW EVERYONE CAN SEE WHAT YOU REALLY ARE. A SNAKE. A LOW-DOWN, DIRTY, ROTTEN SNAKE!›
‹BUT... I'M A HOG.›
RATTLE.
‹HOG, SNAKE, WHATEVER. I WAS THIS CLOSE TO LEAVING YOU DEAD, BOTCHKO, SO HOW ABOUT YOU COUNT YOUR DAMNED BLESSINGS?›
‹SSSURE, SSIZZAJEE, SSURE. I GOTCHA. ALL GOOD HERE. BOTCHKO THE SSSERPENTAUR, READY TO RUMBLE.›
‹LET'S HOPE SO, BUDDY.›
‹'CAUSE I GOT WORK FOR YOU.›

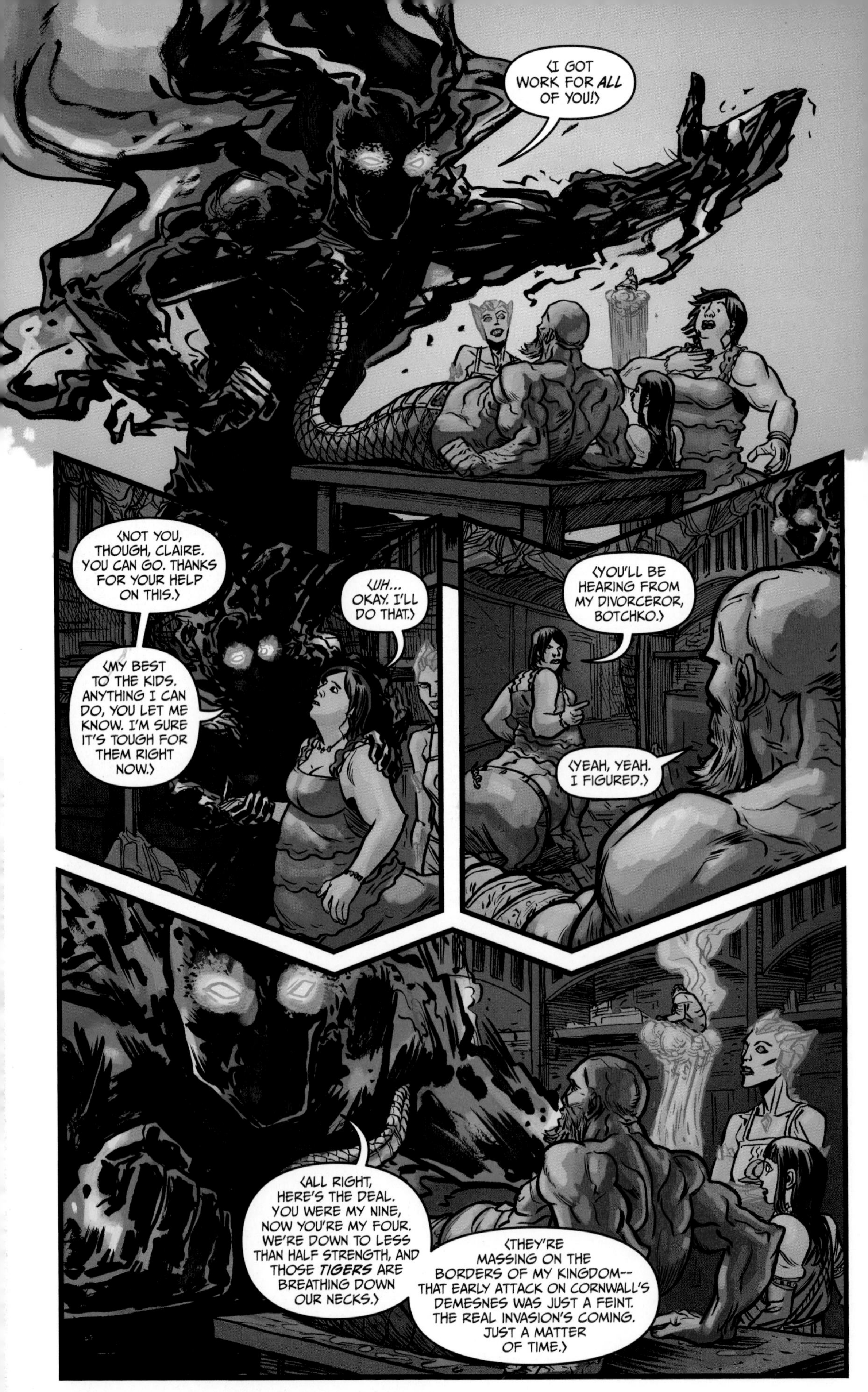
⟨I GOT WORK FOR ALL OF YOU!⟩
⟨NOT YOU, THOUGH, CLAIRE. YOU CAN GO. THANKS FOR YOUR HELP ON THIS.⟩
⟨MY BEST TO THE KIDS. ANYTHING I CAN DO, YOU LET ME KNOW. I'M SURE IT'S TOUGH FOR THEM RIGHT NOW.⟩
⟨UH... OKAY. I'LL DO THAT.⟩
⟨YOU'LL BE HEARING FROM MY DIVORCEROR, BOTCHKO.⟩
⟨YEAH, YEAH. I FIGURED.⟩
⟨ALL RIGHT, HERE'S THE DEAL. YOU WERE MY NINE, NOW YOU'RE MY FOUR. WE'RE DOWN TO LESS THAN HALF STRENGTH, AND THOSE TIGERS ARE BREATHING DOWN OUR NECKS.⟩
⟨THEY'RE MASSING ON THE BORDERS OF MY KINGDOM-- THAT EARLY ATTACK ON CORNWALL'S DEMESNES WAS JUST A FEINT. THE REAL INVASION'S COMING. JUST A MATTER OF TIME.⟩

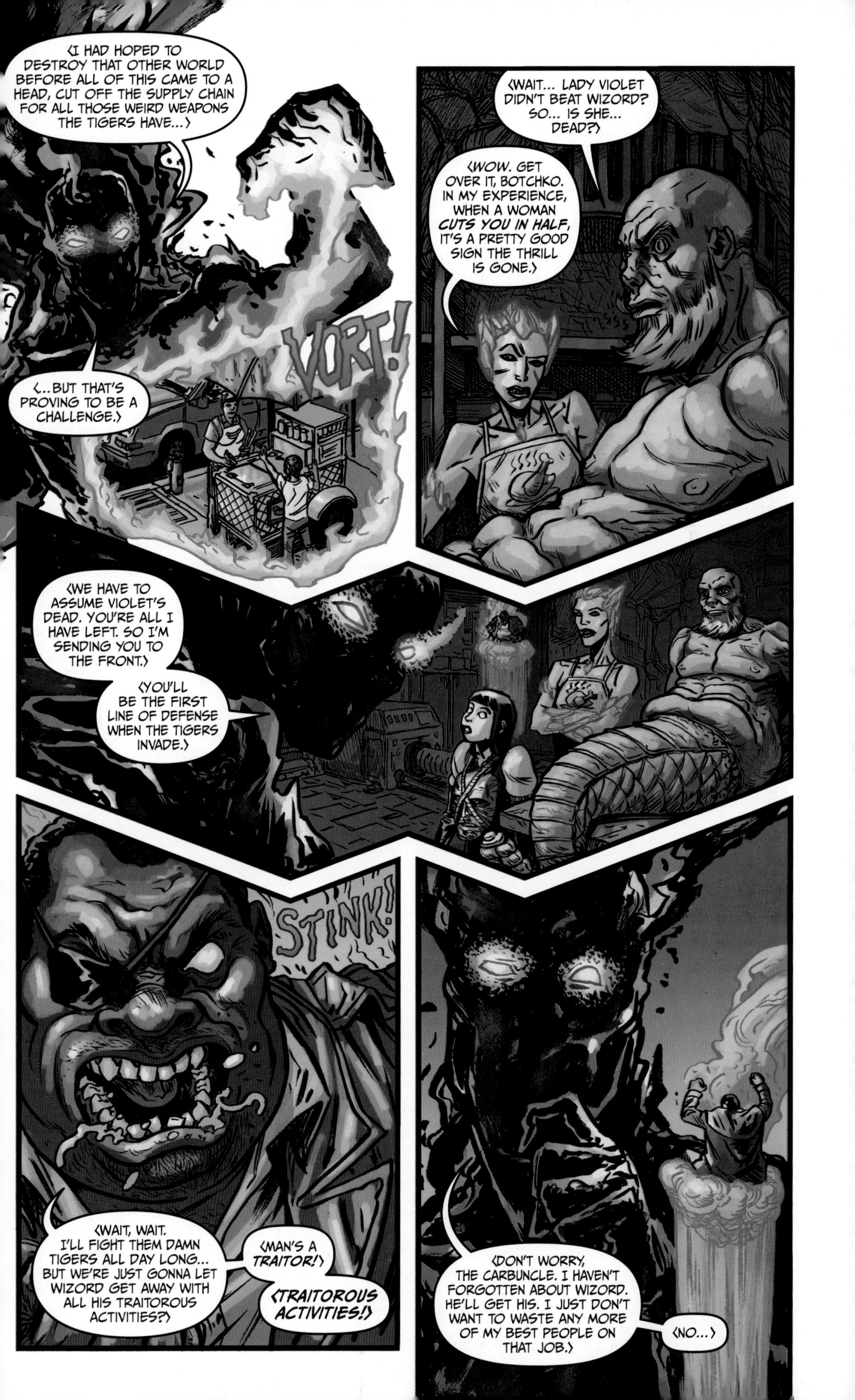

⟨I HAD HOPED TO DESTROY THAT OTHER WORLD BEFORE ALL OF THIS CAME TO A HEAD, CUT OFF THE SUPPLY CHAIN FOR ALL THOSE WEIRD WEAPONS THE TIGERS HAVE...⟩
VORT!
⟨...BUT THAT'S PROVING TO BE A CHALLENGE.⟩
⟨WAIT... LADY VIOLET DIDN'T BEAT WIZORD? SO... IS SHE... DEAD?⟩
⟨WOW. GET OVER IT, BOTCHKO. IN MY EXPERIENCE, WHEN A WOMAN *CUTS YOU IN HALF*, IT'S A PRETTY GOOD SIGN THE THRILL IS GONE.⟩
⟨WE HAVE TO ASSUME VIOLET'S DEAD. YOU'RE ALL I HAVE LEFT. SO I'M SENDING YOU TO THE FRONT.⟩
⟨YOU'LL BE THE FIRST LINE OF DEFENSE WHEN THE TIGERS INVADE.⟩
STINK!
⟨WAIT, WAIT. I'LL FIGHT THEM DAMN TIGERS ALL DAY LONG... BUT WE'RE JUST GONNA LET WIZORD GET AWAY WITH ALL HIS TRAITOROUS ACTIVITIES?⟩
⟨MAN'S A *TRAITOR!*⟩
⟨*TRAITOROUS ACTIVITIES!*⟩
⟨DON'T WORRY, THE CARBUNCLE. I HAVEN'T FORGOTTEN ABOUT WIZORD. HE'LL GET HIS. I JUST DON'T WANT TO WASTE ANY MORE OF MY BEST PEOPLE ON THAT JOB.⟩
⟨NO...⟩

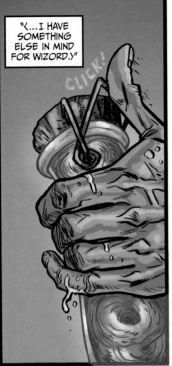

"〈...I HAVE SOMETHING ELSE IN MIND FOR WIZORD.〉"

CLICK!

TINK!

TINK!

WHOA, EASY THERE, PAL!

YOU'VE GOT SOME PRETTY VOLATILE STUFF IN THAT BOTTLE, JACQUES ZACQUES. THAT BREAKS, WE'RE ALL DONE FOR.

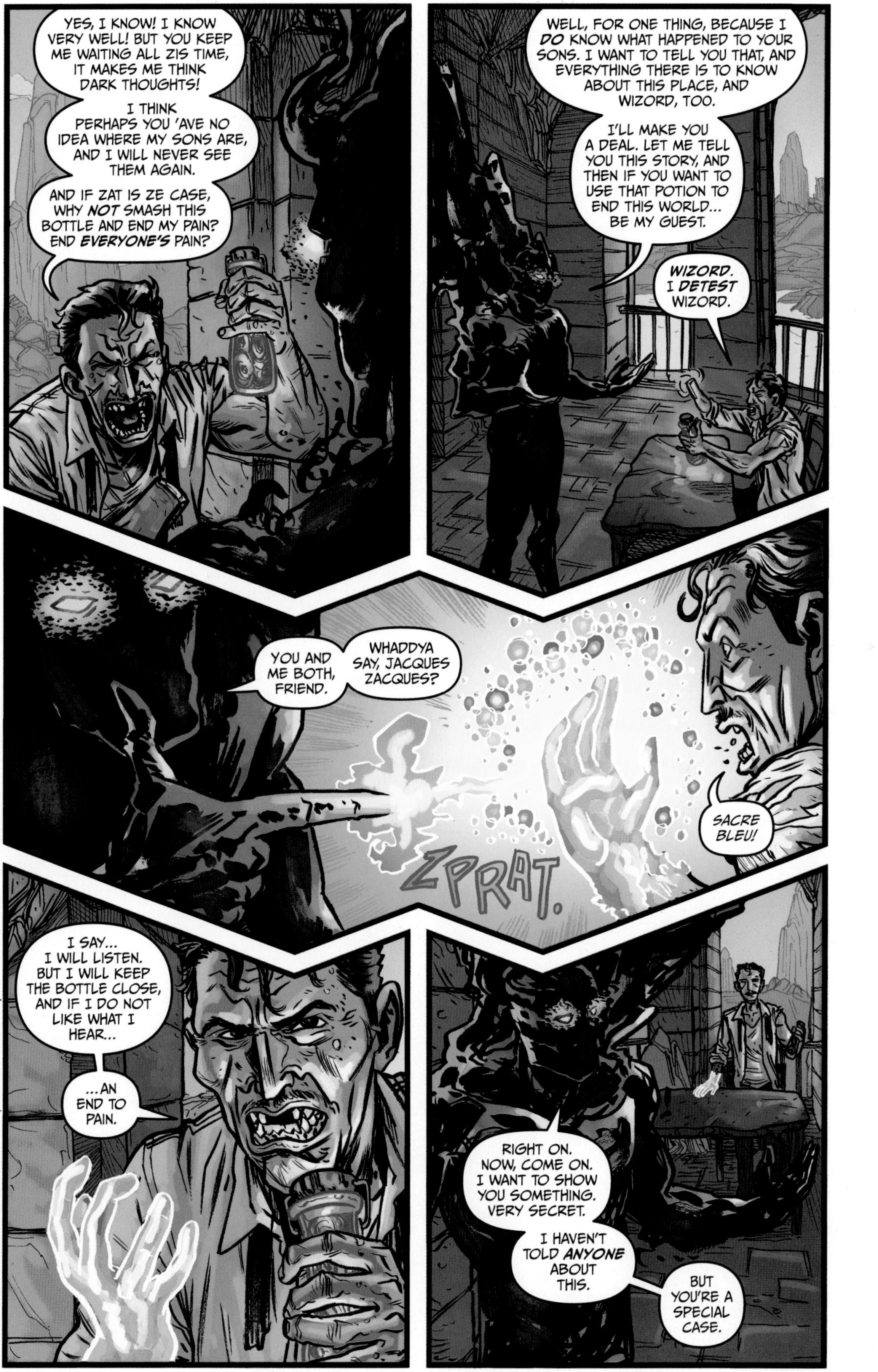
YES, I KNOW! I KNOW VERY WELL! BUT YOU KEEP ME WAITING ALL ZIS TIME, IT MAKES ME THINK DARK THOUGHTS!
I THINK PERHAPS YOU 'AVE NO IDEA WHERE MY SONS ARE, AND I WILL NEVER SEE THEM AGAIN.
AND IF ZAT IS ZE CASE, WHY *NOT* SMASH THIS BOTTLE AND END MY PAIN? END *EVERYONE'S* PAIN?
WELL, FOR ONE THING, BECAUSE I *DO* KNOW WHAT HAPPENED TO YOUR SONS. I WANT TO TELL YOU THAT, AND EVERYTHING THERE IS TO KNOW ABOUT THIS PLACE, AND WIZORD, TOO.
I'LL MAKE YOU A DEAL. LET ME TELL YOU THIS STORY, AND THEN IF YOU WANT TO USE THAT POTION TO END THIS WORLD... BE MY GUEST.
WIZORD. I *DETEST* WIZORD.
YOU AND ME BOTH, FRIEND.
WHADDYA SAY, JACQUES ZACQUES?
ZPRAT.
SACRE BLEU!
I SAY... I WILL LISTEN. BUT I WILL KEEP THE BOTTLE CLOSE, AND IF I DO NOT LIKE WHAT I HEAR...
...AN END TO PAIN.
RIGHT ON. NOW, COME ON. I WANT TO SHOW YOU SOMETHING. VERY SECRET.
I HAVEN'T TOLD *ANYONE* ABOUT THIS.
BUT YOU'RE A SPECIAL CASE.

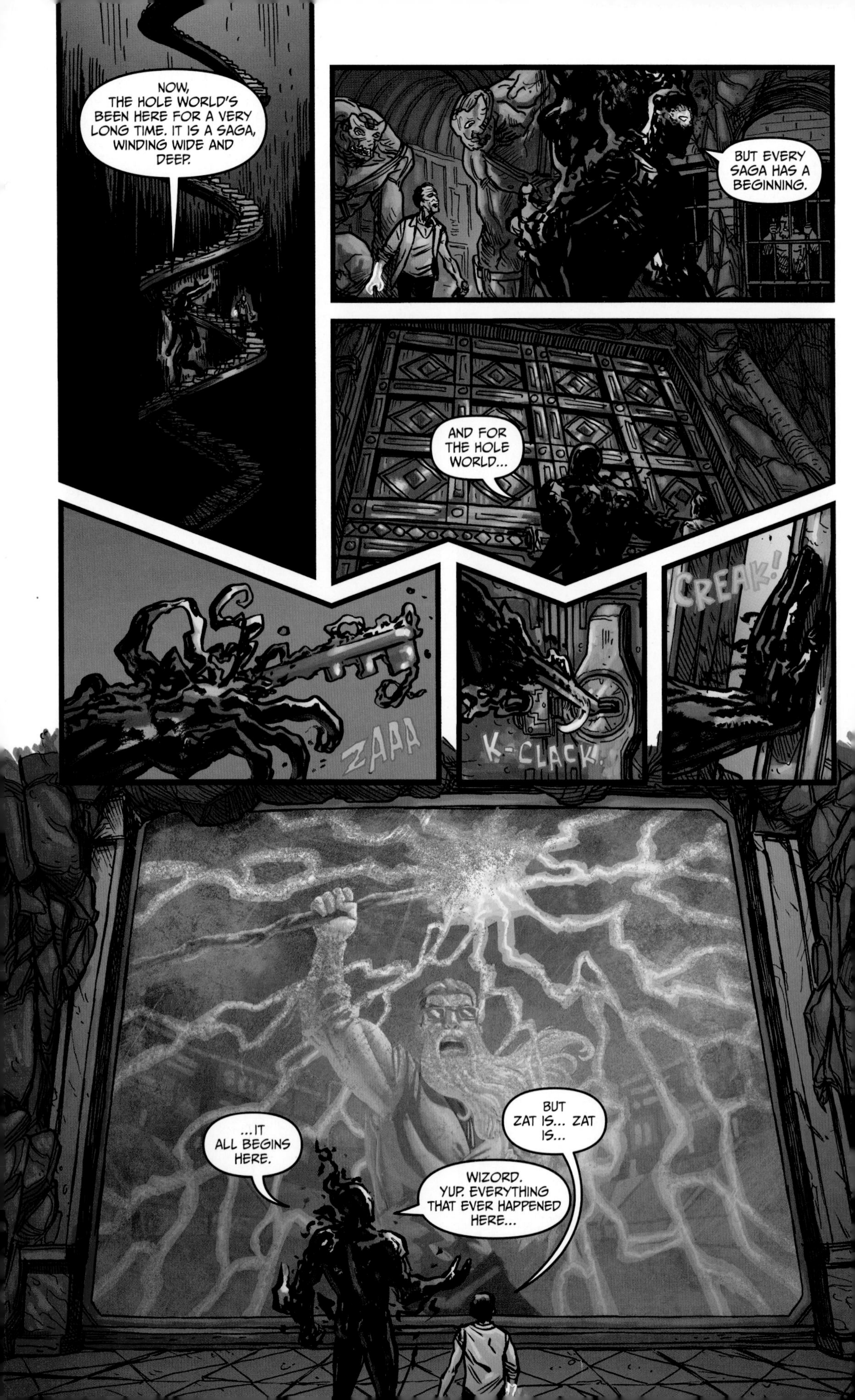
NOW, THE HOLE WORLD'S BEEN HERE FOR A VERY LONG TIME. IT IS A SAGA, WINDING WIDE AND DEEP.
BUT EVERY SAGA HAS A BEGINNING.
AND FOR THE HOLE WORLD...
ZAAA
K-CLACK!
CREAK!
...IT ALL BEGINS HERE.
BUT ZAT IS... ZAT IS...
WIZORD. YUP. EVERYTHING THAT EVER HAPPENED HERE...

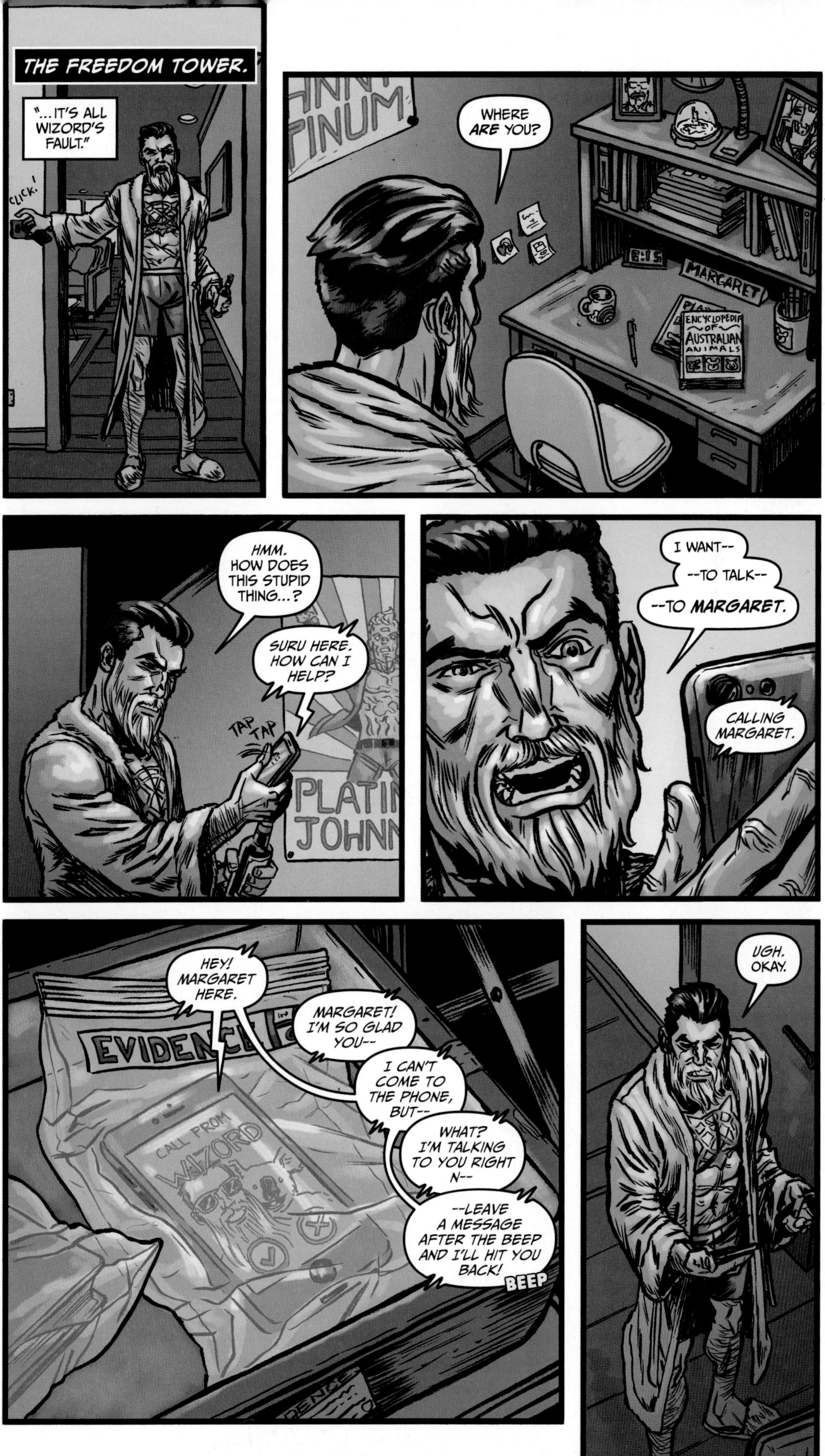
THE FREEDOM TOWER.
"...IT'S ALL WIZORD'S FAULT."
CLICK!
WHERE ARE YOU?
MARGARET
ENCYCLOPEDIA OF AUSTRALIAN ANIMALS
HMM. HOW DOES THIS STUPID THING...?
SURU HERE. HOW CAN I HELP?
TAP TAP
PLATIN JOHNN
I WANT--
--TO TALK--
--TO MARGARET.
CALLING MARGARET.
HEY! MARGARET HERE.
EVIDENCE
CALL FROM WIZORD
MARGARET! I'M SO GLAD YOU--
I CAN'T COME TO THE PHONE, BUT--
WHAT? I'M TALKING TO YOU RIGHT N--
--LEAVE A MESSAGE AFTER THE BEEP AND I'LL HIT YOU BACK!
BEEP
UGH. OKAY.

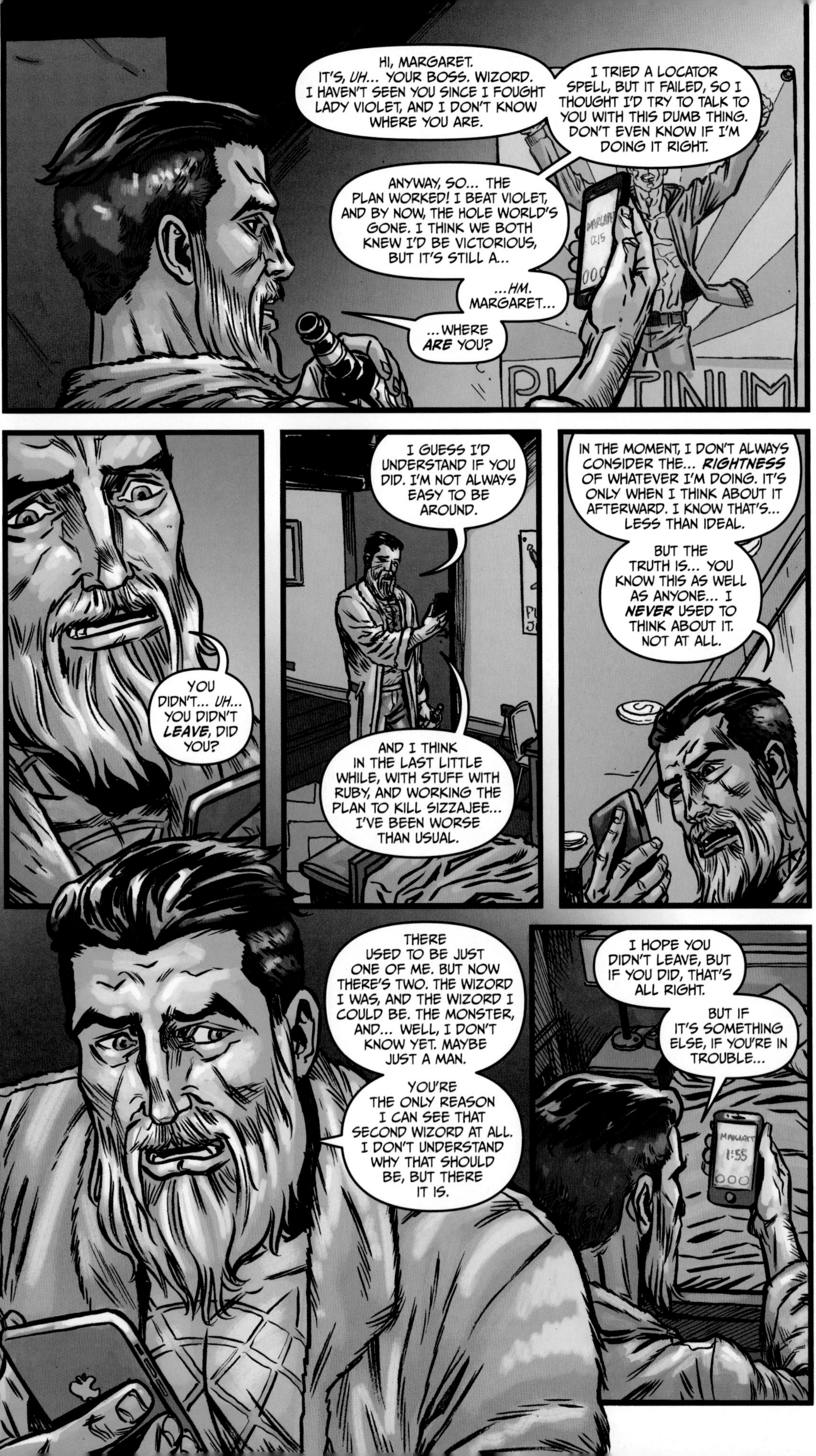
HI, MARGARET. IT'S, *UH*... YOUR BOSS. WIZORD. I HAVEN'T SEEN YOU SINCE I FOUGHT LADY VIOLET, AND I DON'T KNOW WHERE YOU ARE.
I TRIED A LOCATOR SPELL, BUT IT FAILED, SO I THOUGHT I'D TRY TO TALK TO YOU WITH THIS DUMB THING. DON'T EVEN KNOW IF I'M DOING IT RIGHT.
ANYWAY, SO... THE PLAN WORKED! I BEAT VIOLET, AND BY NOW, THE HOLE WORLD'S GONE. I THINK WE BOTH KNEW I'D BE VICTORIOUS, BUT IT'S STILL A...
...*HM*. MARGARET...
...WHERE ***ARE*** YOU?
YOU DIDN'T... *UH*... YOU DIDN'T ***LEAVE***, DID YOU?
I GUESS I'D UNDERSTAND IF YOU DID. I'M NOT ALWAYS EASY TO BE AROUND.
AND I THINK IN THE LAST LITTLE WHILE, WITH STUFF WITH RUBY, AND WORKING THE PLAN TO KILL SIZZAJEE... I'VE BEEN WORSE THAN USUAL.
IN THE MOMENT, I DON'T ALWAYS CONSIDER THE... ***RIGHTNESS*** OF WHATEVER I'M DOING. IT'S ONLY WHEN I THINK ABOUT IT AFTERWARD. I KNOW THAT'S... LESS THAN IDEAL.
BUT THE TRUTH IS... YOU KNOW THIS AS WELL AS ANYONE... I ***NEVER*** USED TO THINK ABOUT IT. NOT AT ALL.
THERE USED TO BE JUST ONE OF ME. BUT NOW THERE'S TWO. THE WIZORD I WAS, AND THE WIZORD I COULD BE. THE MONSTER, AND... WELL, I DON'T KNOW YET. MAYBE JUST A MAN.
YOU'RE THE ONLY REASON I CAN SEE THAT SECOND WIZORD AT ALL. I DON'T UNDERSTAND WHY THAT SHOULD BE, BUT THERE IT IS.
I HOPE YOU DIDN'T LEAVE, BUT IF YOU DID, THAT'S ALL RIGHT.
BUT IF IT'S SOMETHING ELSE, IF YOU'RE IN TROUBLE...

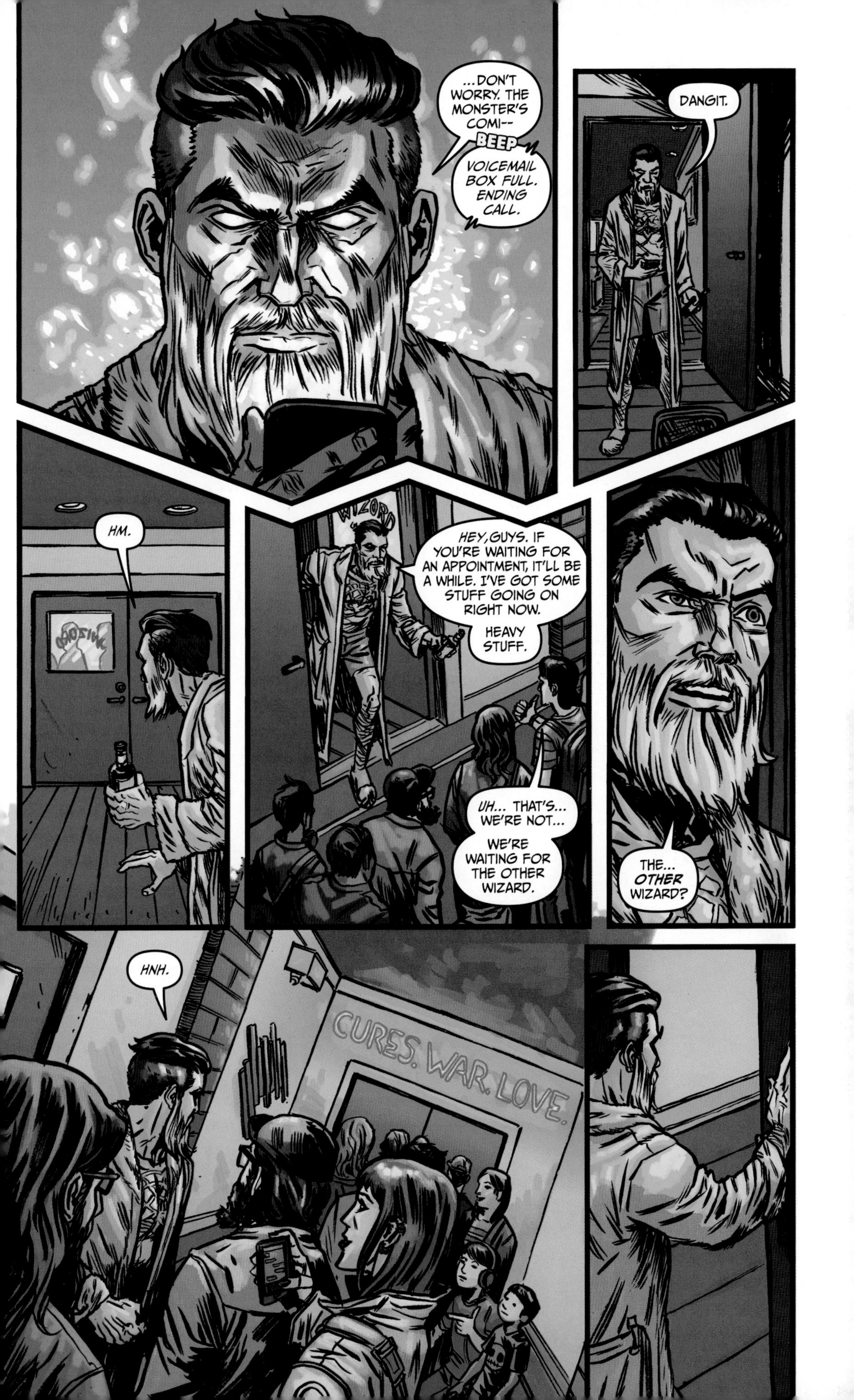
...DON'T WORRY. THE MONSTER'S COMI--
BEEP
VOICEMAIL BOX FULL. ENDING CALL.
DANGIT.
HM.
WIZARD
HEY, GUYS. IF YOU'RE WAITING FOR AN APPOINTMENT, IT'LL BE A WHILE. I'VE GOT SOME STUFF GOING ON RIGHT NOW.
HEAVY STUFF.
UH... THAT'S... WE'RE NOT...
WE'RE WAITING FOR THE OTHER WIZARD.
THE... OTHER WIZARD?
HNH.
CURES. WAR. LOVE.

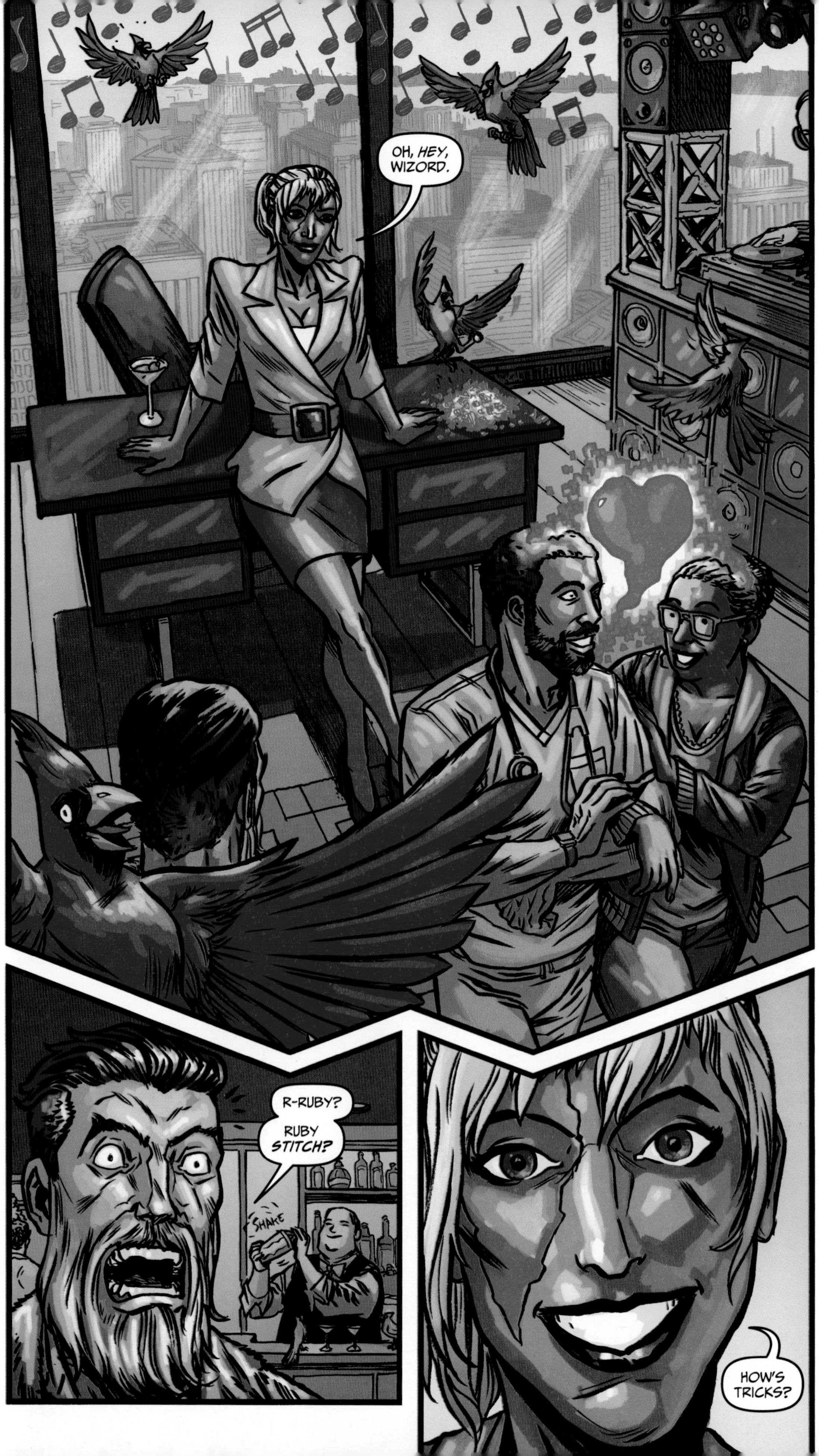
OH, HEY, WIZORD.
R-RUBY?
RUBY STITCH?
SHAKE
HOW'S TRICKS?

TWELVE

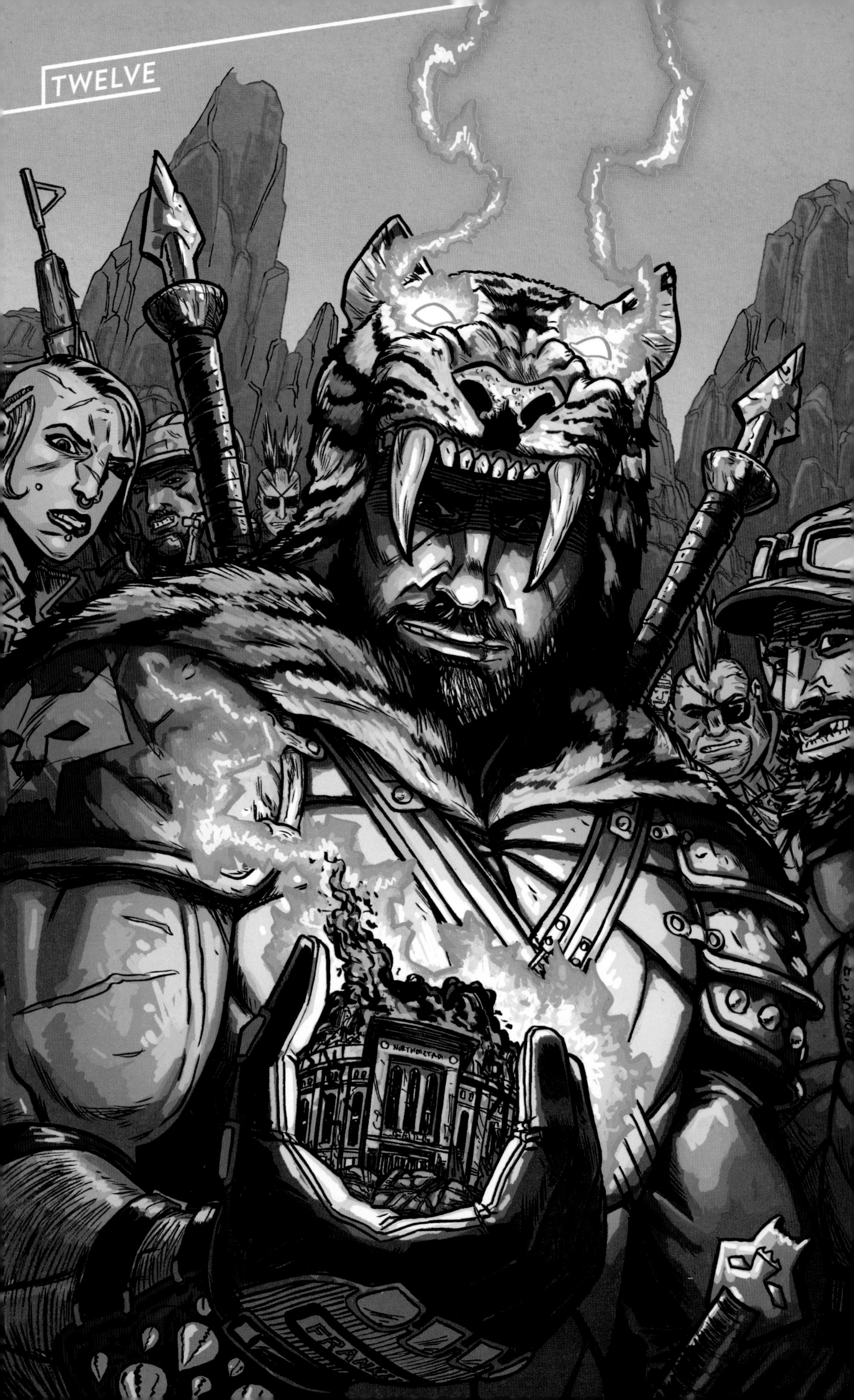

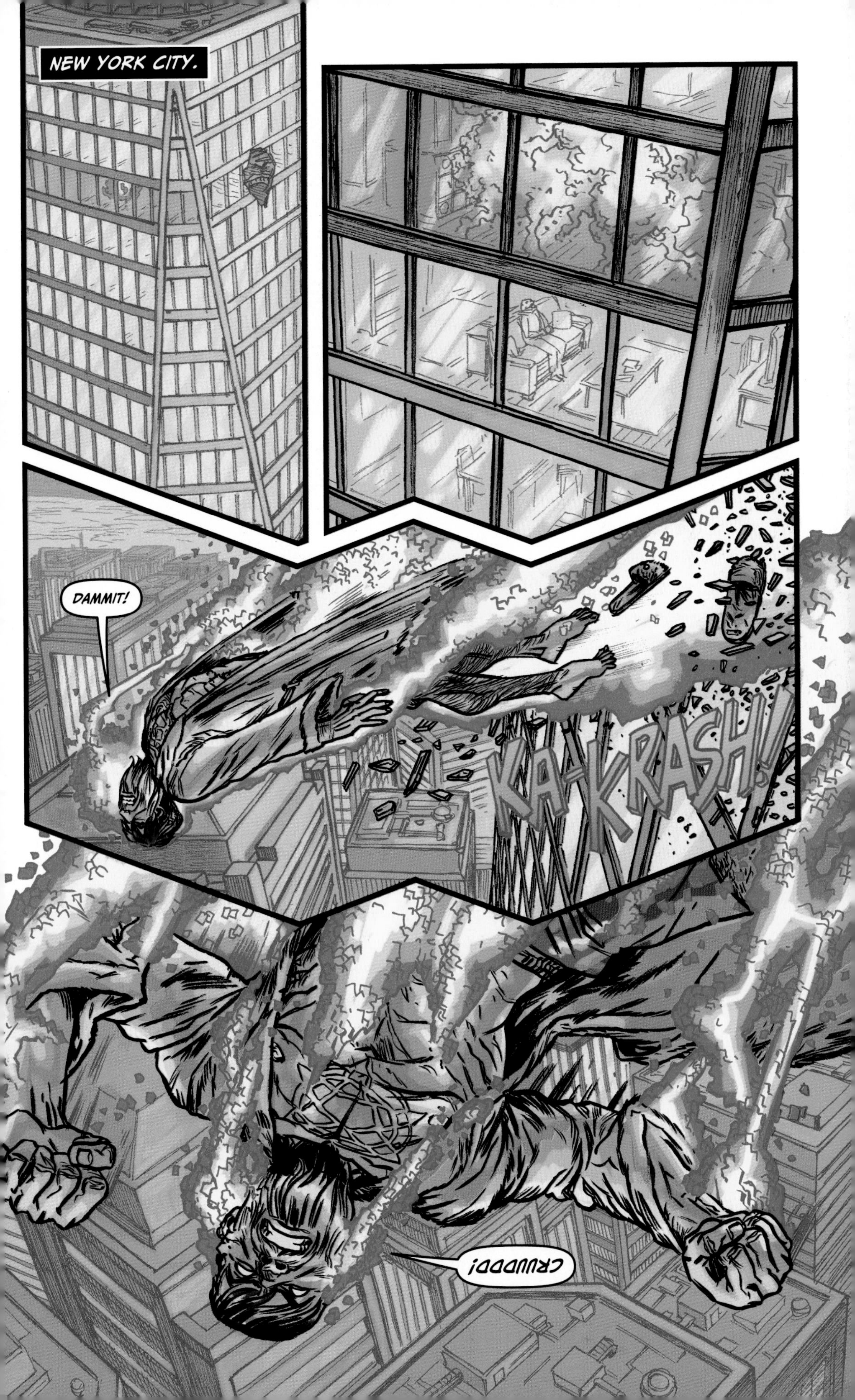

NEW YORK CITY.
DAMMIT!
KA-KRASH!!
CRUDDD!

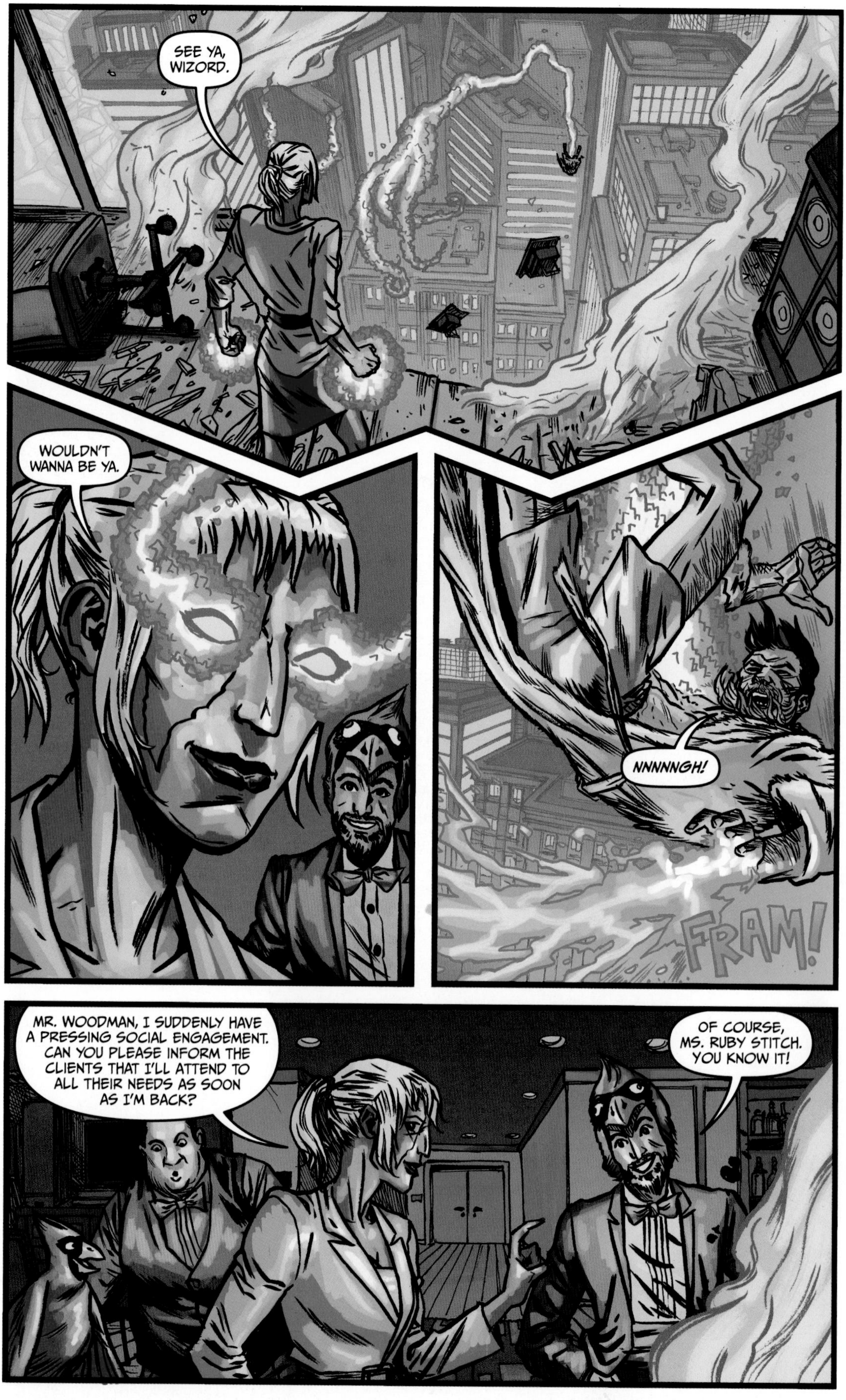
SEE YA, WIZORD.
WOULDN'T WANNA BE YA.
NNNNNGH!
FRAM!
MR. WOODMAN, I SUDDENLY HAVE A PRESSING SOCIAL ENGAGEMENT. CAN YOU PLEASE INFORM THE CLIENTS THAT I'LL ATTEND TO ALL THEIR NEEDS AS SOON AS I'M BACK?
OF COURSE, MS. RUBY STITCH. YOU KNOW IT!

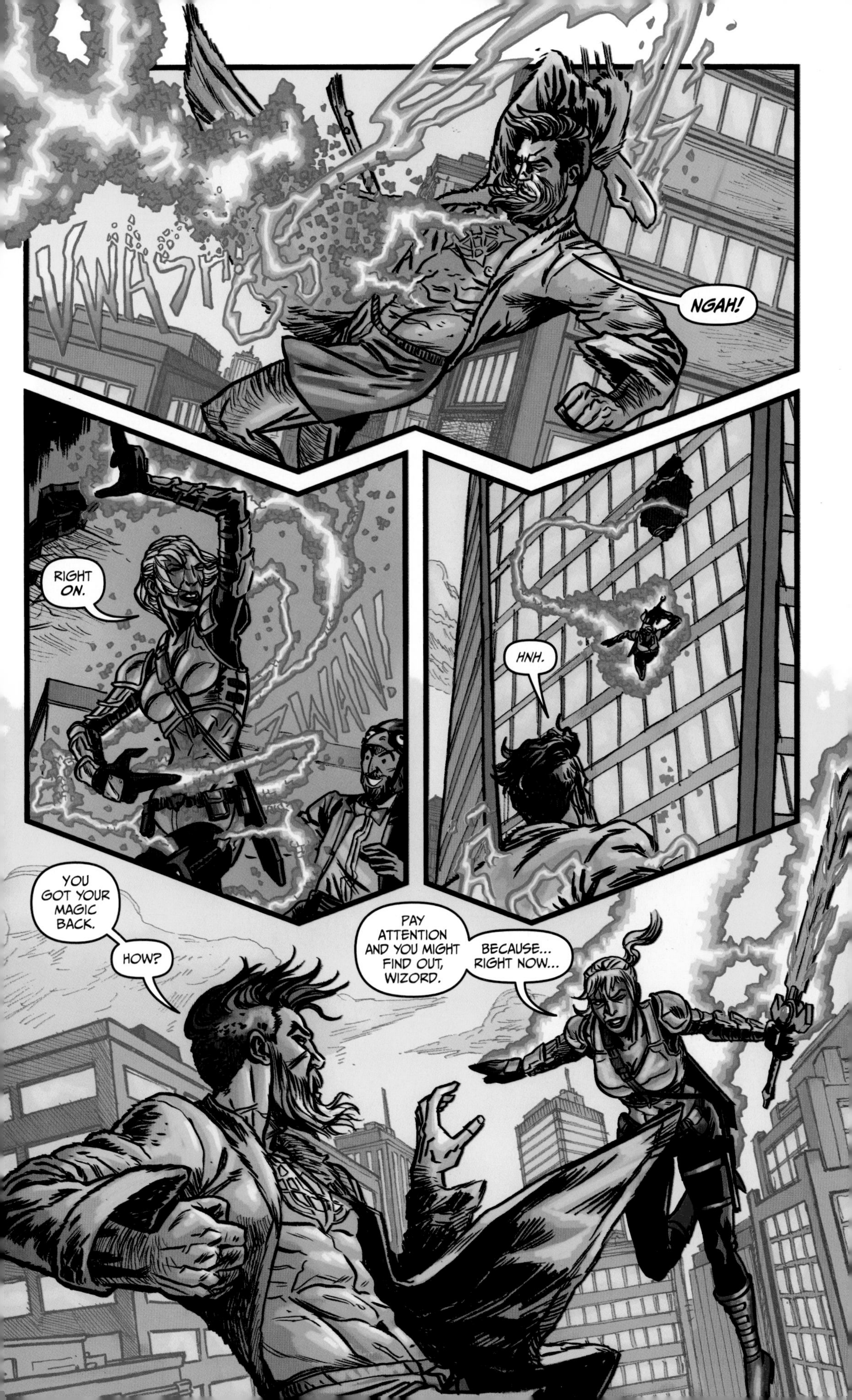
VWASSH
NGAH!
RIGHT ON.
ZWAN!
HNH.
YOU GOT YOUR MAGIC BACK.
HOW?
PAY ATTENTION AND YOU MIGHT FIND OUT, WIZORD.
BECAUSE... RIGHT NOW...

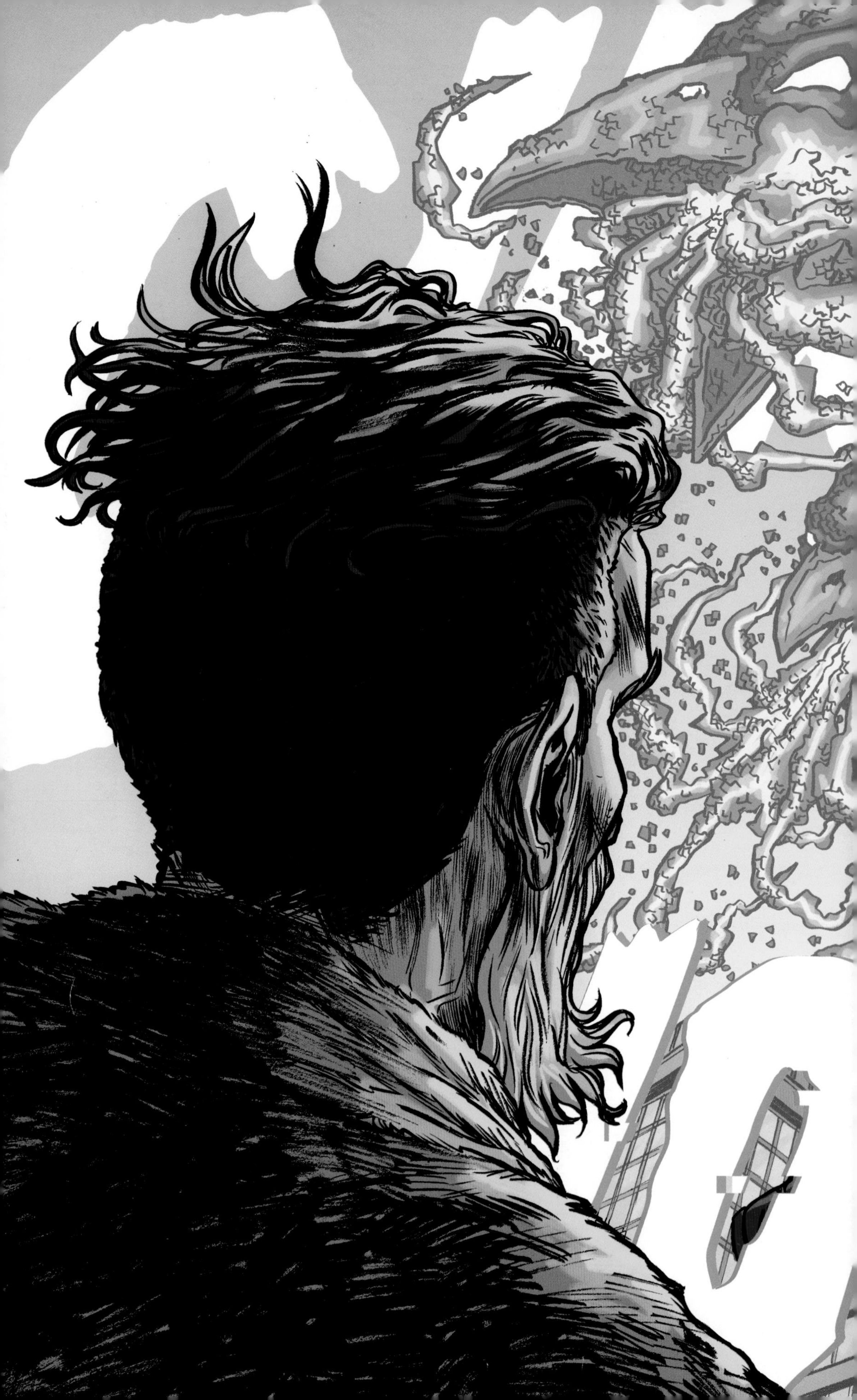

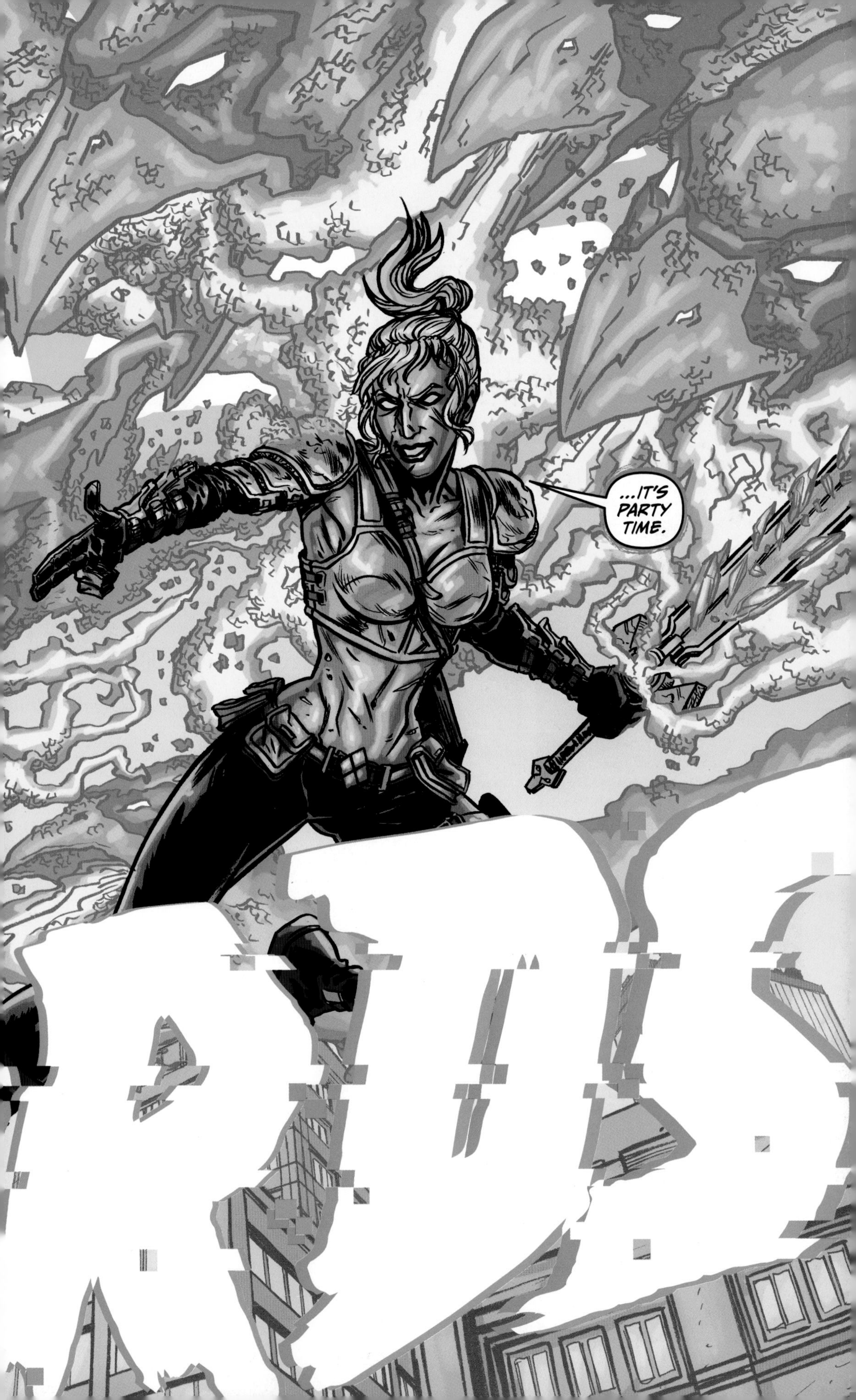
...IT'S PARTY TIME.

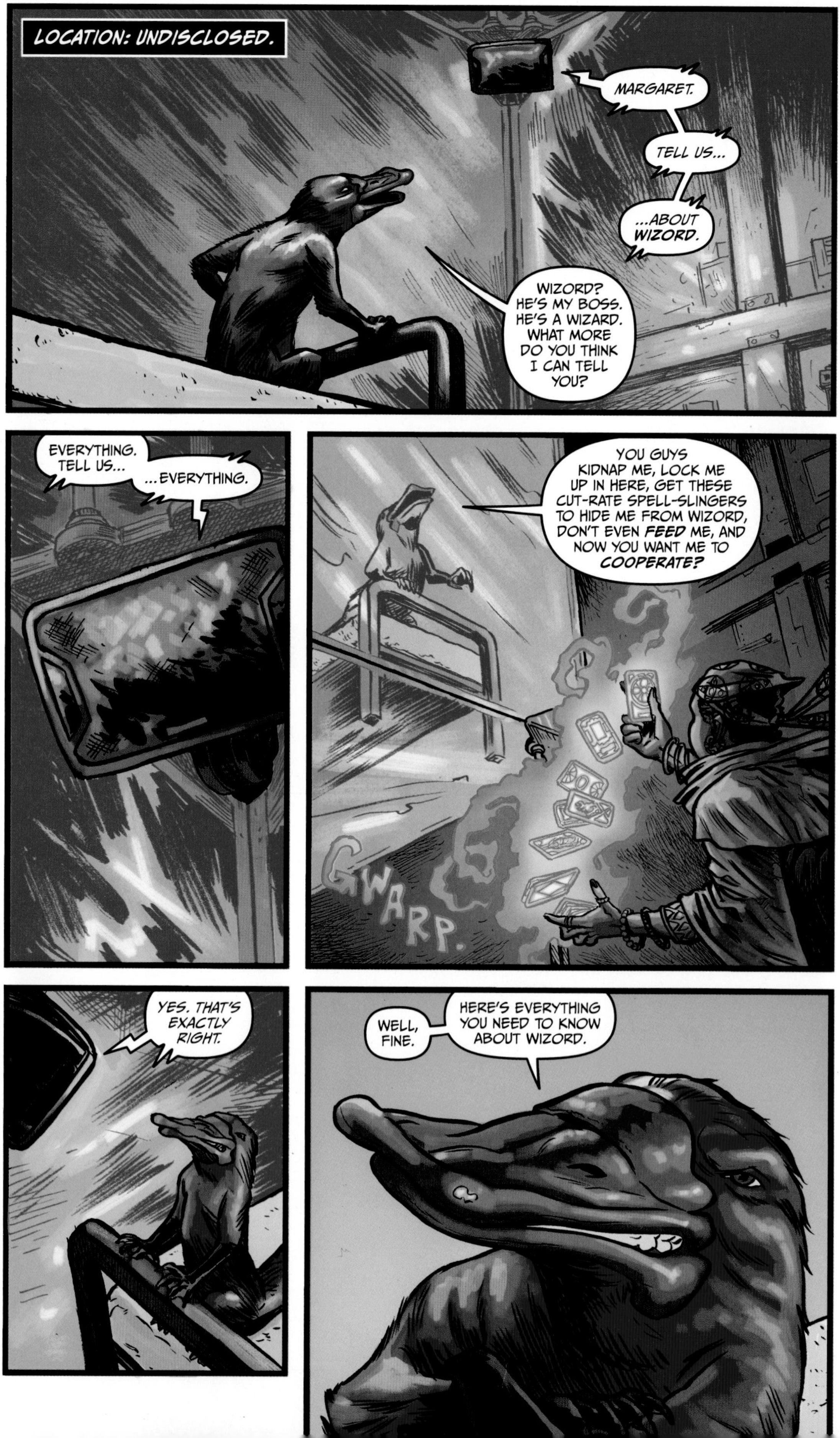
LOCATION: UNDISCLOSED.
MARGARET.
TELL US...
...ABOUT WIZORD.
WIZORD? HE'S MY BOSS. HE'S A WIZARD. WHAT MORE DO YOU THINK I CAN TELL YOU?
EVERYTHING. TELL US...
...EVERYTHING.
YOU GUYS KIDNAP ME, LOCK ME UP IN HERE, GET THESE CUT-RATE SPELL-SLINGERS TO HIDE ME FROM WIZORD, DON'T EVEN FEED ME, AND NOW YOU WANT ME TO COOPERATE?
GWARP.
YES. THAT'S EXACTLY RIGHT.
WELL, FINE.
HERE'S EVERYTHING YOU NEED TO KNOW ABOUT WIZORD.

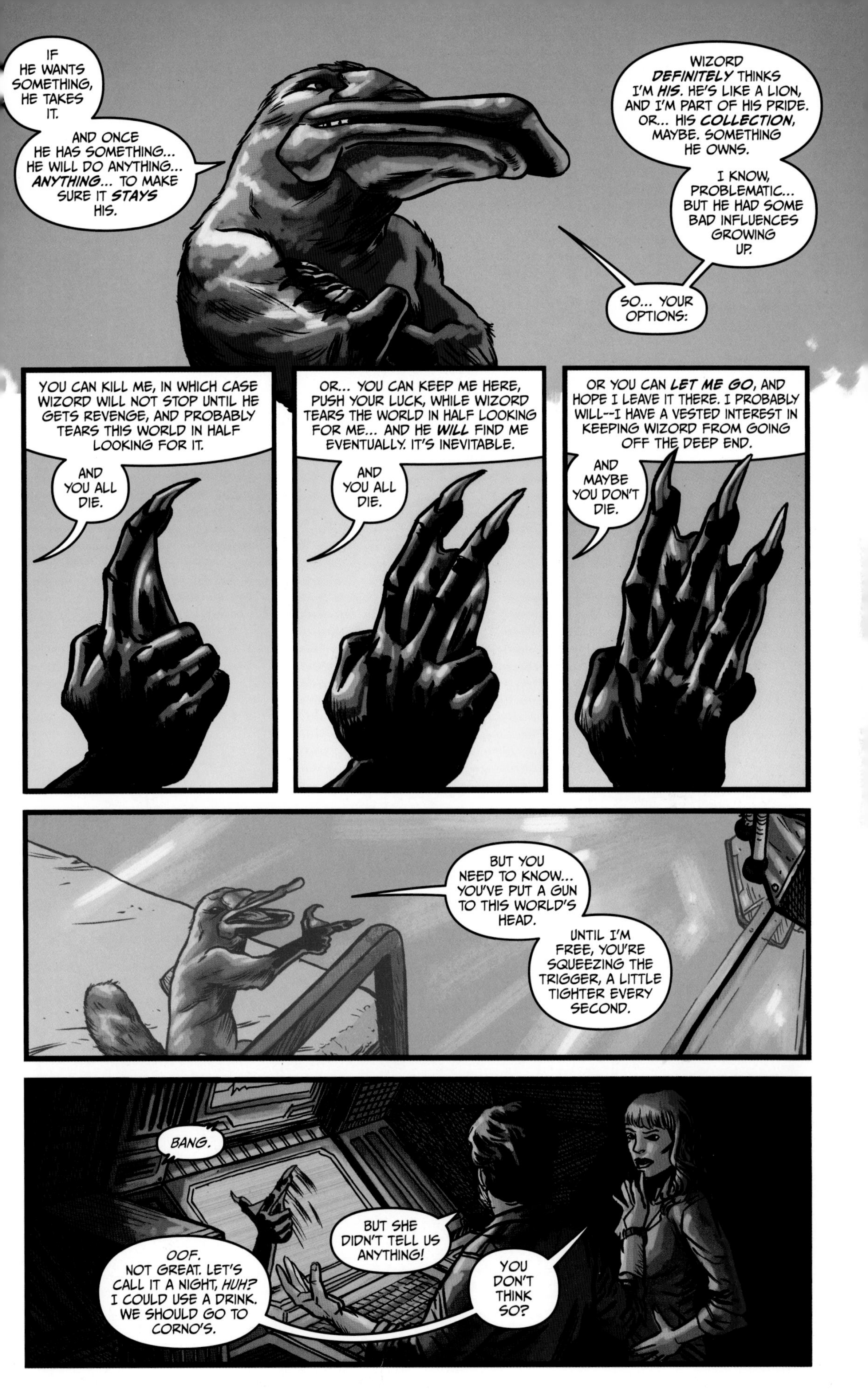

IF HE WANTS SOMETHING, HE TAKES IT.
AND ONCE HE HAS SOMETHING... HE WILL DO ANYTHING... ANYTHING... TO MAKE SURE IT STAYS HIS.
WIZORD DEFINITELY THINKS I'M HIS. HE'S LIKE A LION, AND I'M PART OF HIS PRIDE. OR... HIS COLLECTION, MAYBE. SOMETHING HE OWNS.
I KNOW, PROBLEMATIC... BUT HE HAD SOME BAD INFLUENCES GROWING UP.
SO... YOUR OPTIONS:
YOU CAN KILL ME, IN WHICH CASE WIZORD WILL NOT STOP UNTIL HE GETS REVENGE, AND PROBABLY TEARS THIS WORLD IN HALF LOOKING FOR IT.
AND YOU ALL DIE.
OR... YOU CAN KEEP ME HERE, PUSH YOUR LUCK, WHILE WIZORD TEARS THE WORLD IN HALF LOOKING FOR ME... AND HE WILL FIND ME EVENTUALLY. IT'S INEVITABLE.
AND YOU ALL DIE.
OR YOU CAN LET ME GO, AND HOPE I LEAVE IT THERE. I PROBABLY WILL--I HAVE A VESTED INTEREST IN KEEPING WIZORD FROM GOING OFF THE DEEP END.
AND MAYBE YOU DON'T DIE.
BUT YOU NEED TO KNOW... YOU'VE PUT A GUN TO THIS WORLD'S HEAD.
UNTIL I'M FREE, YOU'RE SQUEEZING THE TRIGGER, A LITTLE TIGHTER EVERY SECOND.
BANG.
OOF. NOT GREAT. LET'S CALL IT A NIGHT, HUH? I COULD USE A DRINK. WE SHOULD GO TO CORNO'S.
BUT SHE DIDN'T TELL US ANYTHING!
YOU DON'T THINK SO?

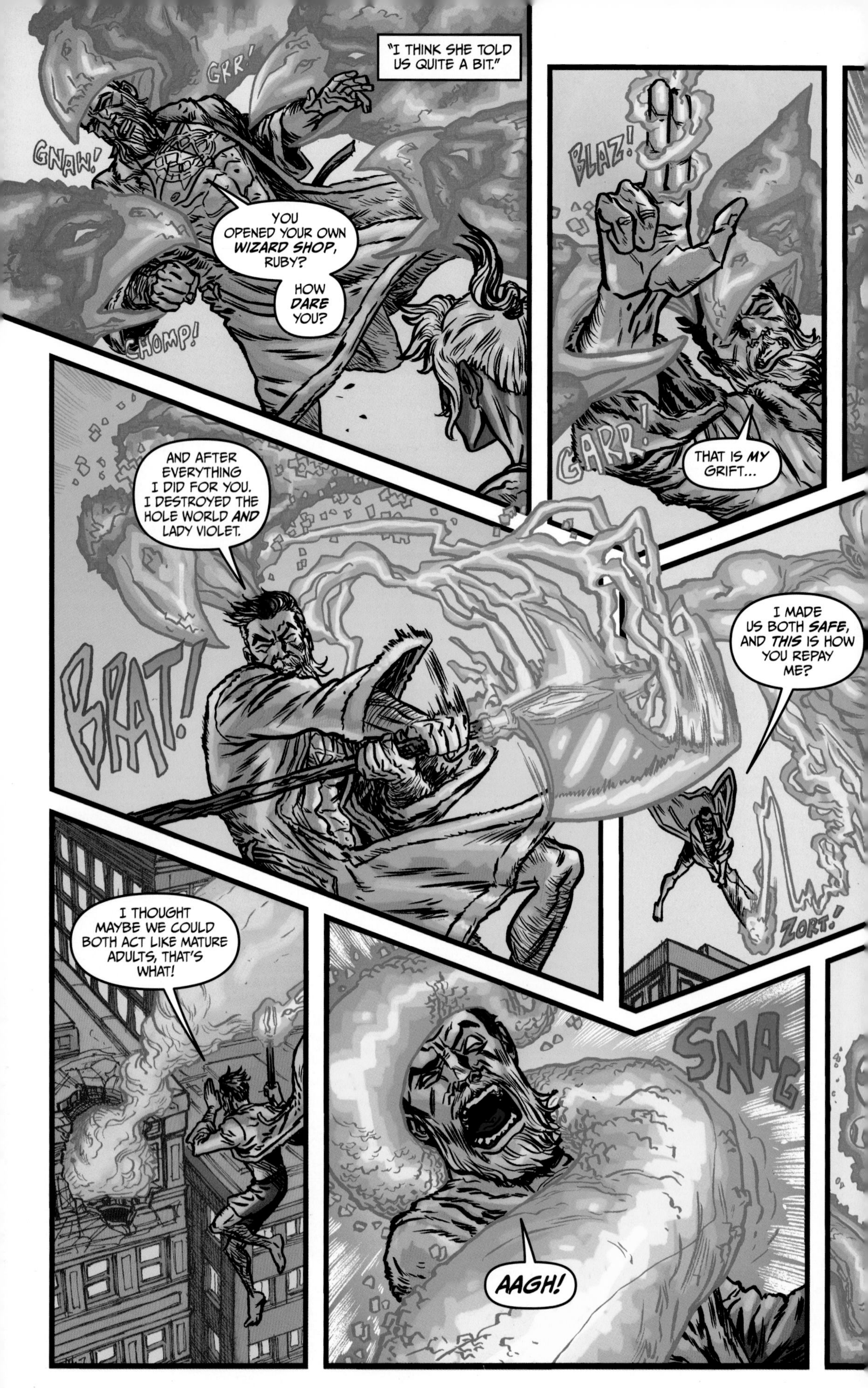
"I THINK SHE TOLD US QUITE A BIT."
GRR!
GNAW!
YOU OPENED YOUR OWN WIZARD SHOP, RUBY?
HOW DARE YOU?
CHOMP!
BLAZ!
GARR!
THAT IS MY GRIFT...
AND AFTER EVERYTHING I DID FOR YOU. I DESTROYED THE HOLE WORLD AND LADY VIOLET.
BRAT!
I MADE US BOTH SAFE, AND THIS IS HOW YOU REPAY ME?
ZORT!
I THOUGHT MAYBE WE COULD BOTH ACT LIKE MATURE ADULTS, THAT'S WHAT!
SNAG
AAGH!

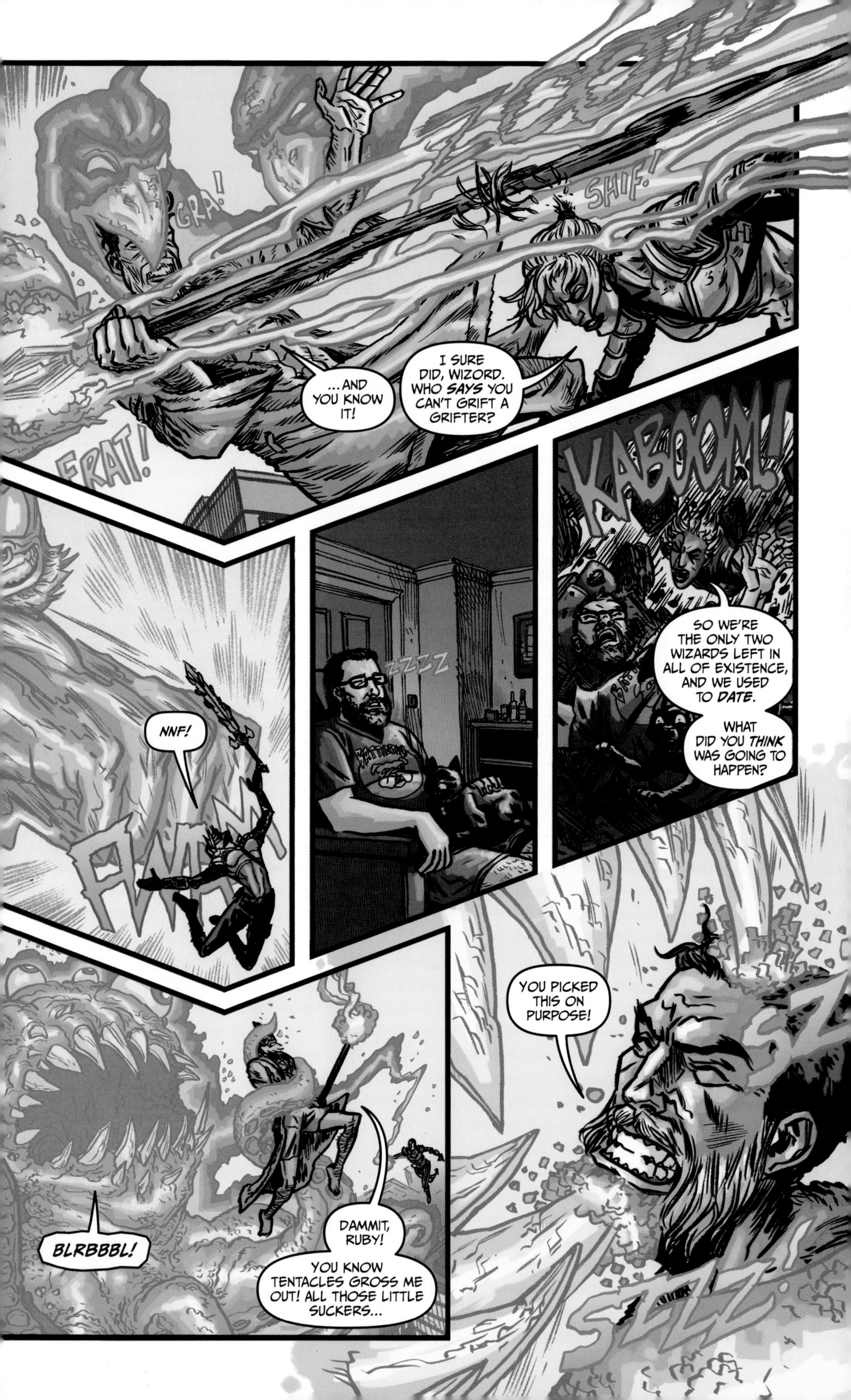
ZOOSH!
GRA!
SHIF!
...AND YOU KNOW IT!
I SURE DID, WIZORD. WHO SAYS YOU CAN'T GRIFT A GRIFTER?
FRAT!
KABOOM!
SO WE'RE THE ONLY TWO WIZARDS LEFT IN ALL OF EXISTENCE, AND WE USED TO DATE.
WHAT DID YOU THINK WAS GOING TO HAPPEN?
ZZZZ
NNF!
YOU PICKED THIS ON PURPOSE!
BLRBBBL!
DAMMIT, RUBY!
YOU KNOW TENTACLES GROSS ME OUT! ALL THOSE LITTLE SUCKERS...
SZZZ!

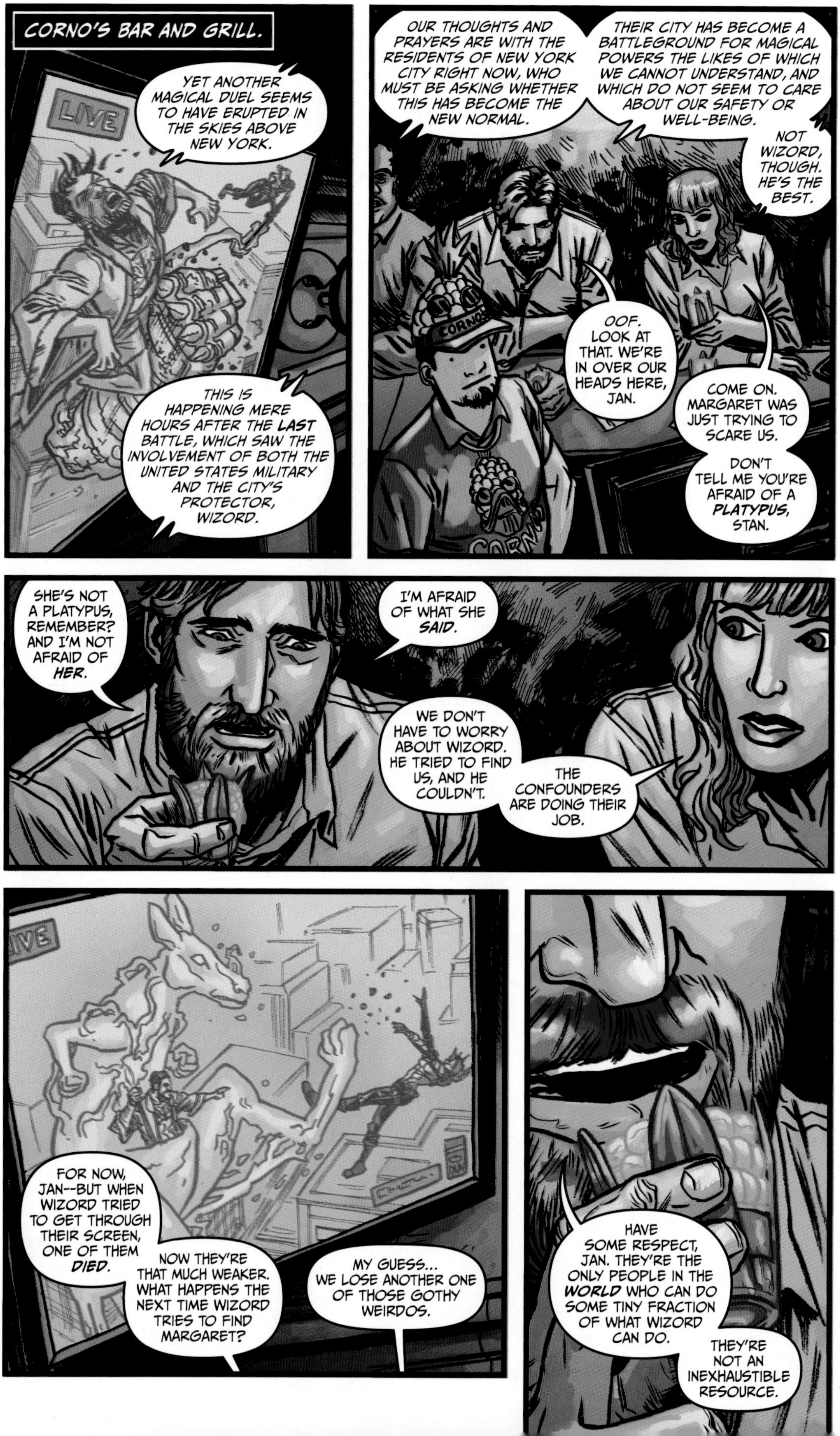
CORNO'S BAR AND GRILL.
YET ANOTHER MAGICAL DUEL SEEMS TO HAVE ERUPTED IN THE SKIES ABOVE NEW YORK.
LIVE
THIS IS HAPPENING MERE HOURS AFTER THE **LAST** BATTLE, WHICH SAW THE INVOLVEMENT OF BOTH THE UNITED STATES MILITARY AND THE CITY'S PROTECTOR, WIZORD.
OUR THOUGHTS AND PRAYERS ARE WITH THE RESIDENTS OF NEW YORK CITY RIGHT NOW, WHO MUST BE ASKING WHETHER THIS HAS BECOME THE NEW NORMAL.
THEIR CITY HAS BECOME A BATTLEGROUND FOR MAGICAL POWERS THE LIKES OF WHICH WE CANNOT UNDERSTAND, AND WHICH DO NOT SEEM TO CARE ABOUT OUR SAFETY OR WELL-BEING.
NOT WIZORD, THOUGH. HE'S THE BEST.
CORNO
OOF. LOOK AT THAT. WE'RE IN OVER OUR HEADS HERE, JAN.
COME ON. MARGARET WAS JUST TRYING TO SCARE US.
DON'T TELL ME YOU'RE AFRAID OF A ***PLATYPUS***, STAN.
SHE'S NOT A PLATYPUS, REMEMBER? AND I'M NOT AFRAID OF ***HER***.
I'M AFRAID OF WHAT SHE ***SAID***.
WE DON'T HAVE TO WORRY ABOUT WIZORD. HE TRIED TO FIND US, AND HE COULDN'T.
THE CONFOUNDERS ARE DOING THEIR JOB.
LIVE
FOR NOW, JAN--BUT WHEN WIZORD TRIED TO GET THROUGH THEIR SCREEN, ONE OF THEM ***DIED***.
NOW THEY'RE THAT MUCH WEAKER. WHAT HAPPENS THE NEXT TIME WIZORD TRIES TO FIND MARGARET?
MY GUESS... WE LOSE ANOTHER ONE OF THOSE GOTHY WEIRDOS.
HAVE SOME RESPECT, JAN. THEY'RE THE ONLY PEOPLE IN THE ***WORLD*** WHO CAN DO SOME TINY FRACTION OF WHAT WIZORD CAN DO.
THEY'RE NOT AN INEXHAUSTIBLE RESOURCE.

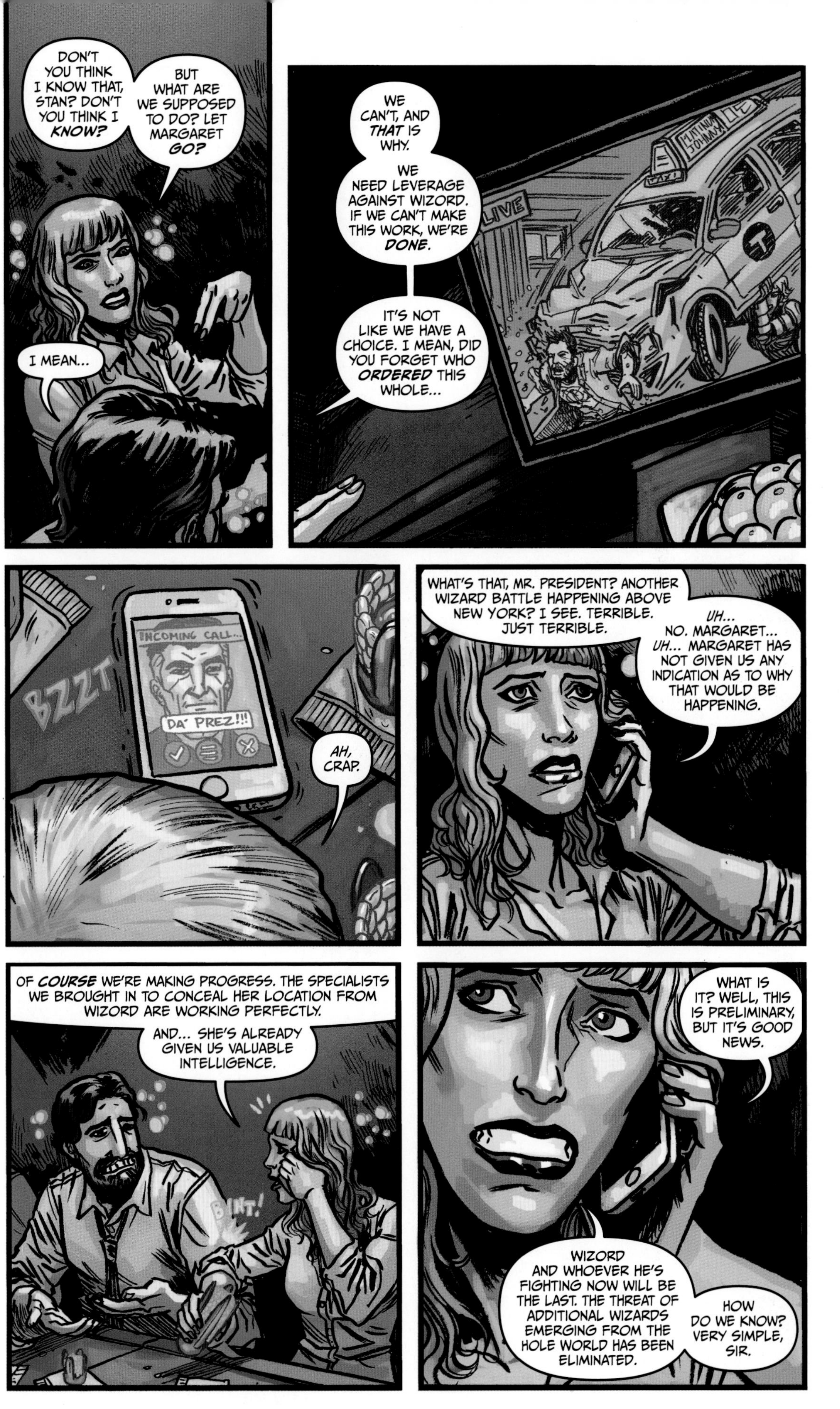
DON'T YOU THINK I KNOW THAT, STAN? DON'T YOU THINK I KNOW?
BUT WHAT ARE WE SUPPOSED TO DO? LET MARGARET GO?
I MEAN...
WE CAN'T, AND THAT IS WHY.
WE NEED LEVERAGE AGAINST WIZORD. IF WE CAN'T MAKE THIS WORK, WE'RE DONE.
IT'S NOT LIKE WE HAVE A CHOICE. I MEAN, DID YOU FORGET WHO ORDERED THIS WHOLE...
LIVE
INCOMING CALL...
DA' PREZ!!!
BZZT
AH, CRAP.
WHAT'S THAT, MR. PRESIDENT? ANOTHER WIZARD BATTLE HAPPENING ABOVE NEW YORK? I SEE. TERRIBLE. JUST TERRIBLE.
UH... NO. MARGARET... UH... MARGARET HAS NOT GIVEN US ANY INDICATION AS TO WHY THAT WOULD BE HAPPENING.
OF COURSE WE'RE MAKING PROGRESS. THE SPECIALISTS WE BROUGHT IN TO CONCEAL HER LOCATION FROM WIZORD ARE WORKING PERFECTLY.
AND... SHE'S ALREADY GIVEN US VALUABLE INTELLIGENCE.
BINT!
WHAT IS IT? WELL, THIS IS PRELIMINARY, BUT IT'S GOOD NEWS.
WIZORD AND WHOEVER HE'S FIGHTING NOW WILL BE THE LAST. THE THREAT OF ADDITIONAL WIZARDS EMERGING FROM THE HOLE WORLD HAS BEEN ELIMINATED.
HOW DO WE KNOW? VERY SIMPLE, SIR.

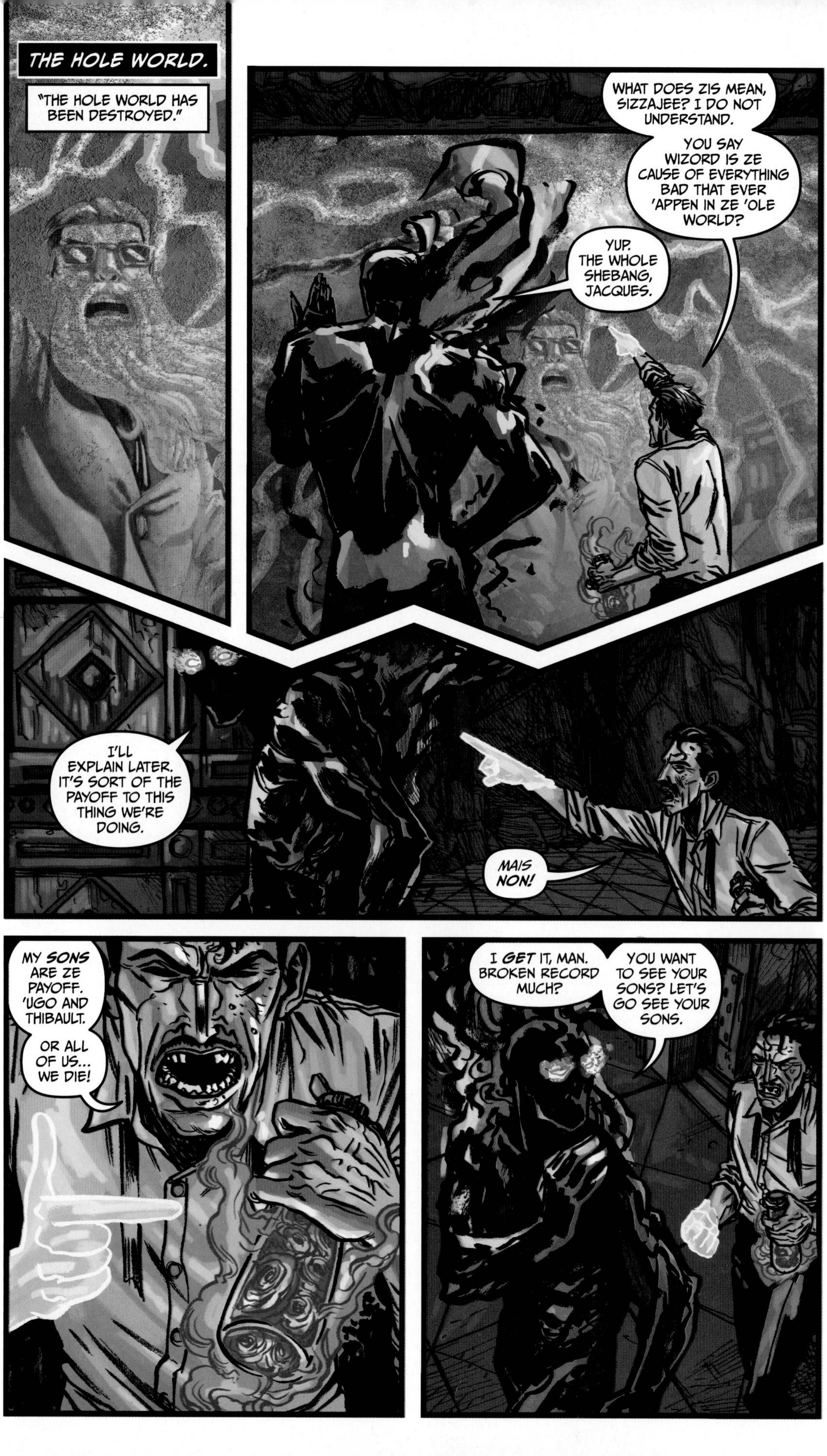
THE HOLE WORLD.
"THE HOLE WORLD HAS BEEN DESTROYED."
WHAT DOES ZIS MEAN, SIZZAJEE? I DO NOT UNDERSTAND.
YOU SAY WIZORD IS ZE CAUSE OF EVERYTHING BAD THAT EVER 'APPEN IN ZE 'OLE WORLD?
YUP. THE WHOLE SHEBANG, JACQUES.
I'LL EXPLAIN LATER. IT'S SORT OF THE PAYOFF TO THIS THING WE'RE DOING.
MAIS NON!
MY SONS ARE ZE PAYOFF. 'UGO AND THIBAULT.
OR ALL OF US... WE DIE!
I GET IT, MAN. BROKEN RECORD MUCH?
YOU WANT TO SEE YOUR SONS? LET'S GO SEE YOUR SONS.

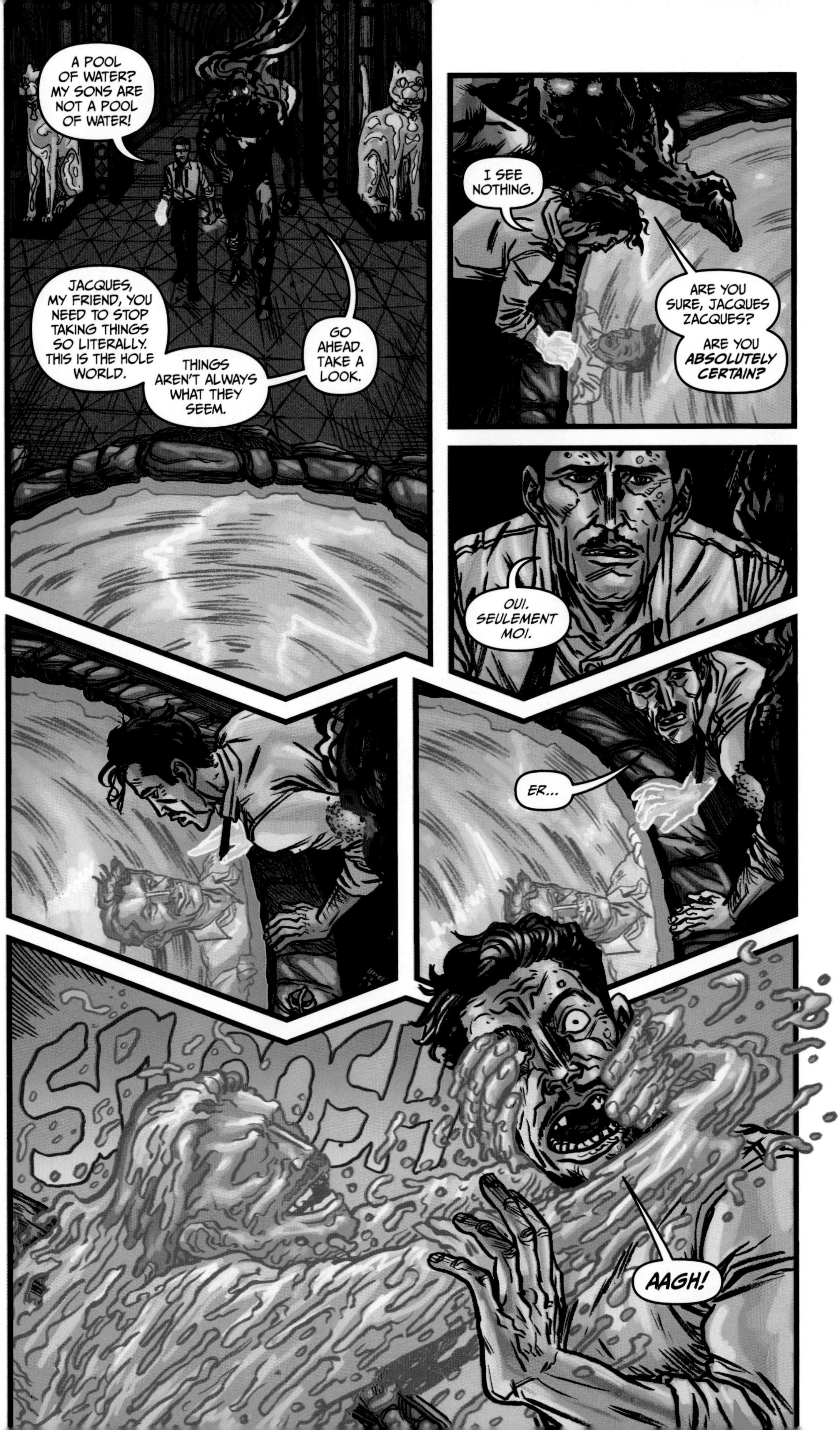
A POOL OF WATER? MY SONS ARE NOT A POOL OF WATER!
JACQUES, MY FRIEND, YOU NEED TO STOP TAKING THINGS SO LITERALLY. THIS IS THE HOLE WORLD.
THINGS AREN'T ALWAYS WHAT THEY SEEM.
GO AHEAD. TAKE A LOOK.
I SEE NOTHING.
ARE YOU SURE, JACQUES ZACQUES?
ARE YOU *ABSOLUTELY CERTAIN?*
OUI. SEULEMENT MOI.
ER...
AAGH!

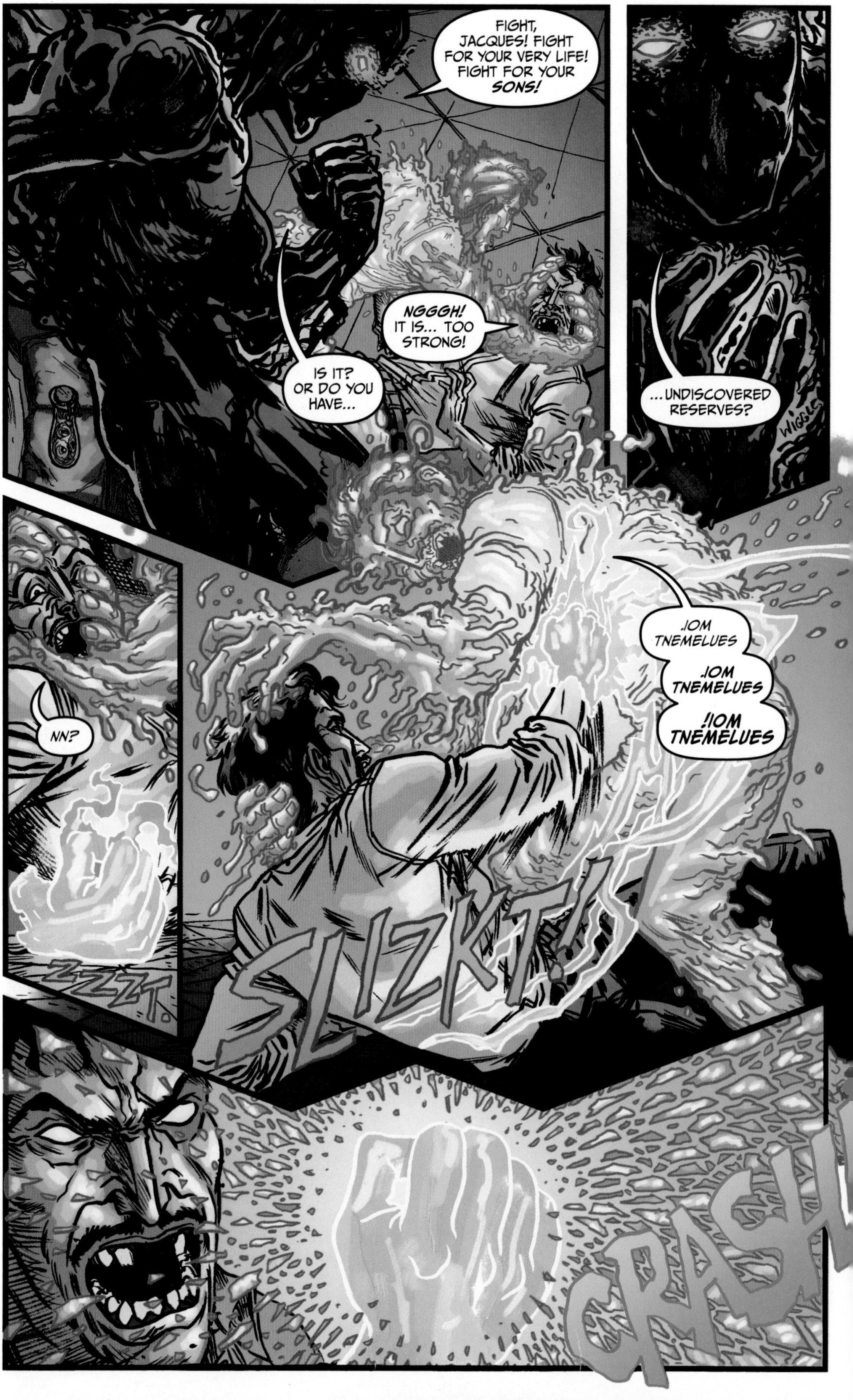
FIGHT, JACQUES! FIGHT FOR YOUR VERY LIFE! FIGHT FOR YOUR SONS!
NGGGH! IT IS... TOO STRONG!
IS IT? OR DO YOU HAVE...
...UNDISCOVERED RESERVES?
WIGGLE
NN?
.IOM TNEMELUES
.IOM TNEMELUES
!IOM TNEMELUES
ZZZZT
SLIZKT!

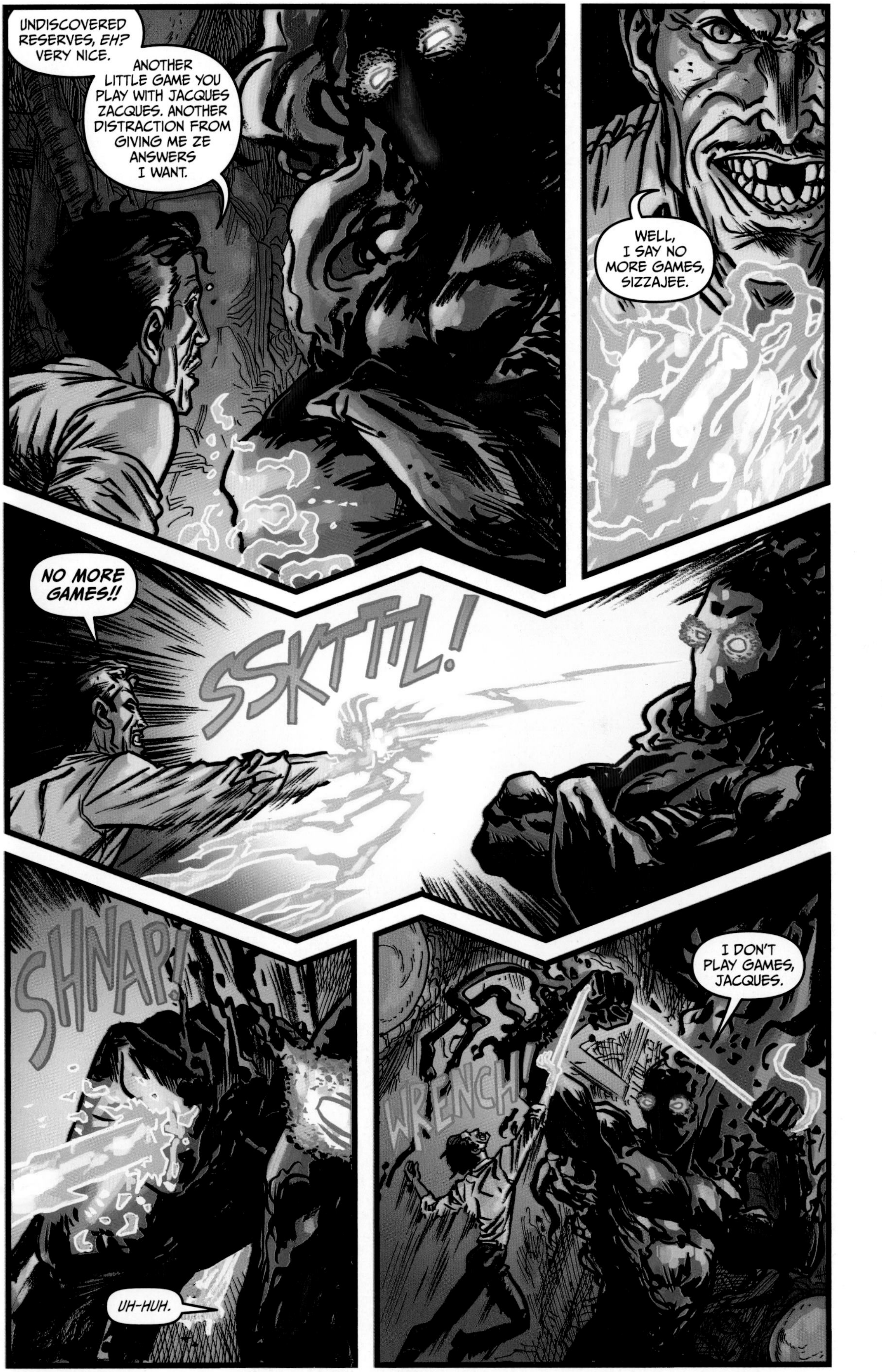
UNDISCOVERED RESERVES, EH? VERY NICE.
ANOTHER LITTLE GAME YOU PLAY WITH JACQUES ZACQUES. ANOTHER DISTRACTION FROM GIVING ME ZE ANSWERS I WANT.
WELL, I SAY NO MORE GAMES, SIZZAJEE.
NO MORE GAMES!!
SSKTTTL!
SHNAP!
UH-HUH.
I DON'T PLAY GAMES, JACQUES.
WRENCH!

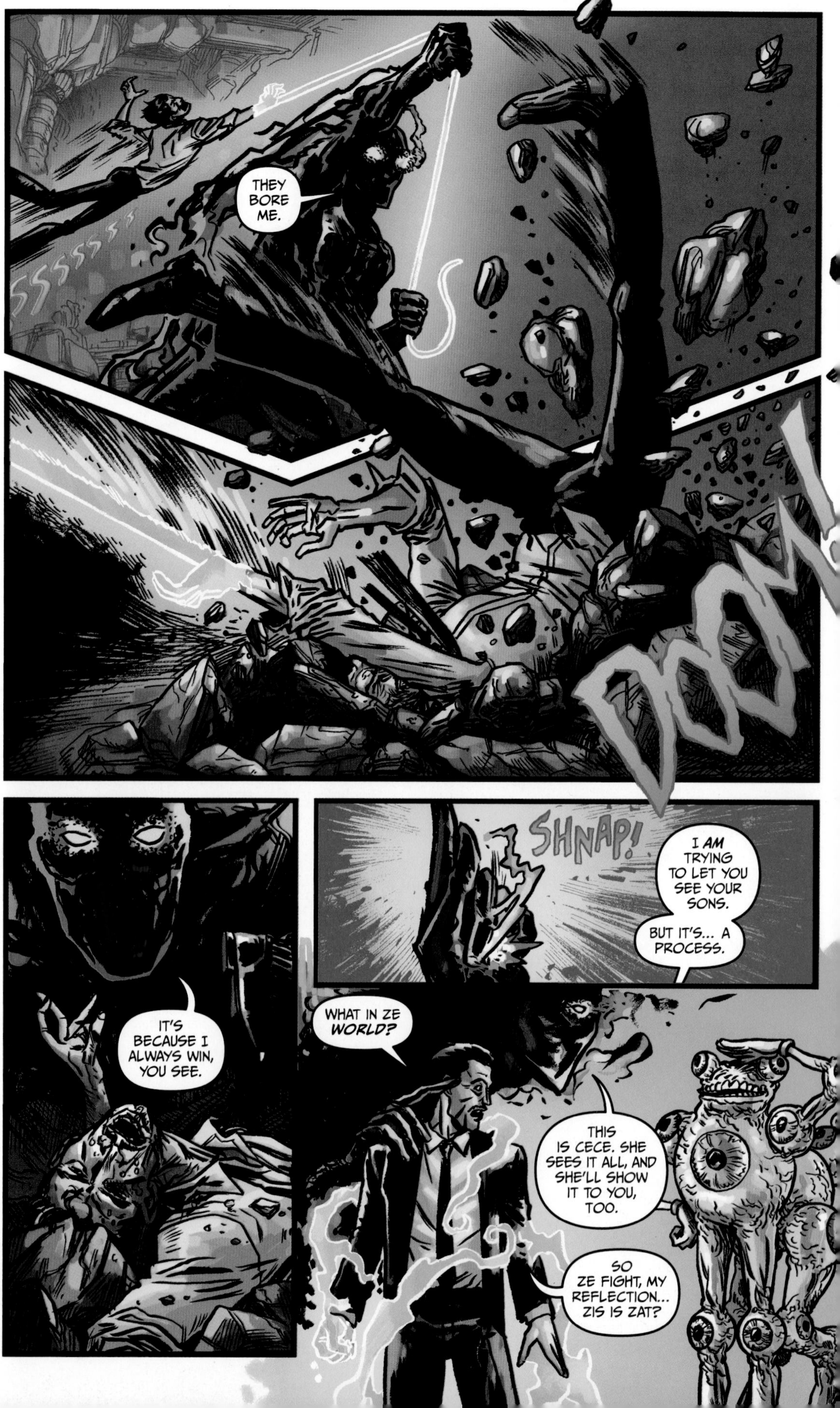

THEY BORE ME.
SSSSSSSSS
DOOM!
IT'S BECAUSE I ALWAYS WIN, YOU SEE.
SHNAP!
I AM TRYING TO LET YOU SEE YOUR SONS.
BUT IT'S... A PROCESS.
WHAT IN ZE WORLD?
THIS IS CECE. SHE SEES IT ALL, AND SHE'LL SHOW IT TO YOU, TOO.
SO ZE FIGHT, MY REFLECTION... ZIS IS ZAT?

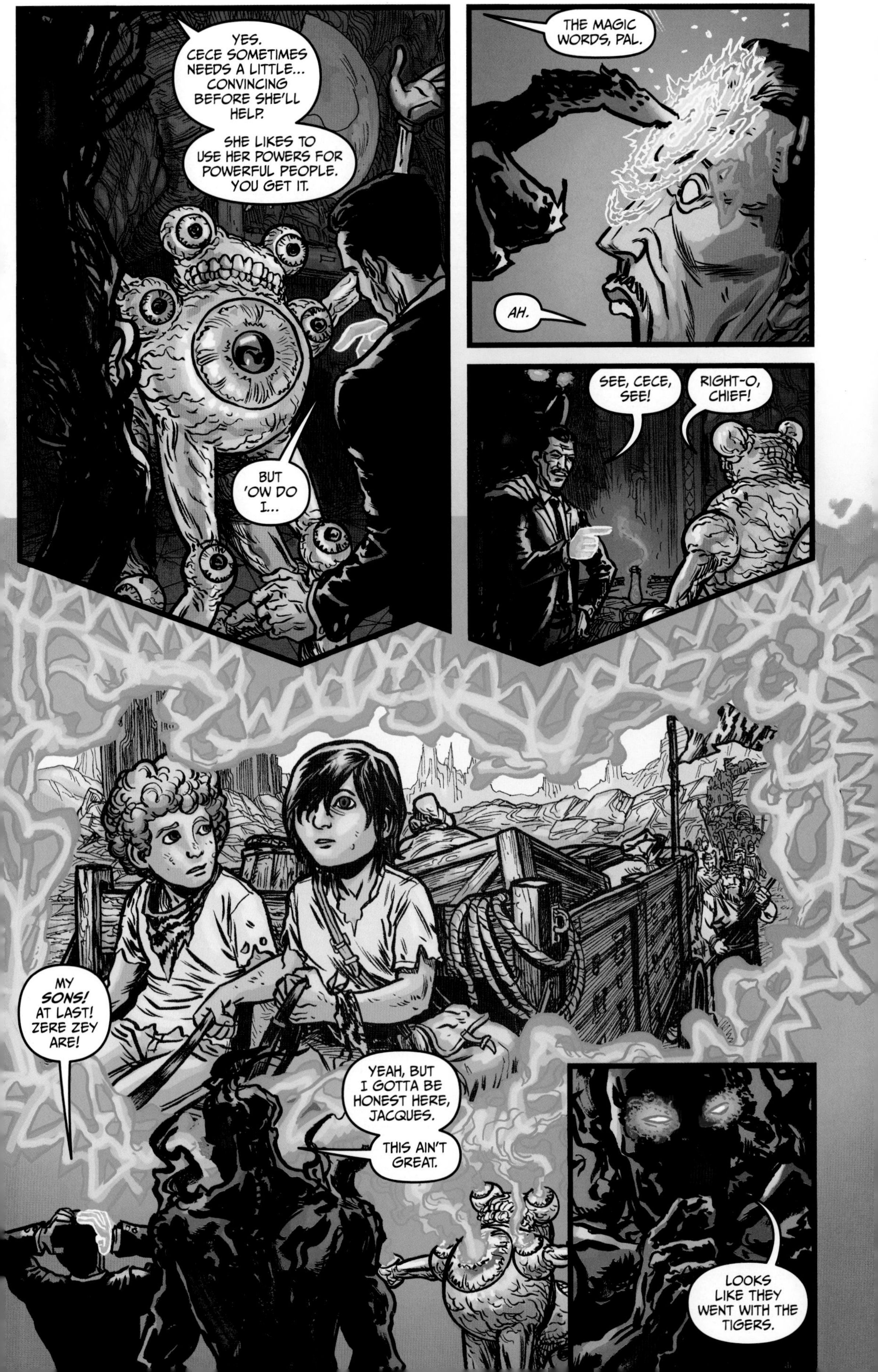
YES. CECE SOMETIMES NEEDS A LITTLE... CONVINCING BEFORE SHE'LL HELP.
SHE LIKES TO USE HER POWERS FOR POWERFUL PEOPLE. YOU GET IT.
BUT 'OW DO I...
THE MAGIC WORDS, PAL.
AH.
SEE, CECE, SEE!
RIGHT-O, CHIEF!
MY *SONS!* AT LAST! ZERE ZEY ARE!
YEAH, BUT I GOTTA BE HONEST HERE, JACQUES.
THIS AIN'T GREAT.
LOOKS LIKE THEY WENT WITH THE TIGERS.

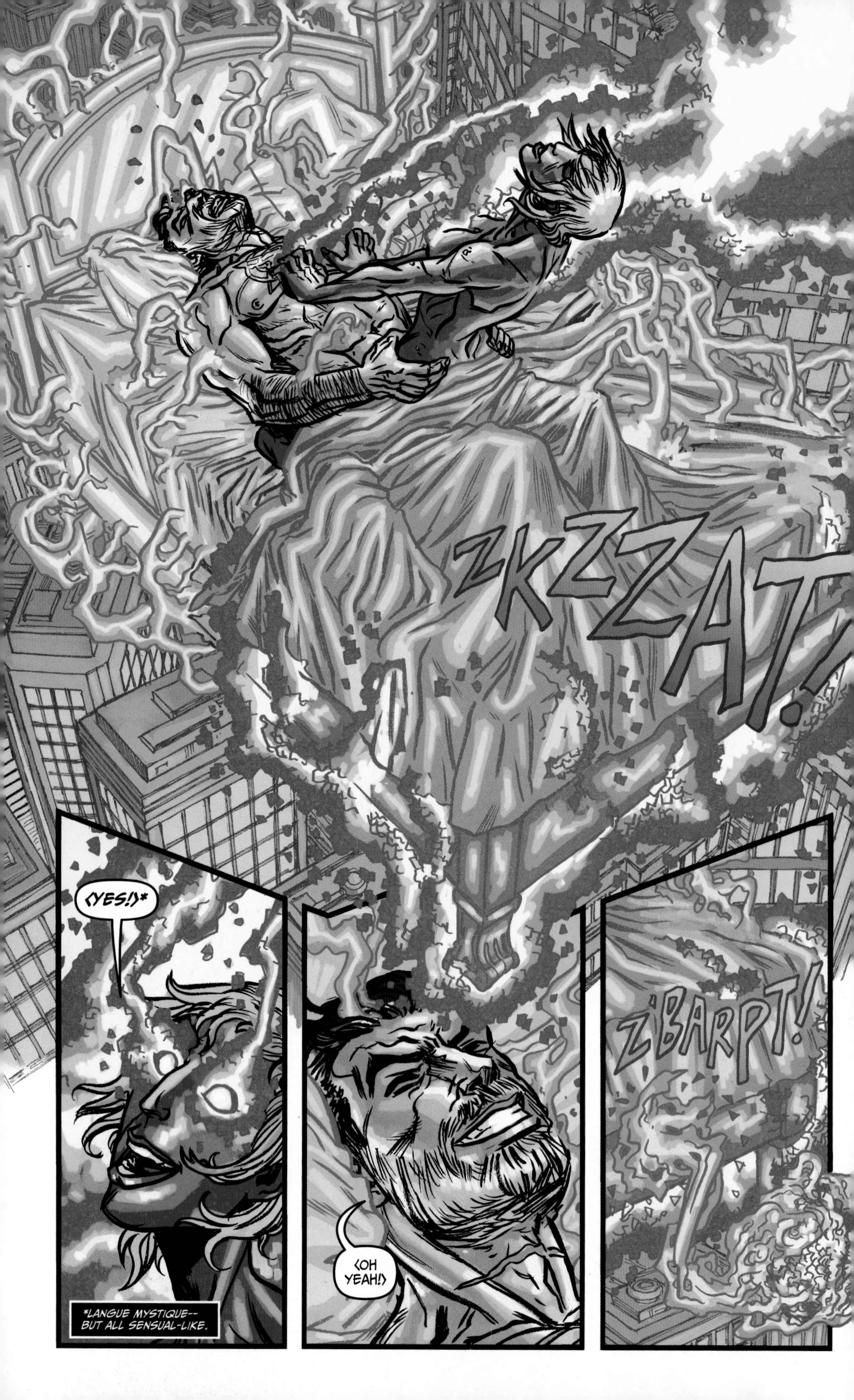
ZKZZZAT!
‹YES!›*
*LANGUE MYSTIQUE--
BUT ALL SENSUAL-LIKE.
‹OH
YEAH!›
Z'BARPT!

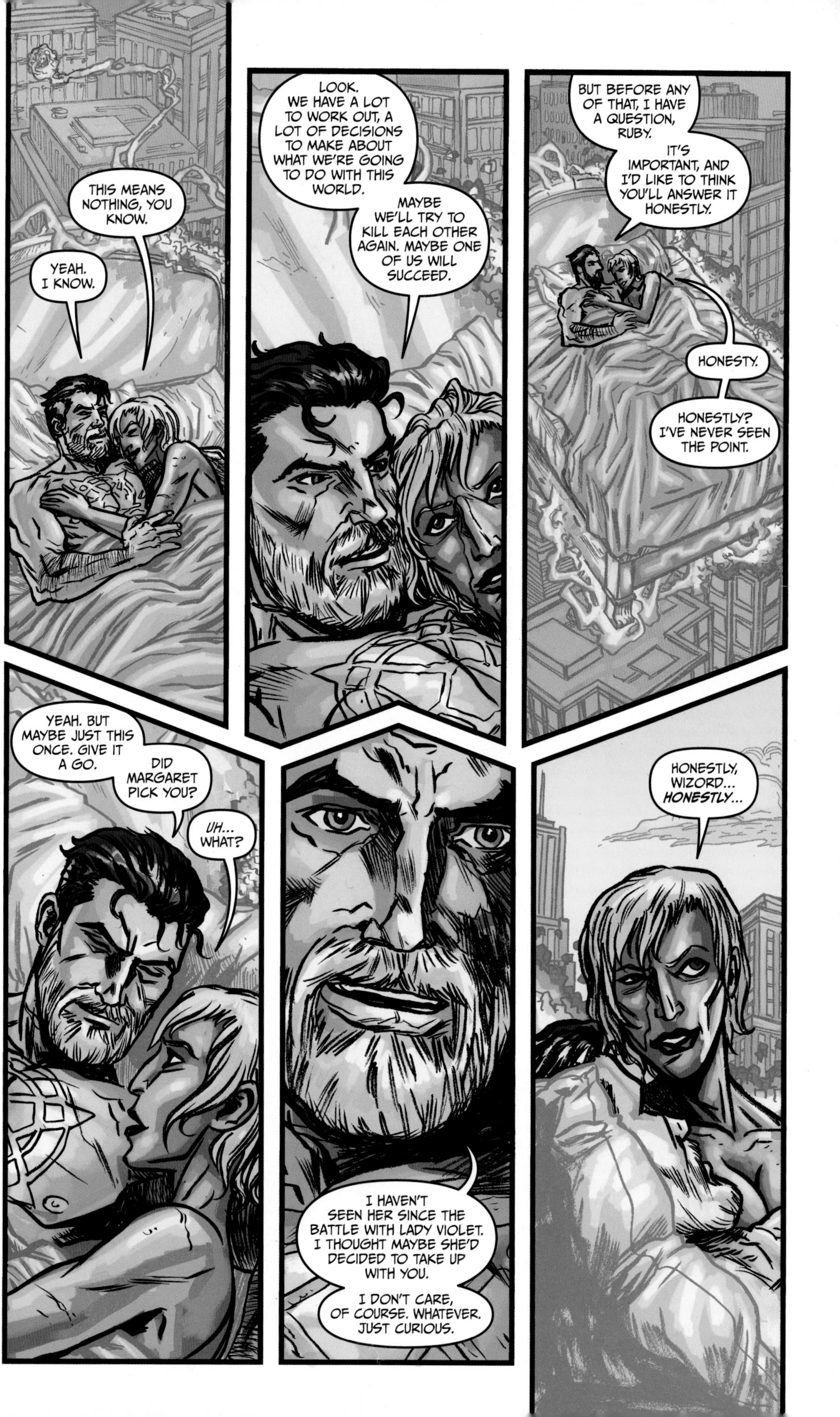
THIS MEANS NOTHING, YOU KNOW.
YEAH. I KNOW.
LOOK. WE HAVE A LOT TO WORK OUT, A LOT OF DECISIONS TO MAKE ABOUT WHAT WE'RE GOING TO DO WITH THIS WORLD.
MAYBE WE'LL TRY TO KILL EACH OTHER AGAIN. MAYBE ONE OF US WILL SUCCEED.
BUT BEFORE ANY OF THAT, I HAVE A QUESTION, RUBY.
IT'S IMPORTANT, AND I'D LIKE TO THINK YOU'LL ANSWER IT HONESTLY.
HONESTY.
HONESTLY? I'VE NEVER SEEN THE POINT.
YEAH. BUT MAYBE JUST THIS ONCE. GIVE IT A GO.
DID MARGARET PICK YOU?
UH... WHAT?
I HAVEN'T SEEN HER SINCE THE BATTLE WITH LADY VIOLET. I THOUGHT MAYBE SHE'D DECIDED TO TAKE UP WITH YOU.
I DON'T CARE, OF COURSE. WHATEVER. JUST CURIOUS.
HONESTLY, WIZORD... HONESTLY...

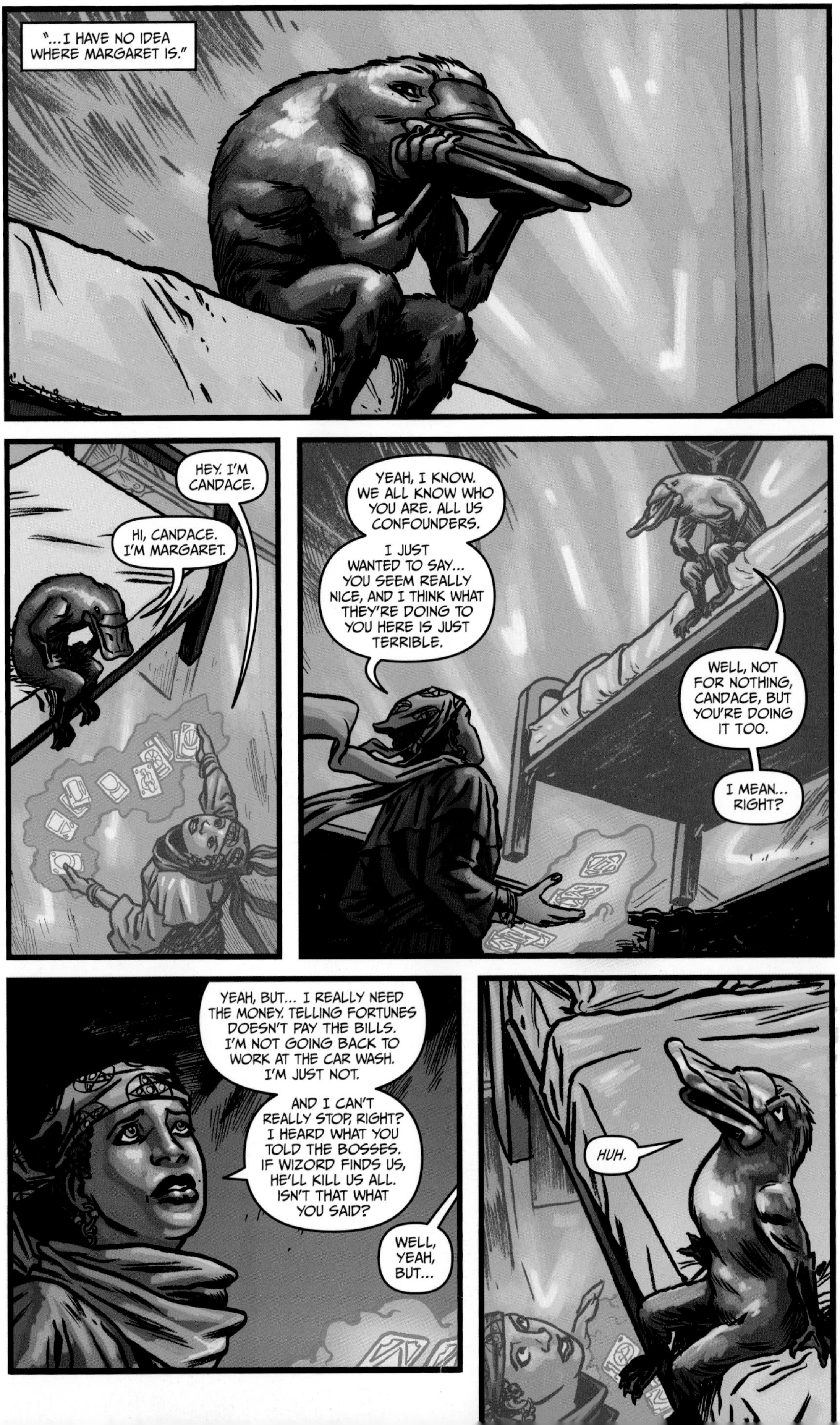
"...I HAVE NO IDEA WHERE MARGARET IS."
HEY. I'M CANDACE.
HI, CANDACE. I'M MARGARET.
YEAH, I KNOW. WE ALL KNOW WHO YOU ARE. ALL US CONFOUNDERS.
I JUST WANTED TO SAY... YOU SEEM REALLY NICE, AND I THINK WHAT THEY'RE DOING TO YOU HERE IS JUST TERRIBLE.
WELL, NOT FOR NOTHING, CANDACE, BUT YOU'RE DOING IT TOO.
I MEAN... RIGHT?
YEAH, BUT... I REALLY NEED THE MONEY. TELLING FORTUNES DOESN'T PAY THE BILLS. I'M NOT GOING BACK TO WORK AT THE CAR WASH. I'M JUST NOT.
AND I CAN'T REALLY STOP, RIGHT? I HEARD WHAT YOU TOLD THE BOSSES. IF WIZORD FINDS US, HE'LL KILL US ALL. ISN'T THAT WHAT YOU SAID?
WELL, YEAH, BUT...
HUH.

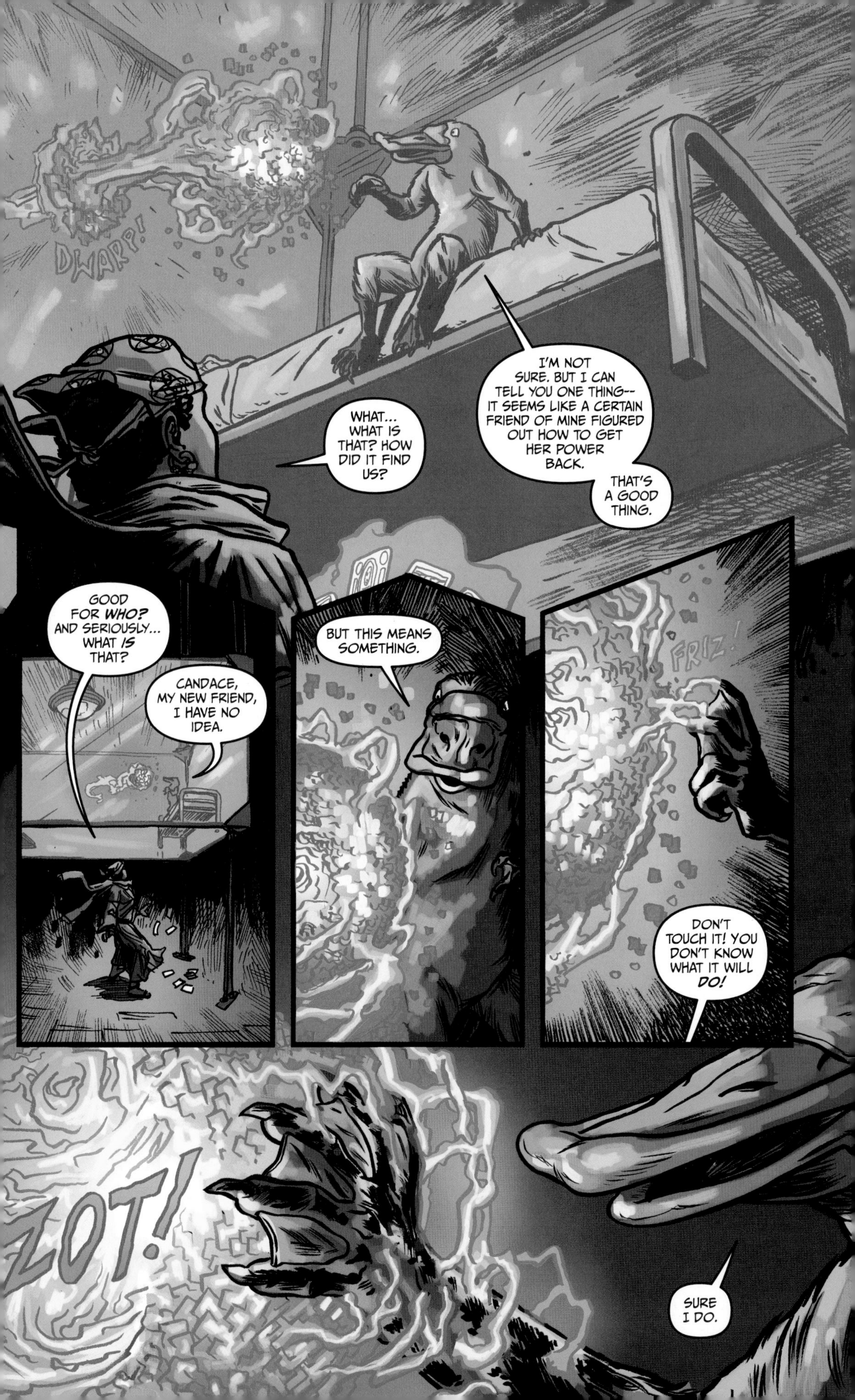
DWARP!
WHAT... WHAT IS THAT? HOW DID IT FIND US?
I'M NOT SURE. BUT I CAN TELL YOU ONE THING-- IT SEEMS LIKE A CERTAIN FRIEND OF MINE FIGURED OUT HOW TO GET HER POWER BACK.
THAT'S A GOOD THING.
GOOD FOR ***WHO?*** AND SERIOUSLY... WHAT ***IS*** THAT?
CANDACE, MY NEW FRIEND, I HAVE NO IDEA.
BUT THIS MEANS SOMETHING.
FRIZ!
DON'T TOUCH IT! YOU DON'T KNOW WHAT IT WILL ***DO!***
ZOT!
SURE I DO.

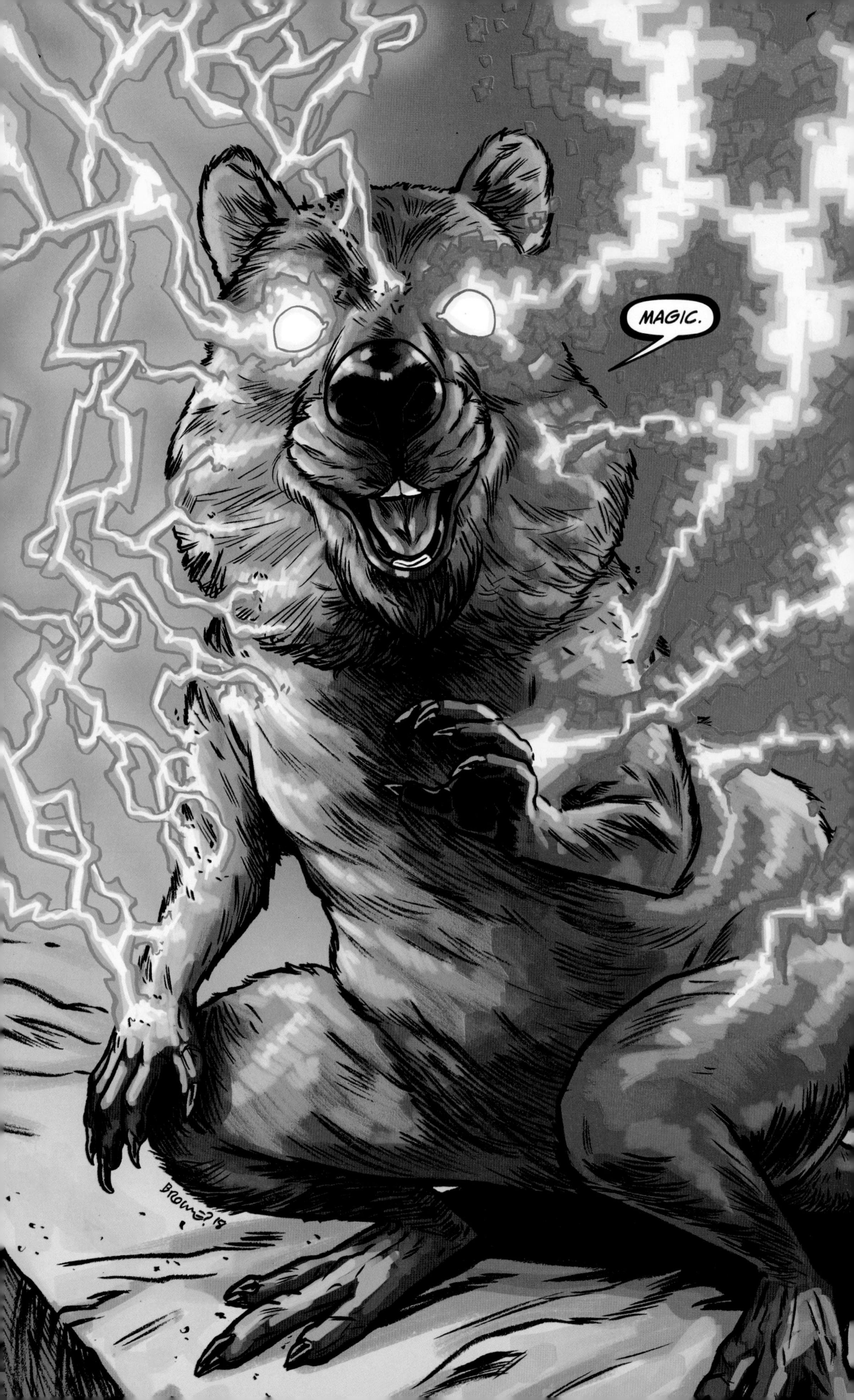
MAGIC.

THIRTEEN

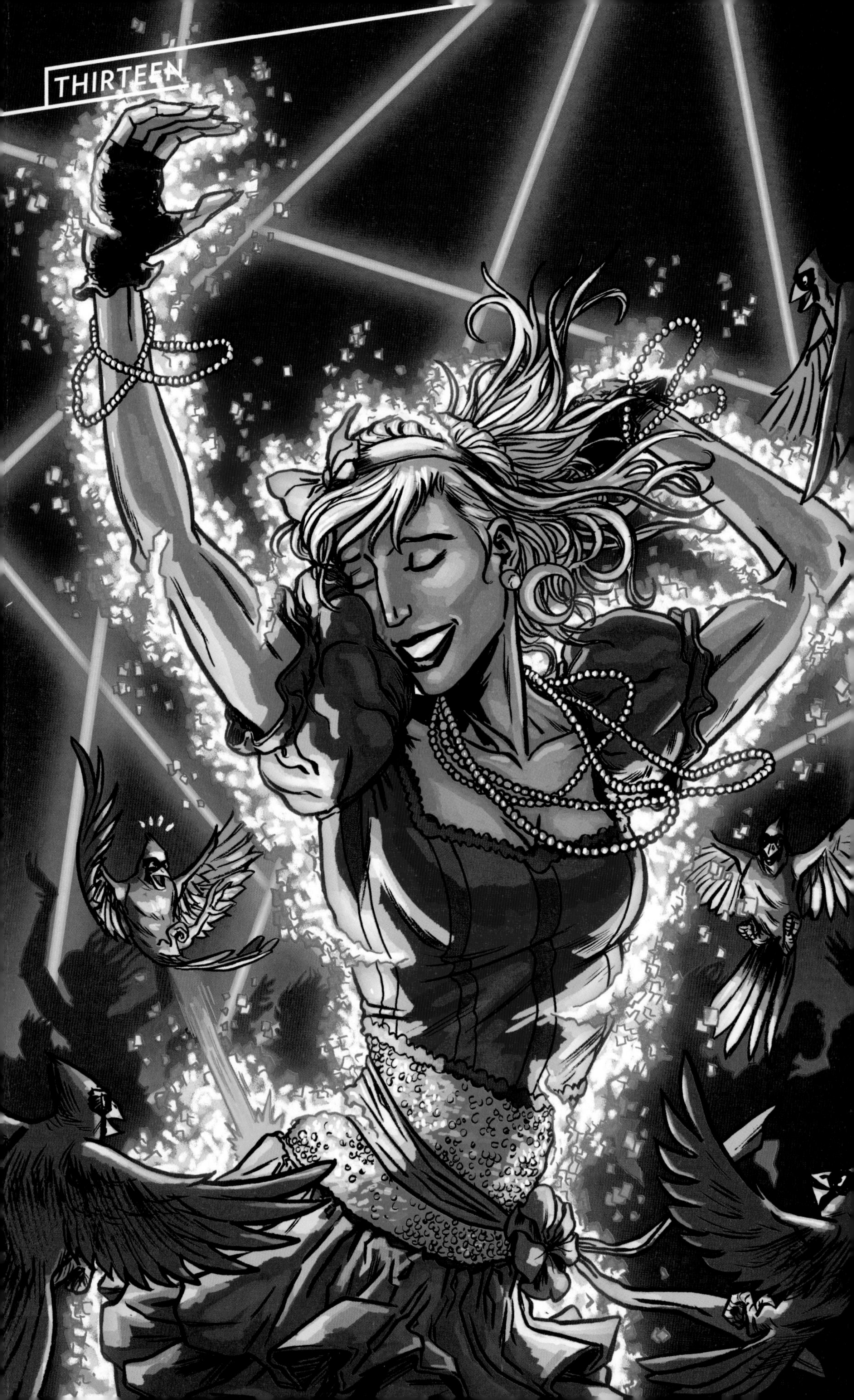

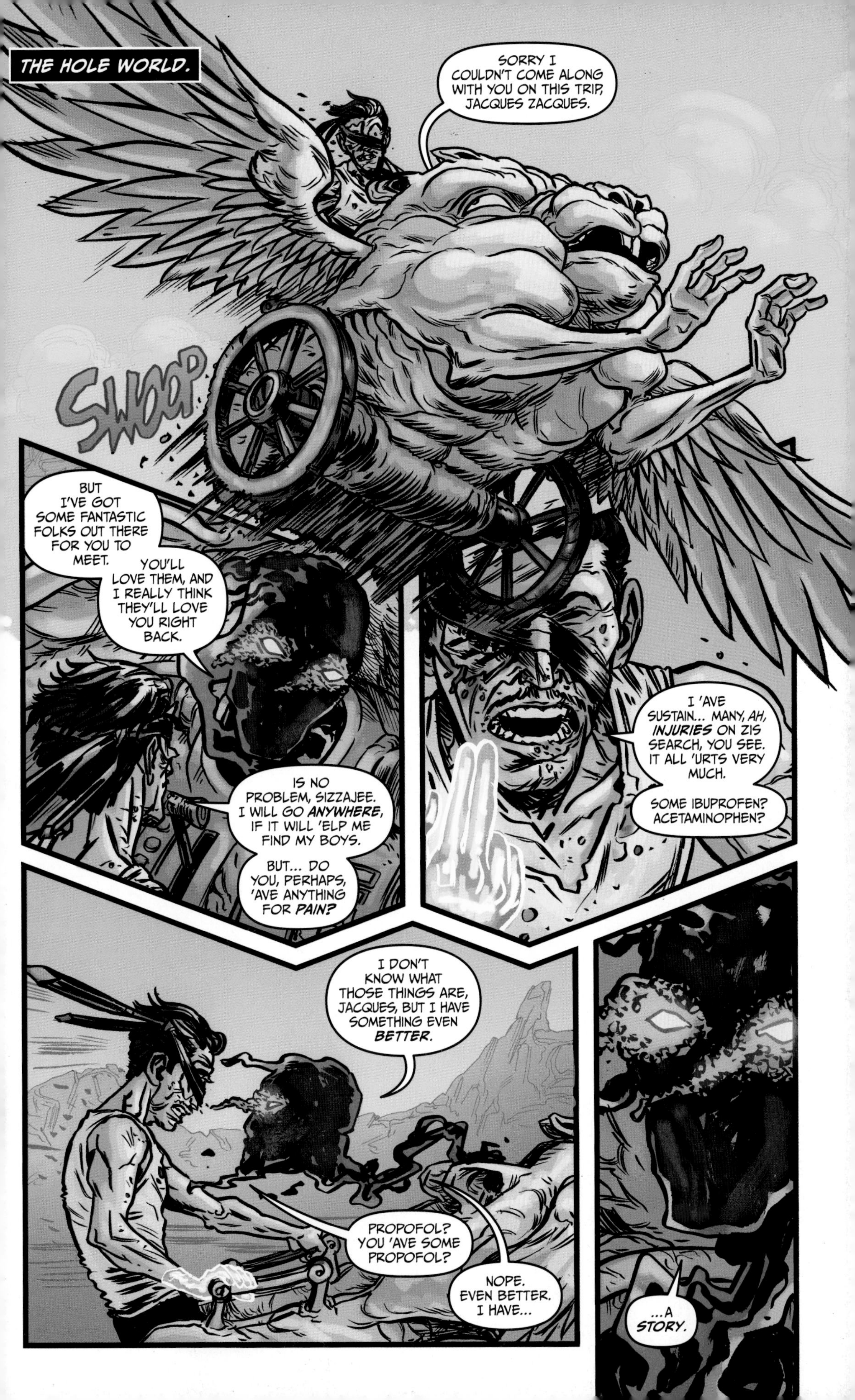
THE HOLE WORLD.
SORRY I COULDN'T COME ALONG WITH YOU ON THIS TRIP, JACQUES ZACQUES.
SWOOP
BUT I'VE GOT SOME FANTASTIC FOLKS OUT THERE FOR YOU TO MEET.
YOU'LL LOVE THEM, AND I REALLY THINK THEY'LL LOVE YOU RIGHT BACK.
IS NO PROBLEM, SIZZAJEE. I WILL GO *ANYWHERE*, IF IT WILL 'ELP ME FIND MY BOYS.
BUT... DO YOU, PERHAPS, 'AVE ANYTHING FOR *PAIN?*
I 'AVE SUSTAIN... MANY, *AH*, *INJURIES* ON ZIS SEARCH, YOU SEE. IT ALL 'URTS VERY MUCH.
SOME IBUPROFEN? ACETAMINOPHEN?
I DON'T KNOW WHAT THOSE THINGS ARE, JACQUES, BUT I HAVE SOMETHING EVEN *BETTER*.
PROPOFOL? YOU 'AVE SOME PROPOFOL?
NOPE. EVEN BETTER. I HAVE...
...A *STORY*.

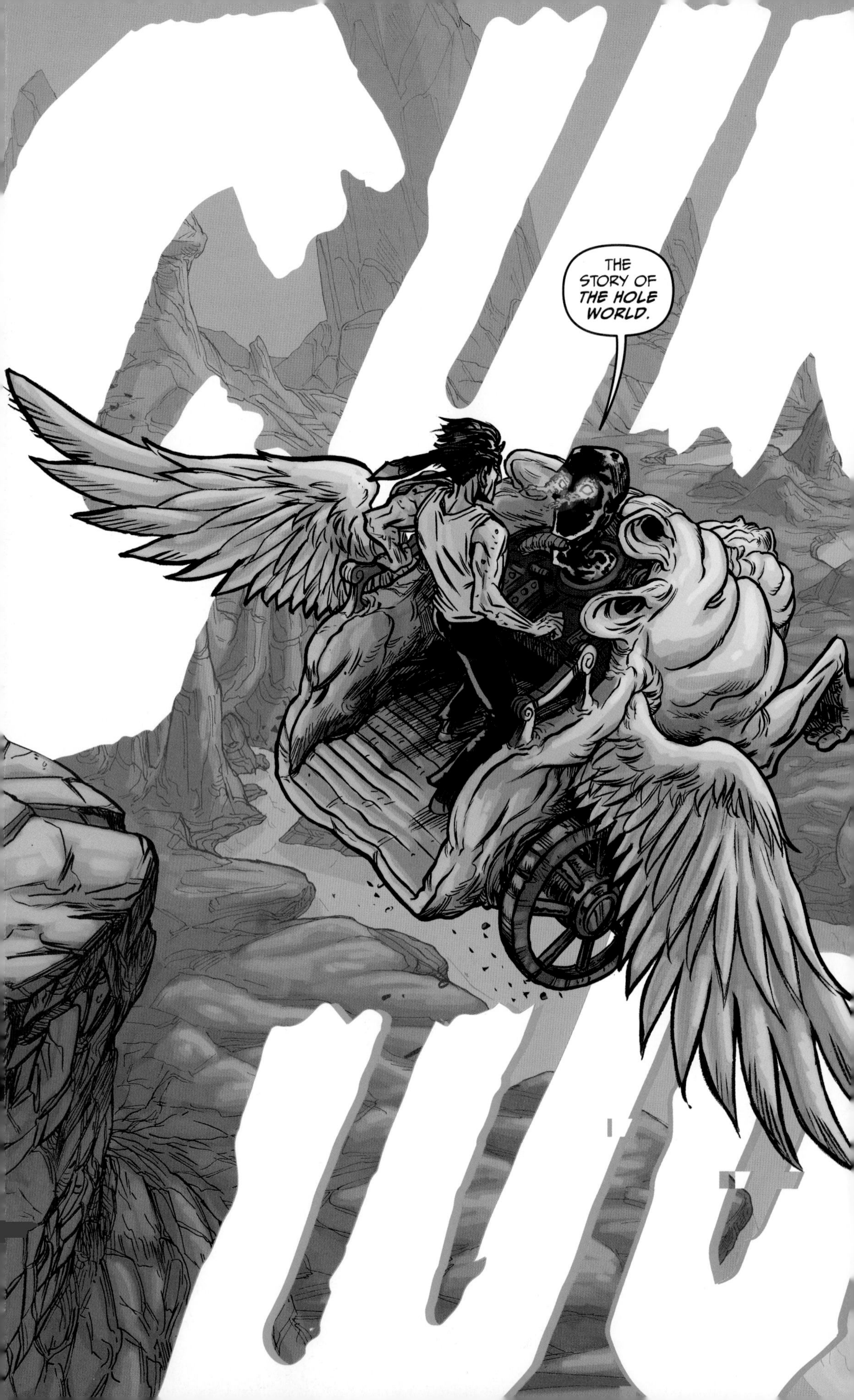
THE STORY OF THE HOLE WORLD.

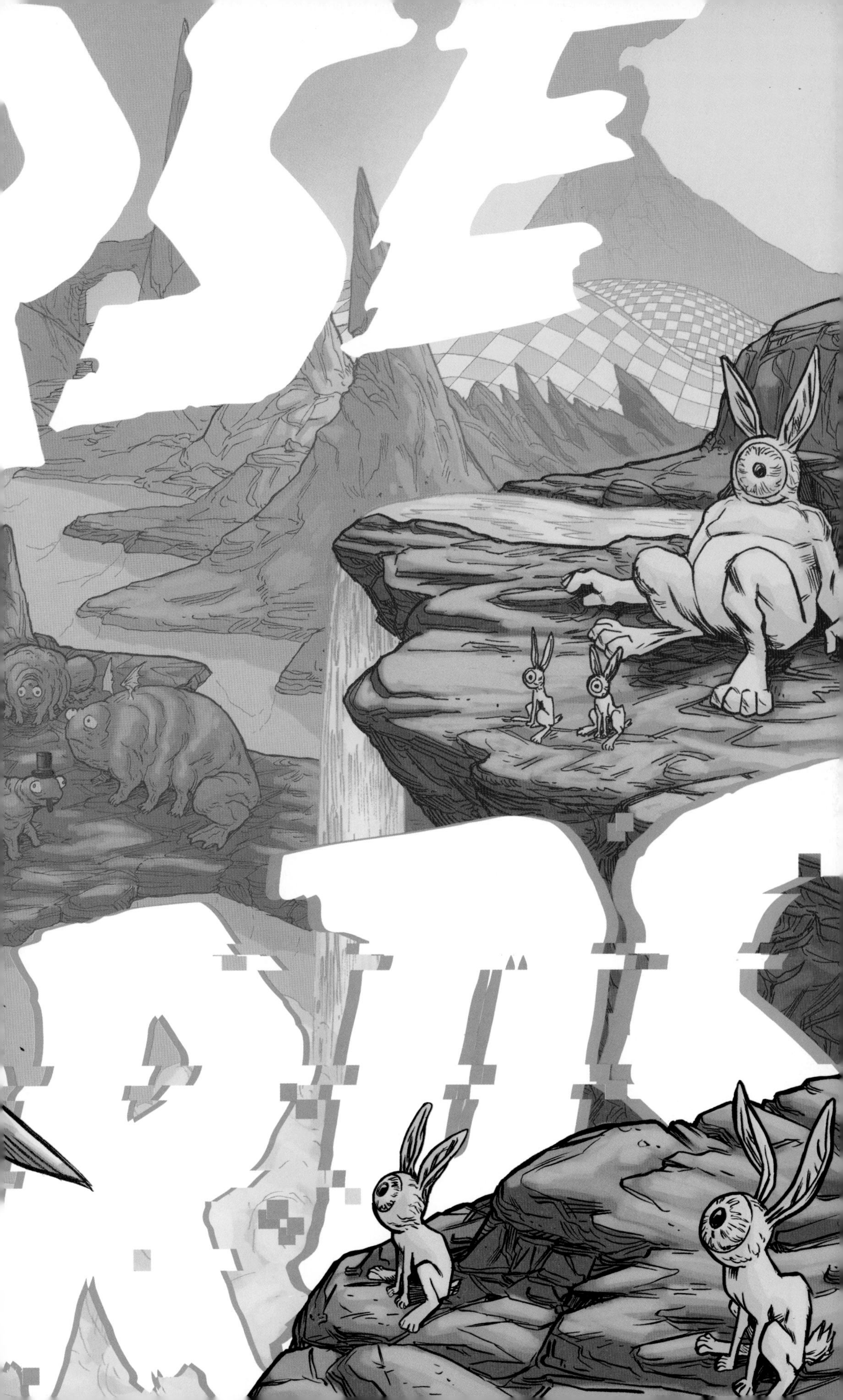

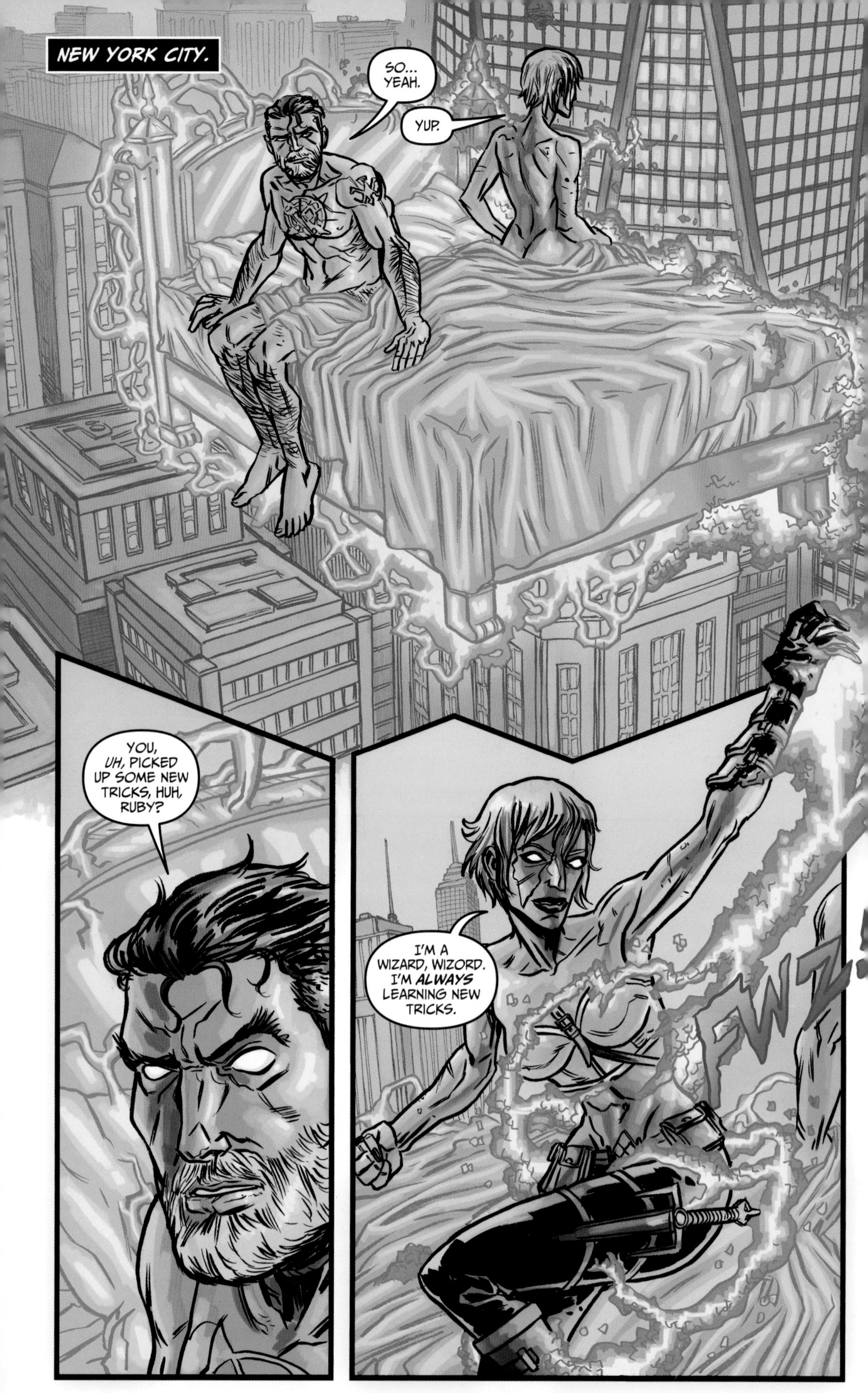

NEW YORK CITY.
SO... YEAH.
YUP.
YOU, UH, PICKED UP SOME NEW TRICKS, HUH, RUBY?
I'M A WIZARD, WIZORD. I'M ALWAYS LEARNING NEW TRICKS.
FWZ

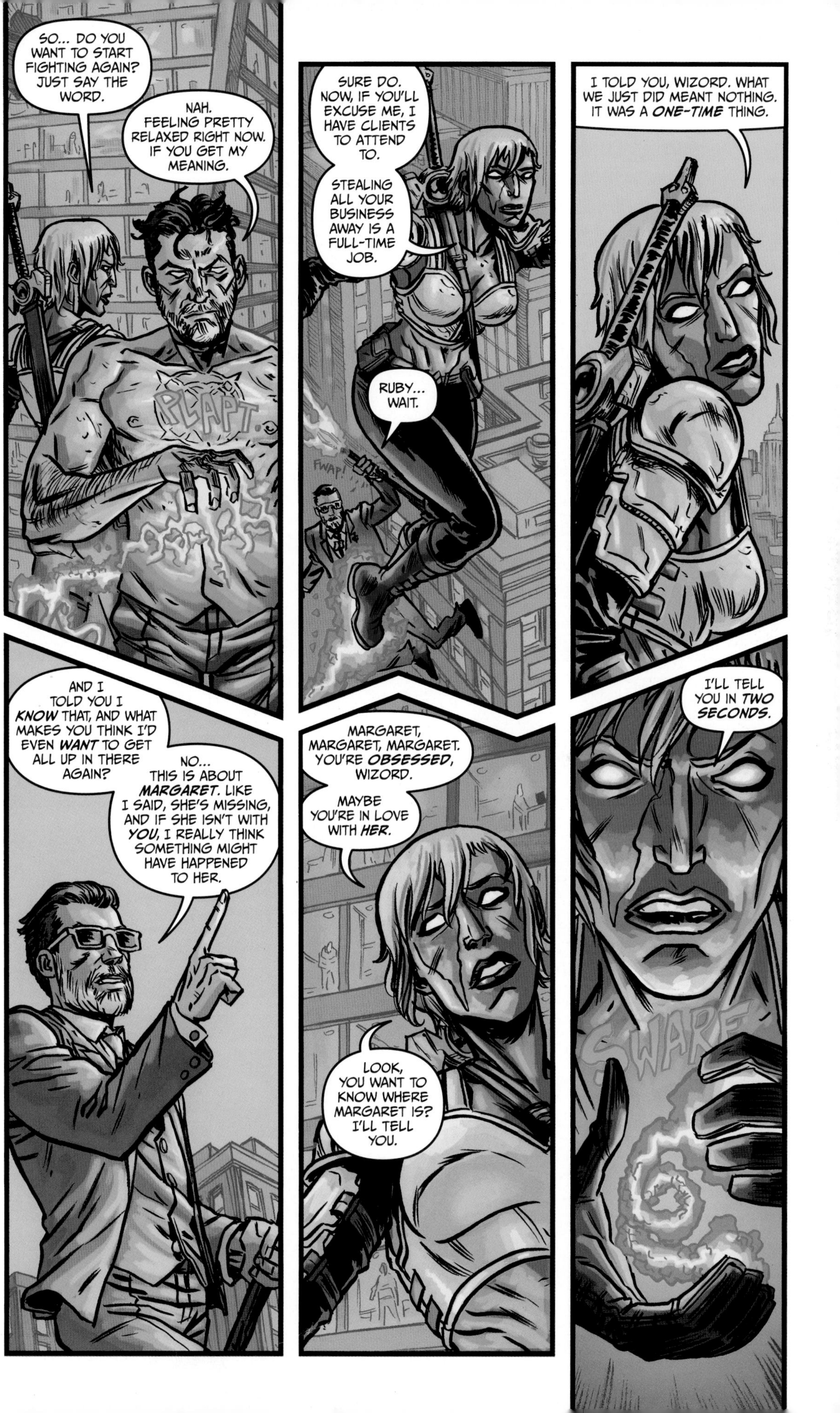
SO... DO YOU WANT TO START FIGHTING AGAIN? JUST SAY THE WORD.
NAH. FEELING PRETTY RELAXED RIGHT NOW. IF YOU GET MY MEANING.
PLAPT
SURE DO. NOW, IF YOU'LL EXCUSE ME, I HAVE CLIENTS TO ATTEND TO.
STEALING ALL YOUR BUSINESS AWAY IS A FULL-TIME JOB.
RUBY... WAIT.
FWAP!
I TOLD YOU, WIZORD. WHAT WE JUST DID MEANT NOTHING. IT WAS A *ONE-TIME* THING.
AND I TOLD YOU I *KNOW* THAT, AND WHAT MAKES YOU THINK I'D EVEN *WANT* TO GET ALL UP IN THERE AGAIN?
NO... THIS IS ABOUT *MARGARET*. LIKE I SAID, SHE'S MISSING, AND IF SHE ISN'T WITH *YOU*, I REALLY THINK SOMETHING MIGHT HAVE HAPPENED TO HER.
MARGARET, MARGARET, MARGARET. YOU'RE *OBSESSED*, WIZORD.
MAYBE YOU'RE IN LOVE WITH *HER*.
LOOK, YOU WANT TO KNOW WHERE MARGARET IS? I'LL TELL YOU.
I'LL TELL YOU IN *TWO SECONDS*.
SWARF

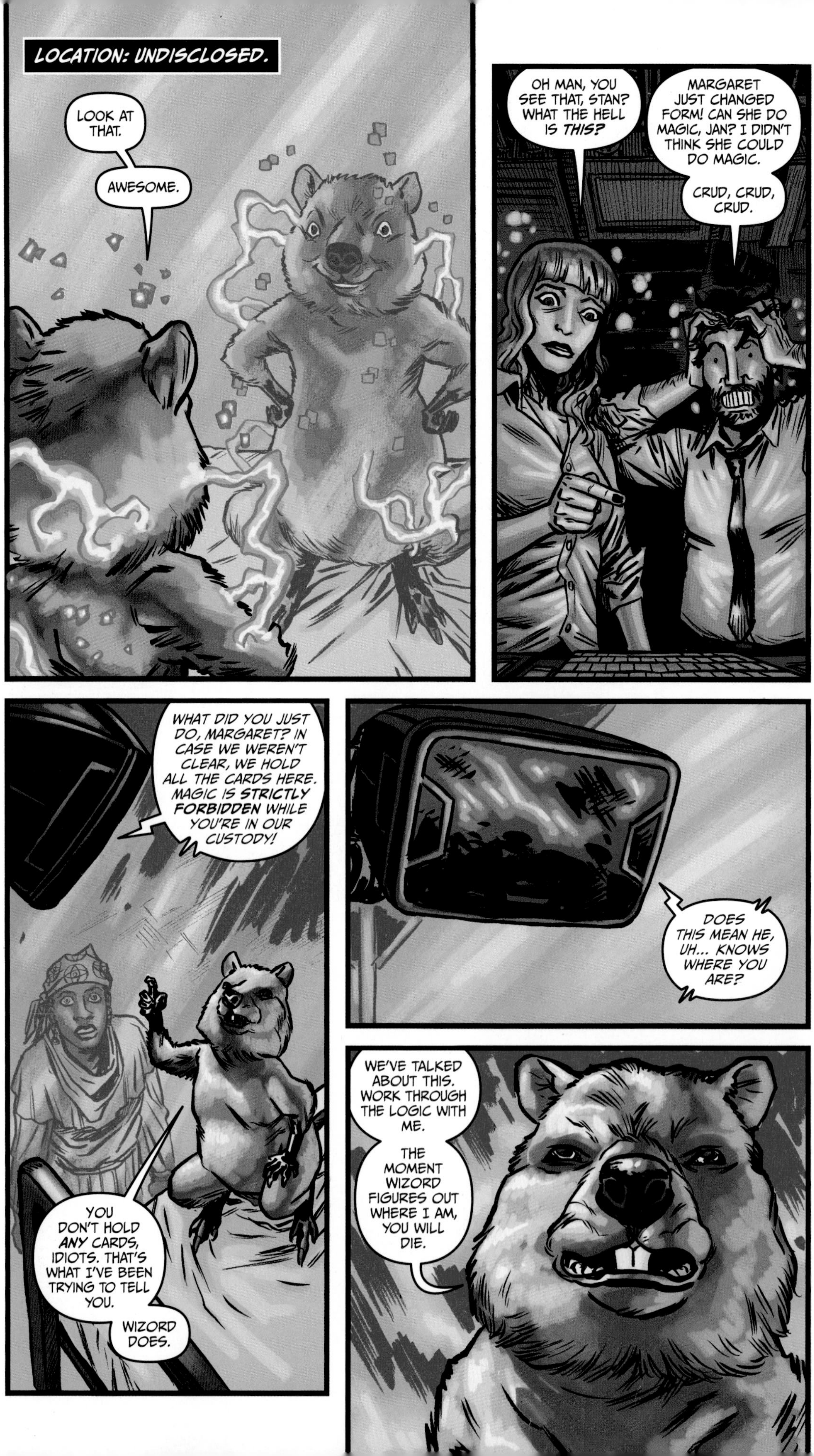
LOCATION: UNDISCLOSED.
LOOK AT THAT.
AWESOME.
OH MAN, YOU SEE THAT, STAN? WHAT THE HELL IS THIS?
MARGARET JUST CHANGED FORM! CAN SHE DO MAGIC, JAN? I DIDN'T THINK SHE COULD DO MAGIC.
CRUD, CRUD, CRUD.
WHAT DID YOU JUST DO, MARGARET? IN CASE WE WEREN'T CLEAR, WE HOLD ALL THE CARDS HERE. MAGIC IS STRICTLY FORBIDDEN WHILE YOU'RE IN OUR CUSTODY!
YOU DON'T HOLD ANY CARDS, IDIOTS. THAT'S WHAT I'VE BEEN TRYING TO TELL YOU.
WIZORD DOES.
DOES THIS MEAN HE, UH... KNOWS WHERE YOU ARE?
WE'VE TALKED ABOUT THIS. WORK THROUGH THE LOGIC WITH ME.
THE MOMENT WIZORD FIGURES OUT WHERE I AM, YOU WILL DIE.

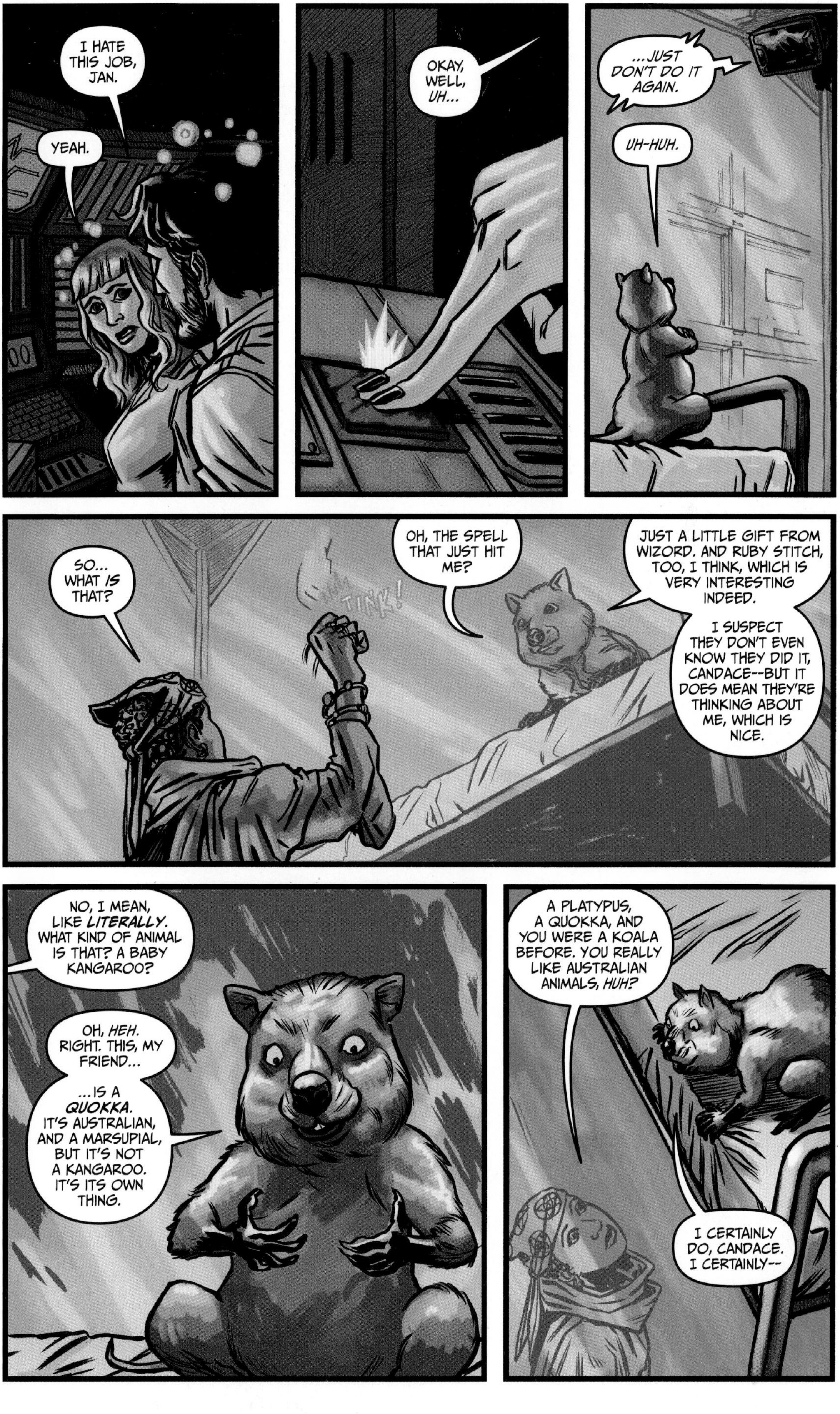
I HATE THIS JOB, JAN.
YEAH.
OKAY, WELL, UH...
...JUST DON'T DO IT AGAIN.
UH-HUH.
SO... WHAT IS THAT?
TINK!
OH, THE SPELL THAT JUST HIT ME?
JUST A LITTLE GIFT FROM WIZORD. AND RUBY STITCH, TOO, I THINK, WHICH IS VERY INTERESTING INDEED.
I SUSPECT THEY DON'T EVEN KNOW THEY DID IT, CANDACE--BUT IT DOES MEAN THEY'RE THINKING ABOUT ME, WHICH IS NICE.
NO, I MEAN, LIKE LITERALLY. WHAT KIND OF ANIMAL IS THAT? A BABY KANGAROO?
OH, HEH. RIGHT. THIS, MY FRIEND...
...IS A QUOKKA. IT'S AUSTRALIAN, AND A MARSUPIAL, BUT IT'S NOT A KANGAROO. IT'S ITS OWN THING.
A PLATYPUS, A QUOKKA, AND YOU WERE A KOALA BEFORE. YOU REALLY LIKE AUSTRALIAN ANIMALS, HUH?
I CERTAINLY DO, CANDACE. I CERTAINLY--

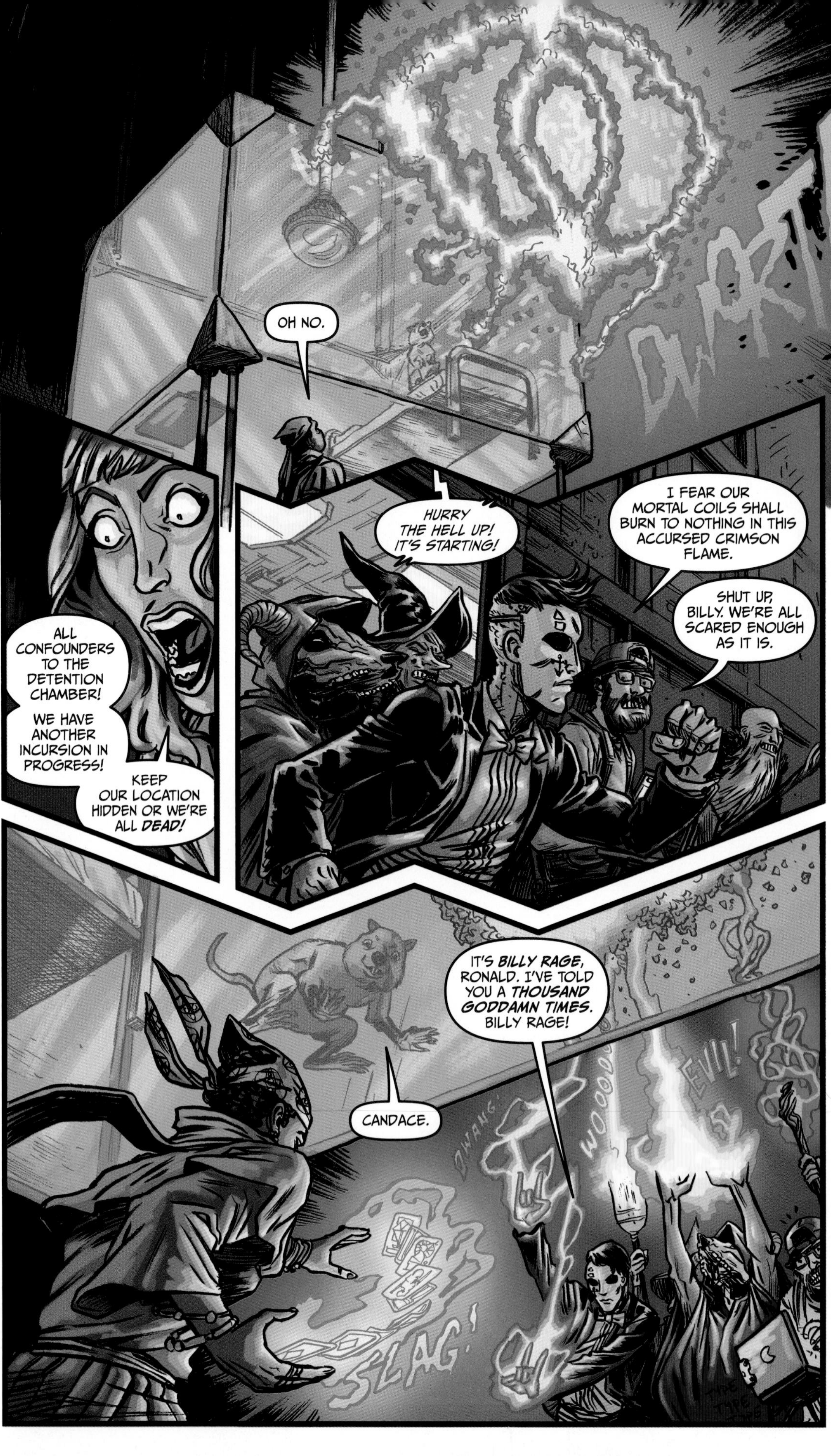

OH NO.
ALL CONFOUNDERS TO THE DETENTION CHAMBER!
WE HAVE ANOTHER INCURSION IN PROGRESS!
KEEP OUR LOCATION HIDDEN OR WE'RE ALL *DEAD!*
HURRY THE HELL UP! IT'S STARTING!
I FEAR OUR MORTAL COILS SHALL BURN TO NOTHING IN THIS ACCURSED CRIMSON FLAME.
SHUT UP, BILLY. WE'RE ALL SCARED ENOUGH AS IT IS.
IT'S ***BILLY RAGE***, RONALD. I'VE TOLD YOU A ***THOUSAND GODDAMN TIMES***. BILLY RAGE!
CANDACE.
EVIL!
SLAG!

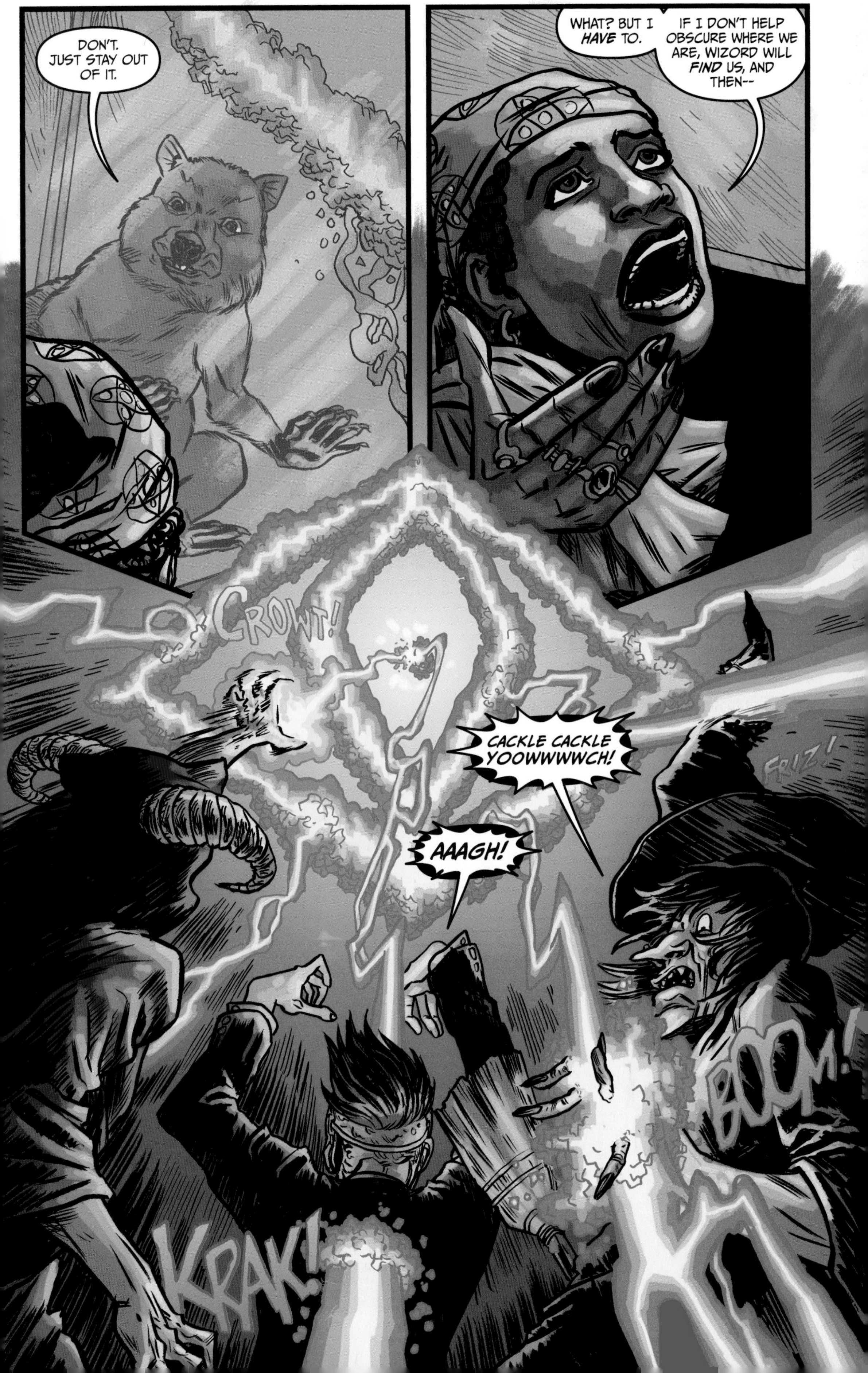
DON'T. JUST STAY OUT OF IT.
WHAT? BUT I HAVE TO.
IF I DON'T HELP OBSCURE WHERE WE ARE, WIZORD WILL FIND US, AND THEN--
CROWT!
CACKLE CACKLE YOOWWWWCH!
FRIZ!
AAAGH!
BOOM!
KRAK!

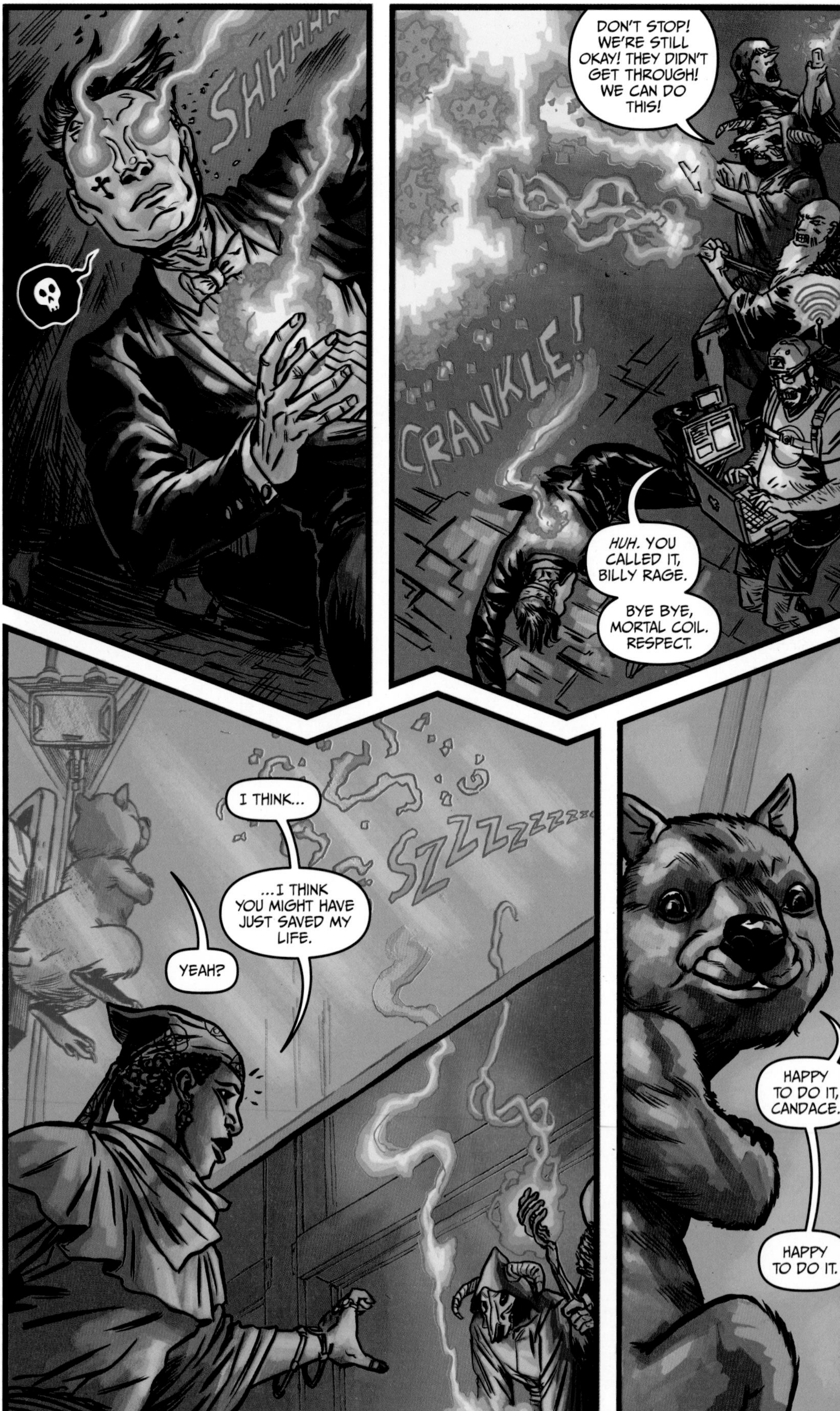
SHHHH
DON'T STOP! WE'RE STILL OKAY! THEY DIDN'T GET THROUGH! WE CAN DO THIS!
CRANKLE!
HUH. YOU CALLED IT, BILLY RAGE.
BYE BYE, MORTAL COIL. RESPECT.
I THINK...
...I THINK YOU MIGHT HAVE JUST SAVED MY LIFE.
SZZZZZZ
YEAH?
HAPPY TO DO IT, CANDACE.
HAPPY TO DO IT.

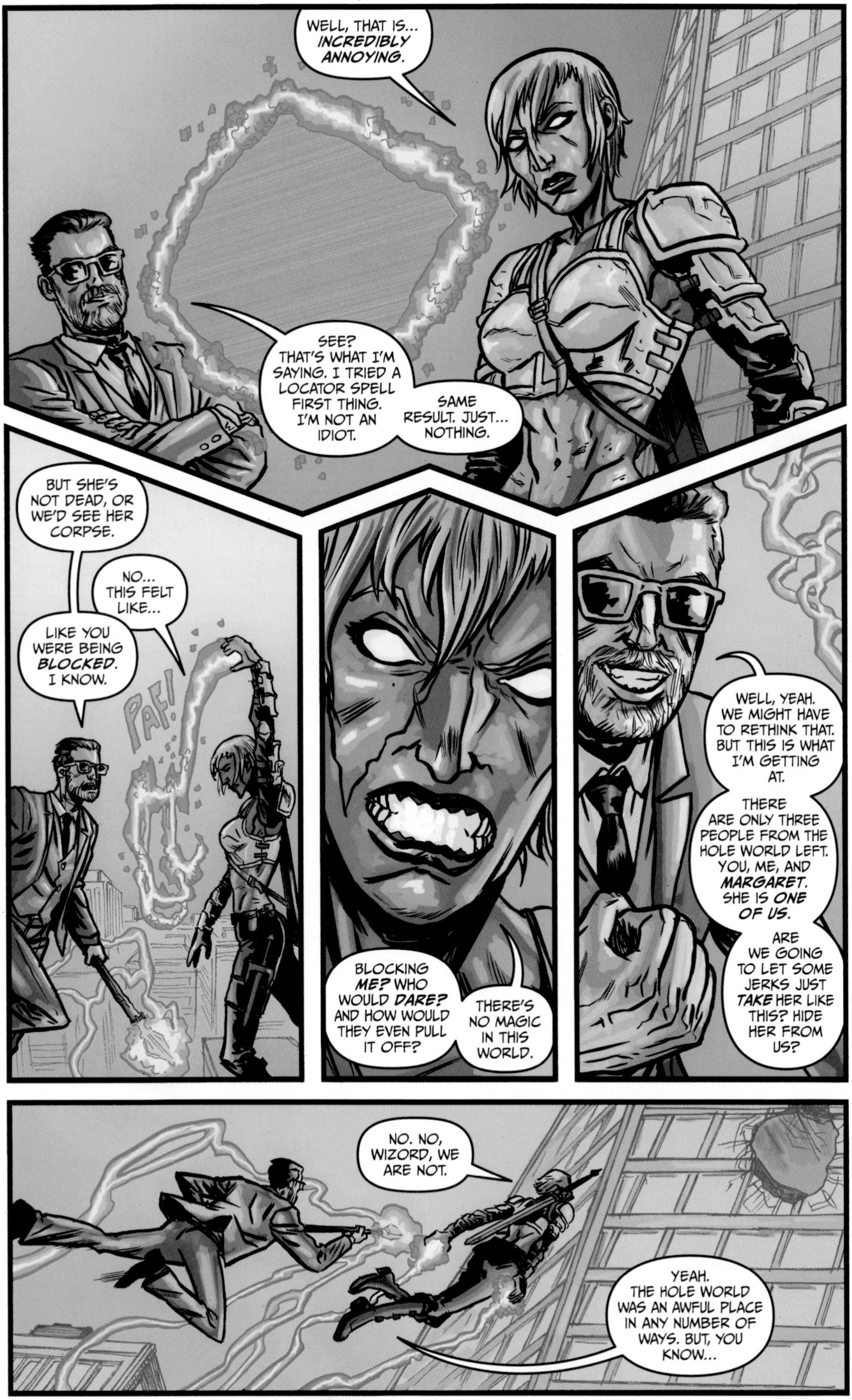
WELL, THAT IS... INCREDIBLY ANNOYING.
SEE? THAT'S WHAT I'M SAYING. I TRIED A LOCATOR SPELL FIRST THING. I'M NOT AN IDIOT.
SAME RESULT. JUST... NOTHING.
BUT SHE'S NOT DEAD, OR WE'D SEE HER CORPSE.
NO... THIS FELT LIKE...
LIKE YOU WERE BEING BLOCKED. I KNOW.
PAF!
BLOCKING ME? WHO WOULD DARE? AND HOW WOULD THEY EVEN PULL IT OFF?
THERE'S NO MAGIC IN THIS WORLD.
WELL, YEAH. WE MIGHT HAVE TO RETHINK THAT. BUT THIS IS WHAT I'M GETTING AT.
THERE ARE ONLY THREE PEOPLE FROM THE HOLE WORLD LEFT. YOU, ME, AND MARGARET. SHE IS ONE OF US.
ARE WE GOING TO LET SOME JERKS JUST TAKE HER LIKE THIS? HIDE HER FROM US?
NO. NO, WIZORD, WE ARE NOT.
YEAH. THE HOLE WORLD WAS AN AWFUL PLACE IN ANY NUMBER OF WAYS. BUT, YOU KNOW...

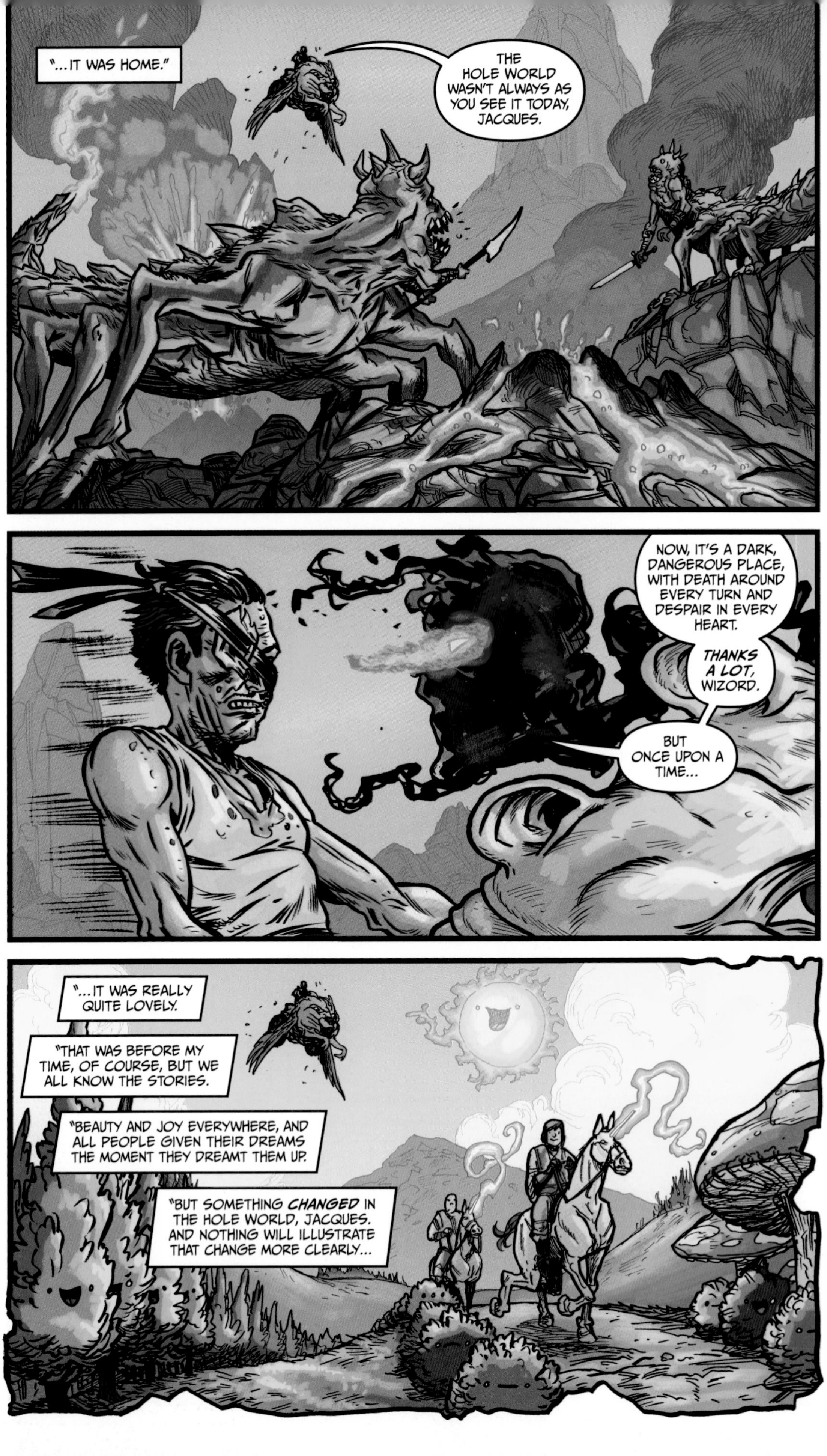

"...IT WAS HOME."
THE HOLE WORLD WASN'T ALWAYS AS YOU SEE IT TODAY, JACQUES.
NOW, IT'S A DARK, DANGEROUS PLACE, WITH DEATH AROUND EVERY TURN AND DESPAIR IN EVERY HEART.
THANKS A LOT, WIZORD.
BUT ONCE UPON A TIME...
"...IT WAS REALLY QUITE LOVELY.
"THAT WAS BEFORE MY TIME, OF COURSE, BUT WE ALL KNOW THE STORIES.
"BEAUTY AND JOY EVERYWHERE, AND ALL PEOPLE GIVEN THEIR DREAMS THE MOMENT THEY DREAMT THEM UP.
"BUT SOMETHING *CHANGED* IN THE HOLE WORLD, JACQUES. AND NOTHING WILL ILLUSTRATE THAT CHANGE MORE CLEARLY...

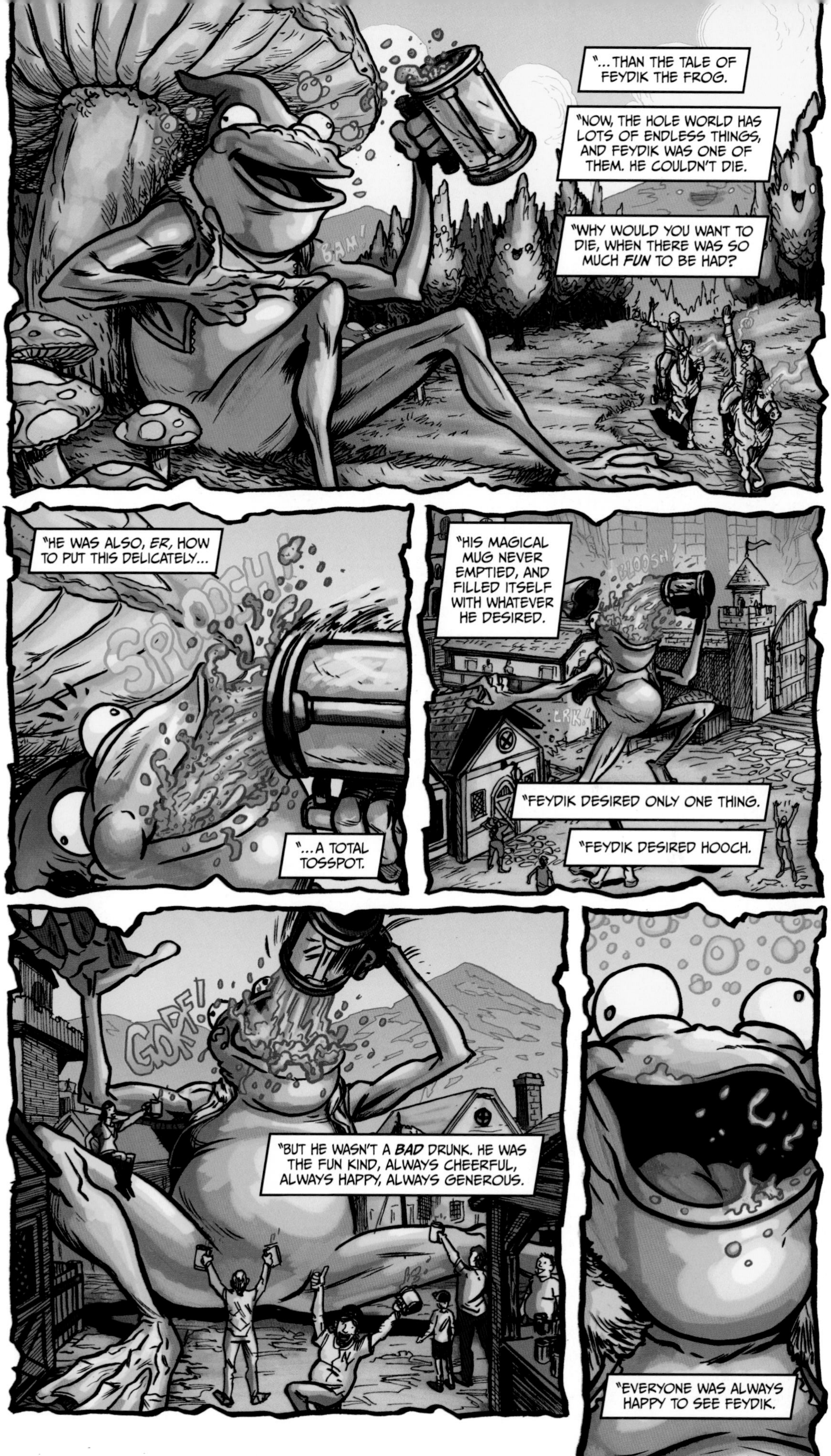
"...THAN THE TALE OF FEYDIK THE FROG.
"NOW, THE HOLE WORLD HAS LOTS OF ENDLESS THINGS, AND FEYDIK WAS ONE OF THEM. HE COULDN'T DIE.
"WHY WOULD YOU WANT TO DIE, WHEN THERE WAS SO MUCH *FUN* TO BE HAD?
"HE WAS ALSO, *ER*, HOW TO PUT THIS DELICATELY...
SPLOOSH!
"...A TOTAL TOSSPOT.
"HIS MAGICAL MUG NEVER EMPTIED, AND FILLED ITSELF WITH WHATEVER HE DESIRED.
BLOOSH!
"FEYDIK DESIRED ONLY ONE THING.
"FEYDIK DESIRED HOOCH.
GORF!
"BUT HE WASN'T A *BAD* DRUNK. HE WAS THE FUN KIND, ALWAYS CHEERFUL, ALWAYS HAPPY, ALWAYS GENEROUS.
"EVERYONE WAS ALWAYS HAPPY TO SEE FEYDIK.

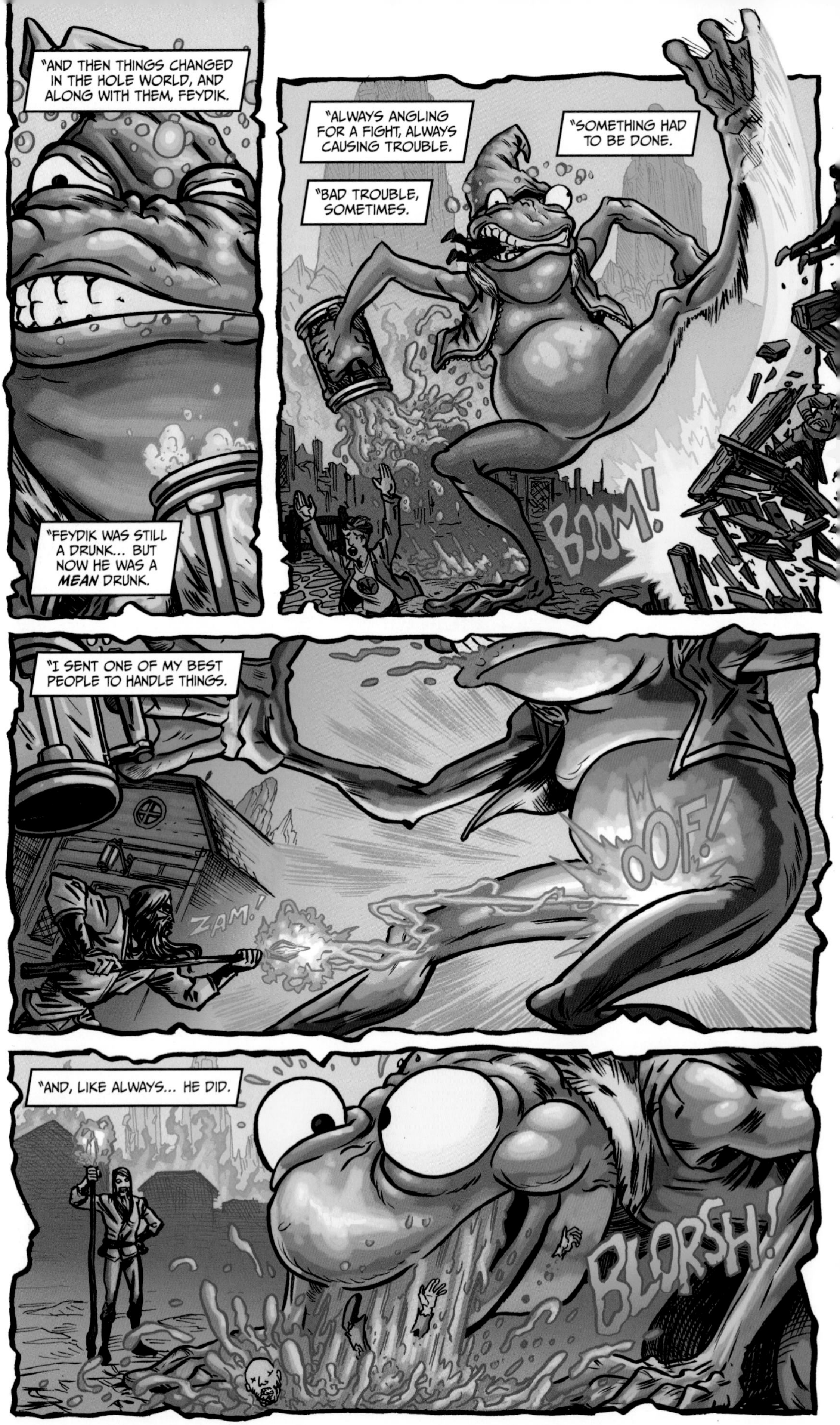
"AND THEN THINGS CHANGED IN THE HOLE WORLD, AND ALONG WITH THEM, FEYDIK.
"FEYDIK WAS STILL A DRUNK... BUT NOW HE WAS A *MEAN* DRUNK.
"ALWAYS ANGLING FOR A FIGHT, ALWAYS CAUSING TROUBLE.
"BAD TROUBLE, SOMETIMES.
"SOMETHING HAD TO BE DONE.
BOOM!
"I SENT ONE OF MY BEST PEOPLE TO HANDLE THINGS.
ZAM!
OOF!
"AND, LIKE ALWAYS... HE DID.
BLORSH!

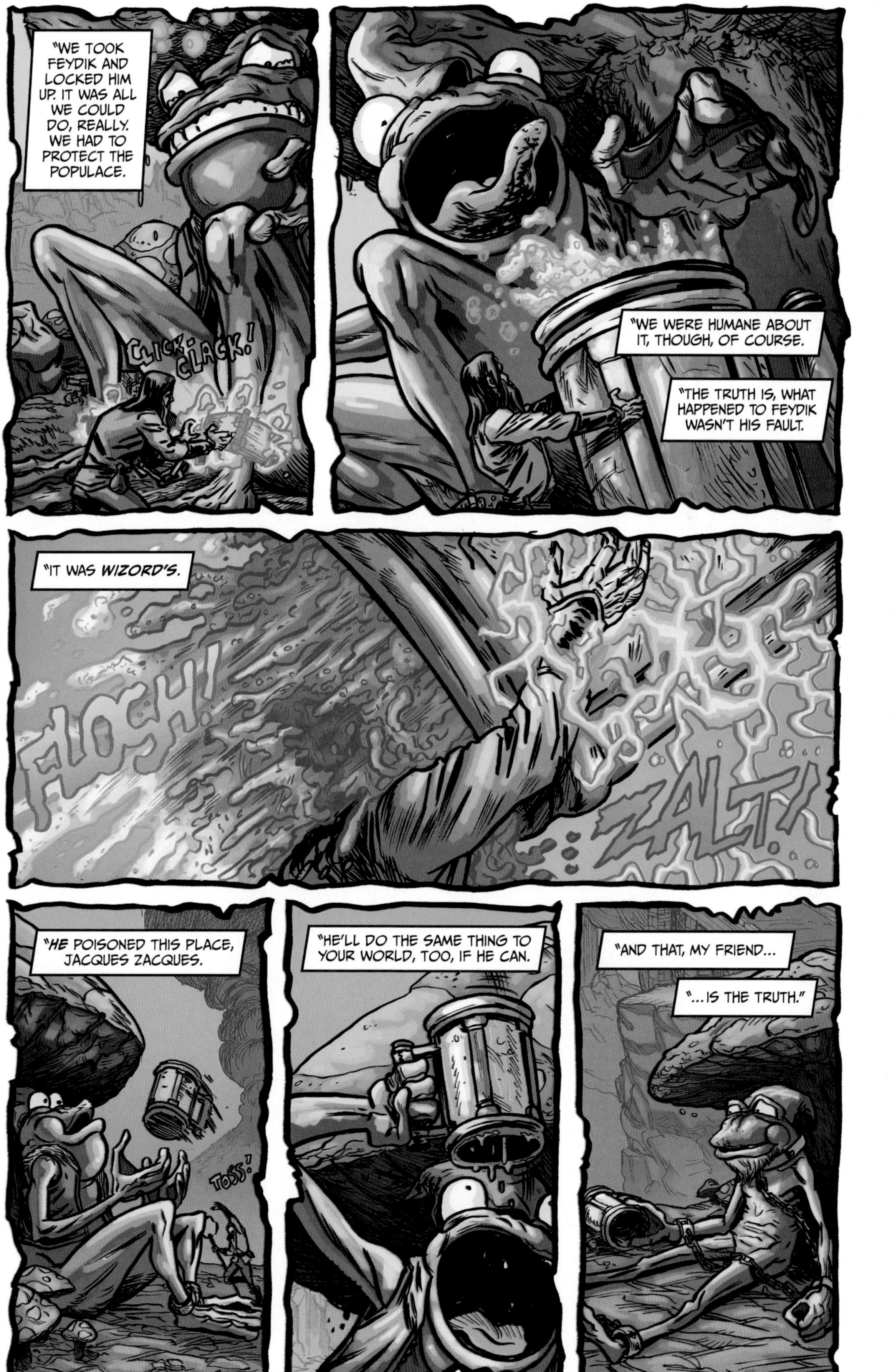
"WE TOOK FEYDIK AND LOCKED HIM UP. IT WAS ALL WE COULD DO, REALLY. WE HAD TO PROTECT THE POPULACE.
CLICK-CLACK!
"WE WERE HUMANE ABOUT IT, THOUGH, OF COURSE.
"THE TRUTH IS, WHAT HAPPENED TO FEYDIK WASN'T HIS FAULT.
"IT WAS WIZORD'S.
FLOOSH!
ZALT!
"HE POISONED THIS PLACE, JACQUES ZACQUES.
TOSS!
"HE'LL DO THE SAME THING TO YOUR WORLD, TOO, IF HE CAN.
"AND THAT, MY FRIEND...
"...IS THE TRUTH."

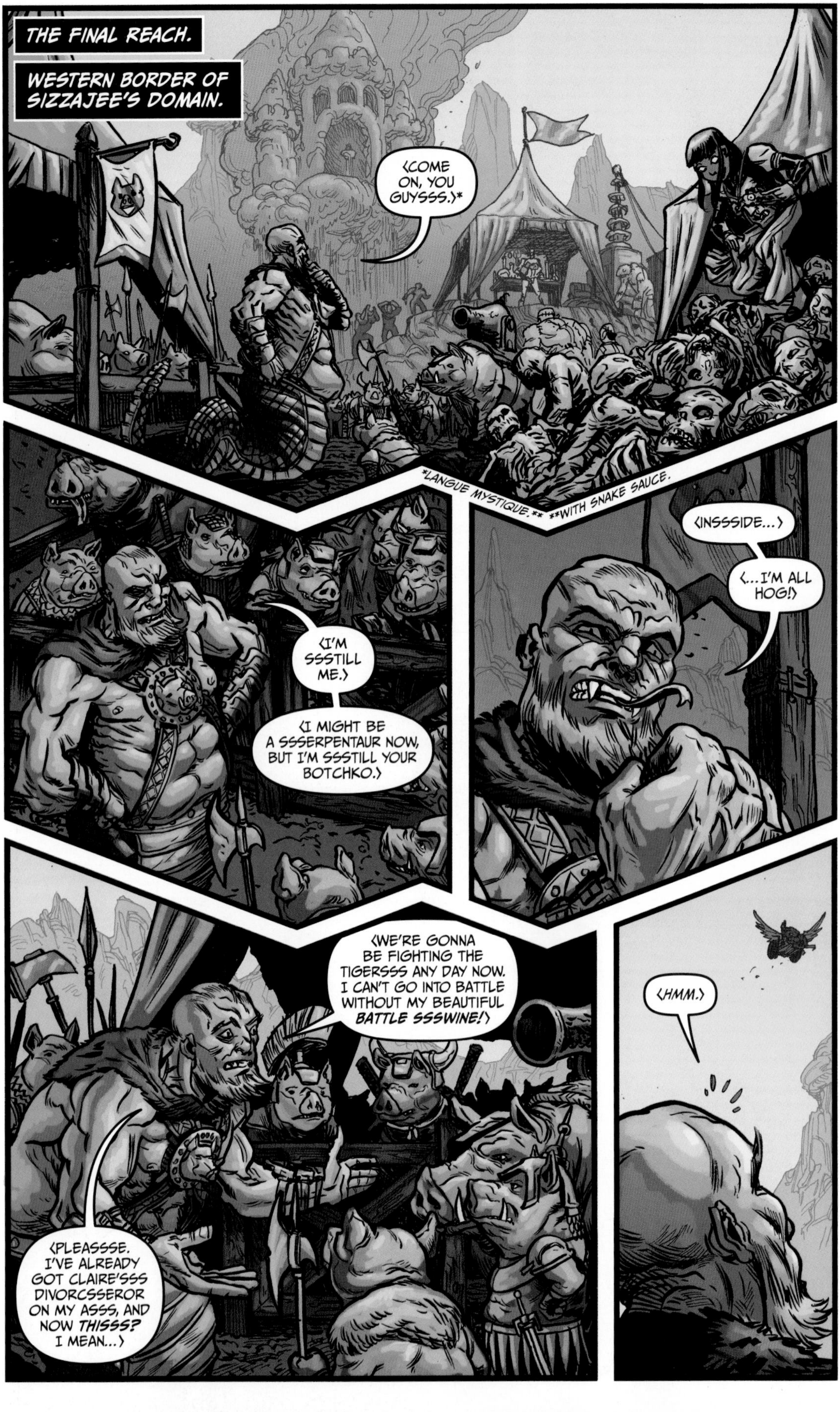
THE FINAL REACH.
WESTERN BORDER OF SIZZAJEE'S DOMAIN.
‹COME ON, YOU GUYSSS.›*
*LANGUE MYSTIQUE.** **WITH SNAKE SAUCE.
‹I'M SSSTILL ME.›
‹I MIGHT BE A SSSERPENTAUR NOW, BUT I'M SSSTILL YOUR BOTCHKO.›
‹INSSSIDE...›
‹...I'M ALL HOG!›
‹WE'RE GONNA BE FIGHTING THE TIGERSSS ANY DAY NOW. I CAN'T GO INTO BATTLE WITHOUT MY BEAUTIFUL BATTLE SSSWINE!›
‹PLEASSSE. I'VE ALREADY GOT CLAIRE'SSS DIVORCSSEROR ON MY ASSS, AND NOW THISSS? I MEAN...›
‹HMM.›

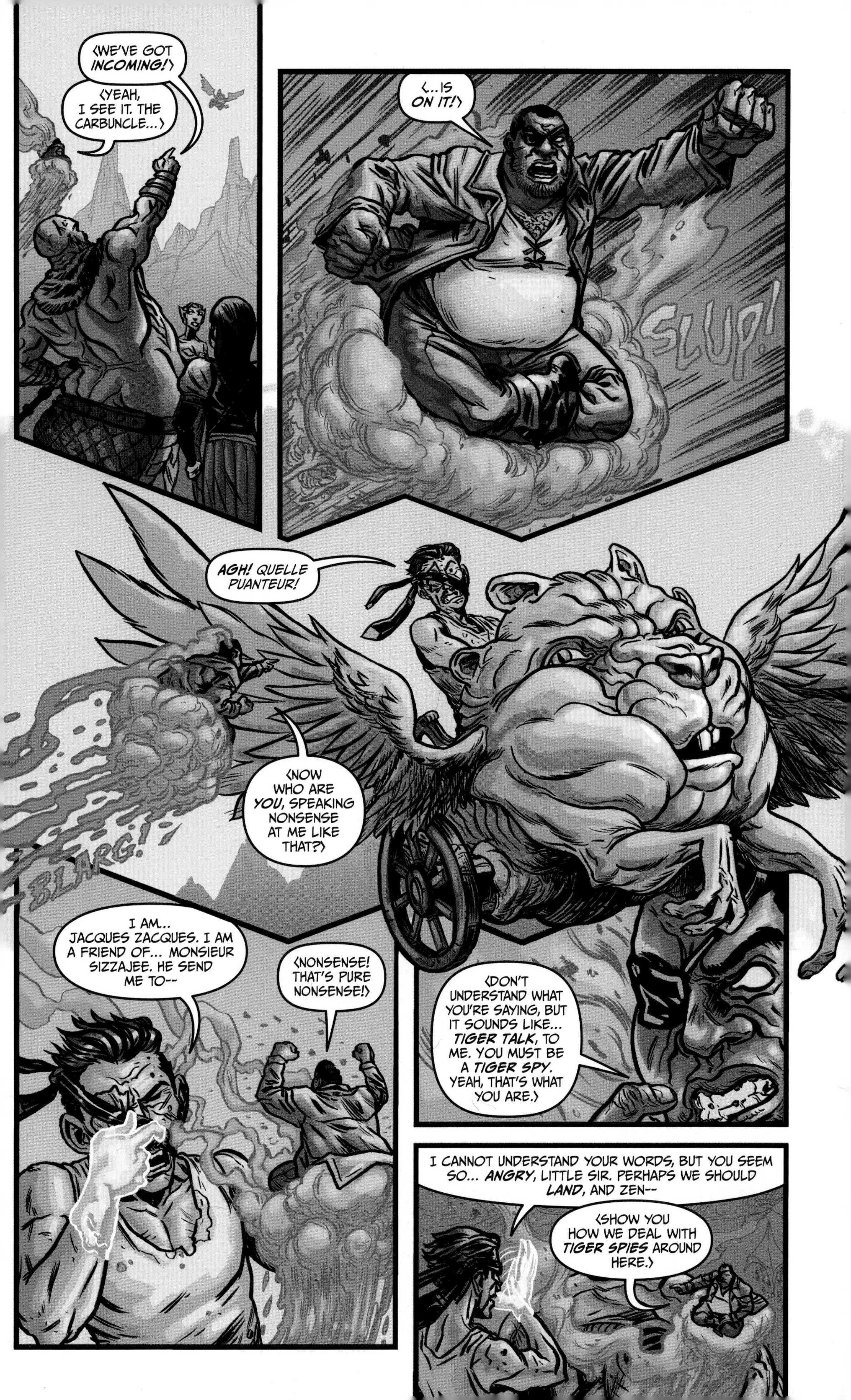

<WE'VE GOT INCOMING!>
<YEAH, I SEE IT. THE CARBUNCLE...>
<...IS ON IT!>
SLUP!
AGH! QUELLE PUANTEUR!
<NOW WHO ARE YOU, SPEAKING NONSENSE AT ME LIKE THAT?>
BLARG!
I AM... JACQUES ZACQUES. I AM A FRIEND OF... MONSIEUR SIZZAJEE. HE SEND ME TO--
<NONSENSE! THAT'S PURE NONSENSE!>
<DON'T UNDERSTAND WHAT YOU'RE SAYING, BUT IT SOUNDS LIKE... TIGER TALK, TO ME. YOU MUST BE A TIGER SPY. YEAH, THAT'S WHAT YOU ARE.>
I CANNOT UNDERSTAND YOUR WORDS, BUT YOU SEEM SO... ANGRY, LITTLE SIR. PERHAPS WE SHOULD LAND, AND ZEN--
<SHOW YOU HOW WE DEAL WITH TIGER SPIES AROUND HERE.>

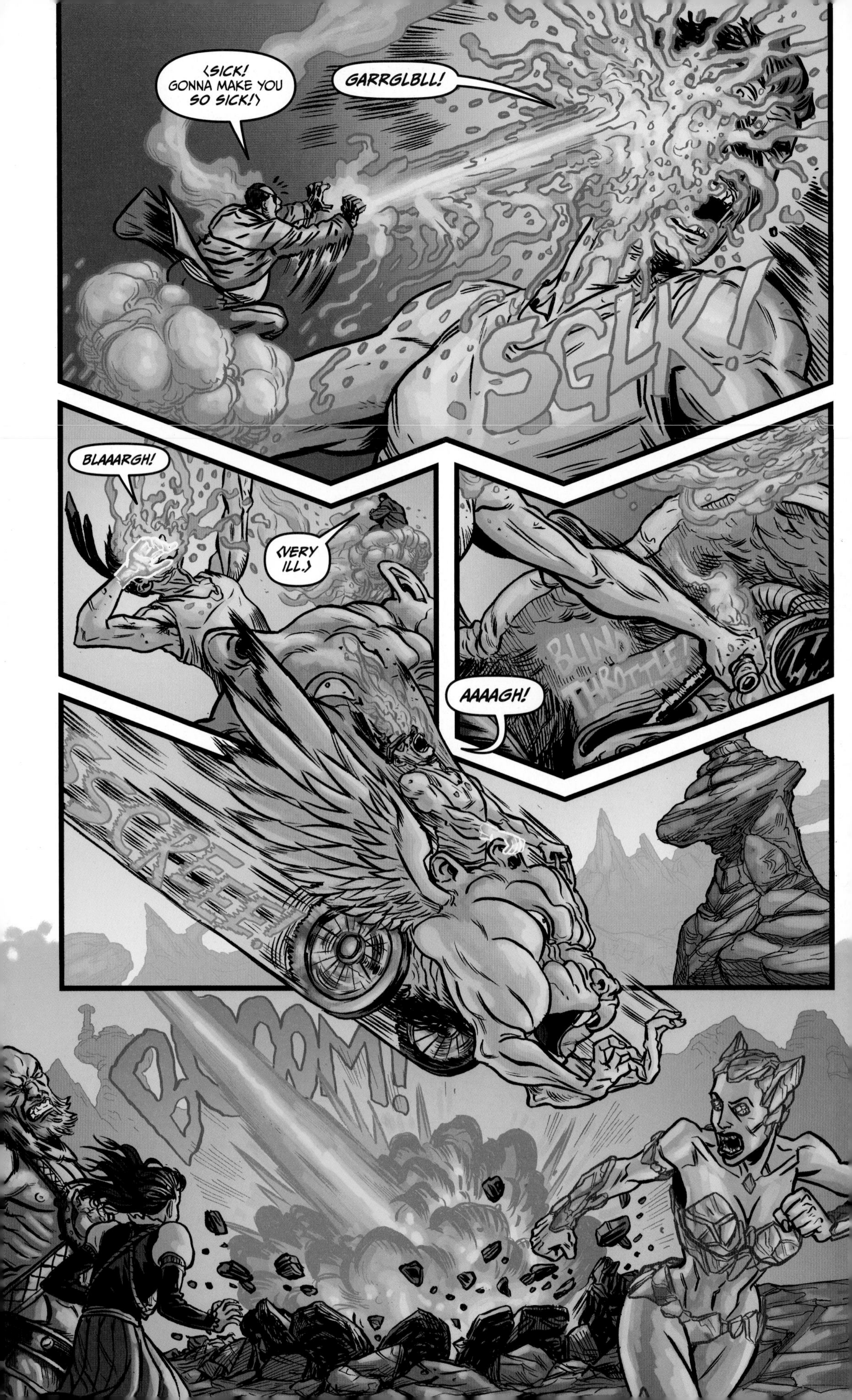

<SICK! GONNA MAKE YOU SO SICK!>
GARRGLBLL!
SGLK!
BLAAARGH!
<VERY ILL.>
BLIND THROTTLE!
AAAAGH!
BOOOM!

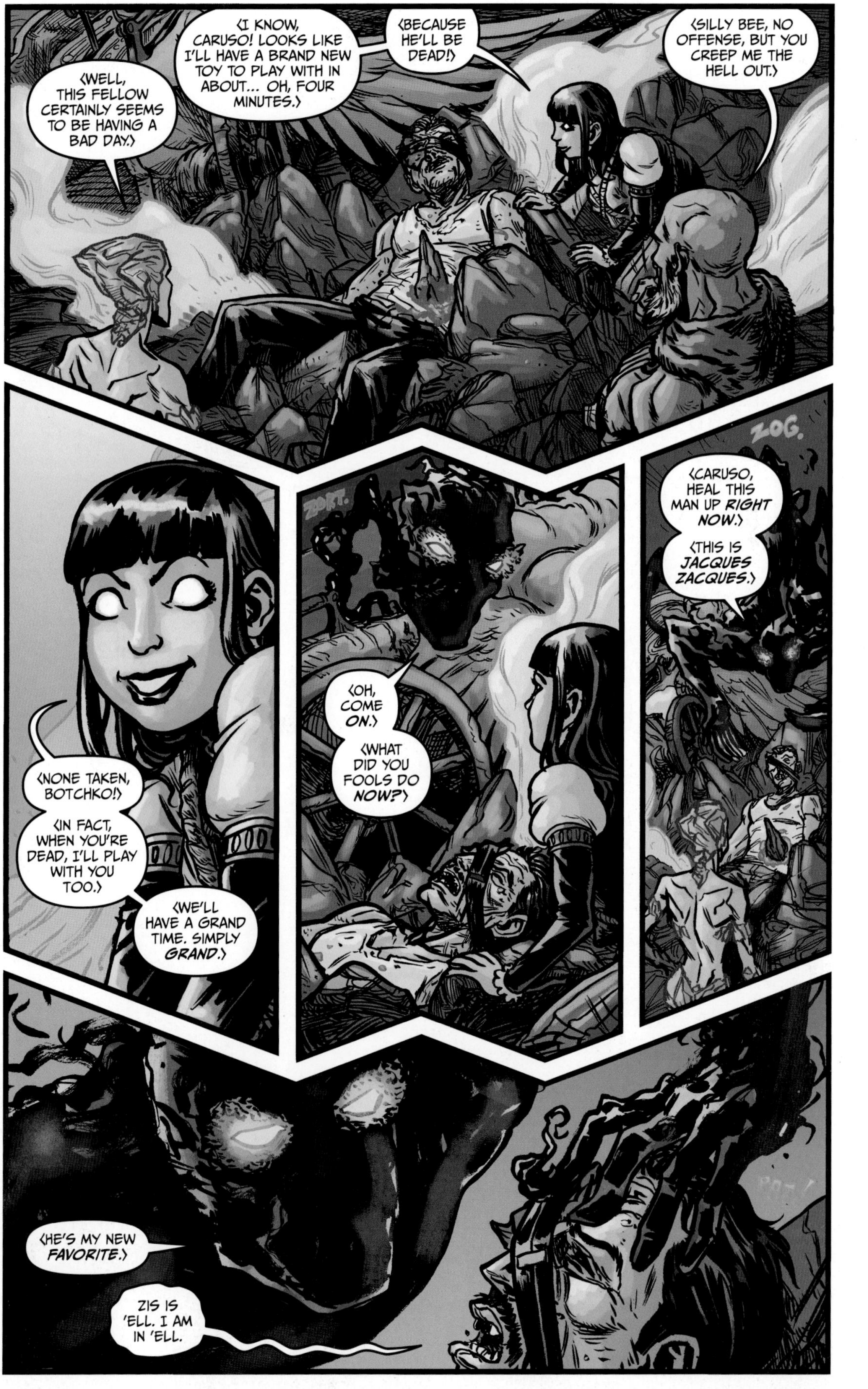

‹WELL, THIS FELLOW CERTAINLY SEEMS TO BE HAVING A BAD DAY.›
‹I KNOW, CARUSO! LOOKS LIKE I'LL HAVE A BRAND NEW TOY TO PLAY WITH IN ABOUT... OH, FOUR MINUTES.›
‹BECAUSE HE'LL BE DEAD!›
‹SILLY BEE, NO OFFENSE, BUT YOU CREEP ME THE HELL OUT.›
‹NONE TAKEN, BOTCHKO!›
‹IN FACT, WHEN YOU'RE DEAD, I'LL PLAY WITH YOU TOO.›
‹WE'LL HAVE A GRAND TIME. SIMPLY *GRAND*.›
ZORT.
‹OH, COME *ON*.›
‹WHAT DID YOU FOOLS DO *NOW?*›
ZOG.
‹CARUSO, HEAL THIS MAN UP *RIGHT NOW*.›
‹THIS IS *JACQUES ZACQUES*.›
‹HE'S MY NEW *FAVORITE*.›
ZIS IS 'ELL. I AM IN 'ELL.

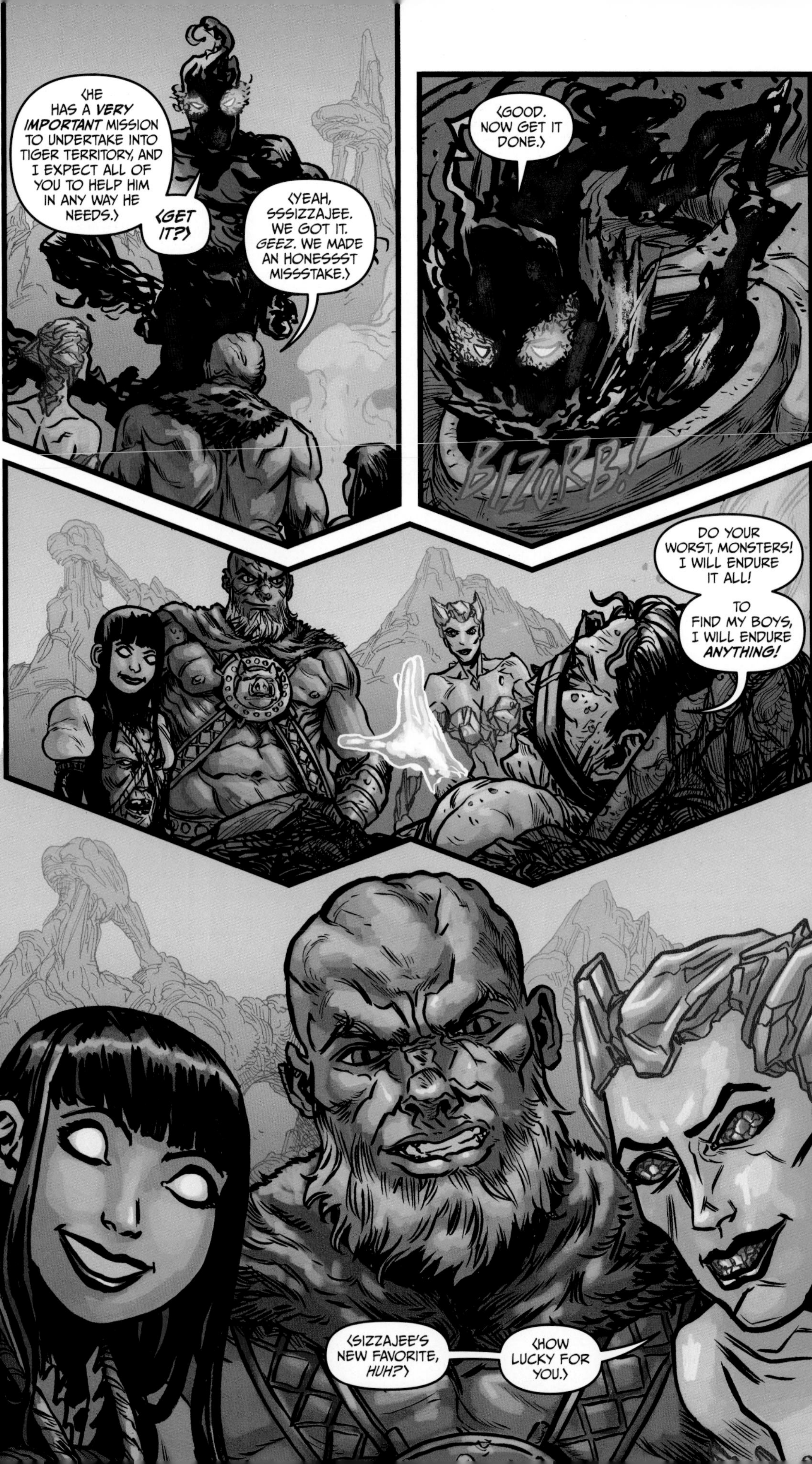
‹HE HAS A VERY IMPORTANT MISSION TO UNDERTAKE INTO TIGER TERRITORY, AND I EXPECT ALL OF YOU TO HELP HIM IN ANY WAY HE NEEDS.›
‹GET IT?›
‹YEAH, SSSIZZAJEE. WE GOT IT. GEEZ. WE MADE AN HONESSST MISSSTAKE.›
‹GOOD. NOW GET IT DONE.›
BIZORB!
DO YOUR WORST, MONSTERS! I WILL ENDURE IT ALL!
TO FIND MY BOYS, I WILL ENDURE ANYTHING!
‹SIZZAJEE'S NEW FAVORITE, HUH?›
‹HOW LUCKY FOR YOU.›

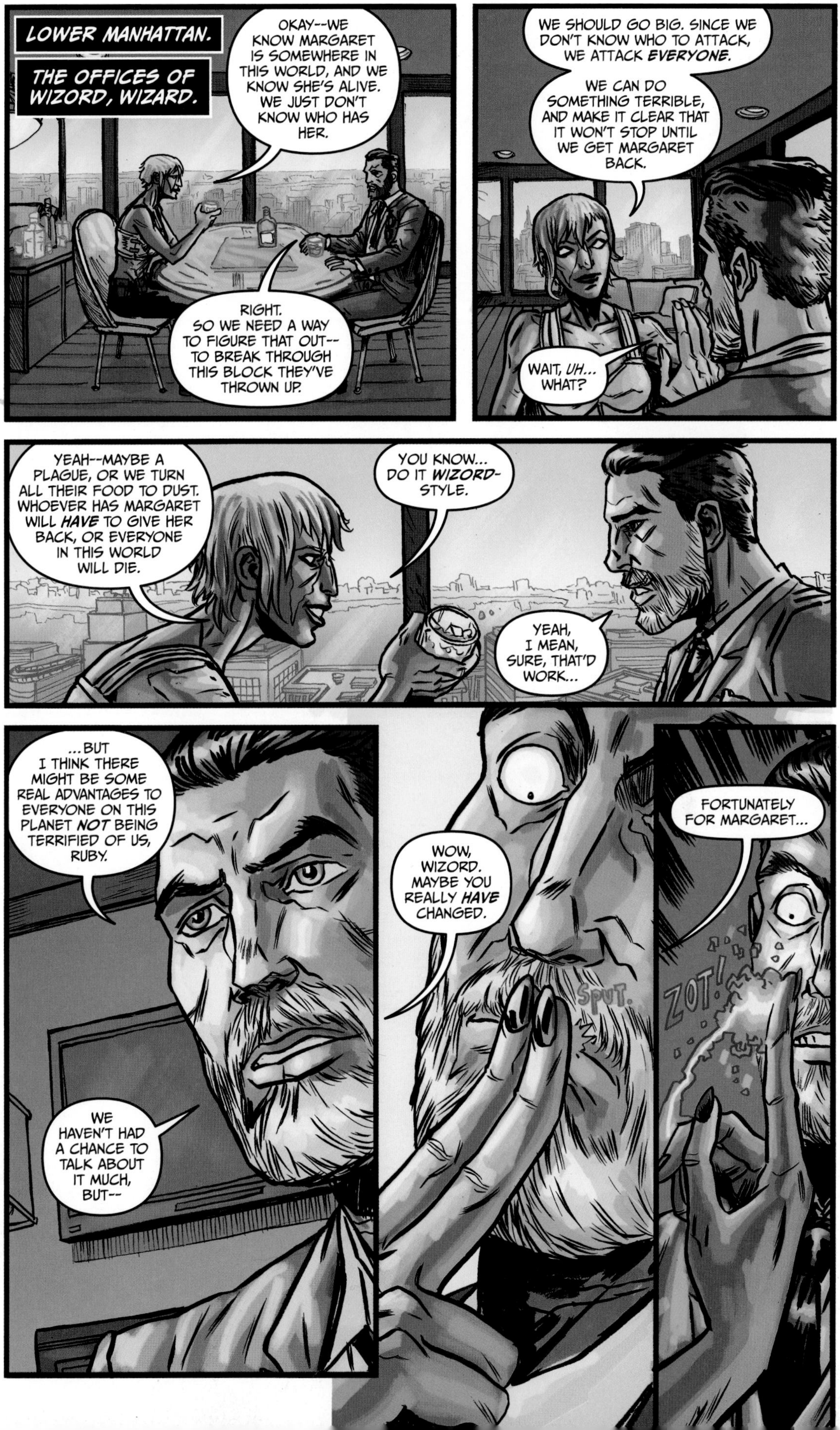

LOWER MANHATTAN.
THE OFFICES OF WIZORD, WIZARD.
OKAY--WE KNOW MARGARET IS SOMEWHERE IN THIS WORLD, AND WE KNOW SHE'S ALIVE. WE JUST DON'T KNOW WHO HAS HER.
RIGHT. SO WE NEED A WAY TO FIGURE THAT OUT-- TO BREAK THROUGH THIS BLOCK THEY'VE THROWN UP.
WE SHOULD GO BIG. SINCE WE DON'T KNOW WHO TO ATTACK, WE ATTACK *EVERYONE.*
WE CAN DO SOMETHING TERRIBLE, AND MAKE IT CLEAR THAT IT WON'T STOP UNTIL WE GET MARGARET BACK.
WAIT, *UH...* WHAT?
YEAH--MAYBE A PLAGUE, OR WE TURN ALL THEIR FOOD TO DUST. WHOEVER HAS MARGARET WILL *HAVE* TO GIVE HER BACK, OR EVERYONE IN THIS WORLD WILL DIE.
YOU KNOW... DO IT *WIZORD*-STYLE.
YEAH, I MEAN, SURE, THAT'D WORK...
...BUT I THINK THERE MIGHT BE SOME REAL ADVANTAGES TO EVERYONE ON THIS PLANET *NOT* BEING TERRIFIED OF US, RUBY.
WE HAVEN'T HAD A CHANCE TO TALK ABOUT IT MUCH, BUT--
WOW, WIZORD. MAYBE YOU REALLY *HAVE* CHANGED.
SPUT.
FORTUNATELY FOR MARGARET...
ZOT!

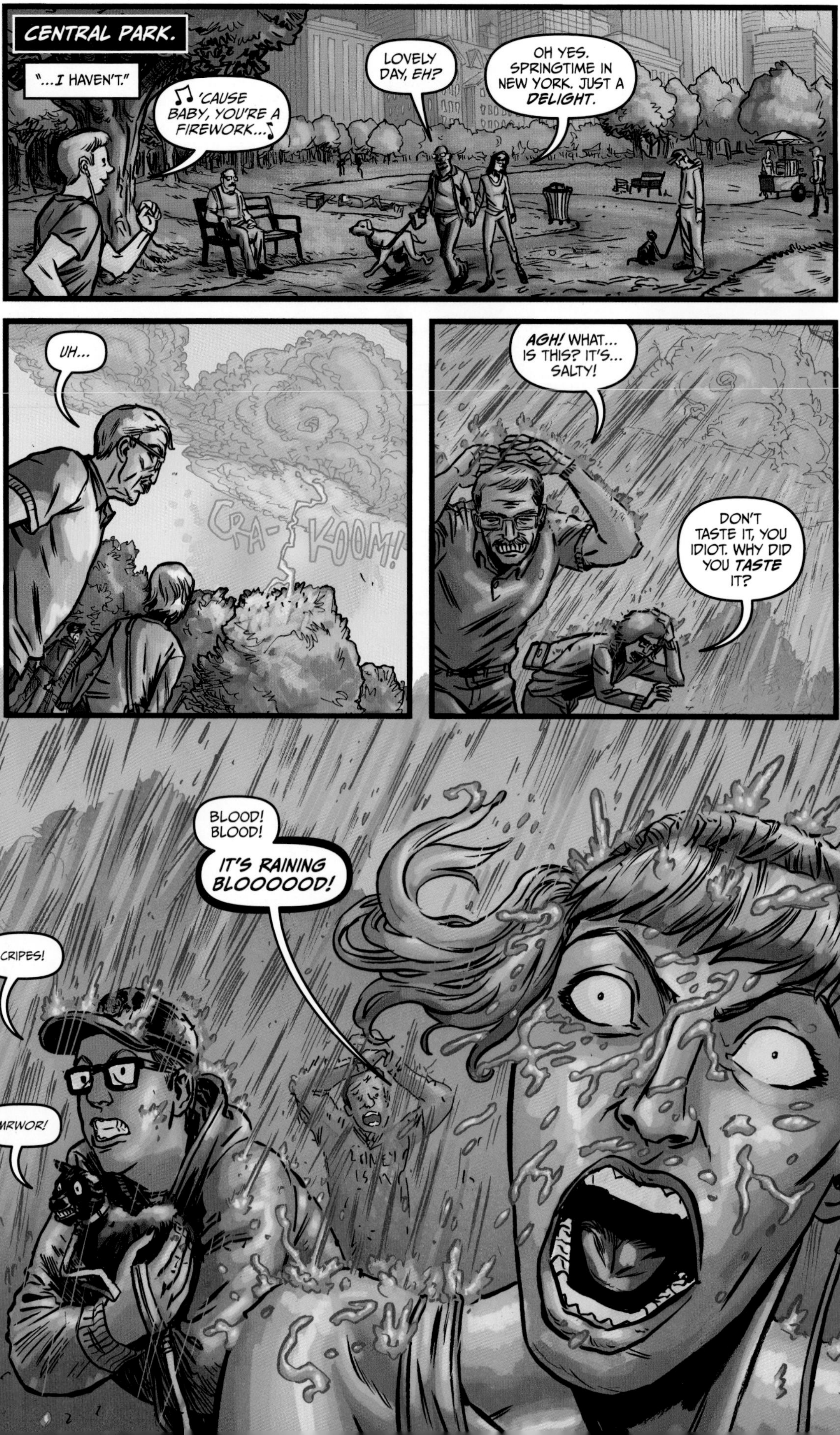
CENTRAL PARK.
"...I HAVEN'T."
'CAUSE BABY, YOU'RE A FIREWORK...
LOVELY DAY, EH?
OH YES. SPRINGTIME IN NEW YORK. JUST A DELIGHT.
UH...
CRA-KOOM!
AGH! WHAT... IS THIS? IT'S... SALTY!
DON'T TASTE IT, YOU IDIOT. WHY DID YOU TASTE IT?
BLOOD! BLOOD!
IT'S RAINING BLOOOOOD!
CRIPES!
MRWOR!

FOURTEEN

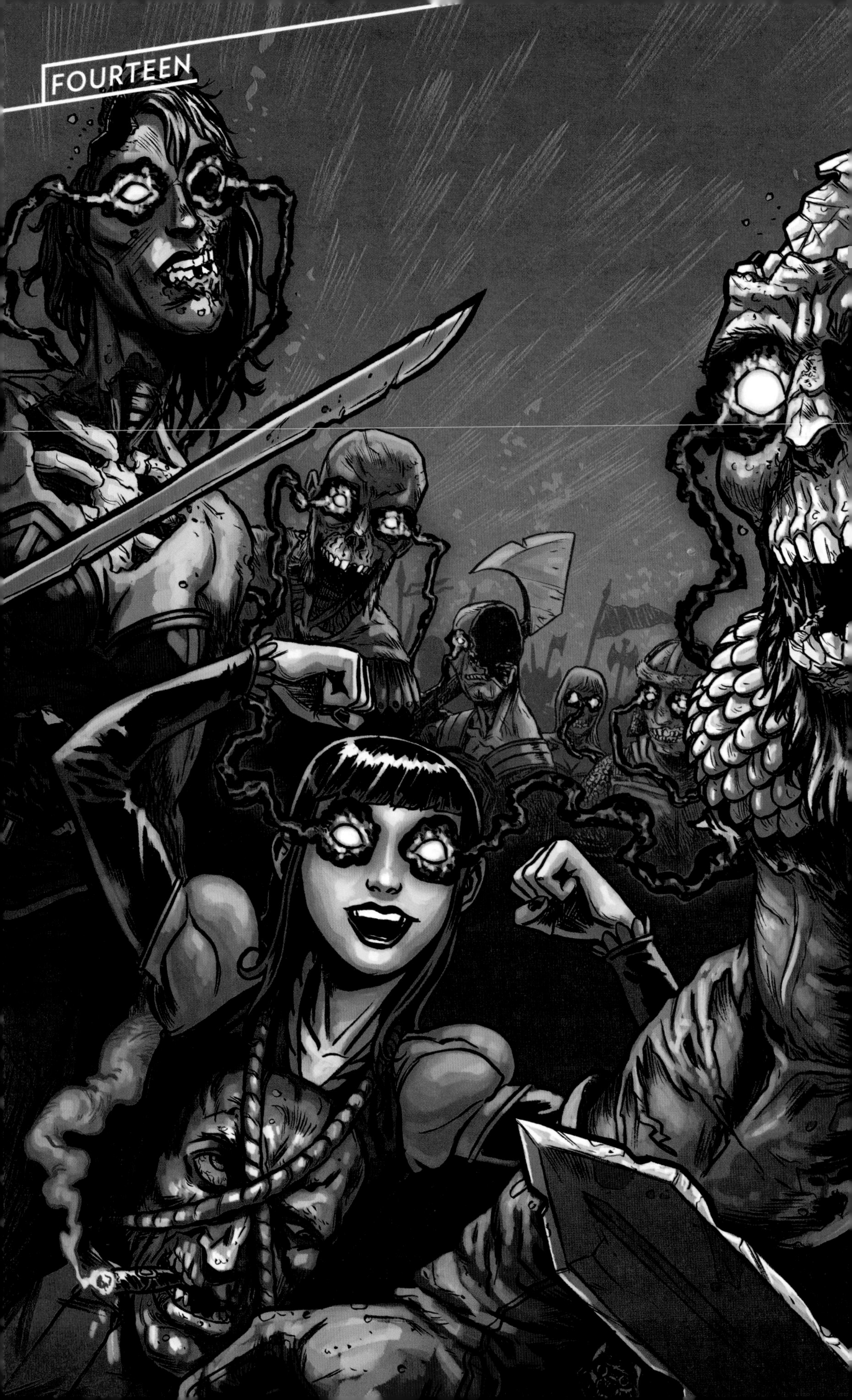

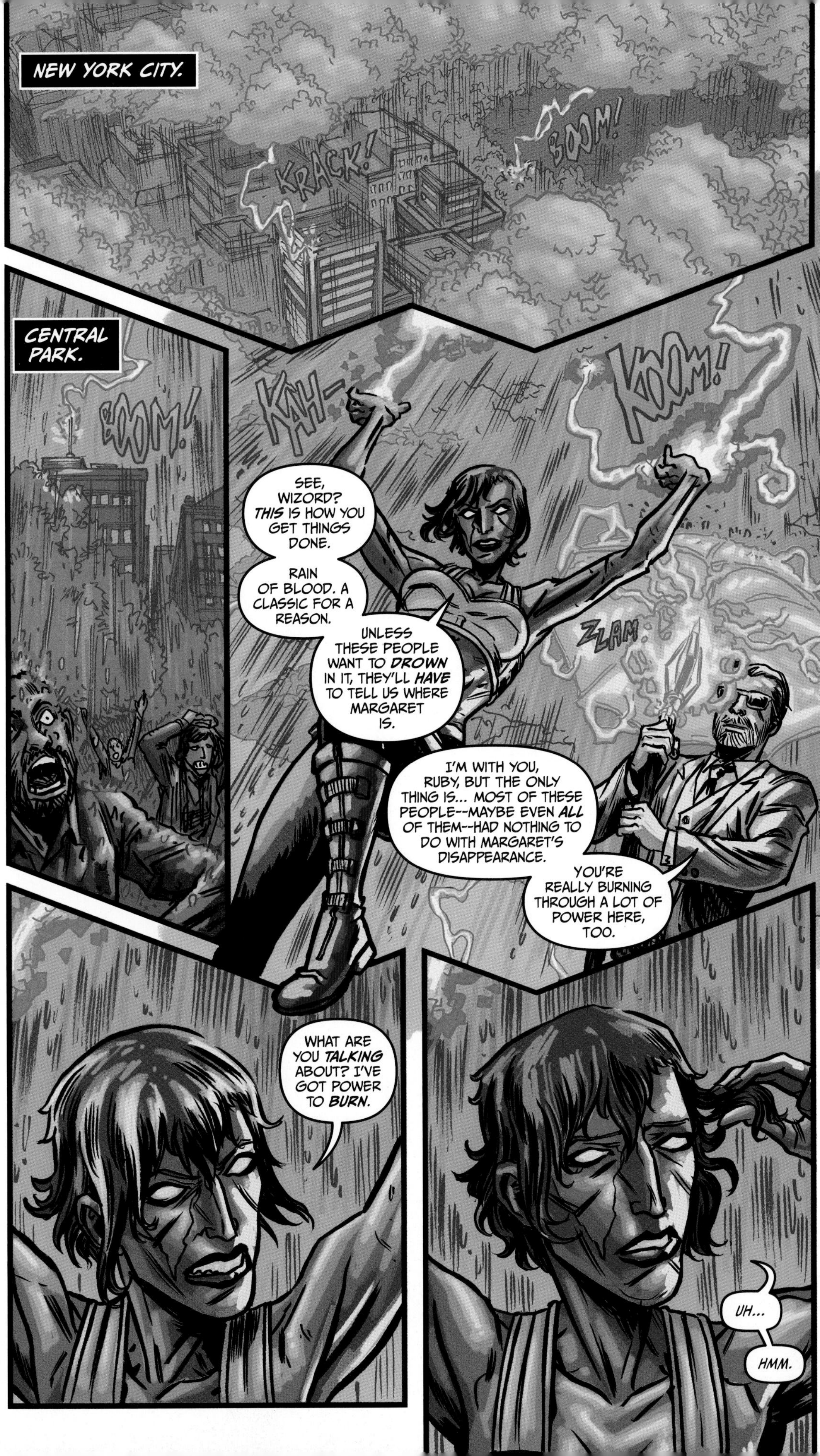
NEW YORK CITY.
KRACK!
BOOM!
CENTRAL PARK.
BOOM!
KAH-
KOOM!
SEE, WIZORD? THIS IS HOW YOU GET THINGS DONE.
RAIN OF BLOOD. A CLASSIC FOR A REASON.
UNLESS THESE PEOPLE WANT TO DROWN IN IT, THEY'LL HAVE TO TELL US WHERE MARGARET IS.
ZLAM
I'M WITH YOU, RUBY, BUT THE ONLY THING IS... MOST OF THESE PEOPLE--MAYBE EVEN ALL OF THEM--HAD NOTHING TO DO WITH MARGARET'S DISAPPEARANCE.
YOU'RE REALLY BURNING THROUGH A LOT OF POWER HERE, TOO.
WHAT ARE YOU TALKING ABOUT? I'VE GOT POWER TO BURN.
UH...
HMM.

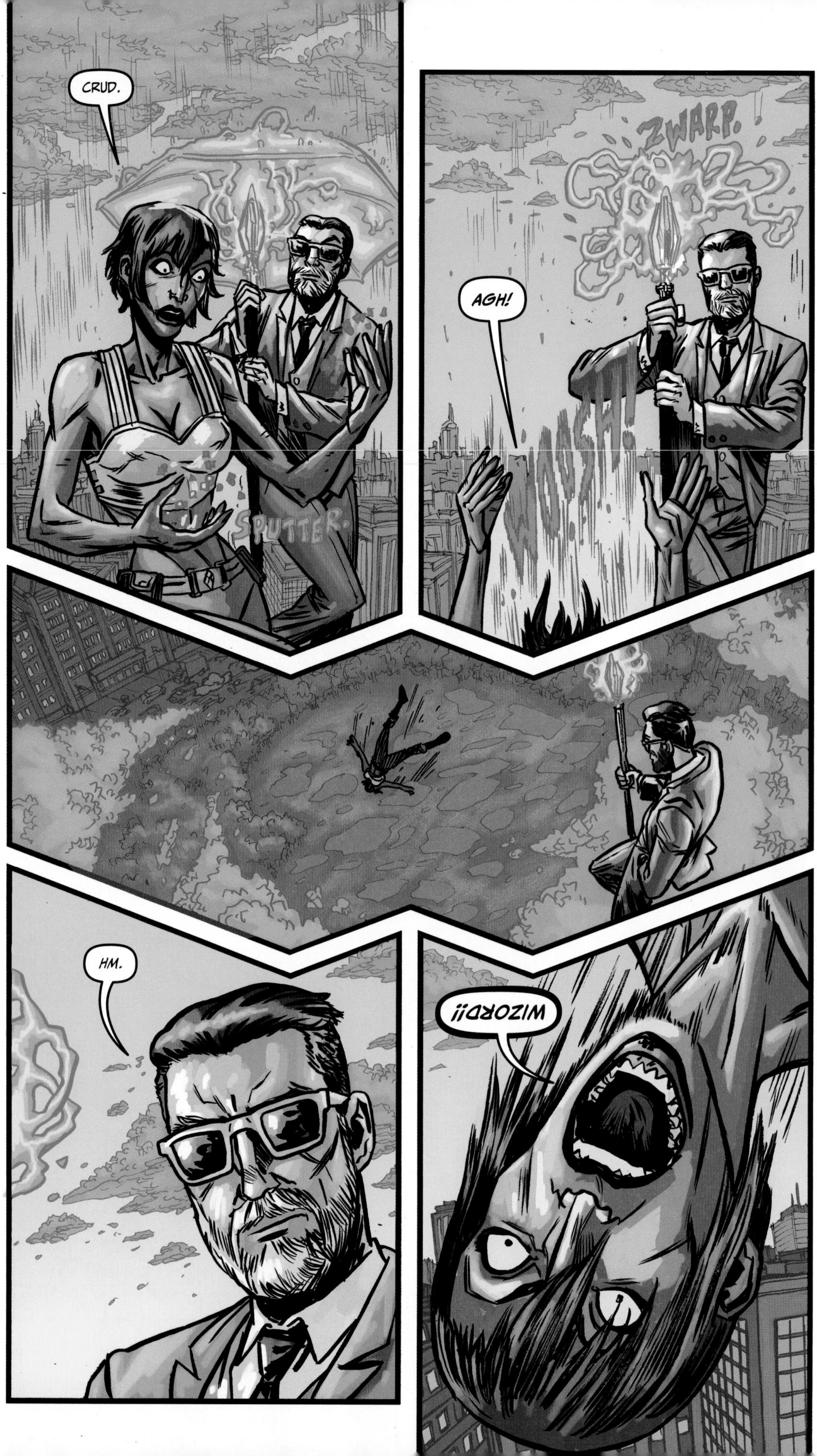
CRUD.
SPUTTER.
ZWARP.
AGH!
WOOSH!
HM.
WIZORD!!

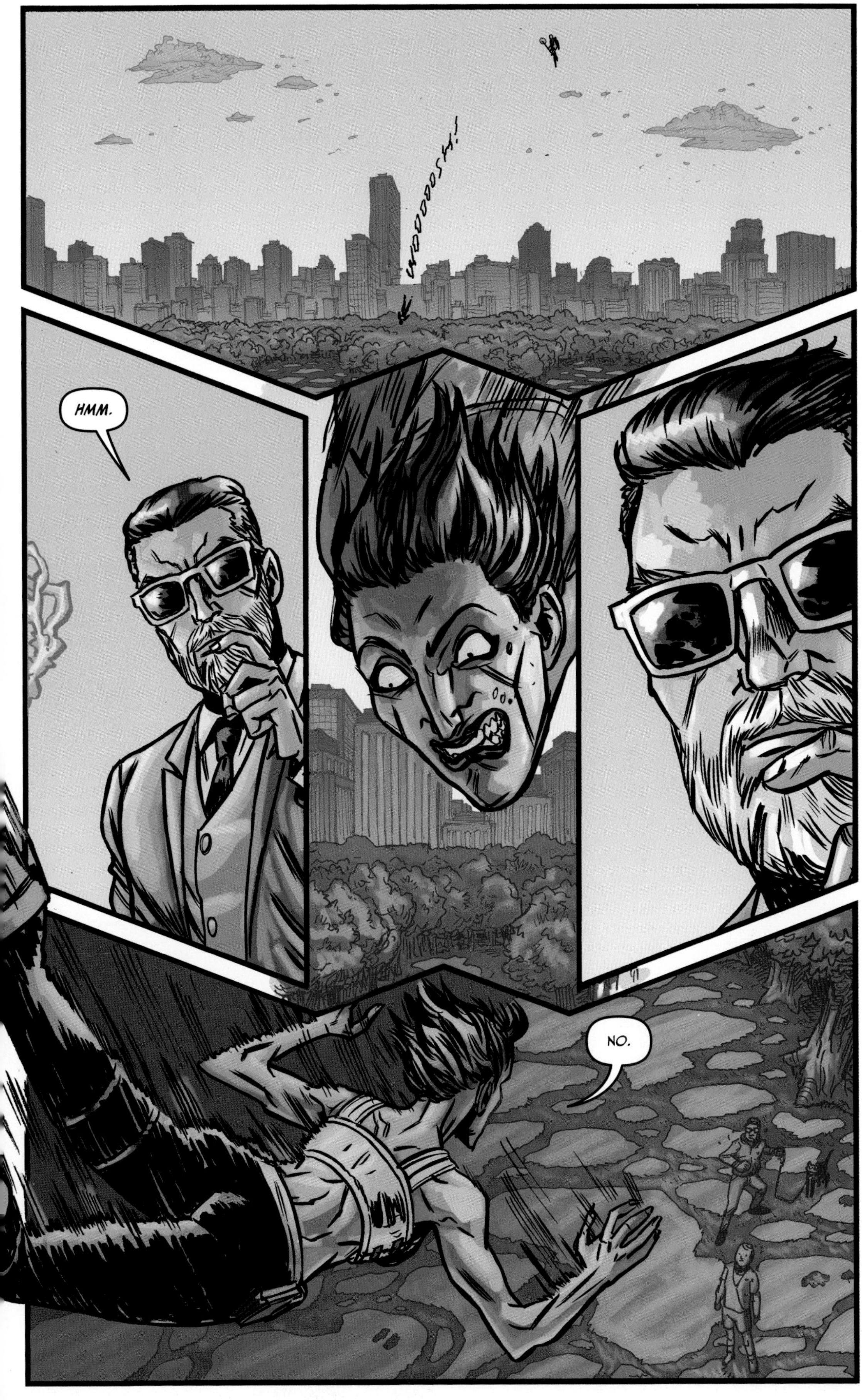
WOOOOOSH!
HMM.
NO.

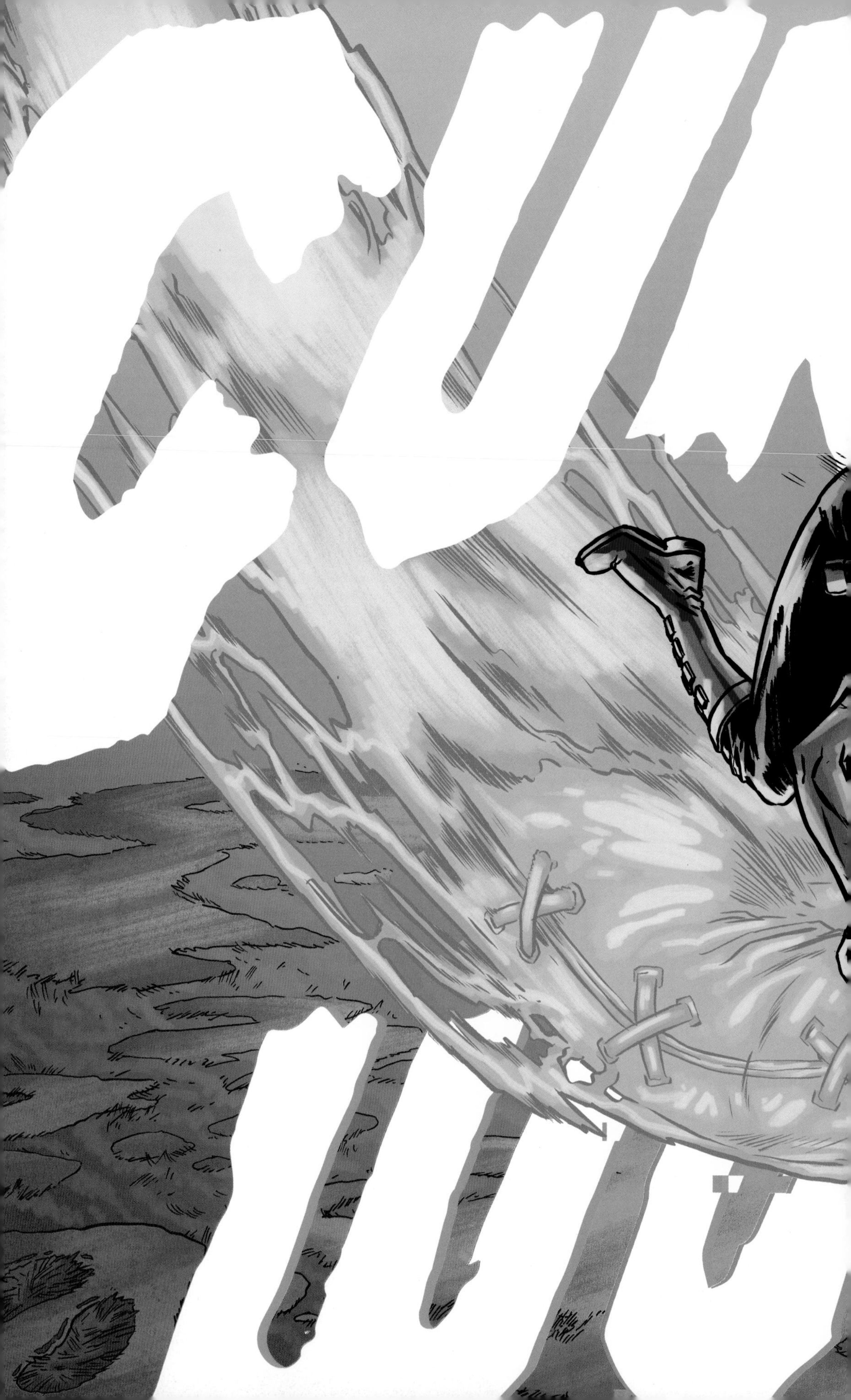

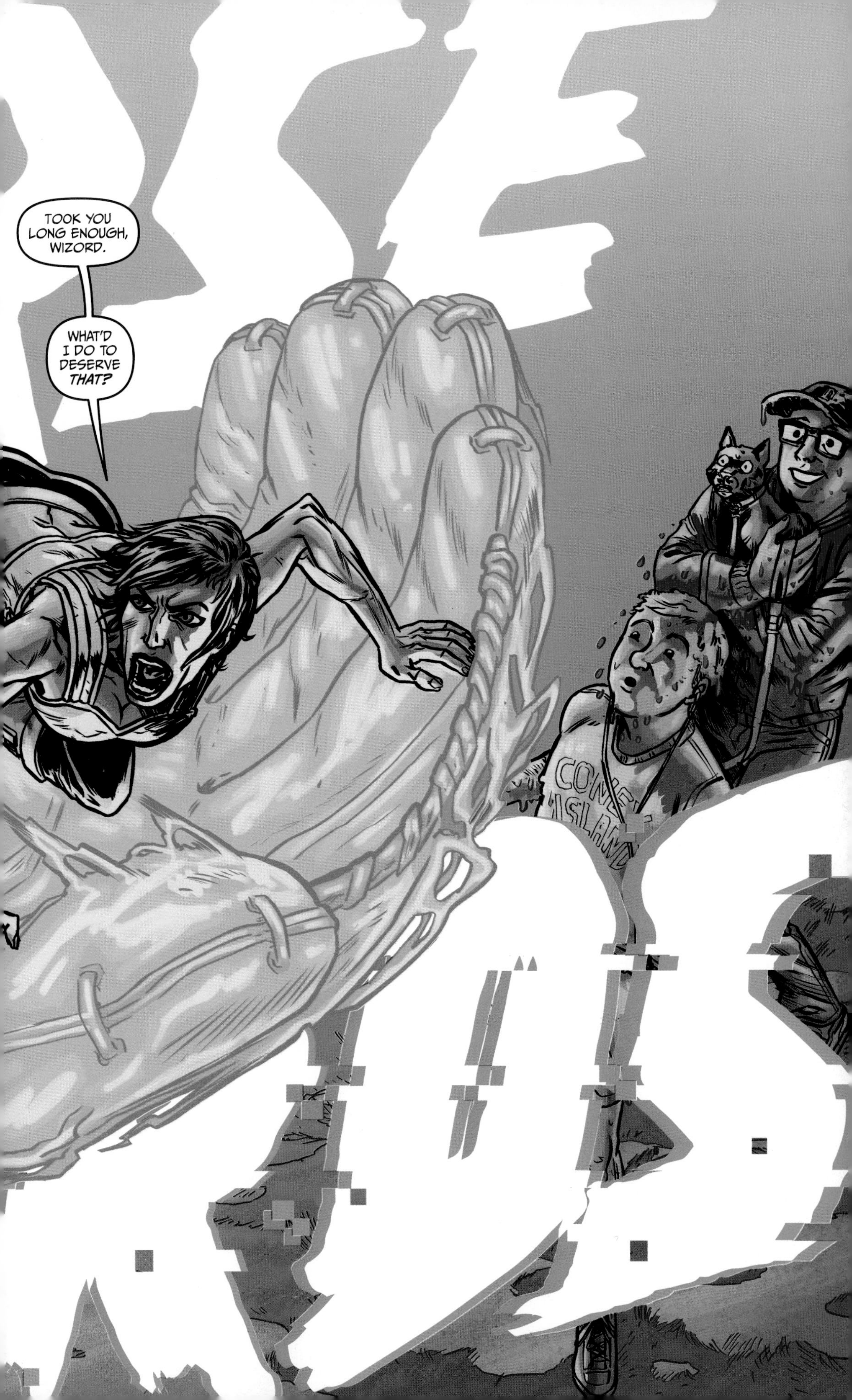

TOOK YOU LONG ENOUGH, WIZORD.
WHAT'D I DO TO DESERVE *THAT?*
CONEY ISLAND

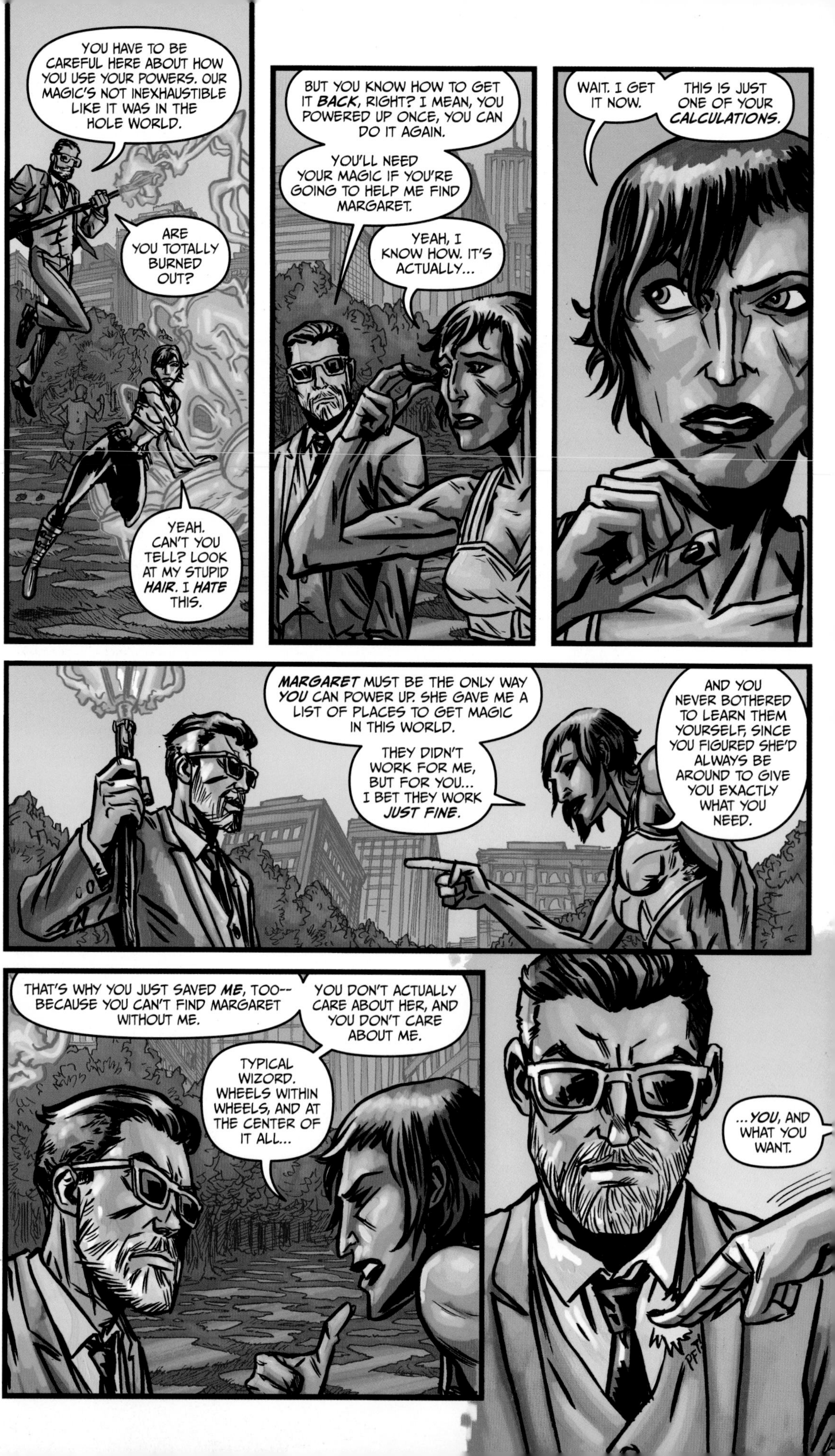
YOU HAVE TO BE CAREFUL HERE ABOUT HOW YOU USE YOUR POWERS. OUR MAGIC'S NOT INEXHAUSTIBLE LIKE IT WAS IN THE HOLE WORLD.
ARE YOU TOTALLY BURNED OUT?
YEAH. CAN'T YOU TELL? LOOK AT MY STUPID HAIR. I HATE THIS.
BUT YOU KNOW HOW TO GET IT BACK, RIGHT? I MEAN, YOU POWERED UP ONCE, YOU CAN DO IT AGAIN.
YOU'LL NEED YOUR MAGIC IF YOU'RE GOING TO HELP ME FIND MARGARET.
YEAH, I KNOW HOW. IT'S ACTUALLY...
WAIT. I GET IT NOW.
THIS IS JUST ONE OF YOUR CALCULATIONS.
MARGARET MUST BE THE ONLY WAY YOU CAN POWER UP. SHE GAVE ME A LIST OF PLACES TO GET MAGIC IN THIS WORLD.
THEY DIDN'T WORK FOR ME, BUT FOR YOU... I BET THEY WORK JUST FINE.
AND YOU NEVER BOTHERED TO LEARN THEM YOURSELF, SINCE YOU FIGURED SHE'D ALWAYS BE AROUND TO GIVE YOU EXACTLY WHAT YOU NEED.
THAT'S WHY YOU JUST SAVED ME, TOO-- BECAUSE YOU CAN'T FIND MARGARET WITHOUT ME.
YOU DON'T ACTUALLY CARE ABOUT HER, AND YOU DON'T CARE ABOUT ME.
TYPICAL WIZORD. WHEELS WITHIN WHEELS, AND AT THE CENTER OF IT ALL...
...YOU, AND WHAT YOU WANT.

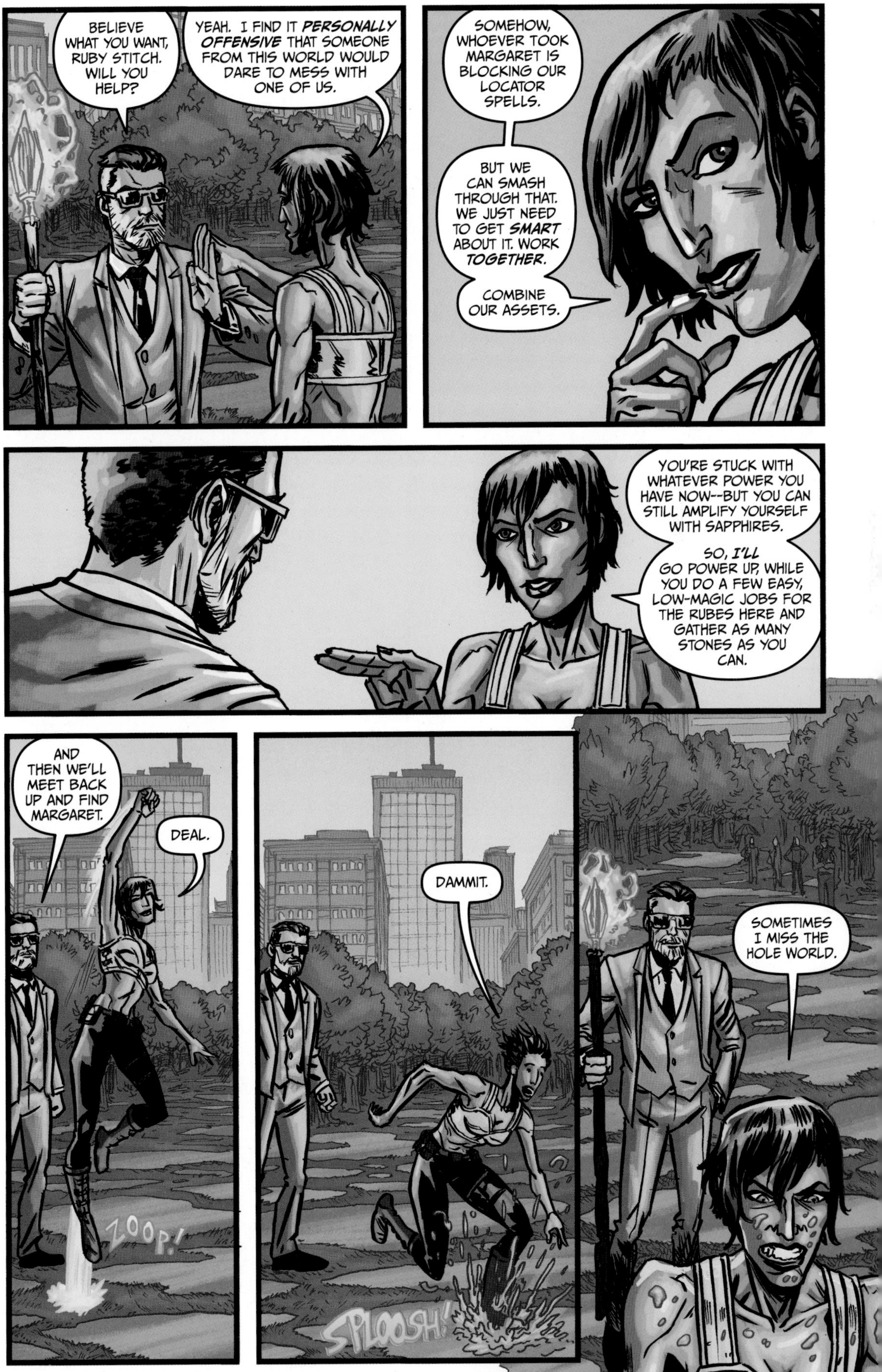
BELIEVE WHAT YOU WANT, RUBY STITCH. WILL YOU HELP?
YEAH. I FIND IT PERSONALLY OFFENSIVE THAT SOMEONE FROM THIS WORLD WOULD DARE TO MESS WITH ONE OF US.
SOMEHOW, WHOEVER TOOK MARGARET IS BLOCKING OUR LOCATOR SPELLS.
BUT WE CAN SMASH THROUGH THAT. WE JUST NEED TO GET SMART ABOUT IT. WORK TOGETHER.
COMBINE OUR ASSETS.
YOU'RE STUCK WITH WHATEVER POWER YOU HAVE NOW--BUT YOU CAN STILL AMPLIFY YOURSELF WITH SAPPHIRES.
SO, I'LL GO POWER UP, WHILE YOU DO A FEW EASY, LOW-MAGIC JOBS FOR THE RUBES HERE AND GATHER AS MANY STONES AS YOU CAN.
AND THEN WE'LL MEET BACK UP AND FIND MARGARET.
DEAL.
ZOOP!
DAMMIT.
SPLOOSH!
SOMETIMES I MISS THE HOLE WORLD.

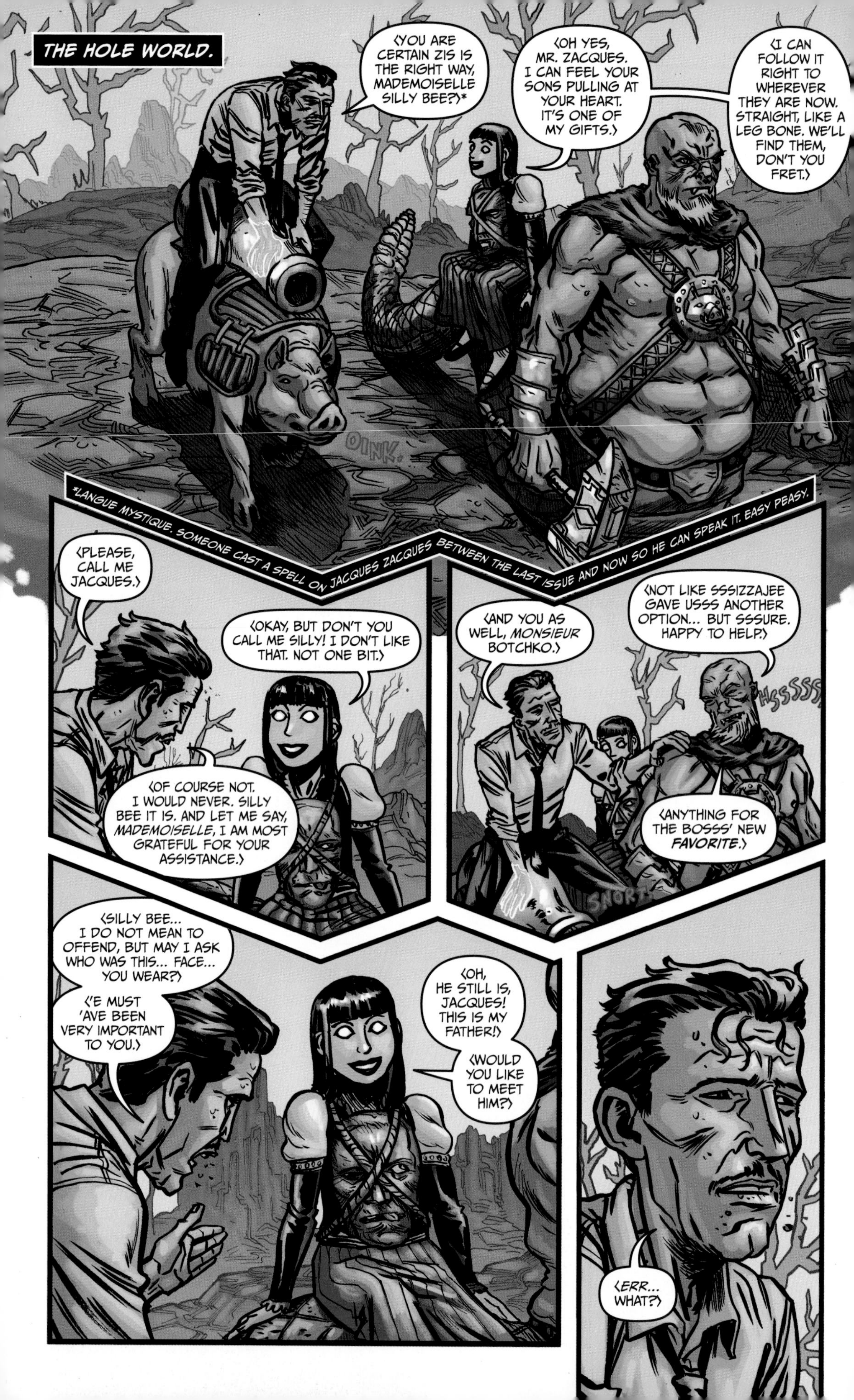
THE HOLE WORLD.
‹YOU ARE CERTAIN ZIS IS THE RIGHT WAY, MADEMOISELLE SILLY BEE?›*
‹OH YES, MR. ZACQUES. I CAN FEEL YOUR SONS PULLING AT YOUR HEART. IT'S ONE OF MY GIFTS.›
‹I CAN FOLLOW IT RIGHT TO WHEREVER THEY ARE NOW. STRAIGHT, LIKE A LEG BONE. WE'LL FIND THEM, DON'T YOU FRET.›
OINK.
*LANGUE MYSTIQUE. SOMEONE CAST A SPELL ON JACQUES ZACQUES BETWEEN THE LAST ISSUE AND NOW SO HE CAN SPEAK IT. EASY PEASY.
‹PLEASE, CALL ME JACQUES.›
‹OKAY, BUT DON'T YOU CALL ME SILLY! I DON'T LIKE THAT. NOT ONE BIT.›
‹OF COURSE NOT. I WOULD NEVER. SILLY BEE IT IS. AND LET ME SAY, *MADEMOISELLE*, I AM MOST GRATEFUL FOR YOUR ASSISTANCE.›
‹AND YOU AS WELL, *MONSIEUR* BOTCHKO.›
‹NOT LIKE SSSIZZAJEE GAVE USSS ANOTHER OPTION... BUT SSSURE. HAPPY TO HELP.›
HSSSSS
‹ANYTHING FOR THE BOSSS' NEW *FAVORITE*.›
SNORT
‹SILLY BEE... I DO NOT MEAN TO OFFEND, BUT MAY I ASK WHO WAS THIS... FACE... YOU WEAR?›
‹'E MUST 'AVE BEEN VERY IMPORTANT TO YOU.›
‹OH, HE STILL IS, JACQUES! THIS IS MY FATHER!›
‹WOULD YOU LIKE TO MEET HIM?›
‹ERR... WHAT?›

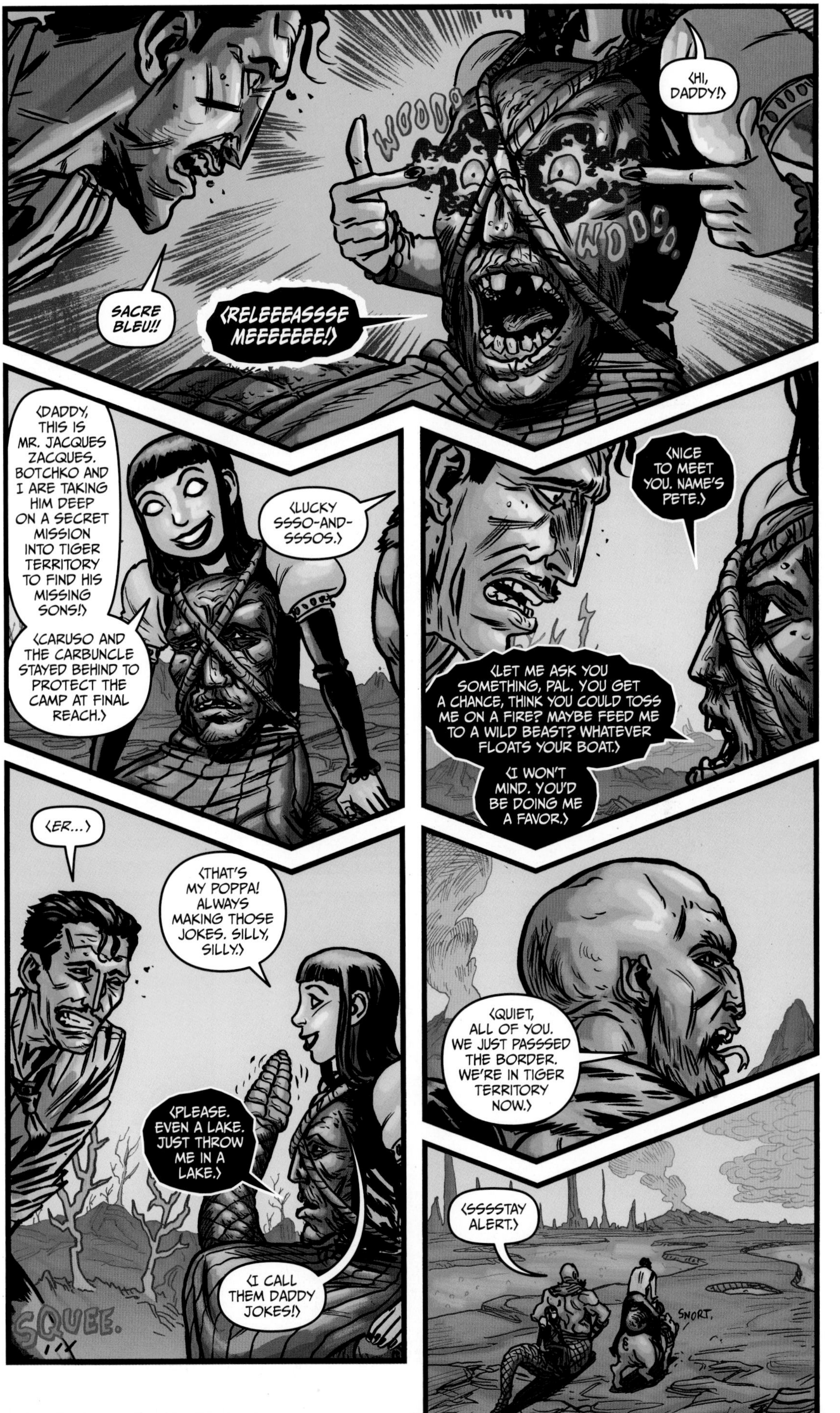
‹HI, DADDY!›
WOOOO
WOOOO.
SACRE BLEU!!
‹RELEEEASSSE MEEEEEEE!›
‹DADDY, THIS IS MR. JACQUES ZACQUES. BOTCHKO AND I ARE TAKING HIM DEEP ON A SECRET MISSION INTO TIGER TERRITORY TO FIND HIS MISSING SONS!›
‹CARUSO AND THE CARBUNCLE STAYED BEHIND TO PROTECT THE CAMP AT FINAL REACH.›
‹LUCKY SSSO-AND-SSSOS.›
‹NICE TO MEET YOU. NAME'S PETE.›
‹LET ME ASK YOU SOMETHING, PAL. YOU GET A CHANCE, THINK YOU COULD TOSS ME ON A FIRE? MAYBE FEED ME TO A WILD BEAST? WHATEVER FLOATS YOUR BOAT.›
‹I WON'T MIND. YOU'D BE DOING ME A FAVOR.›
‹ER...›
‹THAT'S MY POPPA! ALWAYS MAKING THOSE JOKES. SILLY, SILLY.›
‹PLEASE. EVEN A LAKE. JUST THROW ME IN A LAKE.›
‹I CALL THEM DADDY JOKES!›
SQUEE.
‹QUIET, ALL OF YOU. WE JUST PASSSED THE BORDER. WE'RE IN TIGER TERRITORY NOW.›
‹SSSSTAY ALERT.›
SNORT.

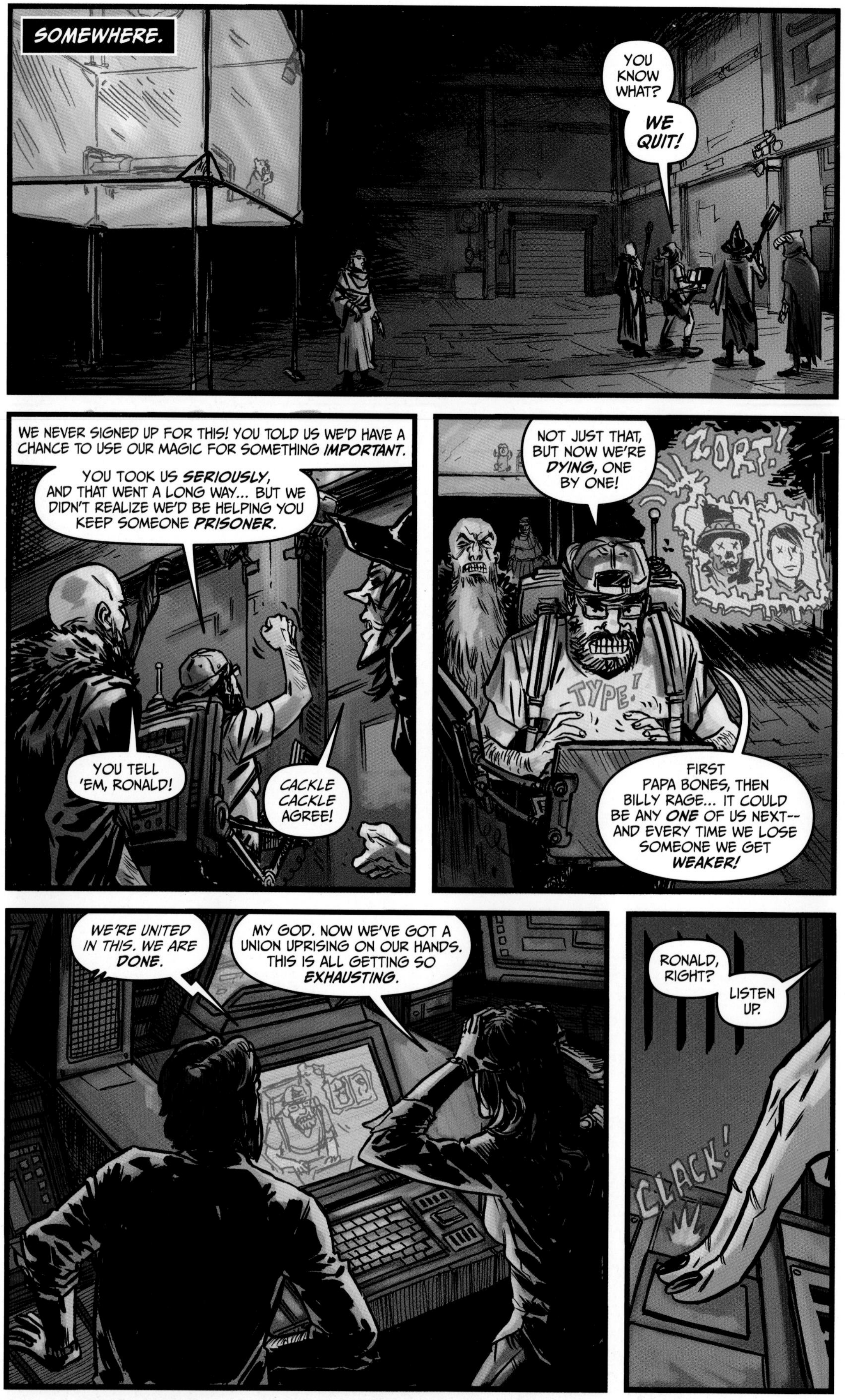
SOMEWHERE.
YOU KNOW WHAT?
WE QUIT!
WE NEVER SIGNED UP FOR THIS! YOU TOLD US WE'D HAVE A CHANCE TO USE OUR MAGIC FOR SOMETHING IMPORTANT.
YOU TOOK US SERIOUSLY, AND THAT WENT A LONG WAY... BUT WE DIDN'T REALIZE WE'D BE HELPING YOU KEEP SOMEONE PRISONER.
YOU TELL 'EM, RONALD!
CACKLE CACKLE AGREE!
NOT JUST THAT, BUT NOW WE'RE DYING, ONE BY ONE!
ZORT!
TYPE!
FIRST PAPA BONES, THEN BILLY RAGE... IT COULD BE ANY ONE OF US NEXT-- AND EVERY TIME WE LOSE SOMEONE WE GET WEAKER!
WE'RE UNITED IN THIS. WE ARE DONE.
MY GOD. NOW WE'VE GOT A UNION UPRISING ON OUR HANDS. THIS IS ALL GETTING SO EXHAUSTING.
RONALD, RIGHT?
LISTEN UP.
CLACK!

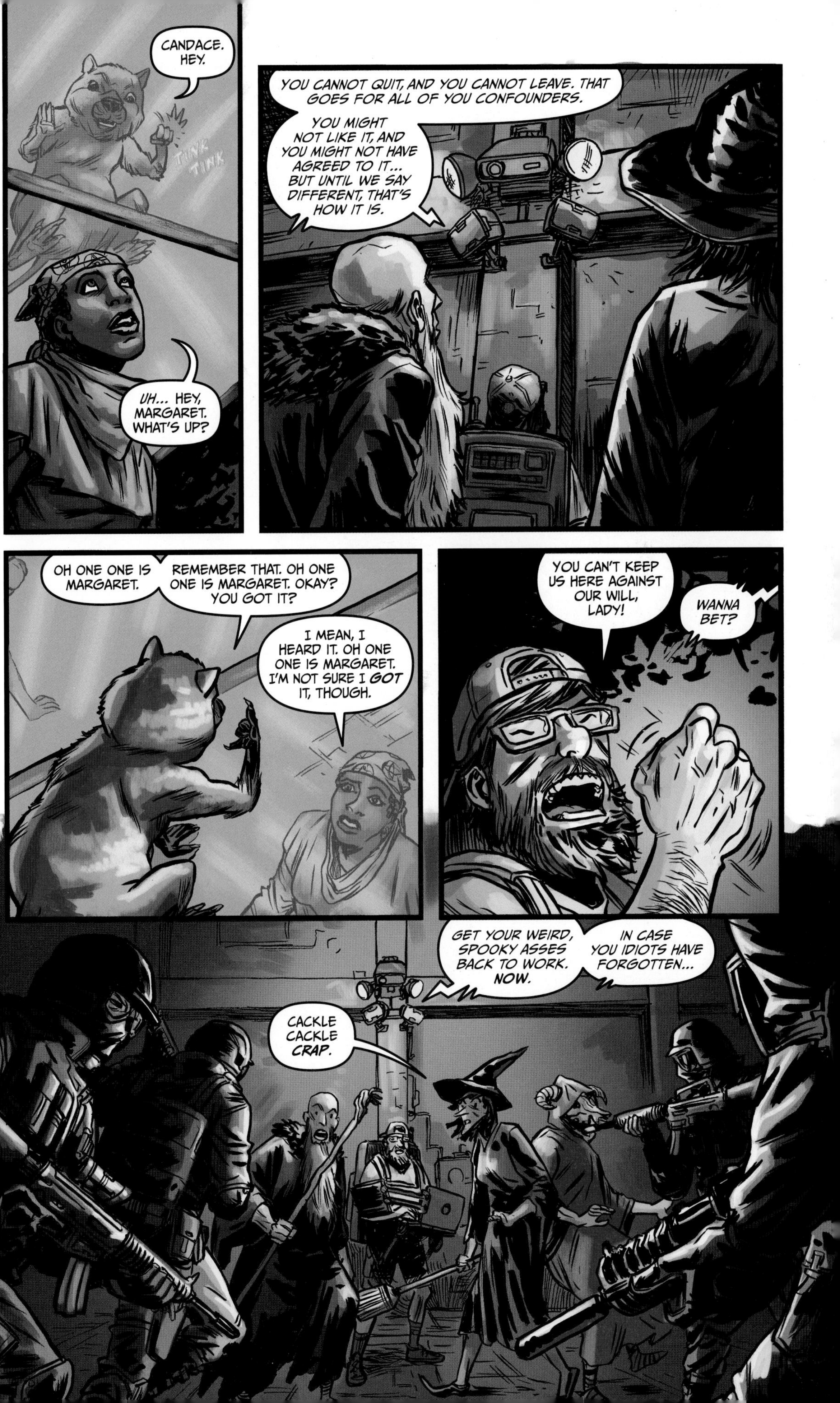
CANDACE. HEY.
TINK TINK
UH... HEY, MARGARET. WHAT'S UP?
YOU CANNOT QUIT, AND YOU CANNOT LEAVE. THAT GOES FOR ALL OF YOU CONFOUNDERS.
YOU MIGHT NOT LIKE IT, AND YOU MIGHT NOT HAVE AGREED TO IT... BUT UNTIL WE SAY DIFFERENT, THAT'S HOW IT IS.
OH ONE ONE IS MARGARET.
REMEMBER THAT. OH ONE ONE IS MARGARET. OKAY? YOU GOT IT?
I MEAN, I HEARD IT. OH ONE ONE IS MARGARET. I'M NOT SURE I GOT IT, THOUGH.
YOU CAN'T KEEP US HERE AGAINST OUR WILL, LADY!
WANNA BET?
IN CASE YOU IDIOTS HAVE FORGOTTEN...
GET YOUR WEIRD, SPOOKY ASSES BACK TO WORK. NOW.
CACKLE CACKLE CRAP.

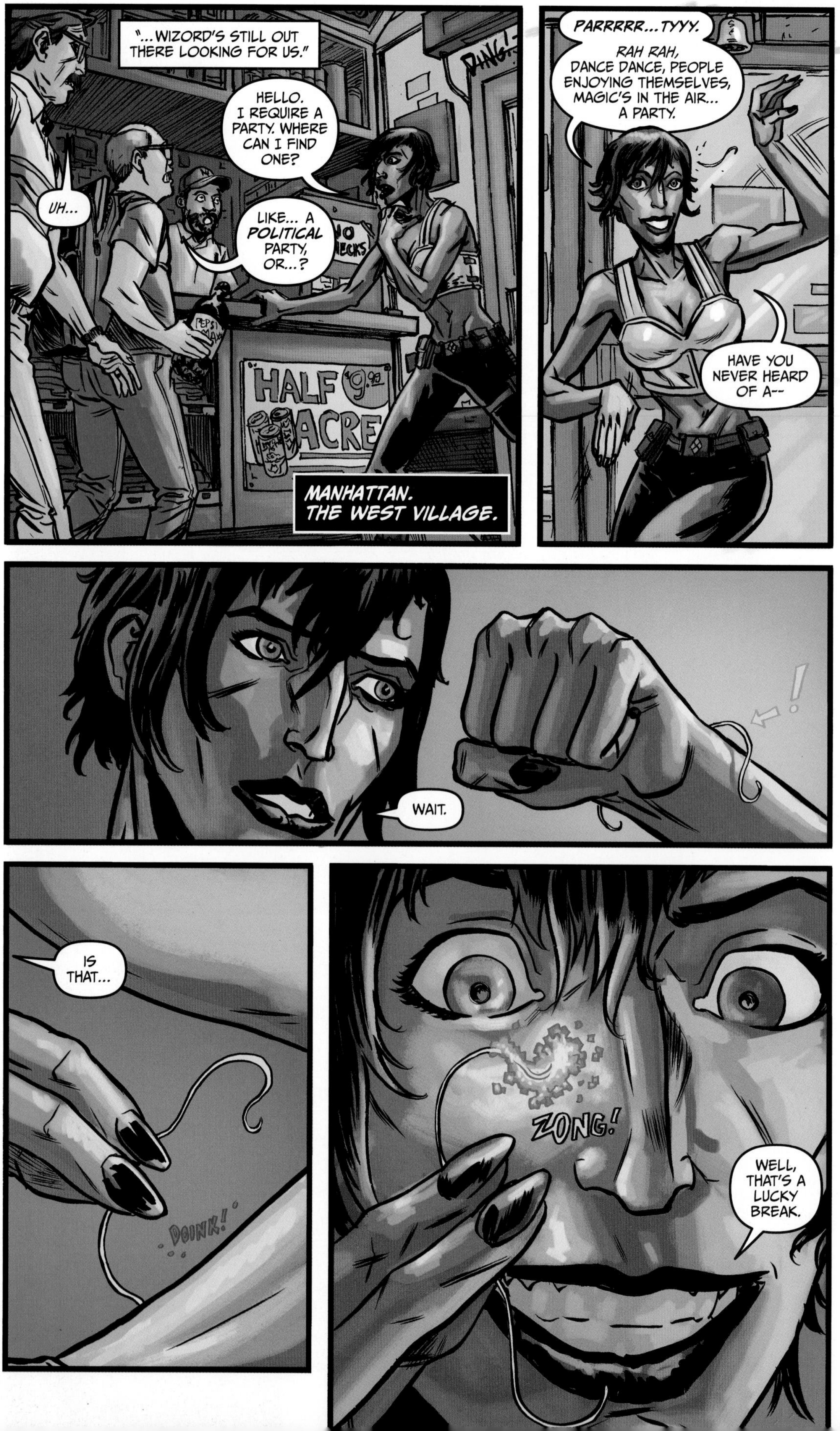
"...WIZORD'S STILL OUT THERE LOOKING FOR US."
HELLO. I REQUIRE A PARTY. WHERE CAN I FIND ONE?
UH...
LIKE... A POLITICAL PARTY, OR...?
HALF ACRE
MANHATTAN. THE WEST VILLAGE.
PARRRRR...TYYY.
RAH RAH, DANCE DANCE, PEOPLE ENJOYING THEMSELVES, MAGIC'S IN THE AIR... A PARTY.
HAVE YOU NEVER HEARD OF A--
WAIT.
IS THAT...
DOINK!
ZONG!
WELL, THAT'S A LUCKY BREAK.

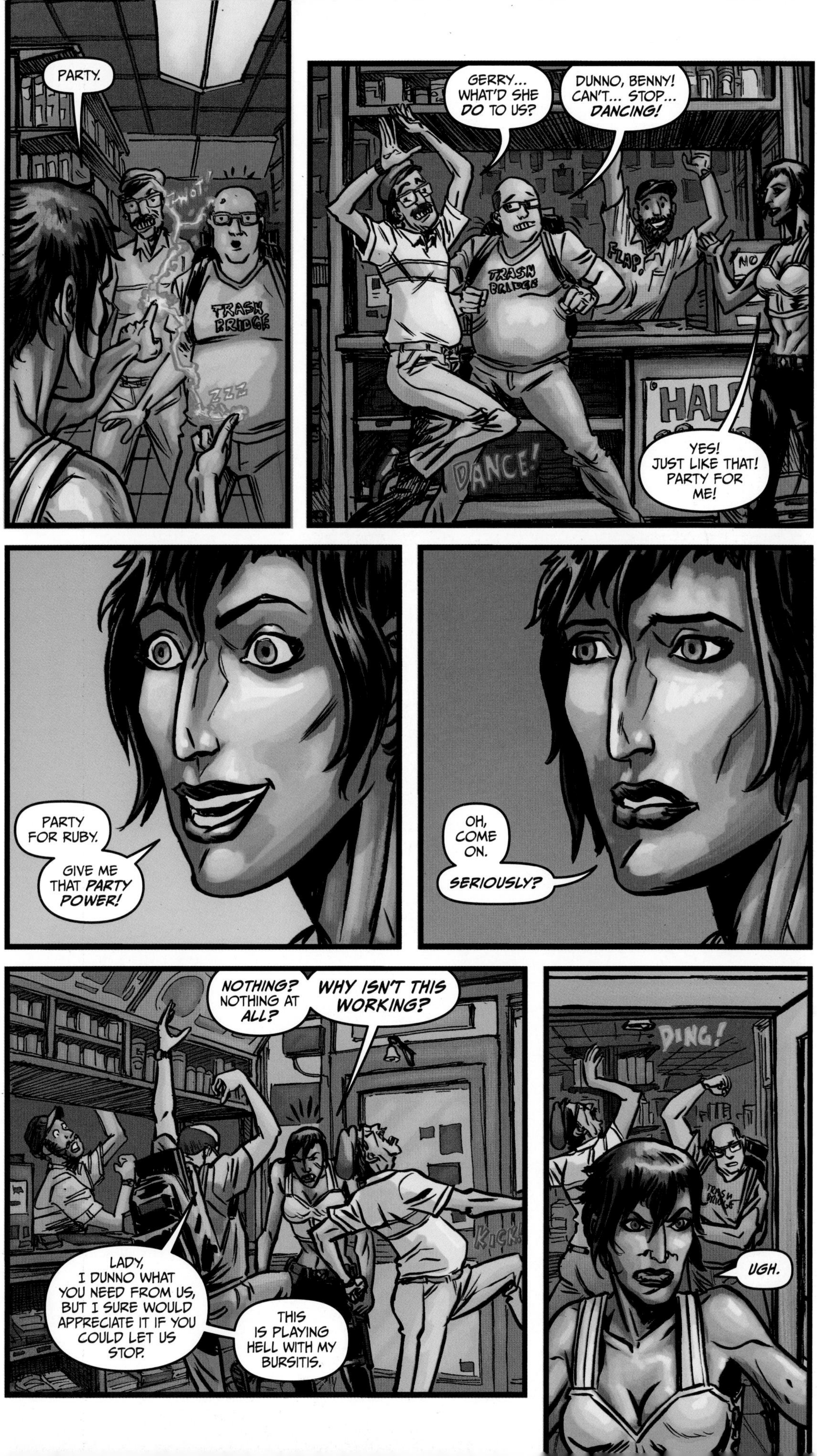
PARTY.
ZZZ
GERRY... WHAT'D SHE *DO* TO US?
DUNNO, BENNY! CAN'T... STOP... *DANCING!*
FLAP!
DANCE!
YES! JUST LIKE THAT! PARTY FOR ME!
PARTY FOR RUBY.
GIVE ME THAT *PARTY POWER!*
OH, COME ON.
SERIOUSLY?
NOTHING? NOTHING AT *ALL?*
WHY ISN'T THIS WORKING?
KICK!
LADY, I DUNNO WHAT YOU NEED FROM US, BUT I SURE WOULD APPRECIATE IT IF YOU COULD LET US STOP.
THIS IS PLAYING HELL WITH MY BURSITIS.
DING!
UGH.

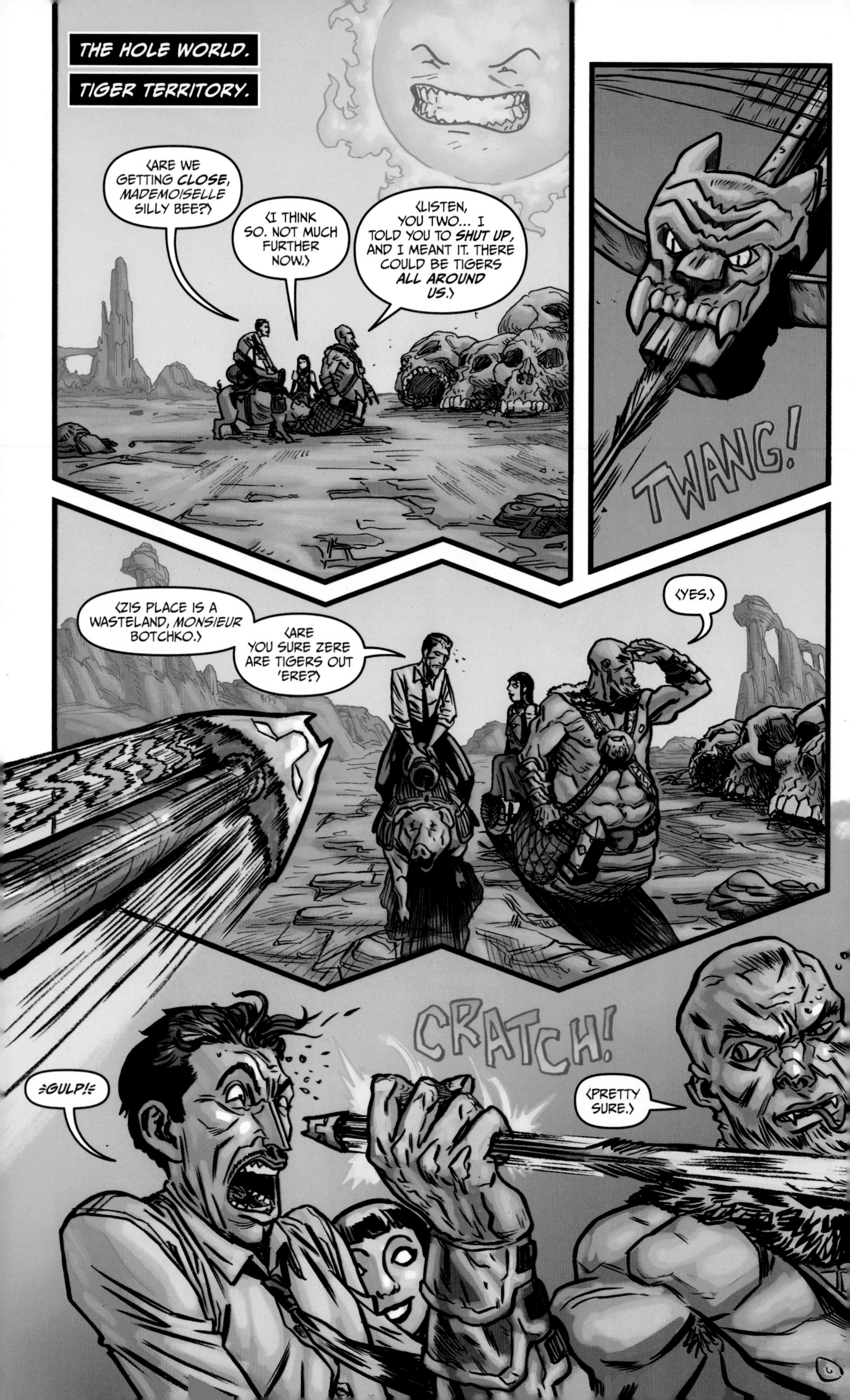
THE HOLE WORLD.
TIGER TERRITORY.
‹ARE WE GETTING CLOSE, MADEMOISELLE SILLY BEE?›
‹I THINK SO. NOT MUCH FURTHER NOW.›
‹LISTEN, YOU TWO... I TOLD YOU TO SHUT UP, AND I MEANT IT. THERE COULD BE TIGERS ALL AROUND US.›
TWANG!
‹ZIS PLACE IS A WASTELAND, MONSIEUR BOTCHKO.›
‹ARE YOU SURE ZERE ARE TIGERS OUT 'ERE?›
‹YES.›
CRATCH!
GULP!
‹PRETTY SURE.›

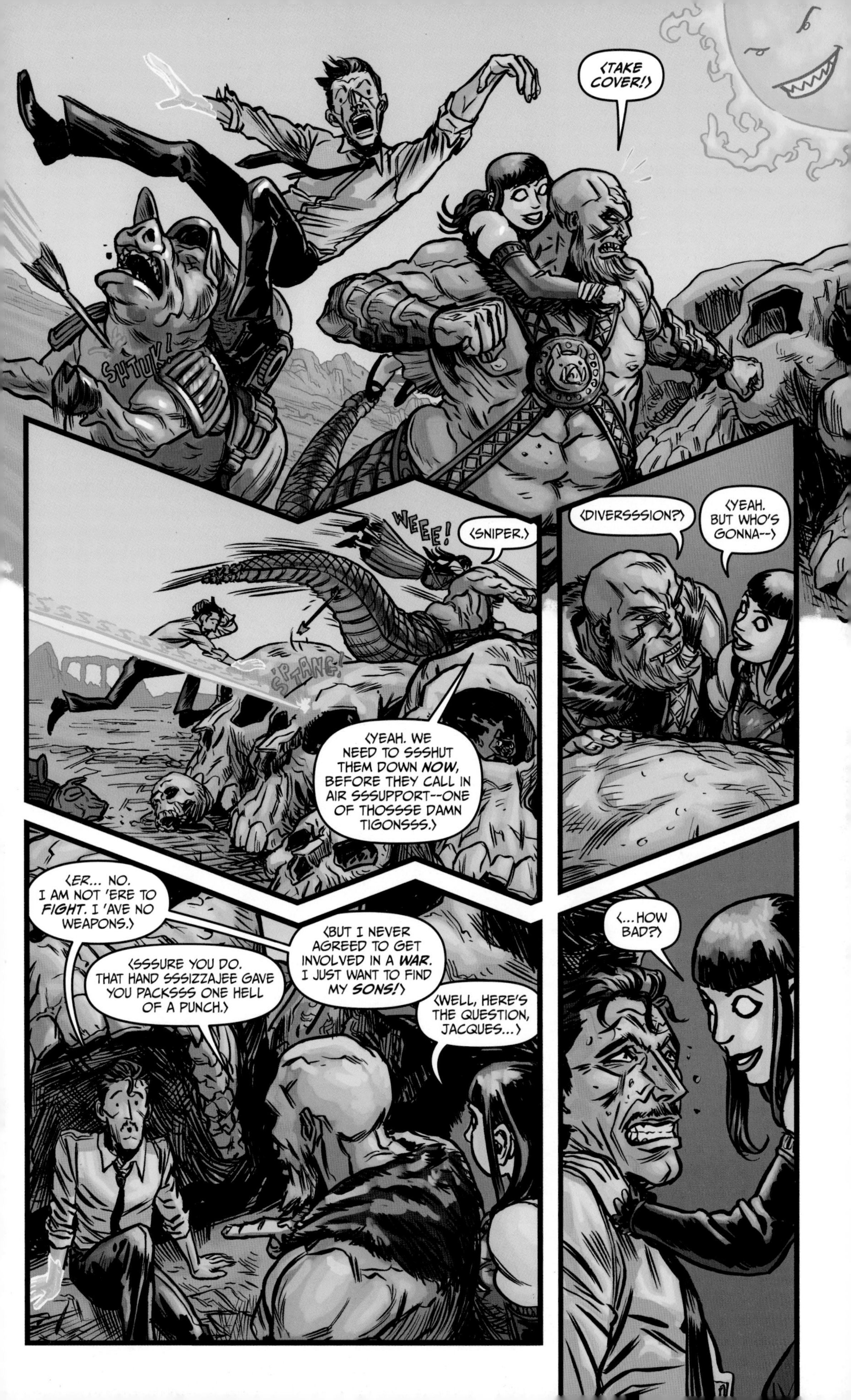
⟨TAKE COVER!⟩
SHTUK!
WEEEE!
⟨SNIPER.⟩
S'PTANG!
⟨YEAH. WE NEED TO SSSHUT THEM DOWN NOW, BEFORE THEY CALL IN AIR SSSUPPORT--ONE OF THOSSSE DAMN TIGONSSS.⟩
⟨DIVERSSSION?⟩
⟨YEAH. BUT WHO'S GONNA--⟩
⟨ER... NO. I AM NOT 'ERE TO FIGHT. I 'AVE NO WEAPONS.⟩
⟨SSSURE YOU DO. THAT HAND SSSIZZAJEE GAVE YOU PACKSSS ONE HELL OF A PUNCH.⟩
⟨BUT I NEVER AGREED TO GET INVOLVED IN A WAR. I JUST WANT TO FIND MY SONS!⟩
⟨WELL, HERE'S THE QUESTION, JACQUES...⟩
⟨...HOW BAD?⟩

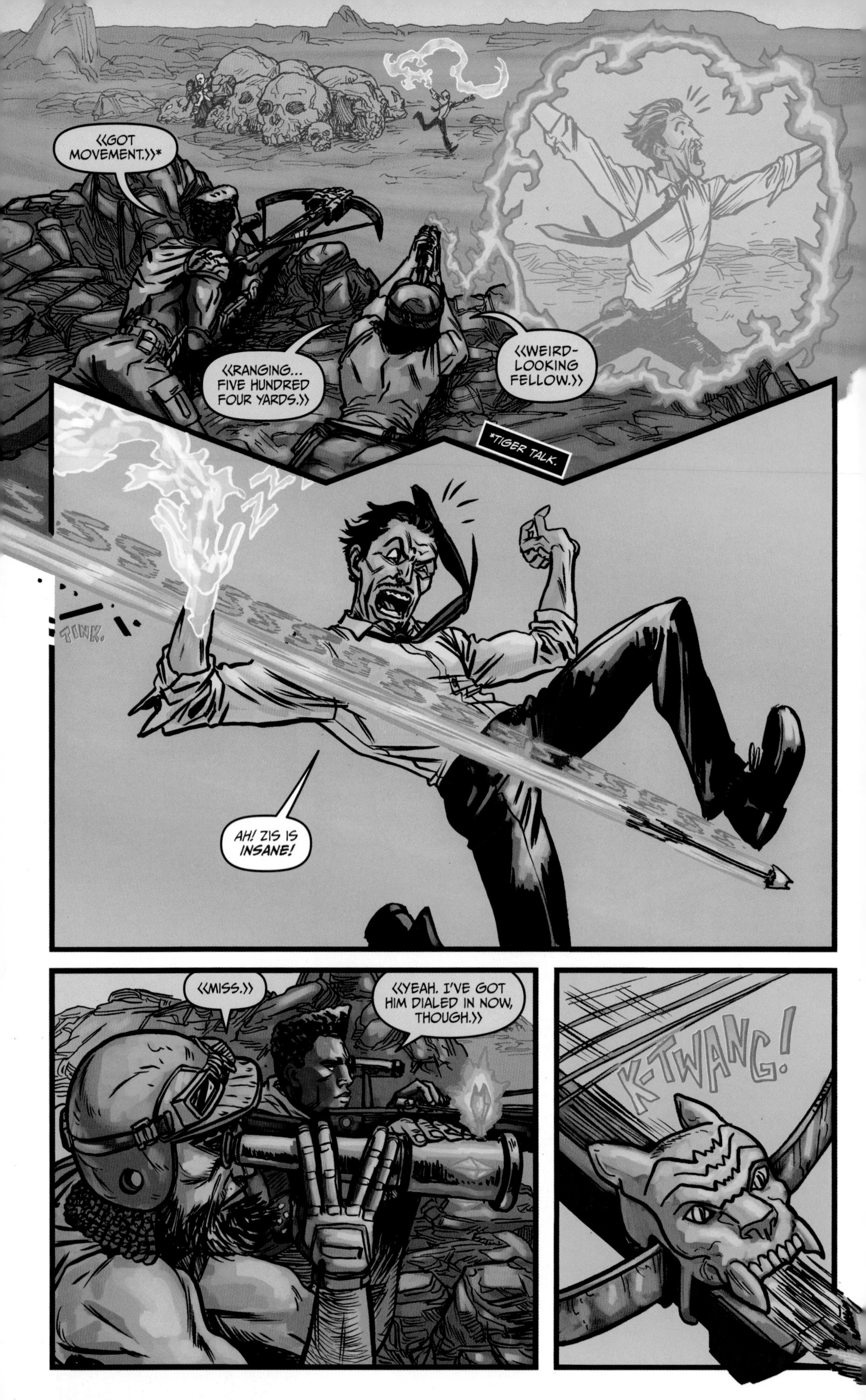

<<GOT MOVEMENT.>>*
<<RANGING... FIVE HUNDRED FOUR YARDS.>>
<<WEIRD-LOOKING FELLOW.>>
*TIGER TALK.
TINK.
AH! ZIS IS INSANE!
<<MISS.>>
<<YEAH. I'VE GOT HIM DIALED IN NOW, THOUGH.>>
K-TWANG!

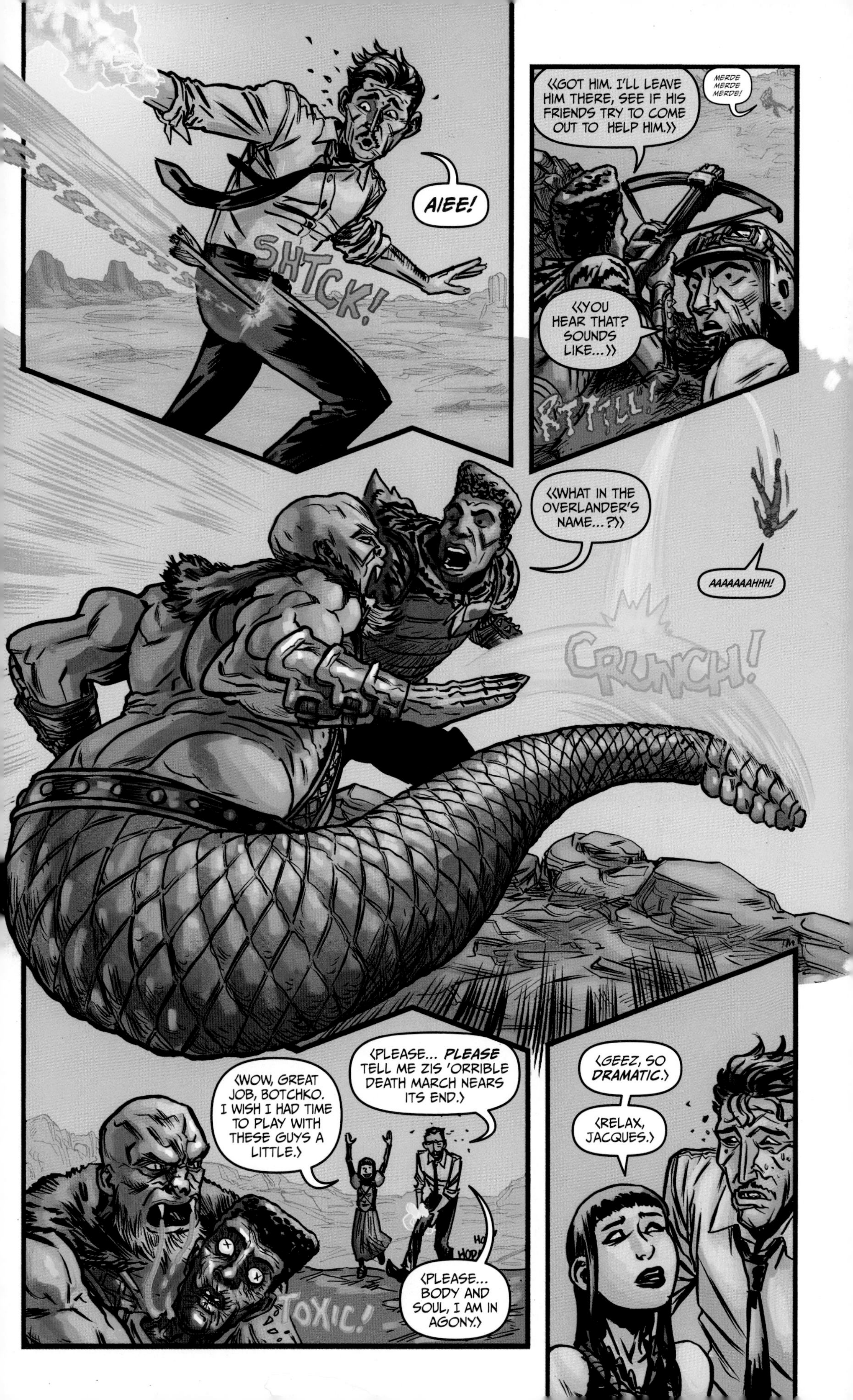
SSSSSSSSS
AIEE!
SHTCK!
<<GOT HIM. I'LL LEAVE HIM THERE, SEE IF HIS FRIENDS TRY TO COME OUT TO HELP HIM.>>
MERDE MERDE MERDE!
<<YOU HEAR THAT? SOUNDS LIKE...>>
RTTTLL!
<<WHAT IN THE OVERLANDER'S NAME...?>>
AAAAAAAHHH!
CRUNCH!
<WOW, GREAT JOB, BOTCHKO. I WISH I HAD TIME TO PLAY WITH THESE GUYS A LITTLE.>
<PLEASE... PLEASE TELL ME ZIS 'ORRIBLE DEATH MARCH NEARS ITS END.>
<PLEASE... BODY AND SOUL, I AM IN AGONY.>
TOXIC!
<GEEZ, SO DRAMATIC.>
<RELAX, JACQUES.>

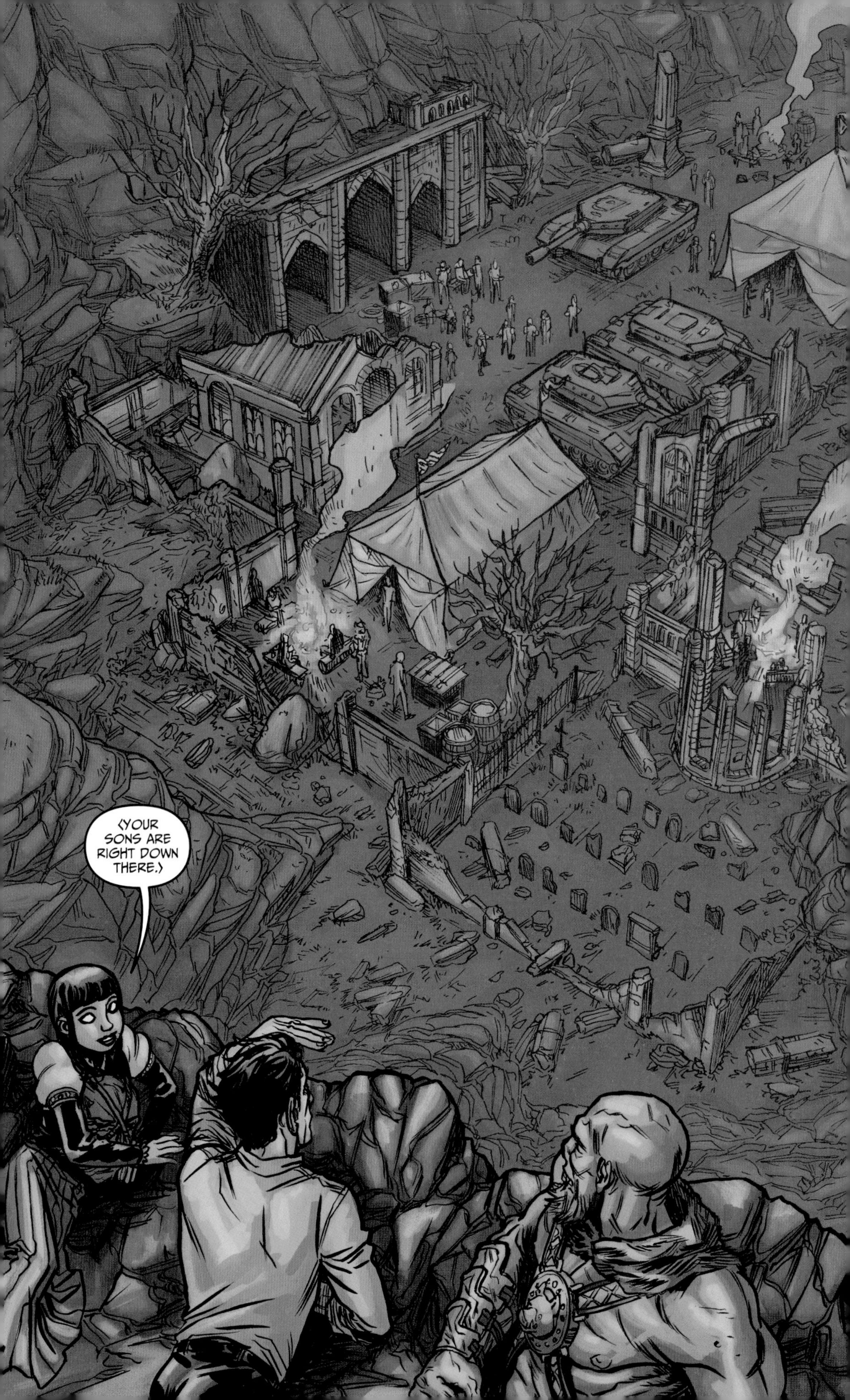

‹YOUR SONS ARE RIGHT DOWN THERE.›

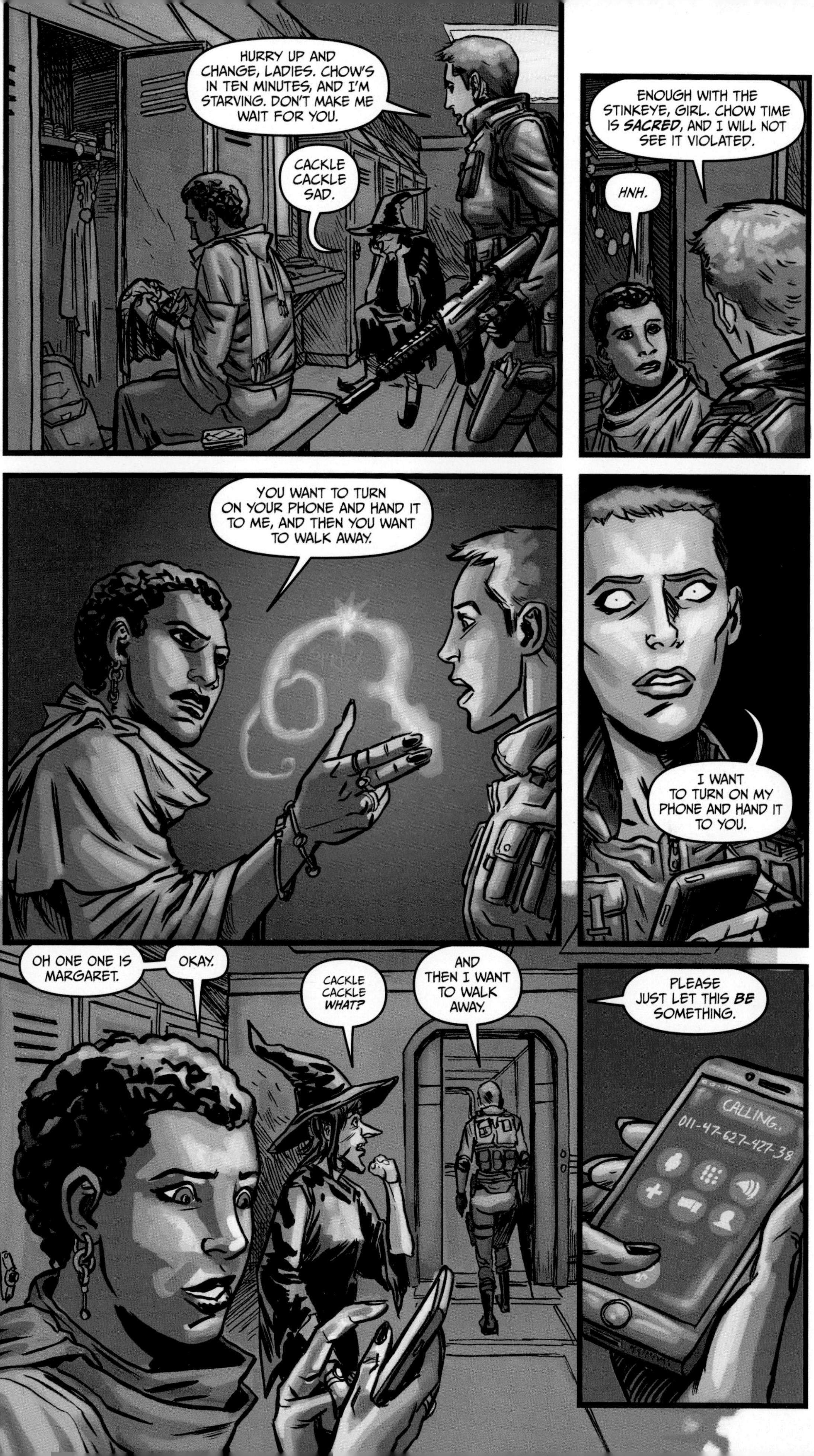
HURRY UP AND CHANGE, LADIES. CHOW'S IN TEN MINUTES, AND I'M STARVING. DON'T MAKE ME WAIT FOR YOU.
CACKLE CACKLE SAD.
ENOUGH WITH THE STINKEYE, GIRL. CHOW TIME IS *SACRED*, AND I WILL NOT SEE IT VIOLATED.
HNH.
YOU WANT TO TURN ON YOUR PHONE AND HAND IT TO ME, AND THEN YOU WANT TO WALK AWAY.
I WANT TO TURN ON MY PHONE AND HAND IT TO YOU.
OH ONE ONE IS MARGARET.
OKAY.
CACKLE CACKLE *WHAT?*
AND THEN I WANT TO WALK AWAY.
PLEASE JUST LET THIS *BE* SOMETHING.
CALLING..
011-47-627-427-38

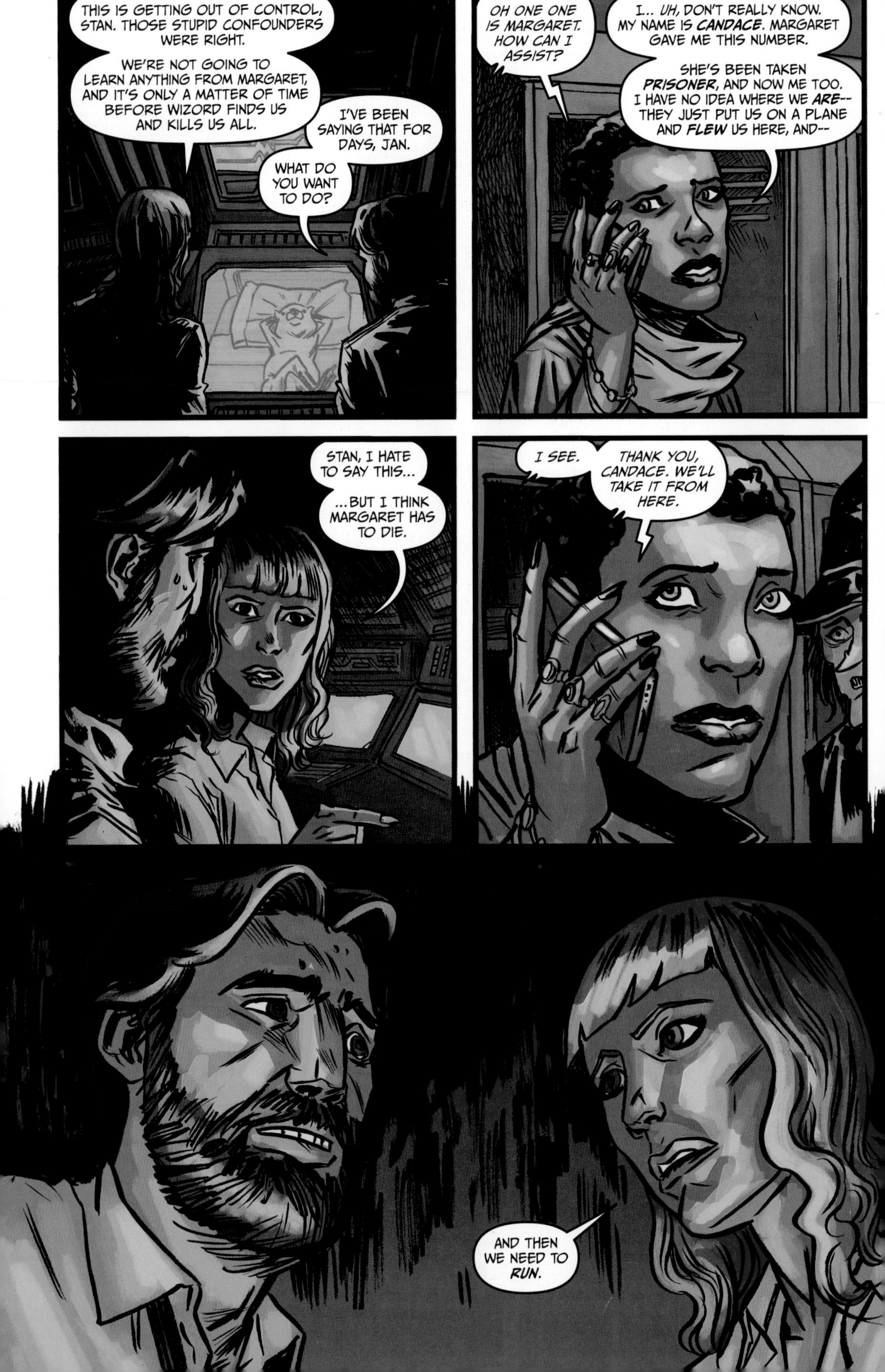
THIS IS GETTING OUT OF CONTROL, STAN. THOSE STUPID CONFOUNDERS WERE RIGHT.
WE'RE NOT GOING TO LEARN ANYTHING FROM MARGARET, AND IT'S ONLY A MATTER OF TIME BEFORE WIZORD FINDS US AND KILLS US ALL.
I'VE BEEN SAYING THAT FOR DAYS, JAN.
WHAT DO YOU WANT TO DO?
OH ONE ONE IS MARGARET. HOW CAN I ASSIST?
I... UH, DON'T REALLY KNOW. MY NAME IS CANDACE. MARGARET GAVE ME THIS NUMBER.
SHE'S BEEN TAKEN PRISONER, AND NOW ME TOO. I HAVE NO IDEA WHERE WE ARE-- THEY JUST PUT US ON A PLANE AND FLEW US HERE, AND--
STAN, I HATE TO SAY THIS...
...BUT I THINK MARGARET HAS TO DIE.
I SEE.
THANK YOU, CANDACE. WE'LL TAKE IT FROM HERE.
AND THEN WE NEED TO RUN.

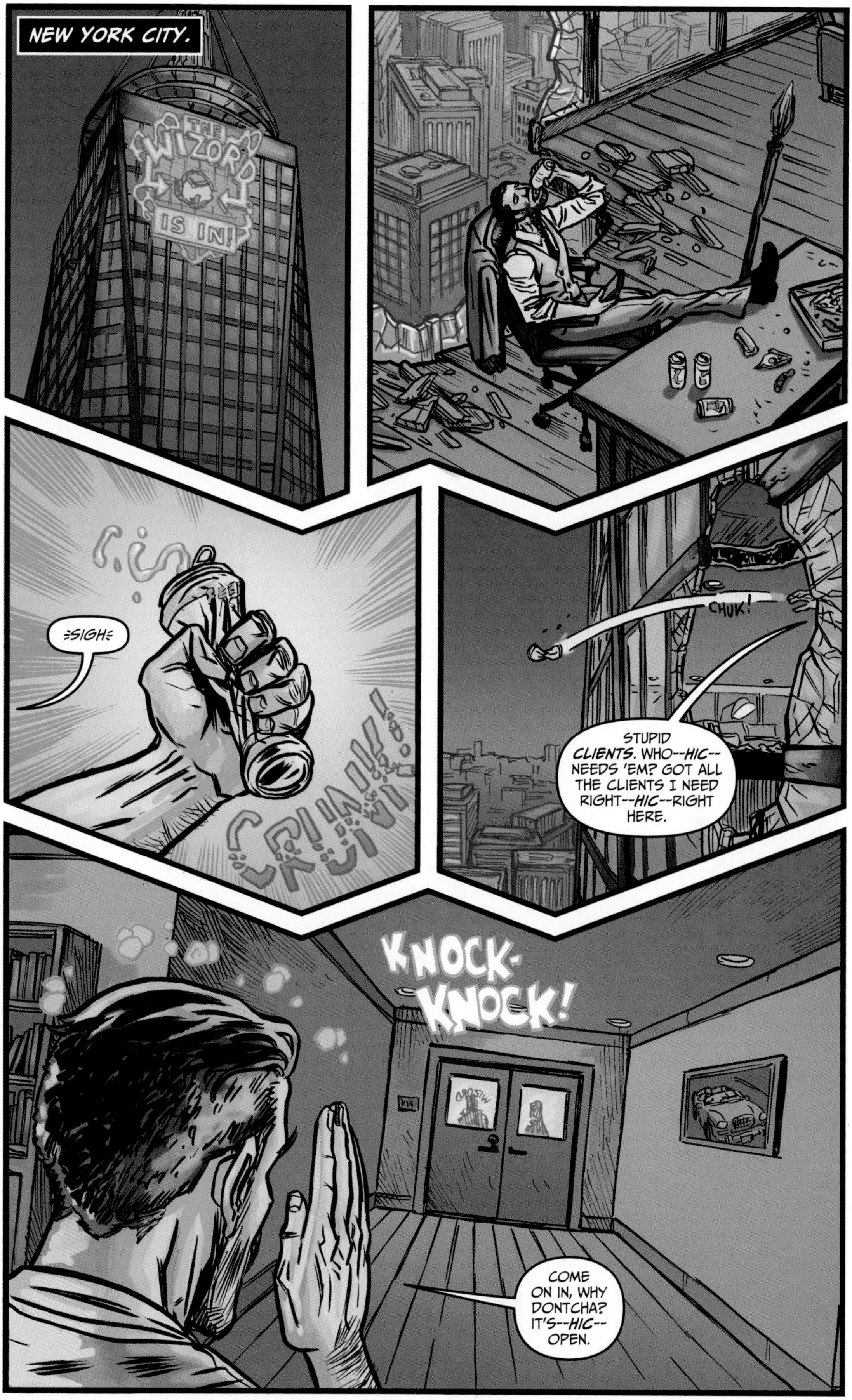
NEW YORK CITY.
THE WIZORD IS IN!
SIGH
CRUNCH!
CHUK!
STUPID CLIENTS. WHO--HIC--NEEDS 'EM? GOT ALL THE CLIENTS I NEED RIGHT--HIC--RIGHT HERE.
KNOCK-KNOCK!
COME ON IN, WHY DONTCHA? IT'S--HIC--OPEN.

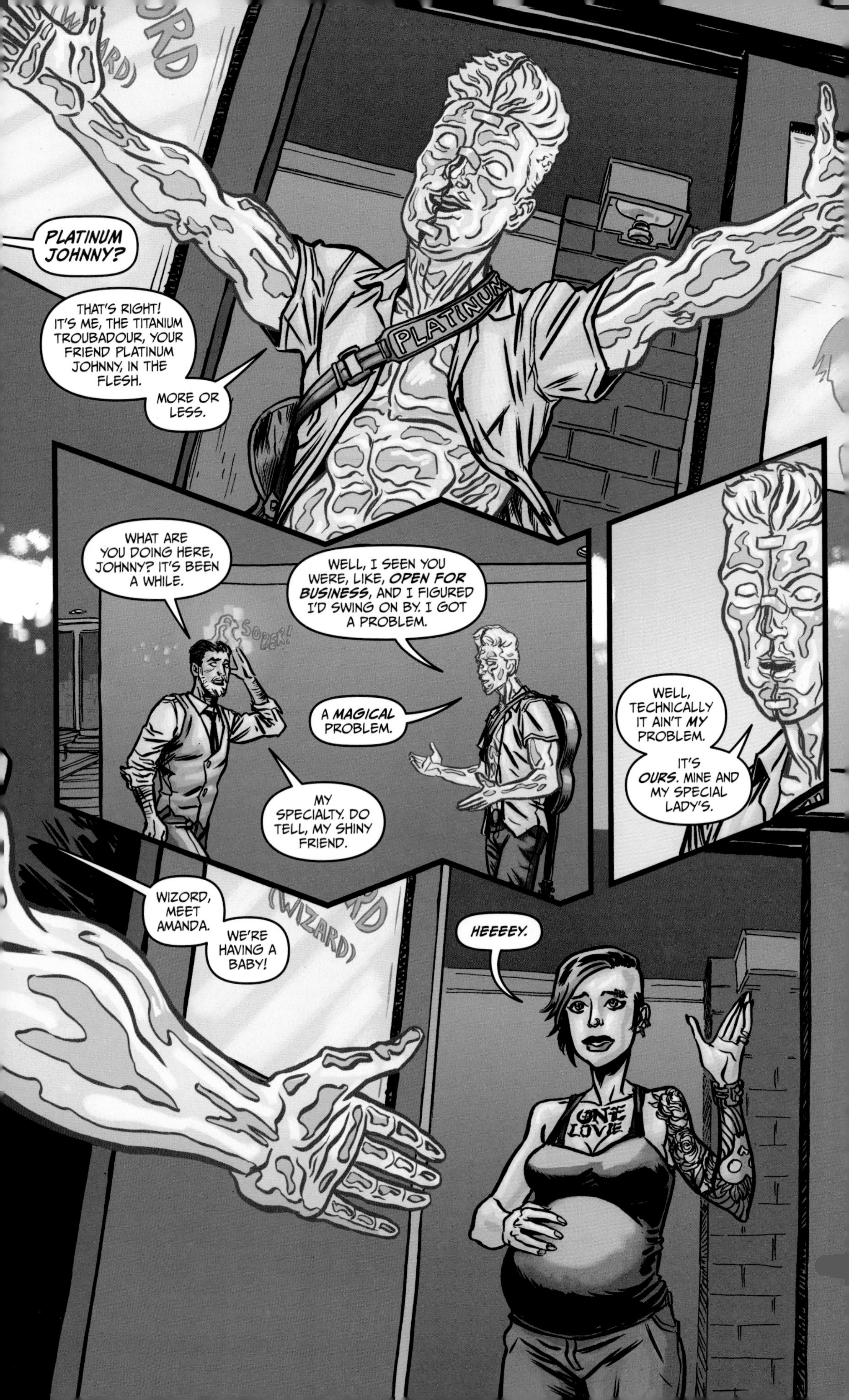
(WIZARD)
PLATINUM JOHNNY?
THAT'S RIGHT! IT'S ME, THE TITANIUM TROUBADOUR, YOUR FRIEND PLATINUM JOHNNY, IN THE FLESH.
MORE OR LESS.
PLATINUM
WHAT ARE YOU DOING HERE, JOHNNY? IT'S BEEN A WHILE.
WELL, I SEEN YOU WERE, LIKE, OPEN FOR BUSINESS, AND I FIGURED I'D SWING ON BY. I GOT A PROBLEM.
SOBER!
A MAGICAL PROBLEM.
MY SPECIALTY. DO TELL, MY SHINY FRIEND.
WELL, TECHNICALLY IT AIN'T MY PROBLEM.
IT'S OURS. MINE AND MY SPECIAL LADY'S.
WIZORD, MEET AMANDA.
WE'RE HAVING A BABY!
(WIZARD)
HEEEEY.
ONE LOVE

FIFTEEN

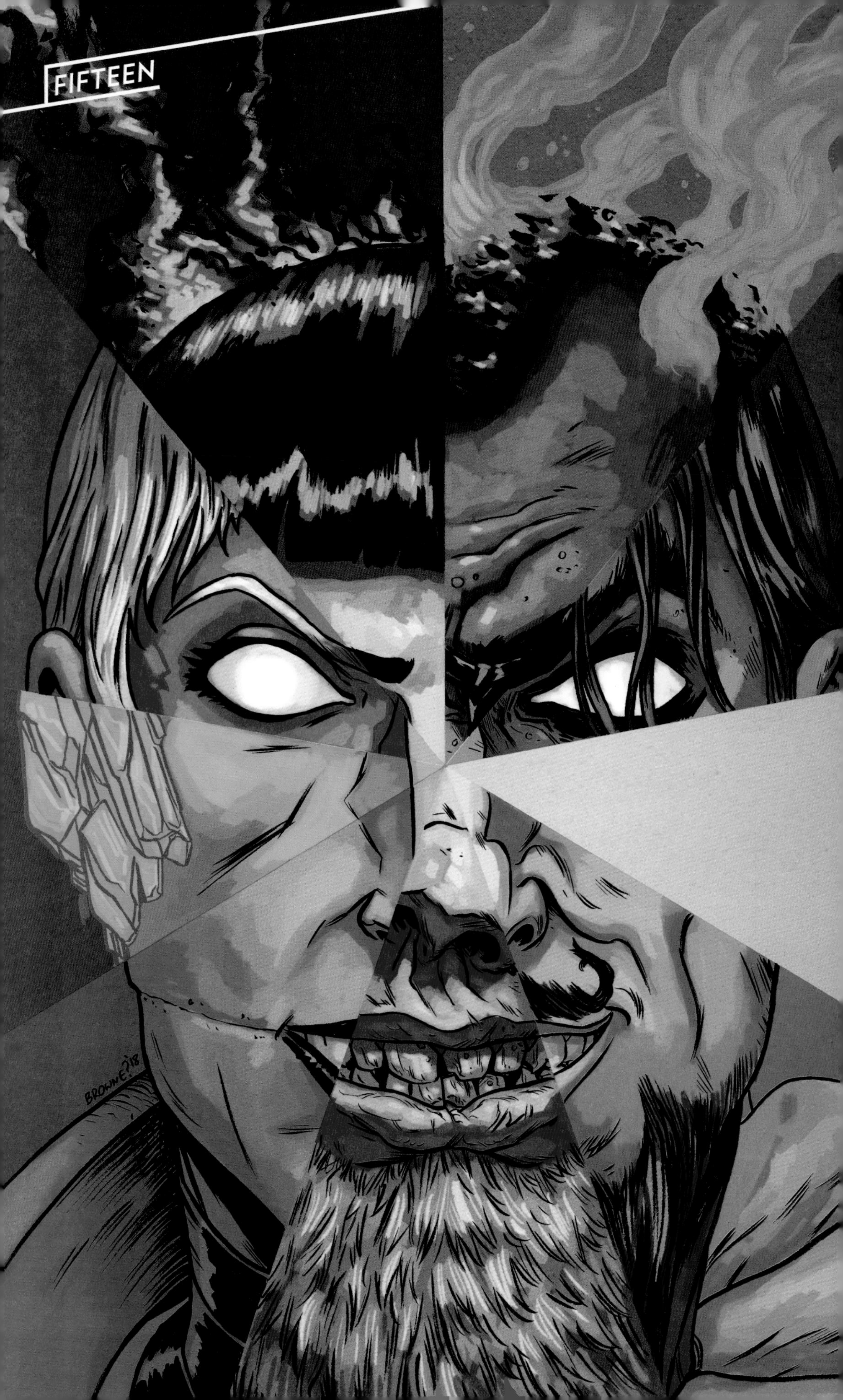
BROWNE '18

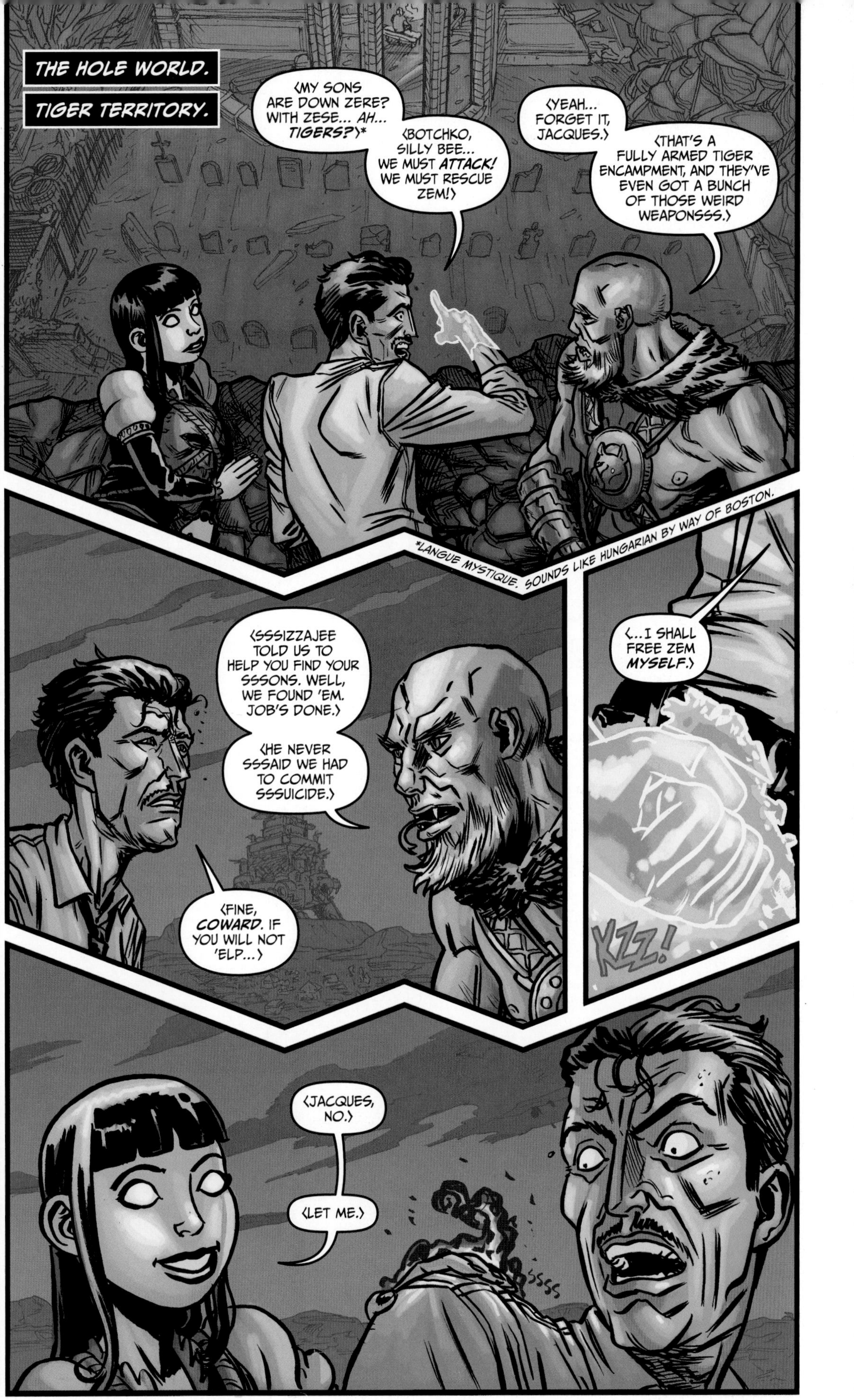
THE HOLE WORLD.
TIGER TERRITORY.
⟨MY SONS ARE DOWN ZERE? WITH ZESE... AH... TIGERS?⟩*
⟨BOTCHKO, SILLY BEE... WE MUST ATTACK! WE MUST RESCUE ZEM!⟩
⟨YEAH... FORGET IT, JACQUES.⟩
⟨THAT'S A FULLY ARMED TIGER ENCAMPMENT, AND THEY'VE EVEN GOT A BUNCH OF THOSE WEIRD WEAPONSSS.⟩
*LANGUE MYSTIQUE. SOUNDS LIKE HUNGARIAN BY WAY OF BOSTON.
⟨SSSIZZAJEE TOLD US TO HELP YOU FIND YOUR SSSONS. WELL, WE FOUND 'EM. JOB'S DONE.⟩
⟨HE NEVER SSSAID WE HAD TO COMMIT SSSUICIDE.⟩
⟨FINE, COWARD. IF YOU WILL NOT 'ELP...⟩
⟨...I SHALL FREE ZEM MYSELF.⟩
KZZ!
⟨JACQUES, NO.⟩
⟨LET ME.⟩
SSSS

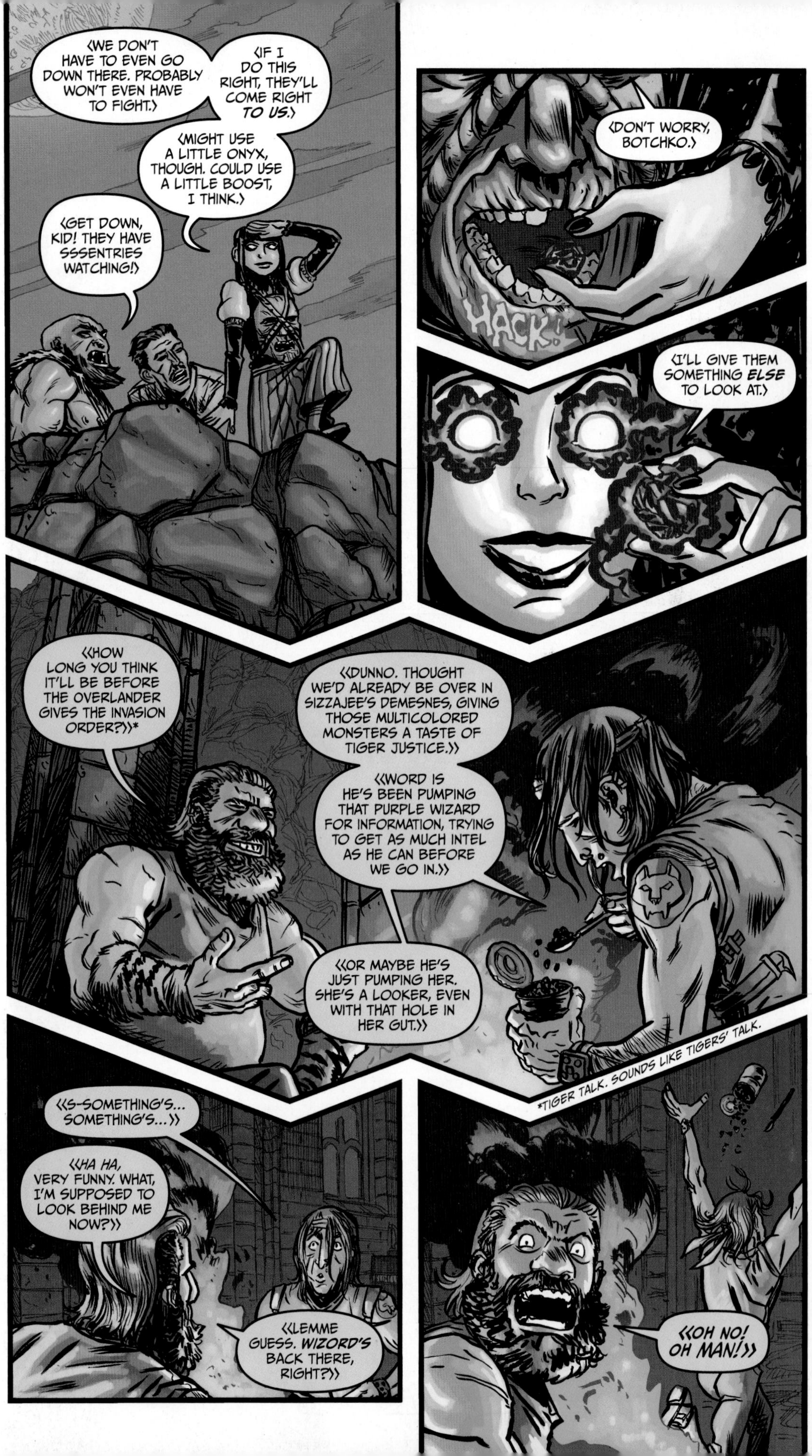
‹WE DON'T HAVE TO EVEN GO DOWN THERE. PROBABLY WON'T EVEN HAVE TO FIGHT.›
‹IF I DO THIS RIGHT, THEY'LL COME RIGHT *TO US*.›
‹MIGHT USE A LITTLE ONYX, THOUGH. COULD USE A LITTLE BOOST, I THINK.›
‹GET DOWN, KID! THEY HAVE SSSENTRIES WATCHING!›
‹DON'T WORRY, BOTCHKO.›
HACK!
‹I'LL GIVE THEM SOMETHING *ELSE* TO LOOK AT.›
‹‹HOW LONG YOU THINK IT'LL BE BEFORE THE OVERLANDER GIVES THE INVASION ORDER?››*
‹‹DUNNO. THOUGHT WE'D ALREADY BE OVER IN SIZZAJEE'S DEMESNES, GIVING THOSE MULTICOLORED MONSTERS A TASTE OF TIGER JUSTICE.››
‹‹WORD IS HE'S BEEN PUMPING THAT PURPLE WIZARD FOR INFORMATION, TRYING TO GET AS MUCH INTEL AS HE CAN BEFORE WE GO IN.››
‹‹OR MAYBE HE'S JUST PUMPING HER. SHE'S A LOOKER, EVEN WITH THAT HOLE IN HER GUT.››
*TIGER TALK. SOUNDS LIKE TIGERS' TALK.
‹‹S-SOMETHING'S... SOMETHING'S...››
‹‹HA HA, VERY FUNNY. WHAT, I'M SUPPOSED TO LOOK BEHIND ME NOW?››
‹‹LEMME GUESS. *WIZORD'S* BACK THERE, RIGHT?››
‹‹OH NO! OH MAN!››

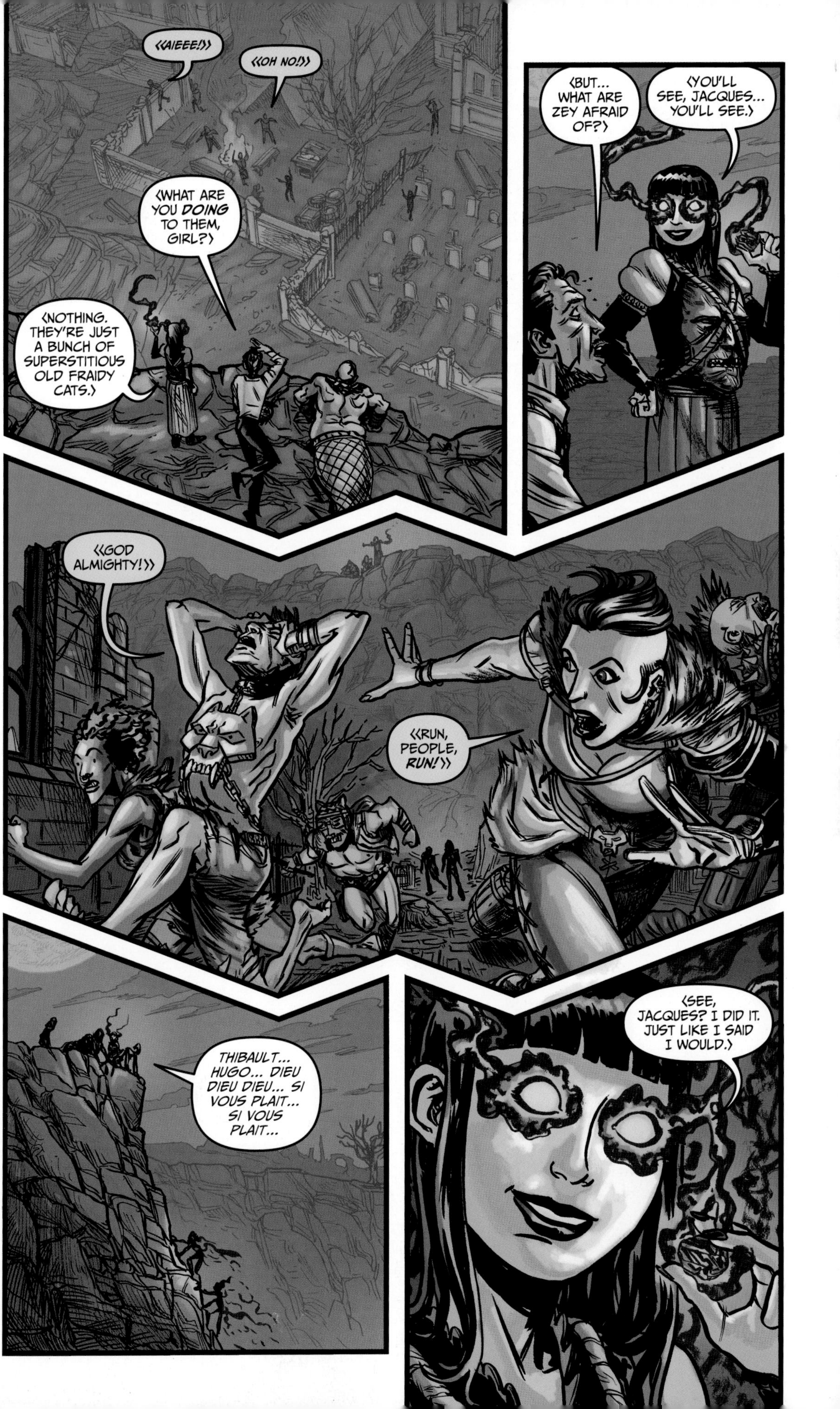

<<AIEEE!>>
<<OH NO!>>
<WHAT ARE YOU *DOING* TO THEM, GIRL?>
<NOTHING. THEY'RE JUST A BUNCH OF SUPERSTITIOUS OLD FRAIDY CATS.>
<BUT... WHAT ARE ZEY AFRAID OF?>
<YOU'LL SEE, JACQUES... YOU'LL SEE.>
<<GOD ALMIGHTY!>>
<<RUN, PEOPLE, *RUN!*>>
THIBAULT... HUGO... DIEU DIEU DIEU... SI VOUS PLAIT... SI VOUS PLAIT...
<SEE, JACQUES? I DID IT. JUST LIKE I SAID I WOULD.>

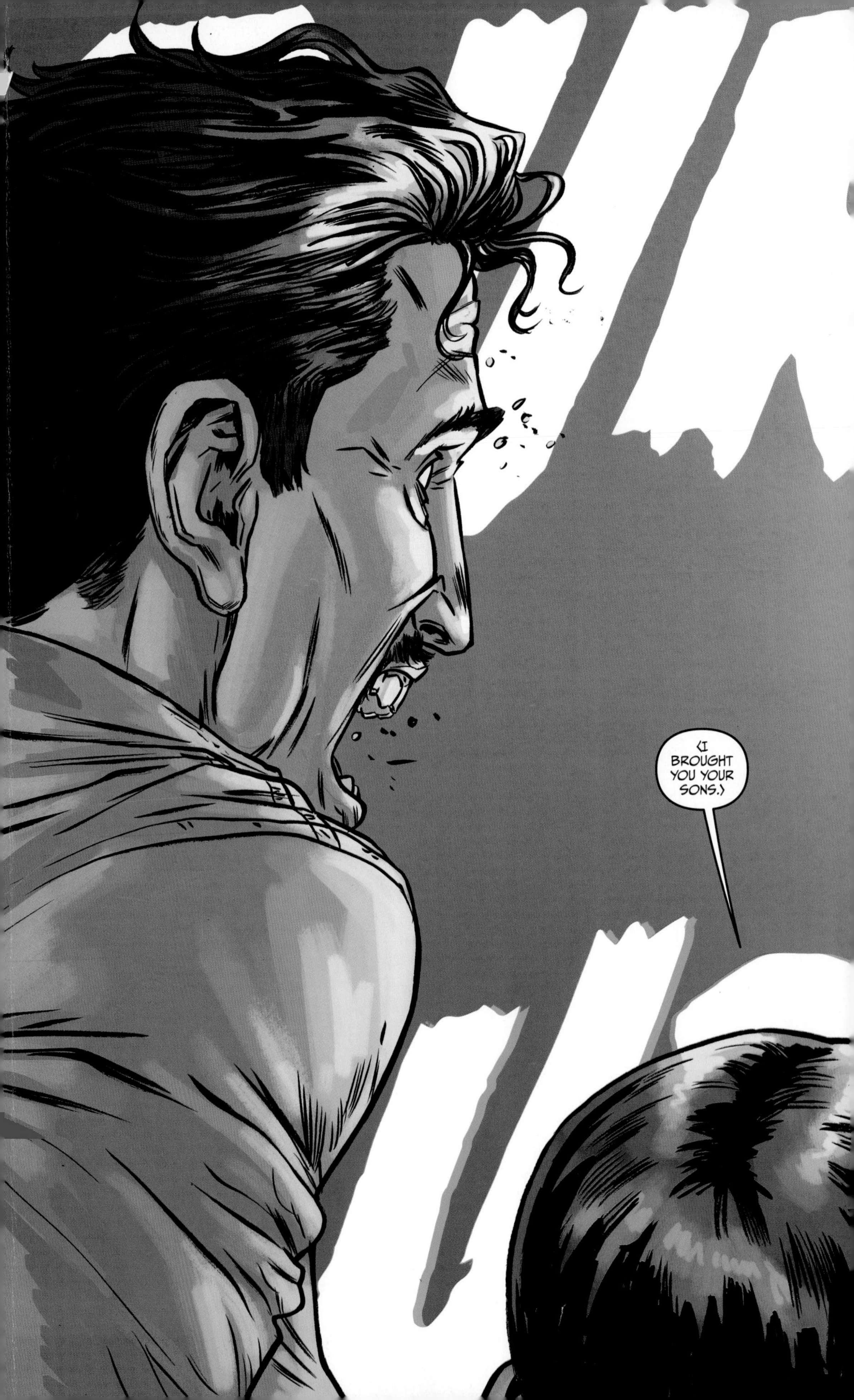
<I BROUGHT YOU YOUR SONS.>

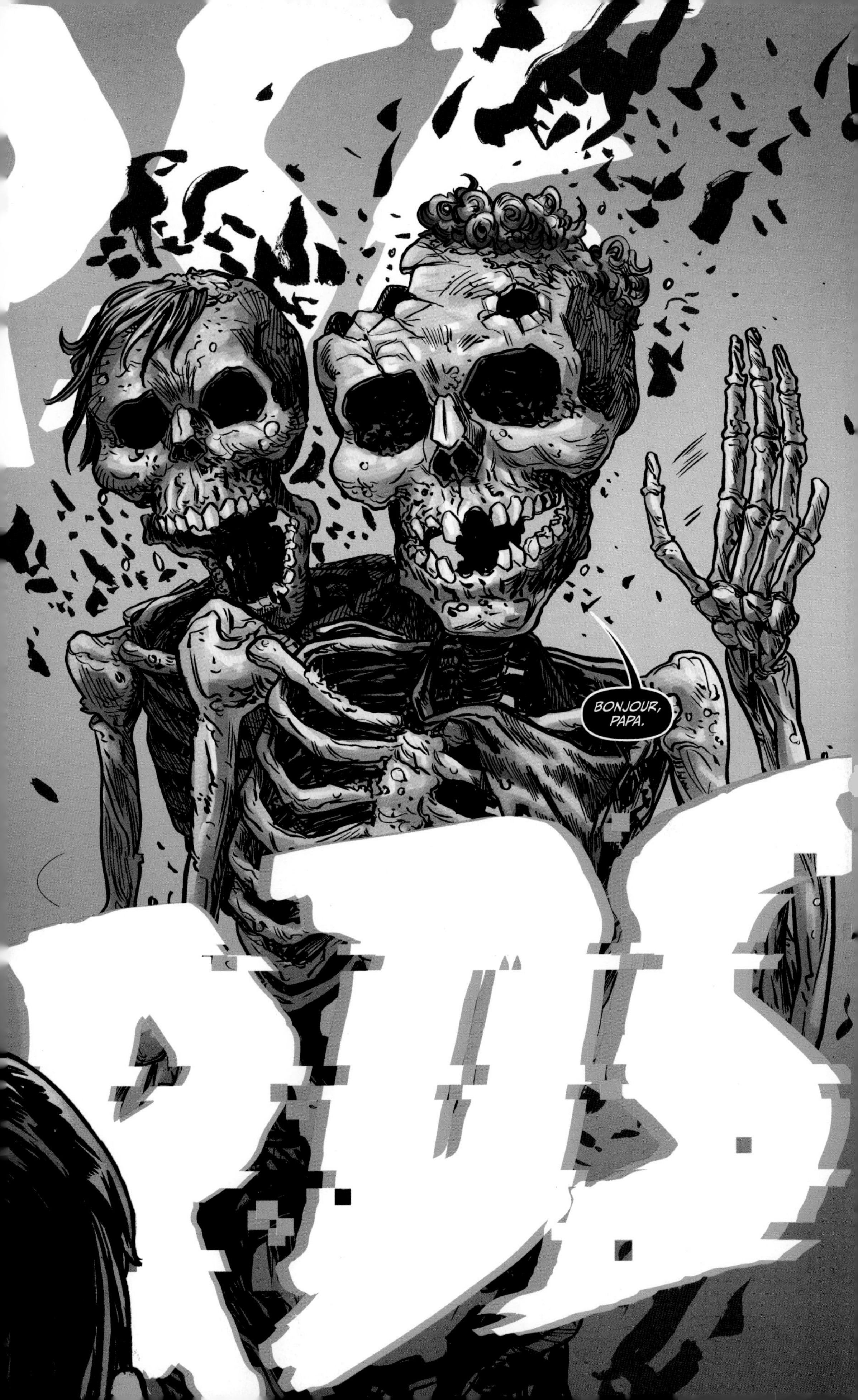
BONJOUR, PAPA.

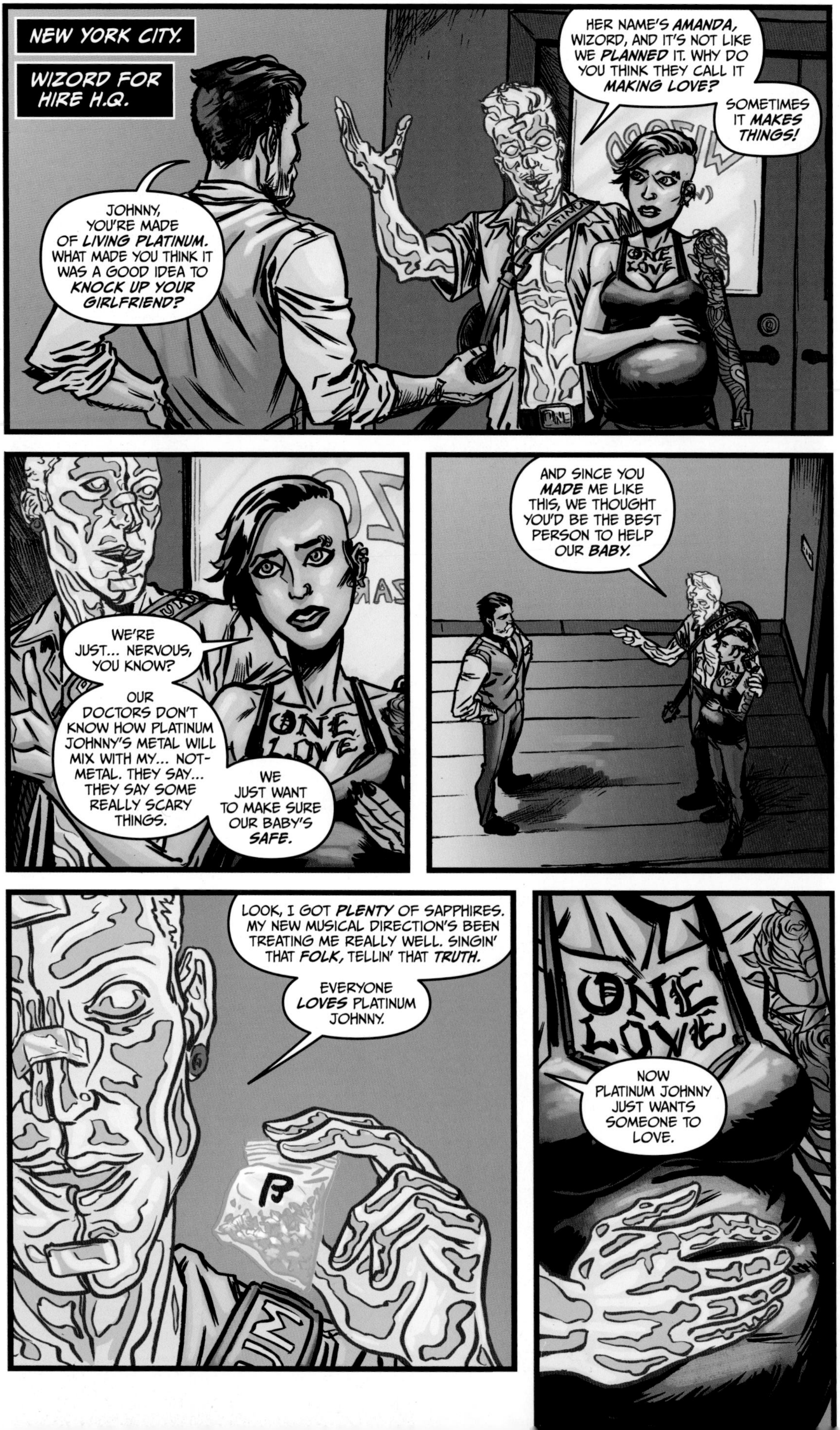
NEW YORK CITY.
WIZORD FOR HIRE H.Q.
JOHNNY, YOU'RE MADE OF LIVING PLATINUM. WHAT MADE YOU THINK IT WAS A GOOD IDEA TO KNOCK UP YOUR GIRLFRIEND?
HER NAME'S AMANDA, WIZORD, AND IT'S NOT LIKE WE PLANNED IT. WHY DO YOU THINK THEY CALL IT MAKING LOVE?
SOMETIMES IT MAKES THINGS!
ONE LOVE
WE'RE JUST... NERVOUS, YOU KNOW?
OUR DOCTORS DON'T KNOW HOW PLATINUM JOHNNY'S METAL WILL MIX WITH MY... NOT-METAL. THEY SAY... THEY SAY SOME REALLY SCARY THINGS.
WE JUST WANT TO MAKE SURE OUR BABY'S SAFE.
AND SINCE YOU MADE ME LIKE THIS, WE THOUGHT YOU'D BE THE BEST PERSON TO HELP OUR BABY.
LOOK, I GOT PLENTY OF SAPPHIRES. MY NEW MUSICAL DIRECTION'S BEEN TREATING ME REALLY WELL. SINGIN' THAT FOLK, TELLIN' THAT TRUTH.
EVERYONE LOVES PLATINUM JOHNNY.
ONE LOVE
NOW PLATINUM JOHNNY JUST WANTS SOMEONE TO LOVE.

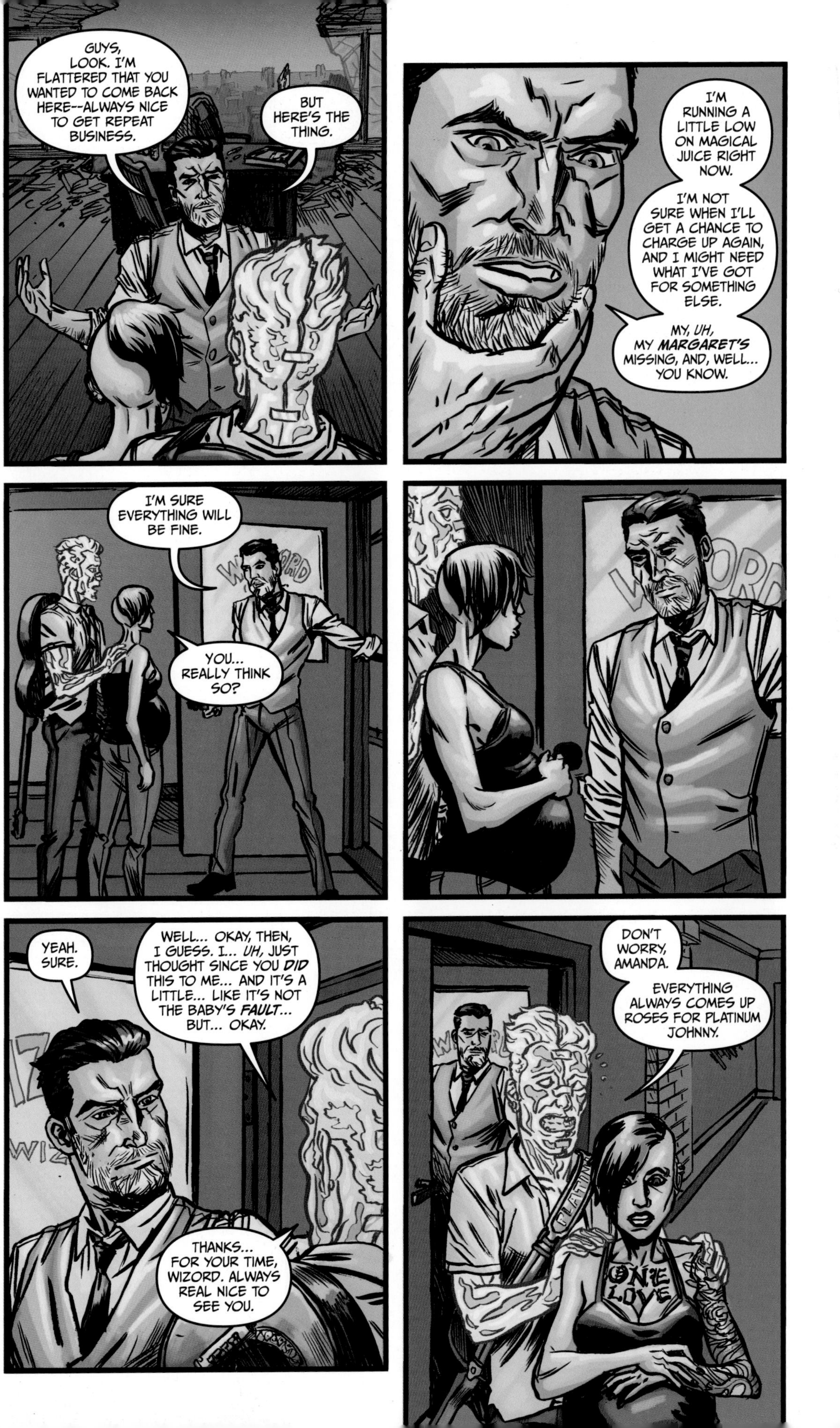
GUYS, LOOK. I'M FLATTERED THAT YOU WANTED TO COME BACK HERE--ALWAYS NICE TO GET REPEAT BUSINESS.
BUT HERE'S THE THING.
I'M RUNNING A LITTLE LOW ON MAGICAL JUICE RIGHT NOW.
I'M NOT SURE WHEN I'LL GET A CHANCE TO CHARGE UP AGAIN, AND I MIGHT NEED WHAT I'VE GOT FOR SOMETHING ELSE.
MY, UH, MY MARGARET'S MISSING, AND, WELL... YOU KNOW.
I'M SURE EVERYTHING WILL BE FINE.
YOU... REALLY THINK SO?
YEAH. SURE.
WELL... OKAY, THEN, I GUESS. I... UH, JUST THOUGHT SINCE YOU DID THIS TO ME... AND IT'S A LITTLE... LIKE IT'S NOT THE BABY'S FAULT... BUT... OKAY.
THANKS... FOR YOUR TIME, WIZORD. ALWAYS REAL NICE TO SEE YOU.
DON'T WORRY, AMANDA.
EVERYTHING ALWAYS COMES UP ROSES FOR PLATINUM JOHNNY.
ONE LOVE

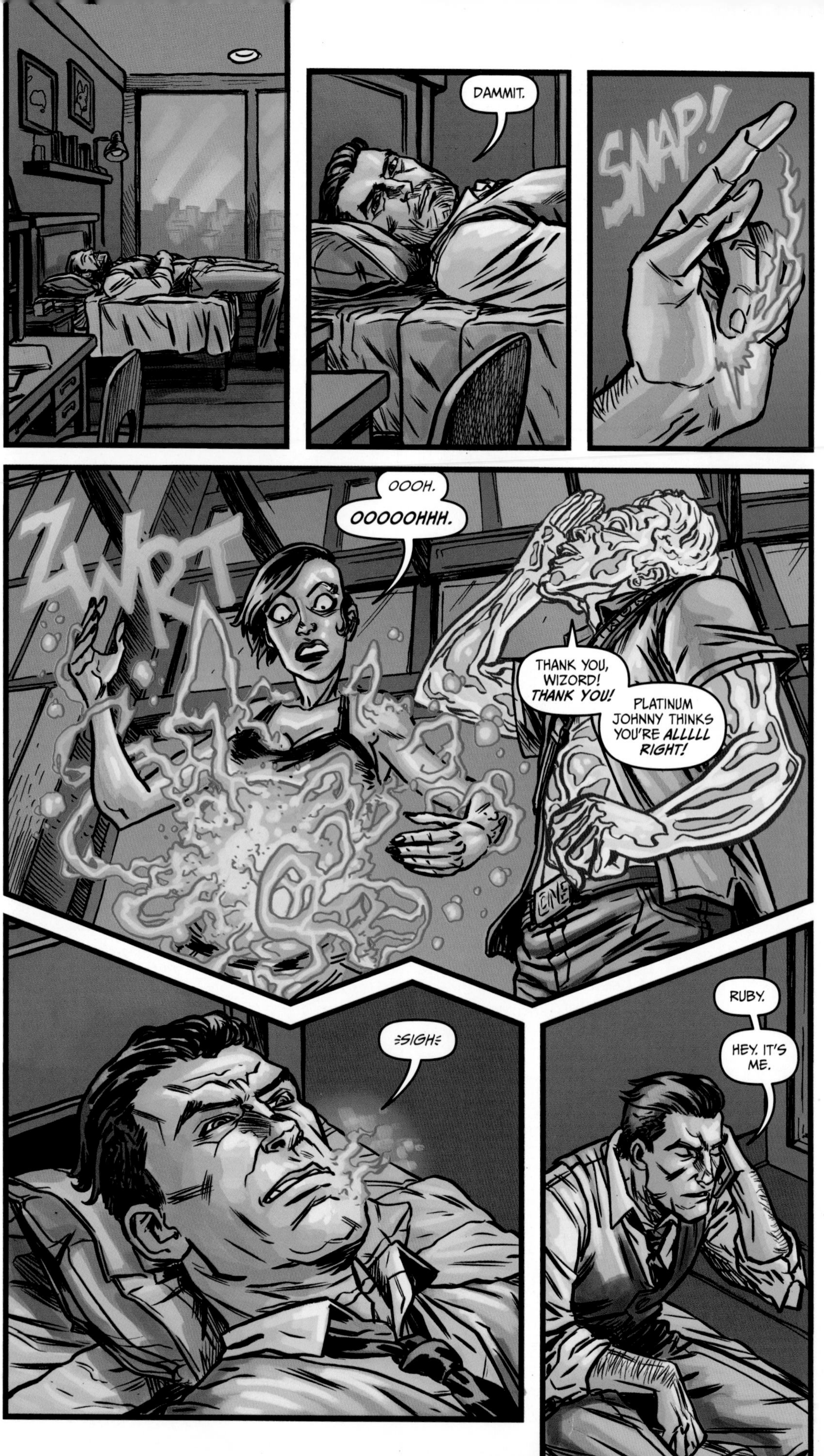
DAMMIT.
SNAP!
ZWRT
OOOH.
OOOOOHHH.
THANK YOU, WIZORD! THANK YOU!
PLATINUM JOHNNY THINKS YOU'RE ALLLLL RIGHT!
SIGH
RUBY.
HEY. IT'S ME.

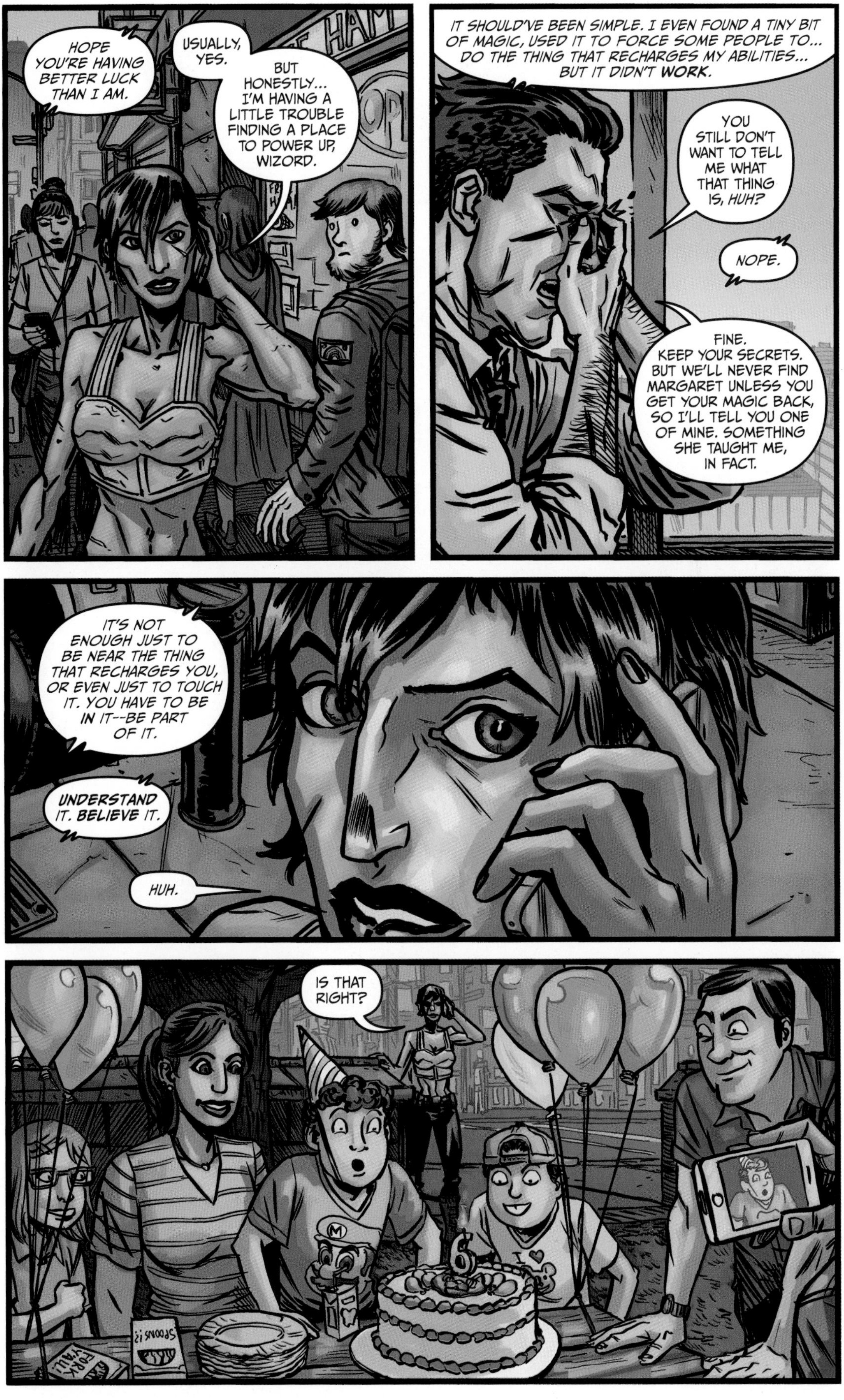
HOPE YOU'RE HAVING BETTER LUCK THAN I AM.
USUALLY, YES.
BUT HONESTLY... I'M HAVING A LITTLE TROUBLE FINDING A PLACE TO POWER UP, WIZORD.
IT SHOULD'VE BEEN SIMPLE. I EVEN FOUND A TINY BIT OF MAGIC, USED IT TO FORCE SOME PEOPLE TO... DO THE THING THAT RECHARGES MY ABILITIES... BUT IT DIDN'T WORK.
YOU STILL DON'T WANT TO TELL ME WHAT THAT THING IS, HUH?
NOPE.
FINE. KEEP YOUR SECRETS. BUT WE'LL NEVER FIND MARGARET UNLESS YOU GET YOUR MAGIC BACK, SO I'LL TELL YOU ONE OF MINE. SOMETHING SHE TAUGHT ME, IN FACT.
IT'S NOT ENOUGH JUST TO BE NEAR THE THING THAT RECHARGES YOU, OR EVEN JUST TO TOUCH IT. YOU HAVE TO BE IN IT--BE PART OF IT.
UNDERSTAND IT. BELIEVE IT.
HUH.
IS THAT RIGHT?

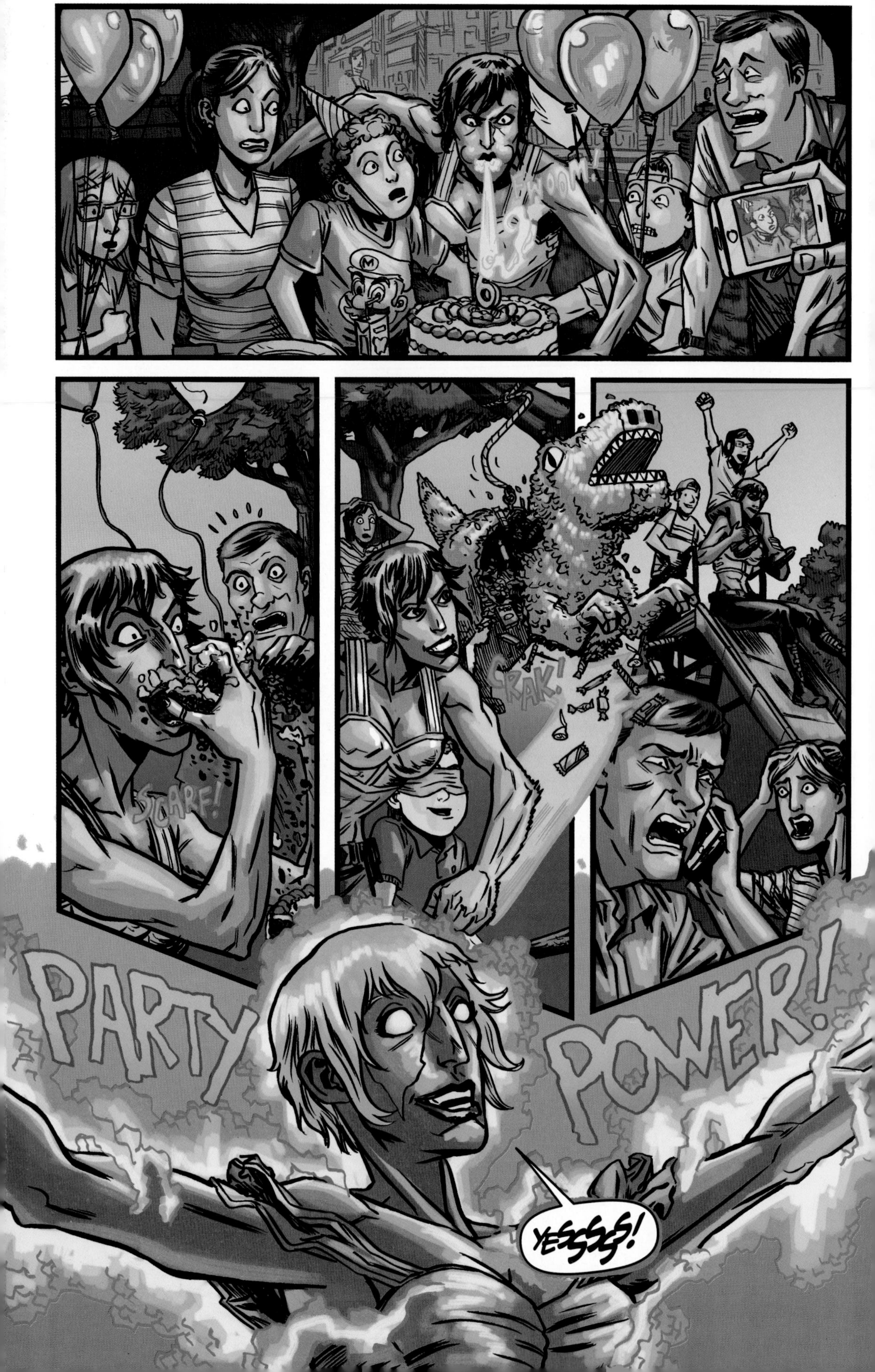
FWOOM!
SCARF!
CRAK!
PARTY POWER!
YESSSS!

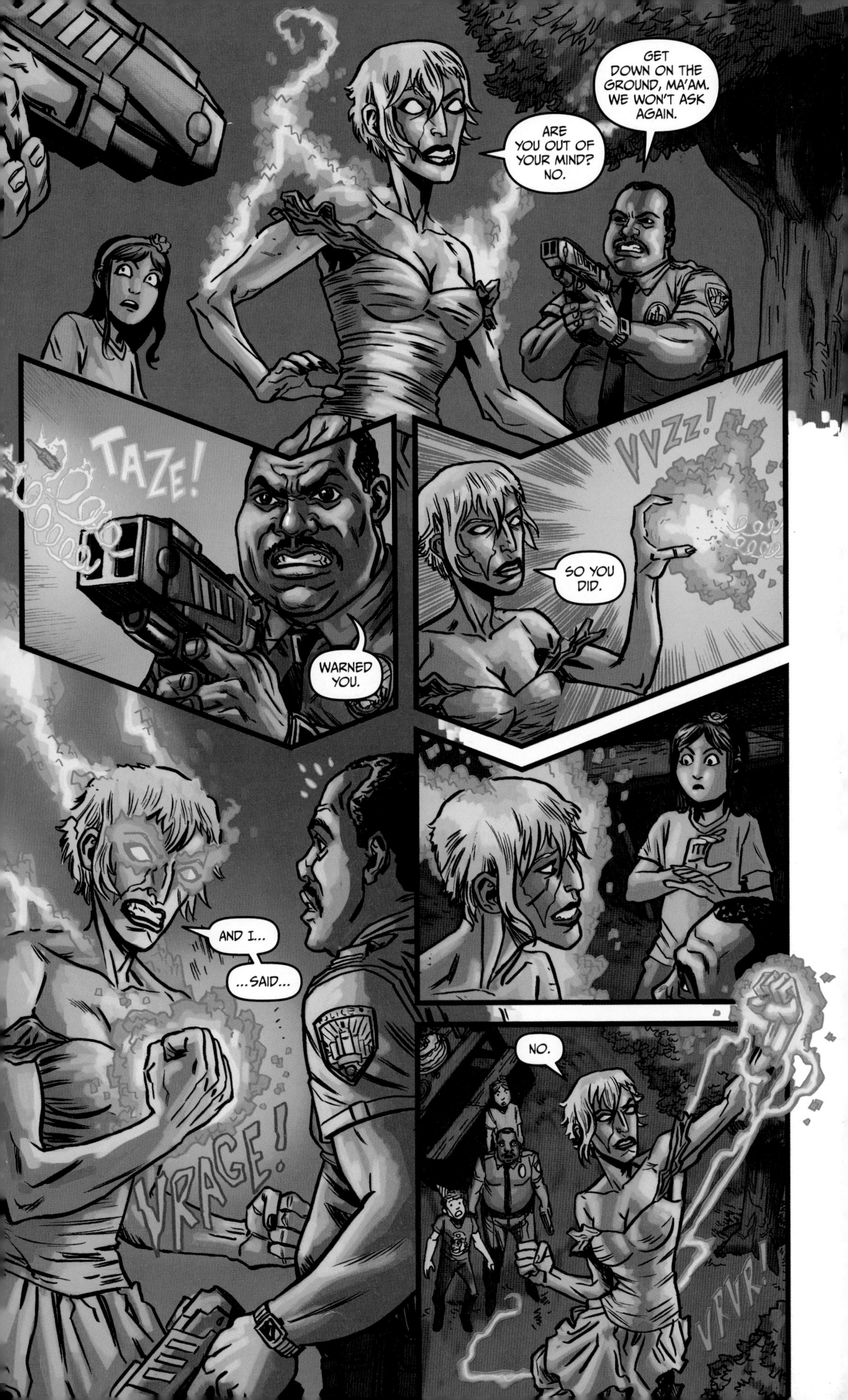
GET DOWN ON THE GROUND, MA'AM. WE WON'T ASK AGAIN.
ARE YOU OUT OF YOUR MIND? NO.
TAZE!
WARNED YOU.
VVZZ!
SO YOU DID.
AND I...
...SAID...
VRAGE!
NO.
VRVR!

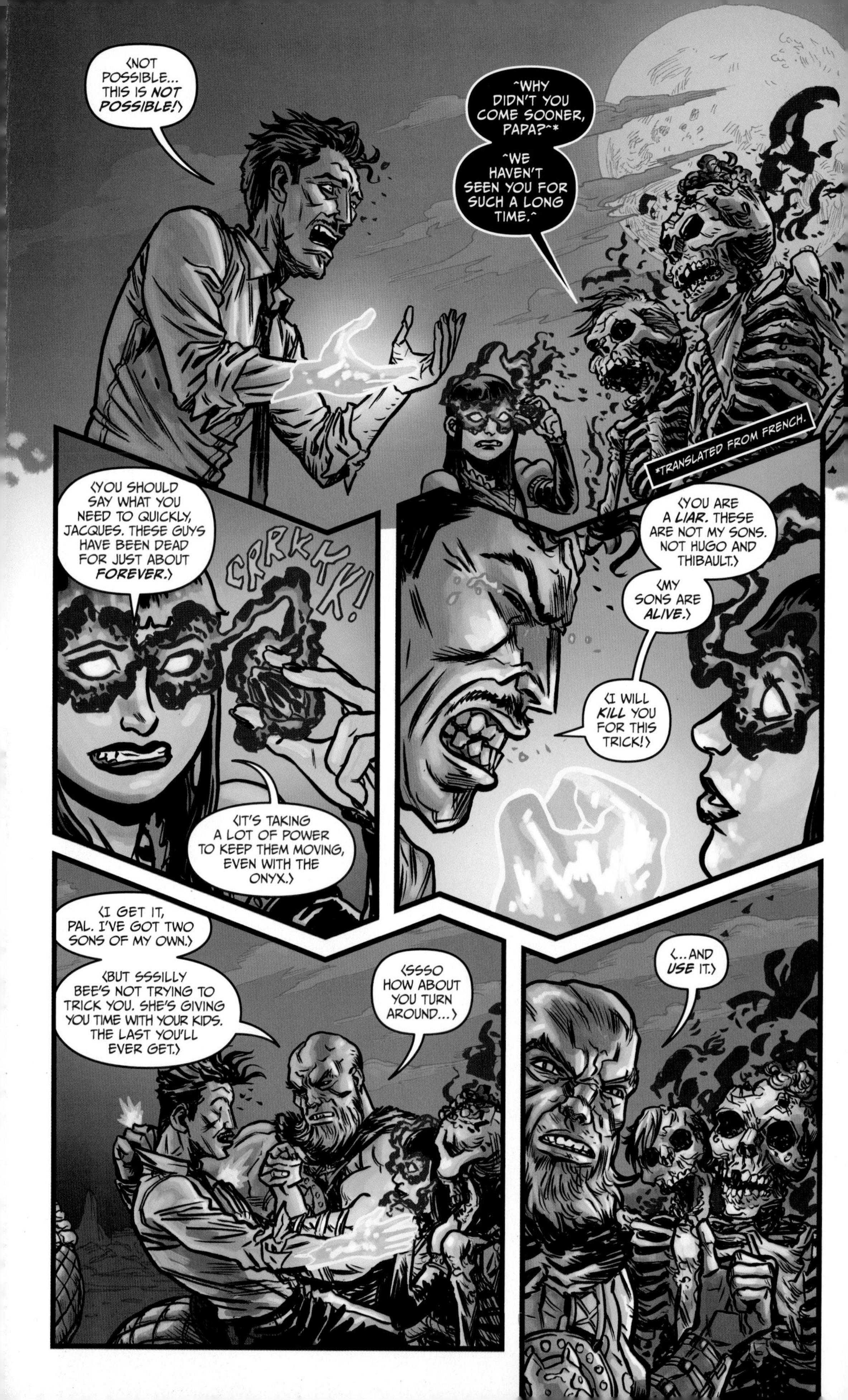

‹NOT POSSIBLE... THIS IS NOT POSSIBLE!›
^WHY DIDN'T YOU COME SOONER, PAPA?^*
^WE HAVEN'T SEEN YOU FOR SUCH A LONG TIME.^
*TRANSLATED FROM FRENCH.
‹YOU SHOULD SAY WHAT YOU NEED TO QUICKLY, JACQUES. THESE GUYS HAVE BEEN DEAD FOR JUST ABOUT FOREVER.›
CRRKKK!
‹IT'S TAKING A LOT OF POWER TO KEEP THEM MOVING, EVEN WITH THE ONYX.›
‹YOU ARE A LIAR. THESE ARE NOT MY SONS. NOT HUGO AND THIBAULT.›
‹MY SONS ARE ALIVE.›
‹I WILL KILL YOU FOR THIS TRICK!›
‹I GET IT, PAL. I'VE GOT TWO SONS OF MY OWN.›
‹BUT SSSILLY BEE'S NOT TRYING TO TRICK YOU. SHE'S GIVING YOU TIME WITH YOUR KIDS. THE LAST YOU'LL EVER GET.›
‹SSSO HOW ABOUT YOU TURN AROUND...›
‹...AND USE IT.›

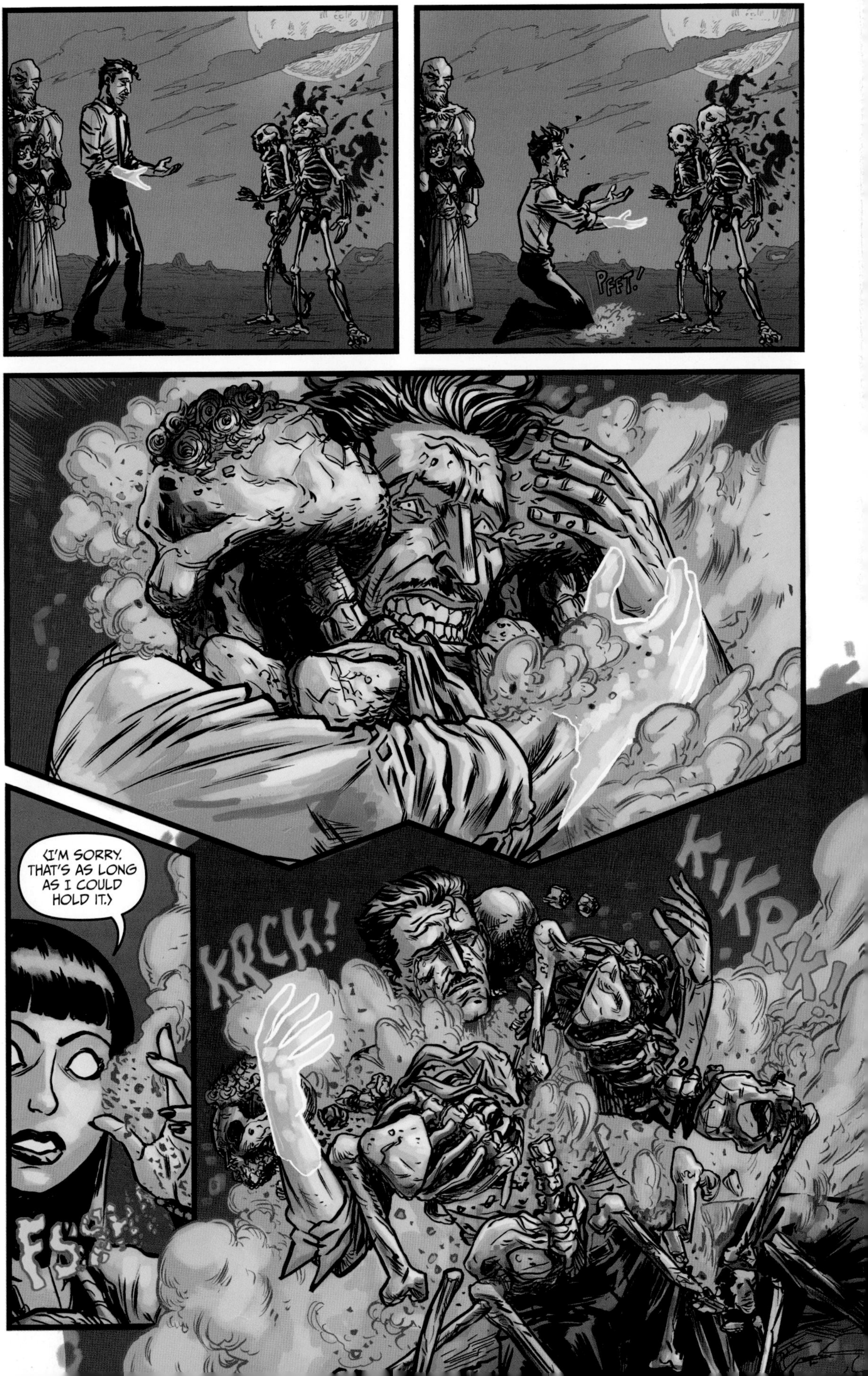
PFFT!
KRCH!
KIKRKK!
‹I'M SORRY. THAT'S AS LONG AS I COULD HOLD IT.›
FSSS

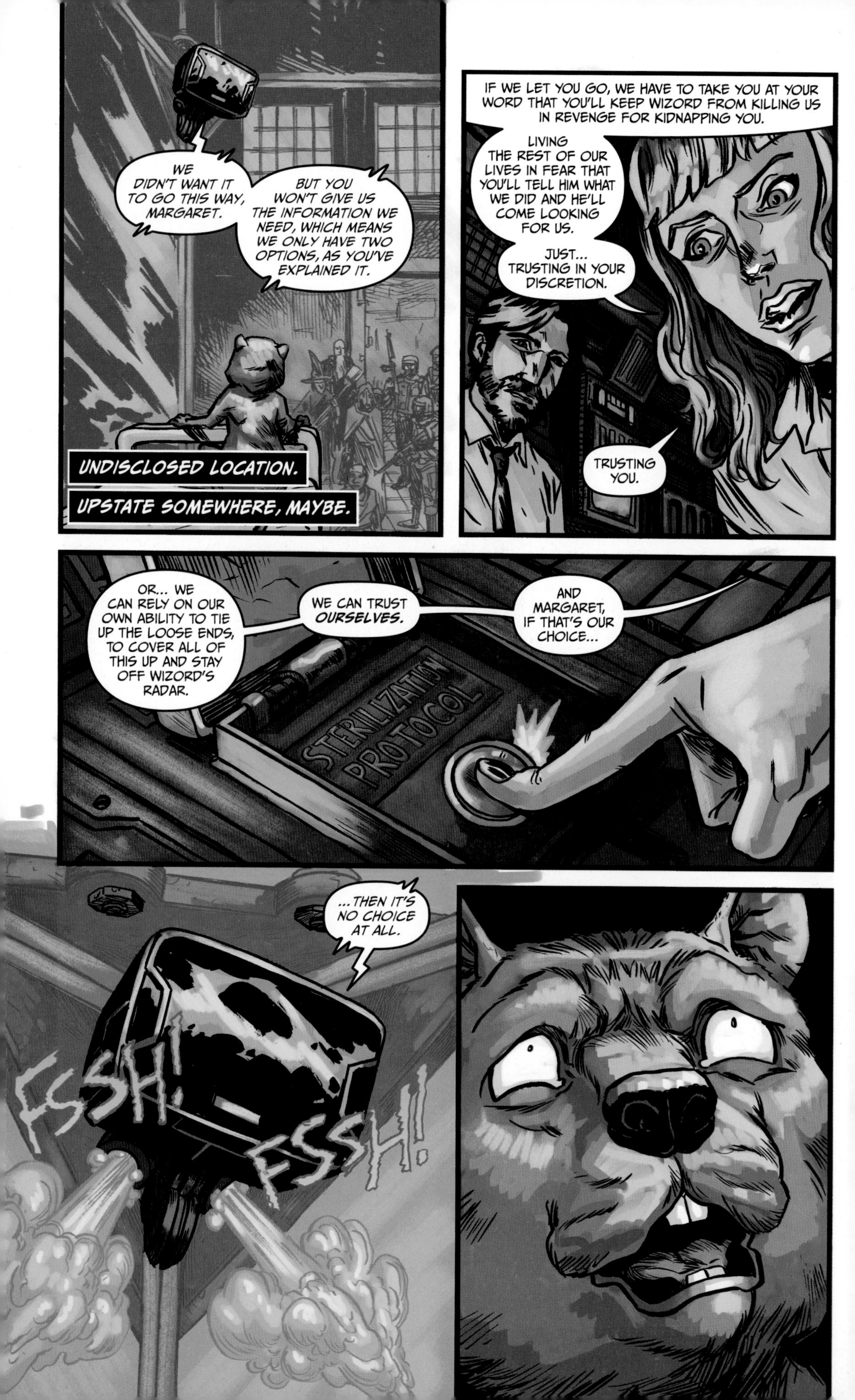
WE DIDN'T WANT IT TO GO THIS WAY, MARGARET.
BUT YOU WON'T GIVE US THE INFORMATION WE NEED, WHICH MEANS WE ONLY HAVE TWO OPTIONS, AS YOU'VE EXPLAINED IT.
UNDISCLOSED LOCATION.
UPSTATE SOMEWHERE, MAYBE.
IF WE LET YOU GO, WE HAVE TO TAKE YOU AT YOUR WORD THAT YOU'LL KEEP WIZORD FROM KILLING US IN REVENGE FOR KIDNAPPING YOU.
LIVING THE REST OF OUR LIVES IN FEAR THAT YOU'LL TELL HIM WHAT WE DID AND HE'LL COME LOOKING FOR US.
JUST... TRUSTING IN YOUR DISCRETION.
TRUSTING YOU.
OR... WE CAN RELY ON OUR OWN ABILITY TO TIE UP THE LOOSE ENDS, TO COVER ALL OF THIS UP AND STAY OFF WIZORD'S RADAR.
WE CAN TRUST OURSELVES.
AND MARGARET, IF THAT'S OUR CHOICE...
STERILIZATION PROTOCOL
...THEN IT'S NO CHOICE AT ALL.
FSSH!
FSSH!

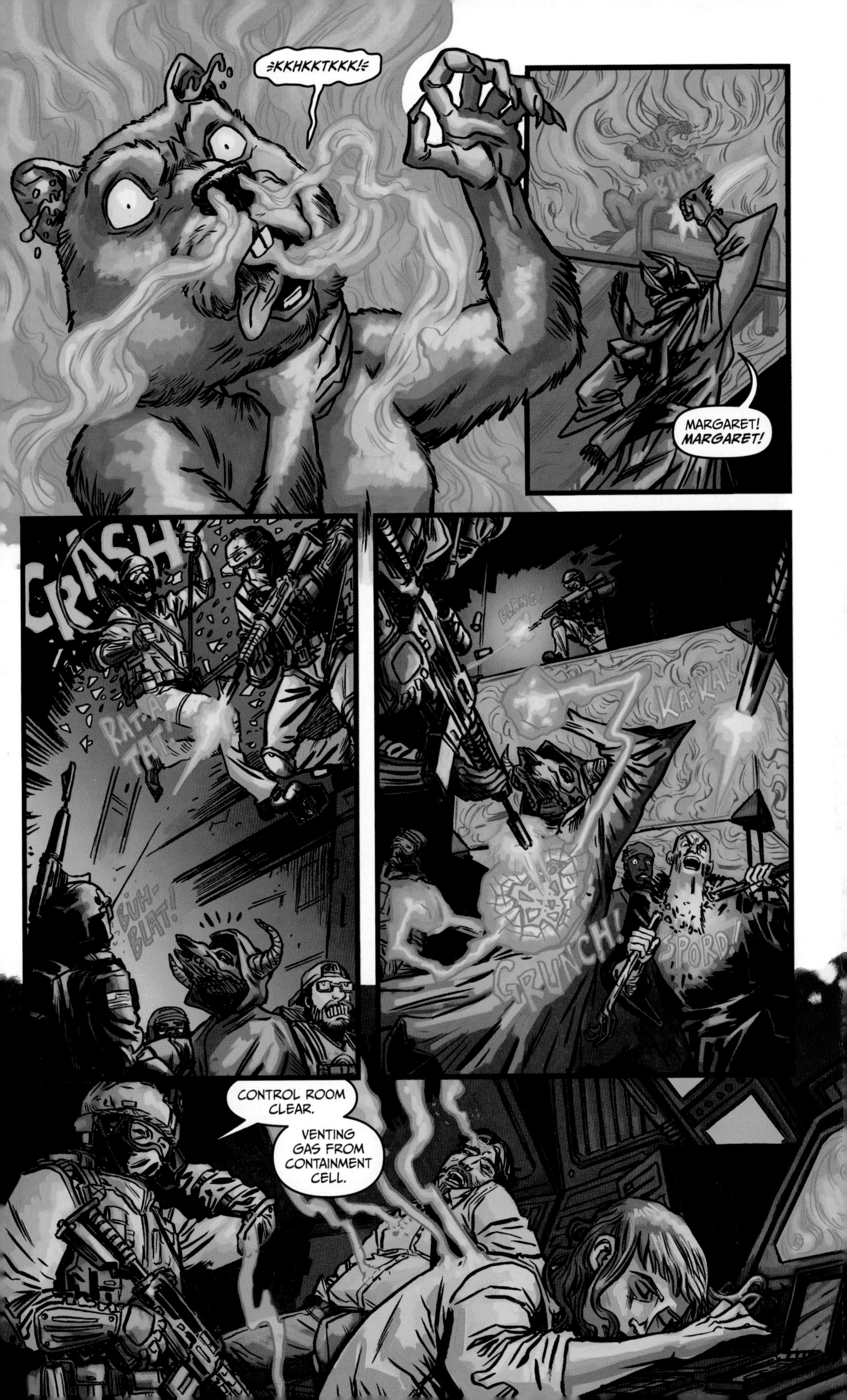

KKHKKTKKK!
BINK!
MARGARET! MARGARET!
CRASH
RAT-A-TAT!
BUH-BLAT!
BLANG!
KA-KAK
GRUNCH!
SPORD!
CONTROL ROOM CLEAR.
VENTING GAS FROM CONTAINMENT CELL.

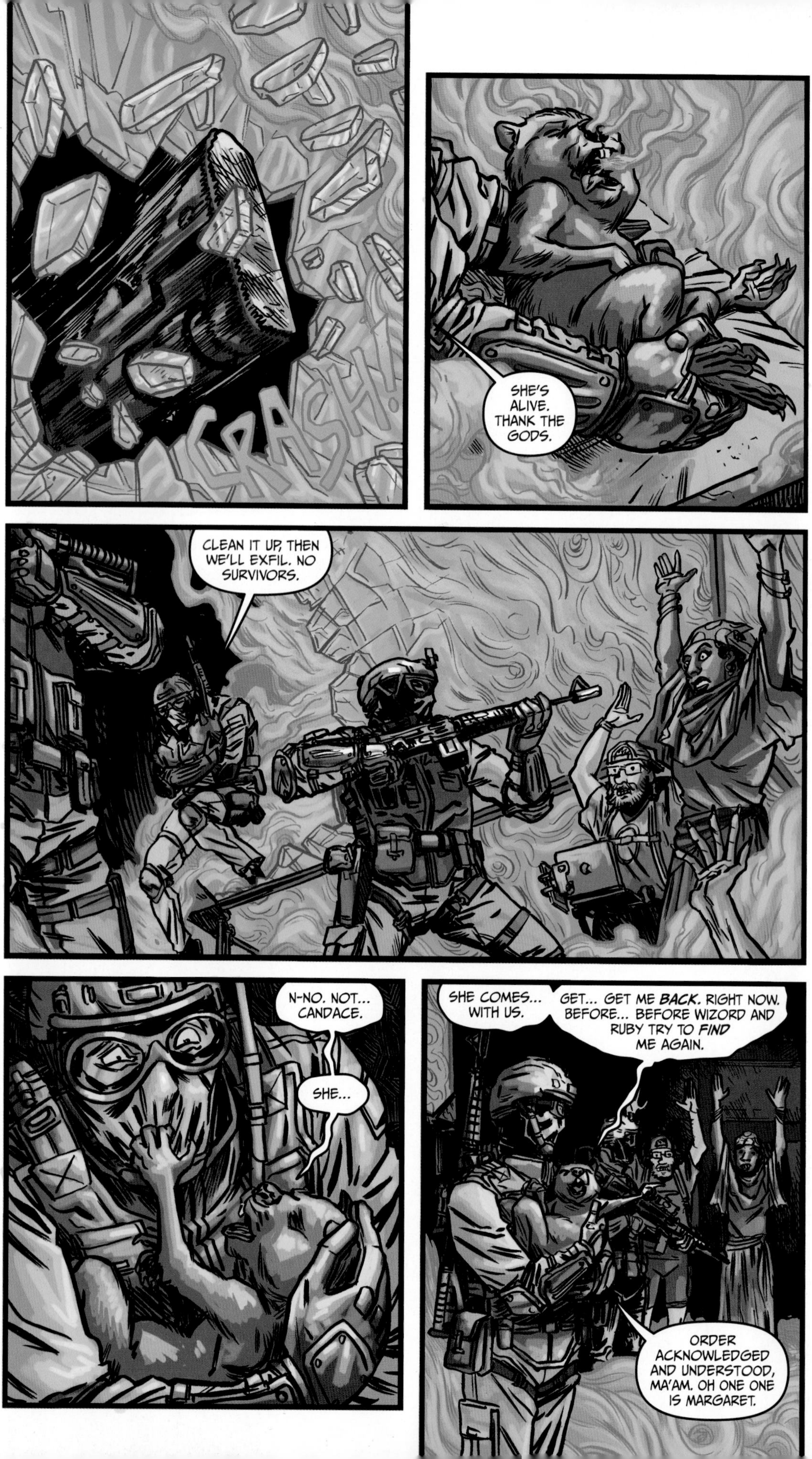
CRASH!
SHE'S ALIVE. THANK THE GODS.
CLEAN IT UP, THEN WE'LL EXFIL. NO SURVIVORS.
N-NO. NOT... CANDACE.
SHE...
SHE COMES... WITH US.
GET... GET ME BACK. RIGHT NOW. BEFORE... BEFORE WIZORD AND RUBY TRY TO FIND ME AGAIN.
ORDER ACKNOWLEDGED AND UNDERSTOOD, MA'AM. OH ONE ONE IS MARGARET.

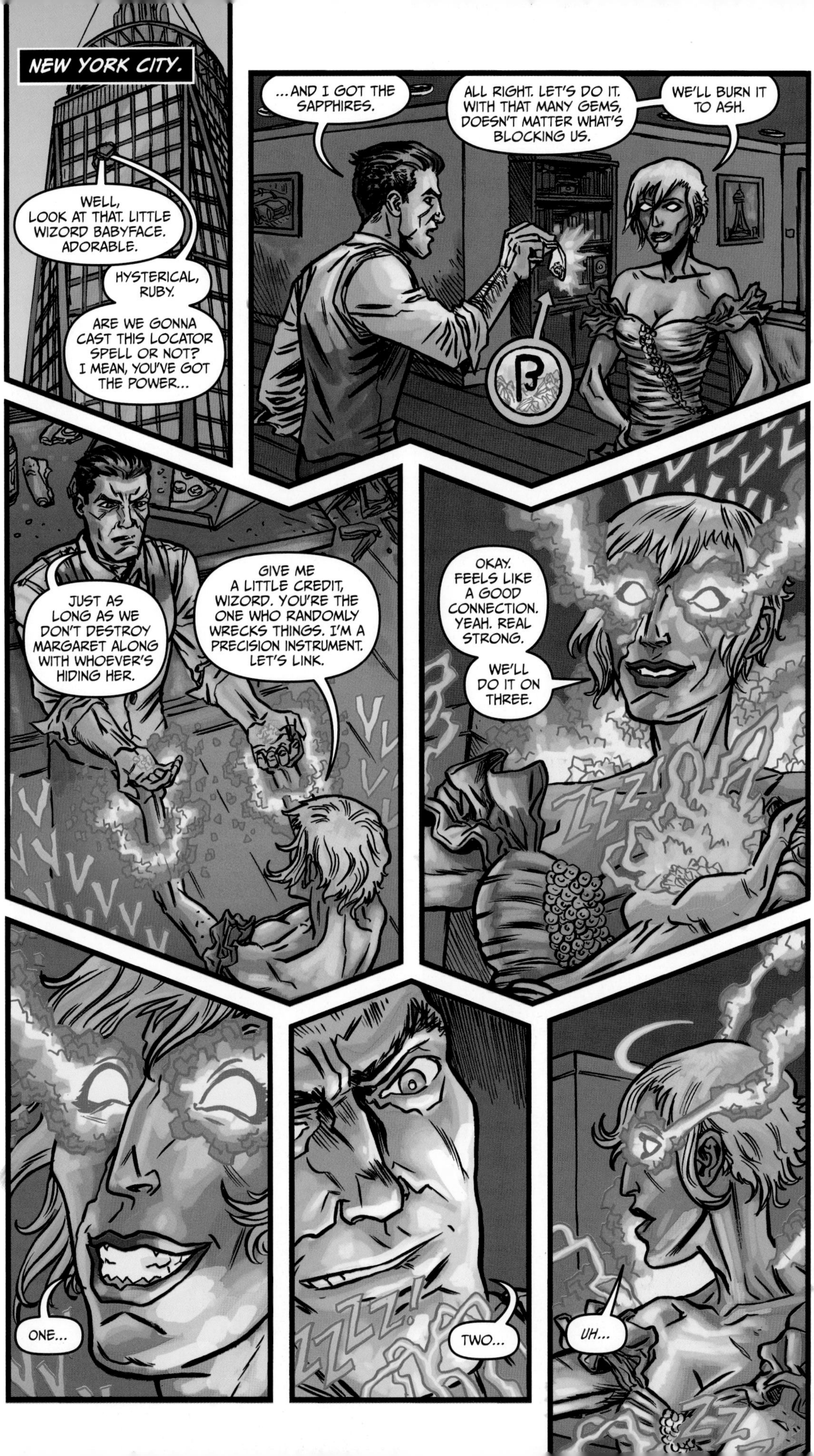
NEW YORK CITY.
WELL, LOOK AT THAT. LITTLE WIZORD BABYFACE. ADORABLE.
HYSTERICAL, RUBY.
ARE WE GONNA CAST THIS LOCATOR SPELL OR NOT? I MEAN, YOU'VE GOT THE POWER...
...AND I GOT THE SAPPHIRES.
ALL RIGHT. LET'S DO IT. WITH THAT MANY GEMS, DOESN'T MATTER WHAT'S BLOCKING US.
WE'LL BURN IT TO ASH.
JUST AS LONG AS WE DON'T DESTROY MARGARET ALONG WITH WHOEVER'S HIDING HER.
GIVE ME A LITTLE CREDIT, WIZORD. YOU'RE THE ONE WHO RANDOMLY WRECKS THINGS. I'M A PRECISION INSTRUMENT. LET'S LINK.
OKAY. FEELS LIKE A GOOD CONNECTION. YEAH. REAL STRONG.
WE'LL DO IT ON THREE.
ZZZ!
ONE...
ZZZZ!
TWO...
UH...

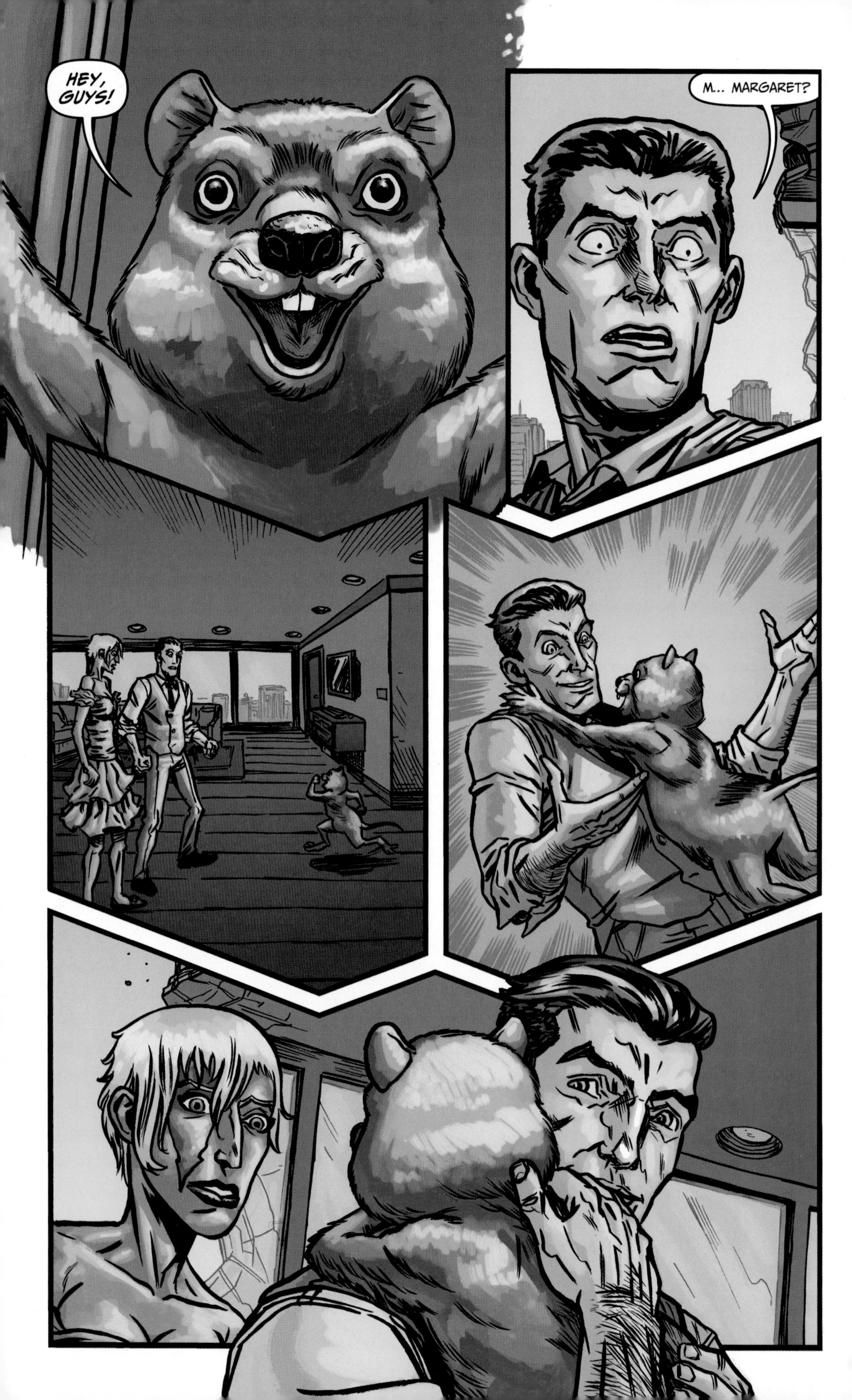
HEY, GUYS!
M... MARGARET?

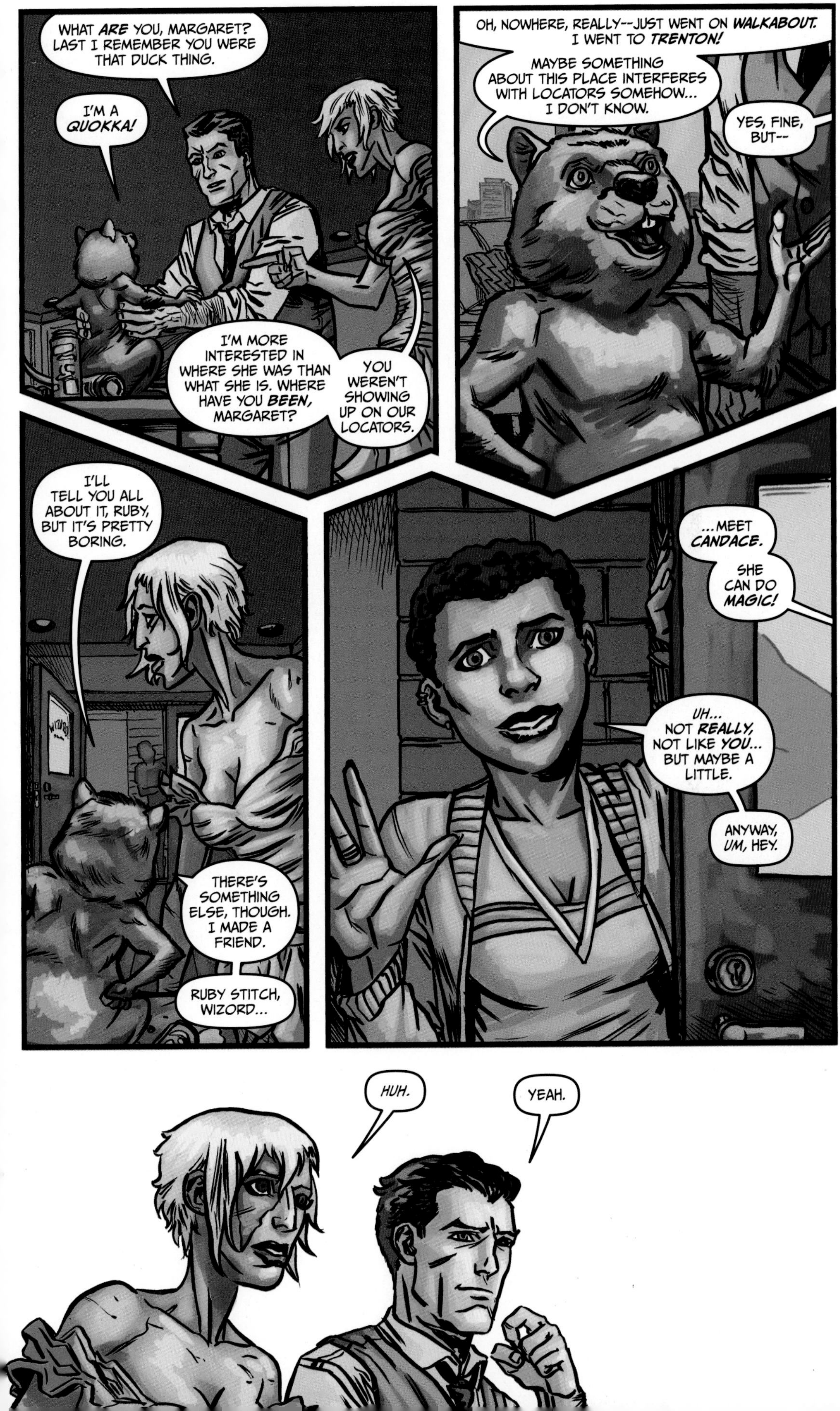
WHAT *ARE* YOU, MARGARET? LAST I REMEMBER YOU WERE THAT DUCK THING.
I'M A *QUOKKA!*
I'M MORE INTERESTED IN WHERE SHE WAS THAN WHAT SHE IS. WHERE HAVE YOU *BEEN,* MARGARET?
YOU WEREN'T SHOWING UP ON OUR LOCATORS.
OH, NOWHERE, REALLY--JUST WENT ON *WALKABOUT.* I WENT TO *TRENTON!*
MAYBE SOMETHING ABOUT THIS PLACE INTERFERES WITH LOCATORS SOMEHOW... I DON'T KNOW.
YES, FINE, BUT--
I'LL TELL YOU ALL ABOUT IT, RUBY, BUT IT'S PRETTY BORING.
THERE'S SOMETHING ELSE, THOUGH. I MADE A FRIEND.
RUBY STITCH, WIZORD...
...MEET *CANDACE.*
SHE CAN DO *MAGIC!*
UH... NOT *REALLY,* NOT LIKE *YOU...* BUT MAYBE A LITTLE.
ANYWAY, *UM,* HEY.
HUH.
YEAH.

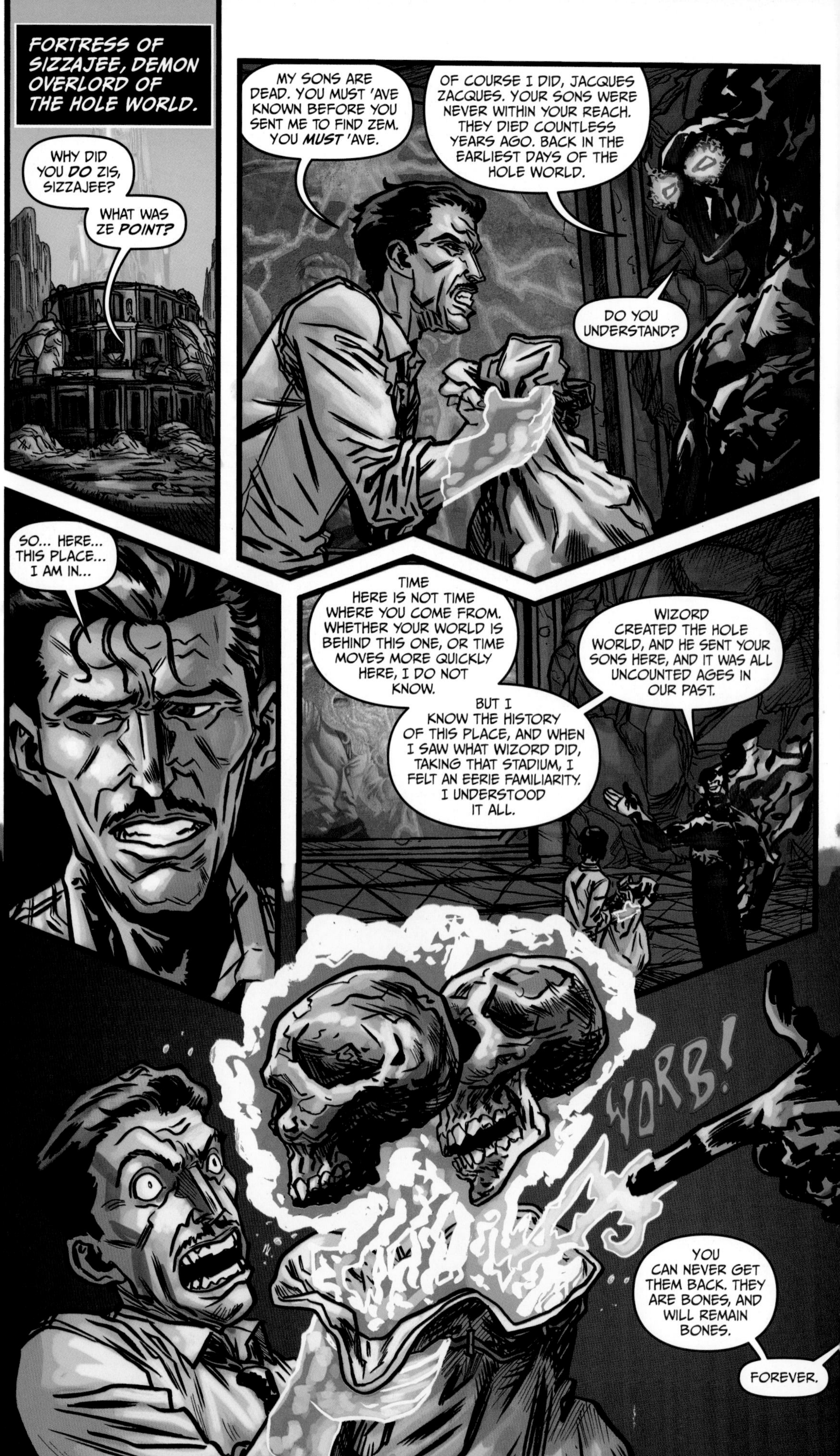
FORTRESS OF SIZZAJEE, DEMON OVERLORD OF THE HOLE WORLD.
WHY DID YOU DO ZIS, SIZZAJEE?
WHAT WAS ZE POINT?
MY SONS ARE DEAD. YOU MUST 'AVE KNOWN BEFORE YOU SENT ME TO FIND ZEM. YOU MUST 'AVE.
OF COURSE I DID, JACQUES ZACQUES. YOUR SONS WERE NEVER WITHIN YOUR REACH. THEY DIED COUNTLESS YEARS AGO. BACK IN THE EARLIEST DAYS OF THE HOLE WORLD.
DO YOU UNDERSTAND?
SO... HERE... THIS PLACE... I AM IN...
TIME HERE IS NOT TIME WHERE YOU COME FROM. WHETHER YOUR WORLD IS BEHIND THIS ONE, OR TIME MOVES MORE QUICKLY HERE, I DO NOT KNOW.
BUT I KNOW THE HISTORY OF THIS PLACE, AND WHEN I SAW WHAT WIZORD DID, TAKING THAT STADIUM, I FELT AN EERIE FAMILIARITY. I UNDERSTOOD IT ALL.
WIZORD CREATED THE HOLE WORLD, AND HE SENT YOUR SONS HERE, AND IT WAS ALL UNCOUNTED AGES IN OUR PAST.
WORB!
YOU CAN NEVER GET THEM BACK. THEY ARE BONES, AND WILL REMAIN BONES.
FOREVER.

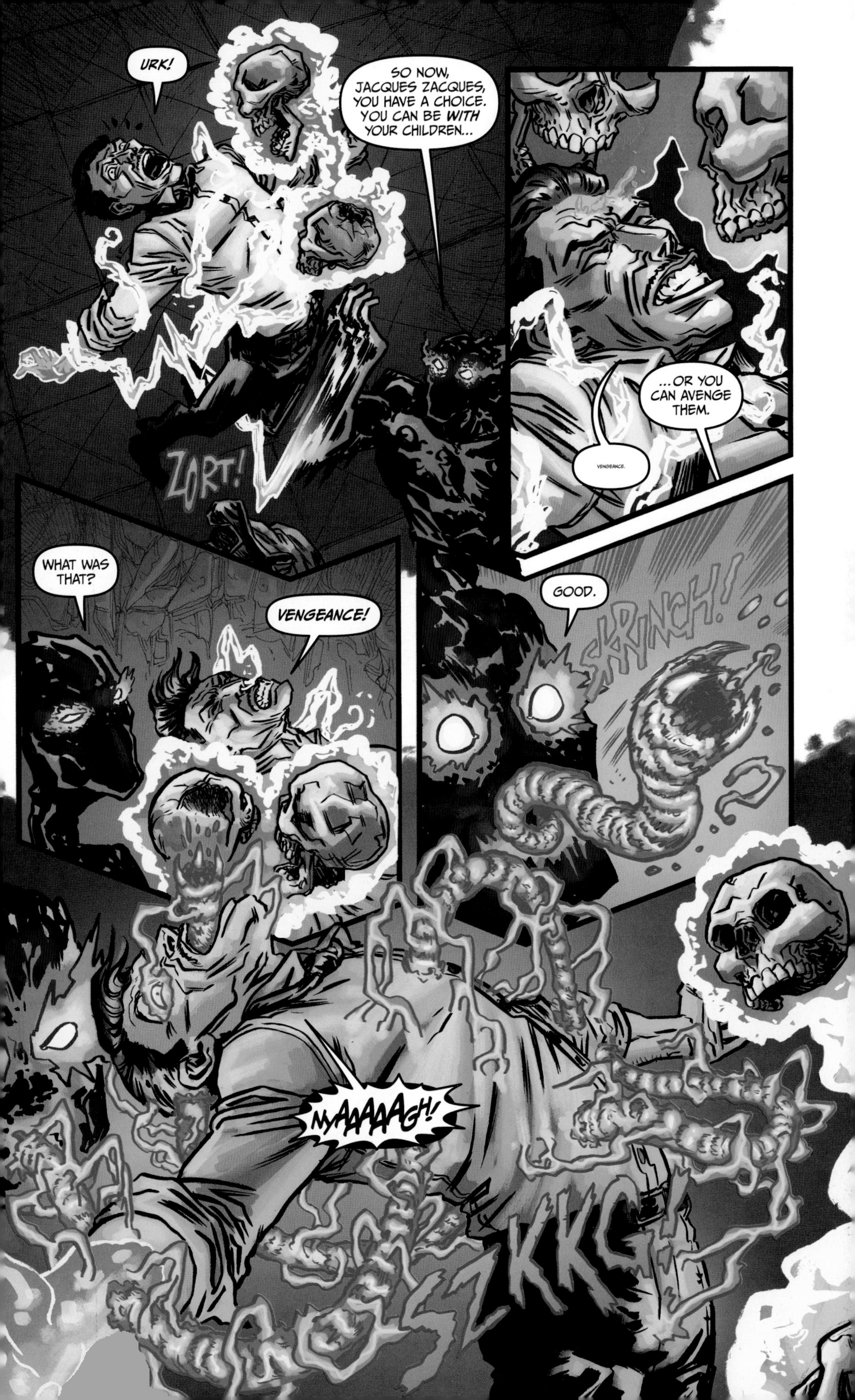
URK!
SO NOW, JACQUES ZACQUES, YOU HAVE A CHOICE. YOU CAN BE WITH YOUR CHILDREN...
...OR YOU CAN AVENGE THEM.
VENGEANCE.
ZORT!
WHAT WAS THAT?
VENGEANCE!
GOOD.
SKRUNCH!
NYAAAAAGH!
KKG!

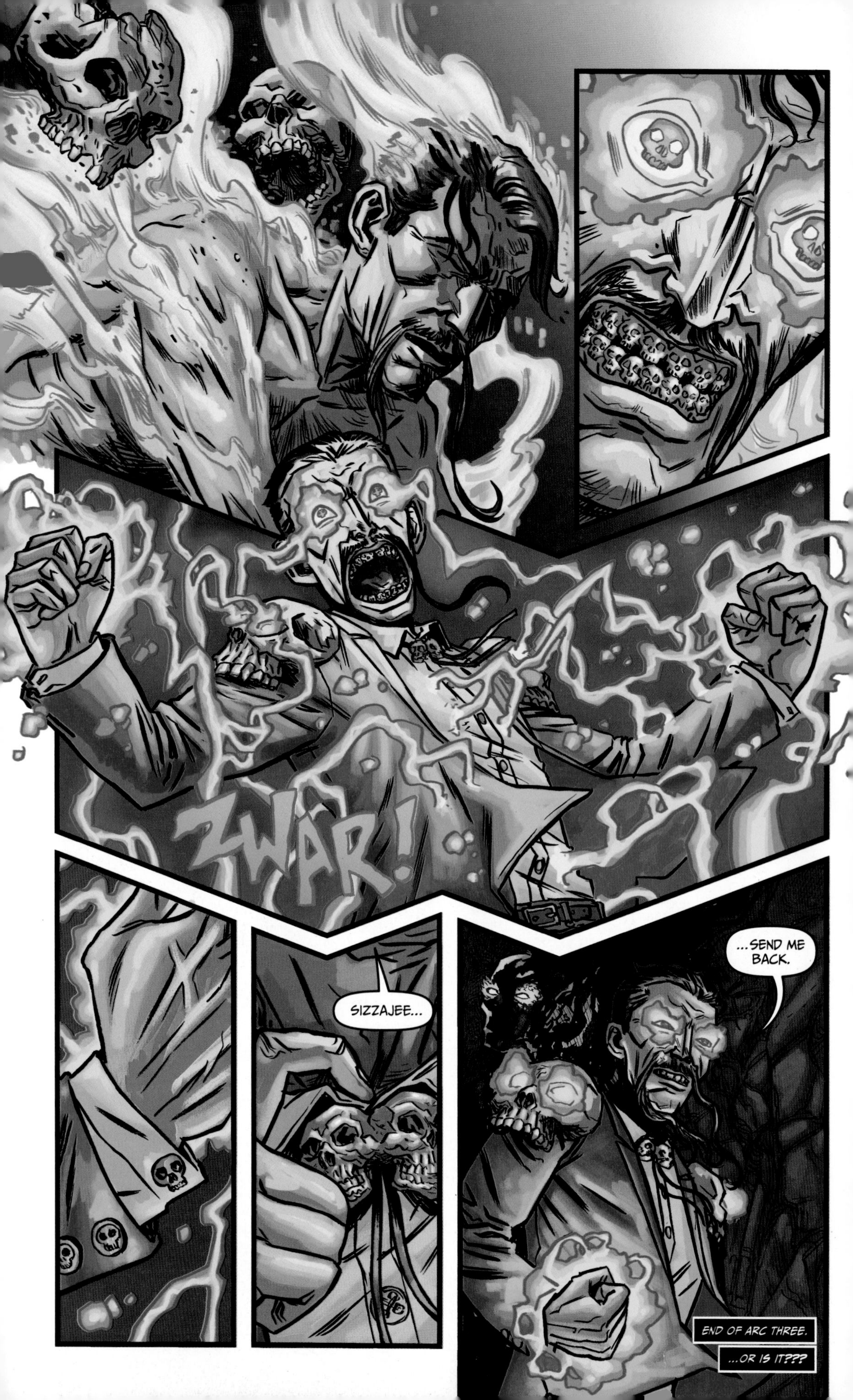
ZWAR!
SIZZAJEE...
...SEND ME BACK.
END OF ARC THREE.
...OR IS IT???

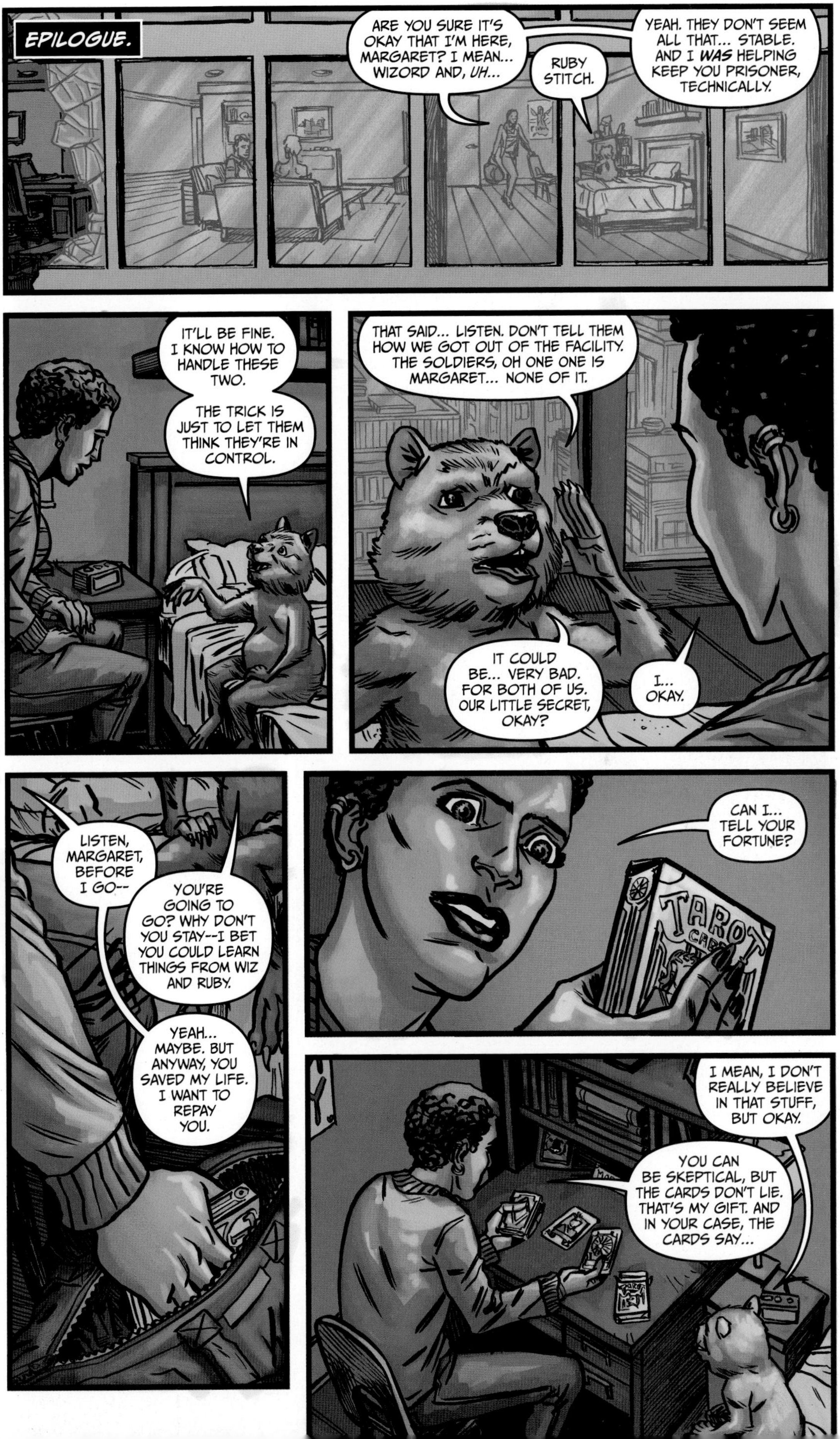
EPILOGUE.
ARE YOU SURE IT'S OKAY THAT I'M HERE, MARGARET? I MEAN... WIZORD AND, UH...
RUBY STITCH.
YEAH. THEY DON'T SEEM ALL THAT... STABLE. AND I WAS HELPING KEEP YOU PRISONER, TECHNICALLY.
IT'LL BE FINE. I KNOW HOW TO HANDLE THESE TWO.
THE TRICK IS JUST TO LET THEM THINK THEY'RE IN CONTROL.
THAT SAID... LISTEN. DON'T TELL THEM HOW WE GOT OUT OF THE FACILITY. THE SOLDIERS, OH ONE ONE IS MARGARET... NONE OF IT.
IT COULD BE... VERY BAD. FOR BOTH OF US. OUR LITTLE SECRET, OKAY?
I... OKAY.
LISTEN, MARGARET, BEFORE I GO--
YOU'RE GOING TO GO? WHY DON'T YOU STAY--I BET YOU COULD LEARN THINGS FROM WIZ AND RUBY.
YEAH... MAYBE. BUT ANYWAY, YOU SAVED MY LIFE. I WANT TO REPAY YOU.
CAN I... TELL YOUR FORTUNE?
TAROT CARDS
I MEAN, I DON'T REALLY BELIEVE IN THAT STUFF, BUT OKAY.
YOU CAN BE SKEPTICAL, BUT THE CARDS DON'T LIE. THAT'S MY GIFT. AND IN YOUR CASE, THE CARDS SAY...

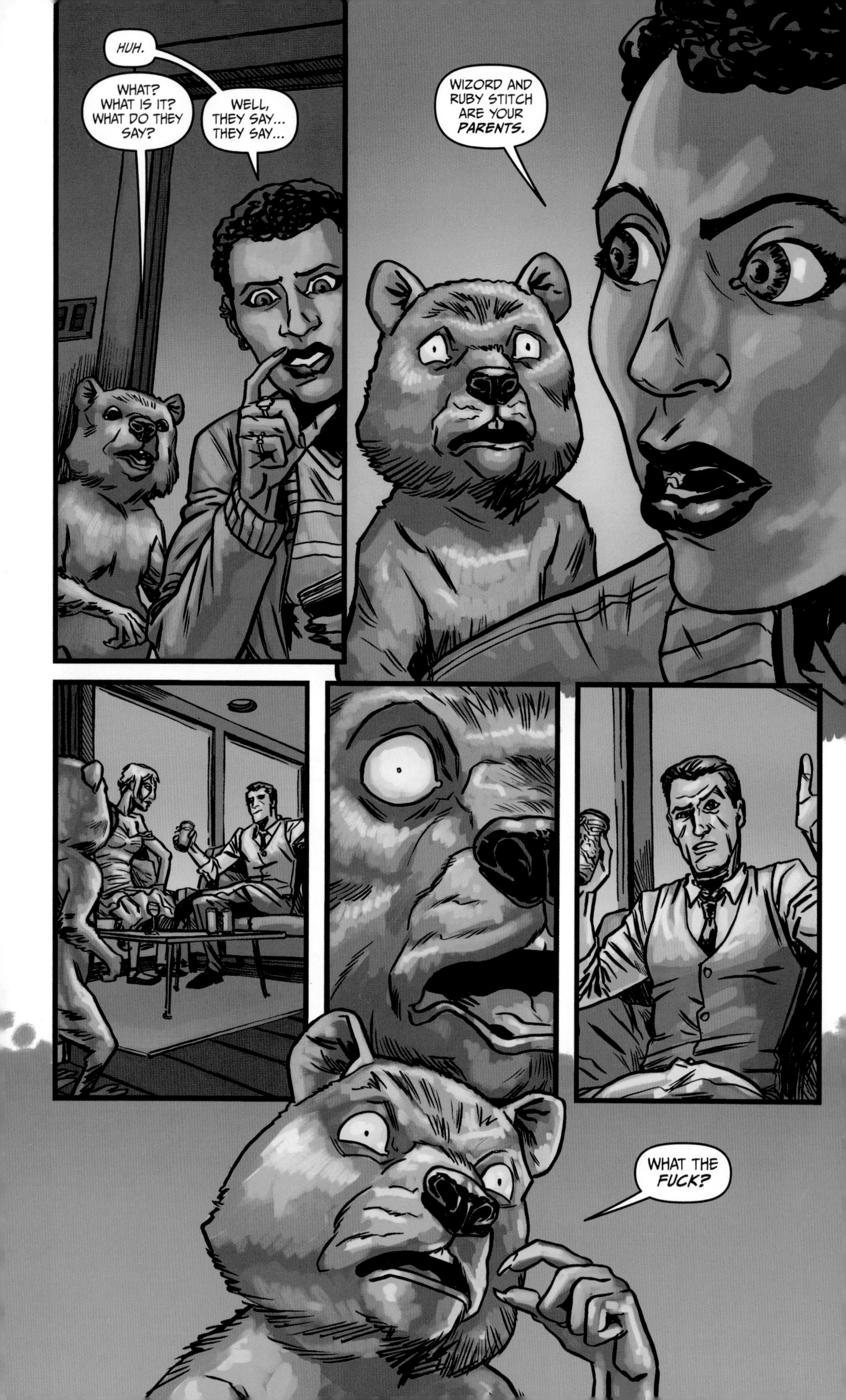
HUH.
WHAT? WHAT IS IT? WHAT DO THEY SAY?
WELL, THEY SAY... THEY SAY...
WIZORD AND RUBY STITCH ARE YOUR *PARENTS.*
WHAT THE *FUCK?*

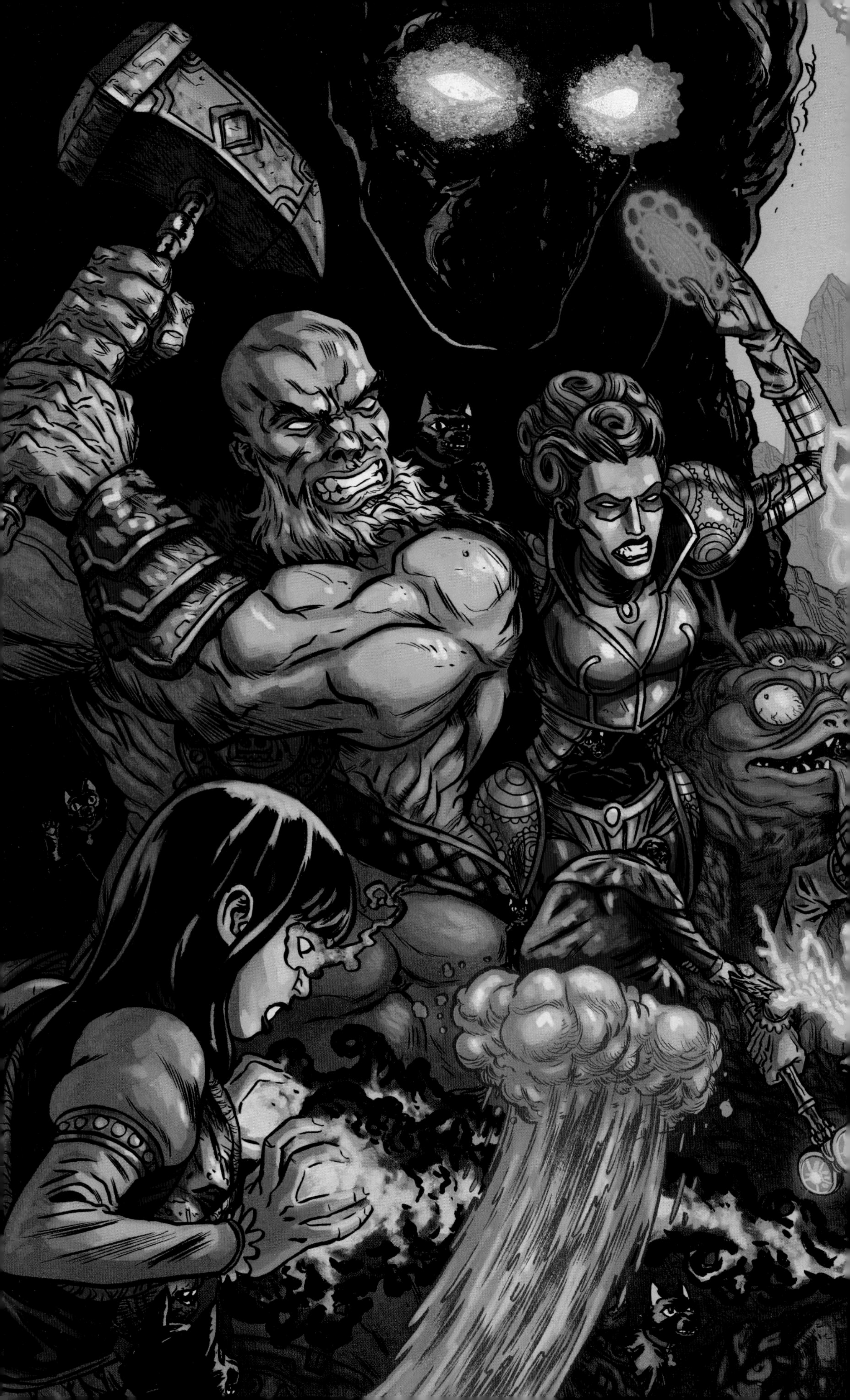

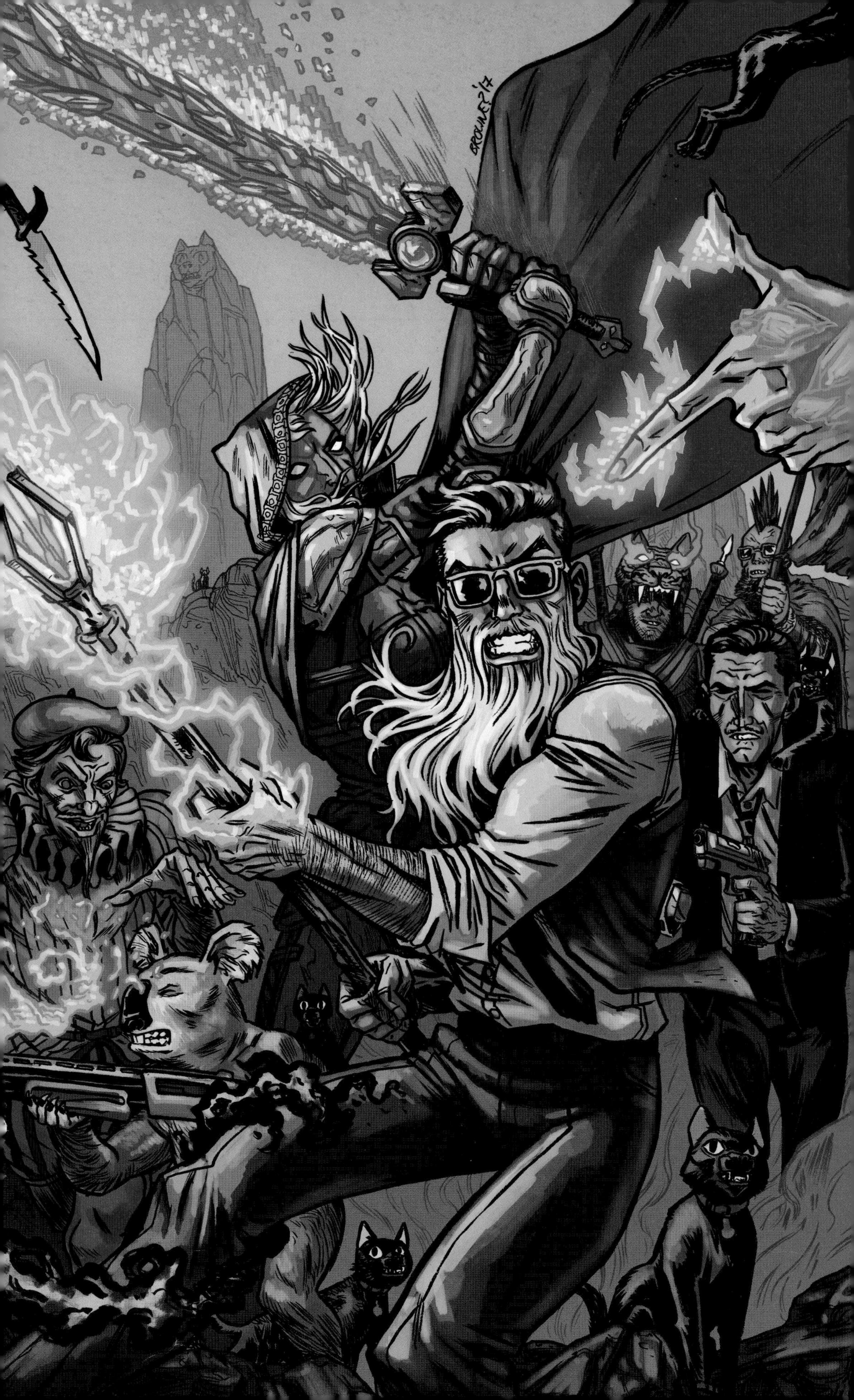

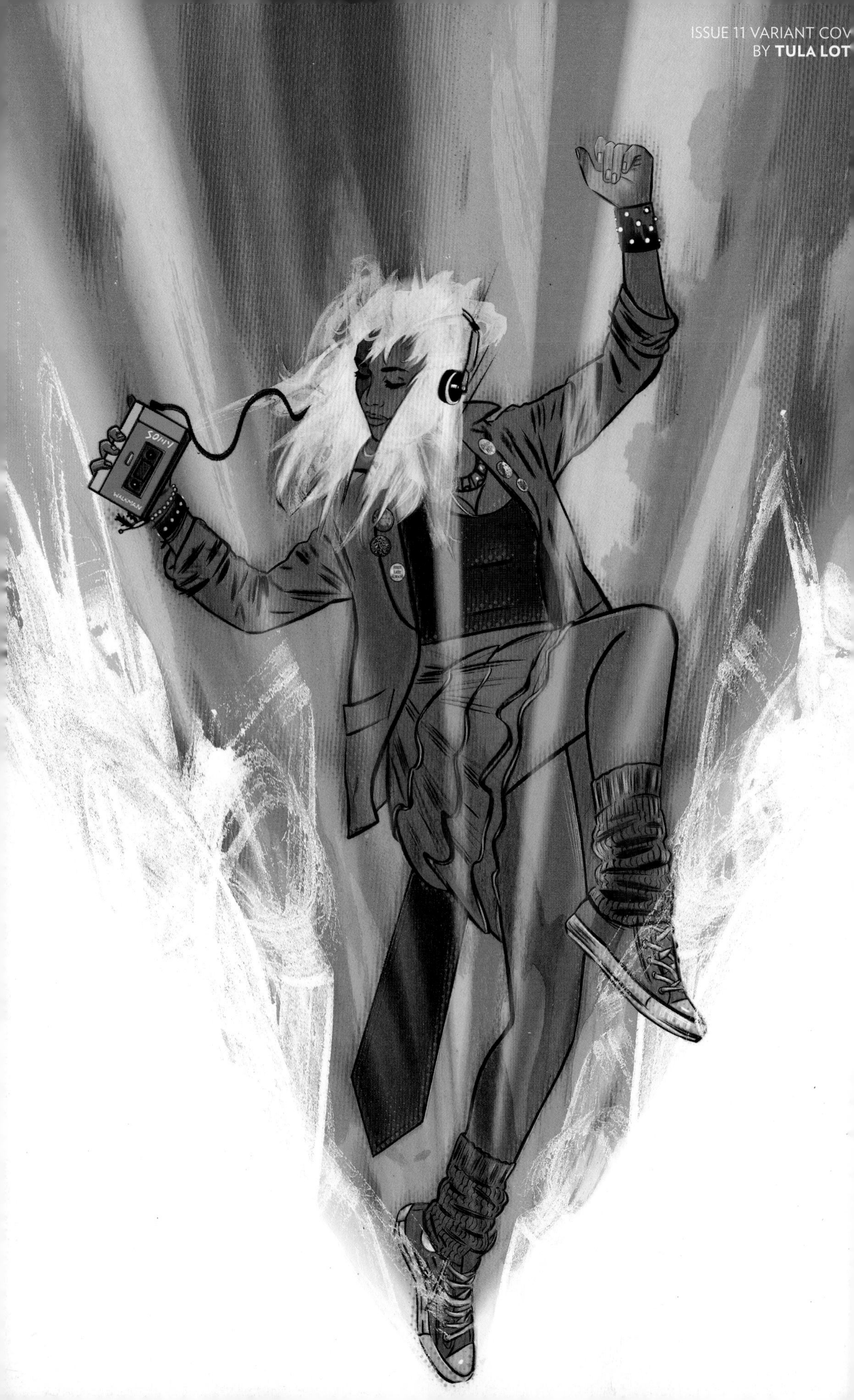

ISSUE 11 VARIANT COV
BY **TULA LOT**